bittersweet

SARAH OCKLER

Simon Pulse

New York London Toronto Sydney New Delhi

SIMON PULSE
An imprint of Simon & Schuster Children's Publishing Division
1230 Avenue of the Americas, New York, NY 10020
First Simon Pulse hardcover edition January 2012
Copyright © 2012 by Sarah Ockler
All rights reserved, including the right of reproduction
in whole or in part in any form.
SIMON PULSE and colophon are registered
trademarks of Simon & Schuster, Inc.
For information about special discounts for bulk purchases,
please contact Simon & Schuster Special Sales at 1-866-506-1949
or business@simonandschuster.com.
The Simon & Schuster Speakers Bureau can bring authors to your live event.
For more information or to book an event contact the
Simon & Schuster Speakers Bureau at 1-866-248-3049
or visit our website at www.simonspeakers.com.
Designed by Karina Granda
The text of this book was set in Adobe Caslon.
Manufactured in the United States of America
2 4 6 8 10 9 7 5 3 1
Library of Congress Cataloging-in-Publication Data
Ockler, Sarah.
Bittersweet / by Sarah Ockler. — 1st Simon Pulse hardcover ed.
p. cm.
Summary: Hudson Avery gave up a promising competitive ice-skating career after her parents divorced when she was fourteen years old, and now spends her time baking cupcakes and helping out in her mother's upstate New York diner, but when she gets a chance at a scholarship and starts coaching the boys' hockey team, she realizes that she is not through with ice-skating after all.
ISBN 978-1-4424-3035-8
[1. Divorce—Fiction. 2. Ice skating—Fiction. 3. Diners (Restaurants)—Fiction. 4. Cupcakes—Fiction. 5. New York (State)—Fiction.] I. Title.
PZ7.O168Lan 2012
[Fic]—dc23
2011024193
ISBN 978-1-4424-3037-2 (eBook)

For Ted Malawer,
who always finds a way to let me
have my cupcakes and eat them, too.

'Twas the Month Before Cupcakes

Three years ago . . .

It was the biggest competition night of my life, but all I could think about was the cheetah bra.

I'd found it a few hours earlier, tucked into a pile of folded laundry on the end of my bed. It was just *there*, two perfect C-cups trimmed in black, nestled between my jeans with the butterfly on the pocket and the faded Buffalo Sabres hoodie I'd swiped from Dad.

Mom was in her bedroom ironing, decked out in her yellow robe and those hard-bottomed slippers that are supposed to be good for your back. I dangled the bra off my finger, because Mom + cheetah = *eww*, and dropped it on her dresser.

"It was mixed in with my stuff," I said when she looked up.

I flopped on her bed, tossing a pillow in the air and catching it. *Toss. Catch. Toss. Catch.* "Are we leaving soon?" *Toss. Catch.*

"It's not . . . yours?" She stood in front of the dresser then, looking down at the bra with her fingers spread out on either side of it like she was scanning the day's headlines.

"Ma." I met her eyes in the mirror, motioning toward my barely noticeable A-cups. No way it could've been mine; as resident bra-buyer of the family, she ought to know my size. I laughed and grabbed the pillow again, but the look that flashed across her face stopped me cold. It was like the aftermath of an ice storm, black and treacherous, yet eerily calm.

I swallowed hard.

After all the late-night arguments, the separate bedrooms, the unspoken glares, things between my parents had just gone from pretty bad to unfixably worse.

"Mom?" I said quietly, still clutching the pillow. "Are you—"

"Almost ready, Hudson. Go down and tell your . . ." She almost choked on the word, clearing her throat as she opened the top drawer and swept in the bra like crumbs from the breakfast table. "Your *father* . . . ask him to start the car."

"But whose—"

"It's an hour and a half drive to Rochester and we still need to take Max to the sitter's." She bumped the drawer closed with her hip, turning toward me with a pinched grin as the mirror shook behind her. "Big night tonight, baby. Let's get moving!"

After we dropped off my little brother, Mom gave me the

front seat next to Dad. He quizzed me on my routine, and as I verbally walked through each step, guilt jabbed me in the chest. He's the one who supported my ice-skating, who told Mom they *had* to find a way to make it work, even if it meant selling Hurley's, the old diner she'd owned since before they were married. He'd said if I made it to nationals later that year, we'd probably have to move anyway—find a bigger city with better access to private ice time. Interview special coaches and home tutors. Look for sponsorships. Whatever it took, Dad was ready and willing, my cheerleader, my number one sideline support system. Still, there was something off between us that night—something uncomfortable I'd never felt before I discovered the bra. Mom hadn't said anything else about it, and from the backseat en route to Rochester's Luby Arena, she stared silently out her window as the highway exits passed.

"You okay?" Kara Shipley asked later, squeezing my hand. My best friend and I were practically twins, and together in the prep area at Luby, we looked the part. Two fourteen-year-olds from Watonka, New York. Slick, strawberry blond buns pinned and sprayed into place. Red-and-gray warm-up jackets with our local club logo—a bison, for Buffalo Bisonettes—embroidered like a badge near the top right shoulder. On our skating dresses underneath, we each wore a silver rabbit pin—our personal good luck charms for every event.

I nodded. "Just . . . nerves." I wanted to tell her about what I'd found, what I suspected, but when I thought of my mother, stopping her ironing to inspect the offending item and then whisking it into the dark of the dresser drawer, my insides burned.

Kara gave me another squeeze. "Don't worry, Hud. You'll rock this place tonight. Just ignore the cameras and breathe." With her free hand she rubbed my back, her palm soft and warm through the nylon dress. I'd almost forgotten about the cameras. Tonight's Empire Games was just a recreational competition, but the sponsor had invited the media to spotlight me since I was the favorite for next month's North Atlantic regionals—the gateway to everything I'd ever trained for. Tonight would be my big public debut—I'd show off my signature moves on live TV, turn more than a few heads, and fire a warning shot to my upcoming regional competition.

Ladies and gentlemen, Hudson Avery! Remember this night, and you'll be able to tell your kids that you knew her when!

"Hudson?" Kara frowned in the mirror, her hand still warm on my back. I took a deep breath as instructed and flashed her a tight smile—the same kind Mom had given me in her bedroom earlier. The same one she'd given my dad as she shuffled me to the front seat and arranged herself in the back. The same one she was probably giving him then, all the way up in the stands.

As the announcer called our names, we glided onto the ice like a long red-and-gray snake. I found my parents in their seats and waved. Mom had the video camera trained on the rink, but she was turned away, looking at the side doors where the event officials had gathered. There were directors from all the regional rinks, and most of the girls had private coaches, too; mine was there with the others, chatting up the CEO of

4

Empire Icehouse, Western New York's largest pro shop. He was an honorary judge.

I looked back at the stands as Dad gave me a small wave. His leg was bouncing up and down like he'd had too much coffee. My parents were sitting right next to each other, shoulders almost touching, but for all the miles between them, they might as well have been in different arenas.

After the parade of skaters, we settled into our reserved seats. Alternating with girls from eight other local clubs, we slid out one at a time to perform our programs—first round. Just as my club predicted, I owned it.

Hours later, seven of us remained in the final round to compete for the big prize: five thousand dollars cash, plus new equipment and upgrades for the entire club—an invaluable sponsorship courtesy of Empire Icehouse.

I was the only one left from the Buffalo club. The last shot. The sure thing.

As the opening chords of my music floated onto the ice, I felt the cameras zoom in on my face, and I forced a smile. My skating friends and coaches were counting on me. I was counting on me. The whole *city* was counting on me, its lone Bisonette, twirling like a ballerina in the spotlight.

By this time next year, I'd be famous, and everyone would know where I'd come from.

I skated over the smooth, white rink and sped up for the first jump. Nailed it. Slid into a long, leaning glide, sailing across the ice on one skate and picking up speed for my double axel.

Nailed that one, too. After months of intense workouts with my coach and choreographer, I'd learned my program impossibly well—memorized it until it was absolutely error-proof. Maybe that's why, as my feet glided across the ice like poured water, my thoughts had the space to stretch and wander. With four minutes to spare, my mind walked home, straight into the muffled arguments that had splintered our family like cracks in the ice—*We can't afford this. She needs to stay in school. I'm not selling the diner. What about Max? We can't just move.* It found Dad in the family room on the couch. It took notice of his late nights at the office and Mom's at Hurley's. It cataloged all the uncorrelated evidence, all the way up to tonight. Mom knew that bra wasn't mine the second she found it in the laundry, but she'd folded it and put it in my room anyway, as if burying it between my girlishly straight jeans and baggy sweatshirt would change the inevitable truth.

I leaned in for my next combination, and suddenly I could see into our future—it was all there, right before me. Dad would leave. Mom would get stuck with me and Max, who was only five and wouldn't understand. We'd probably have to move anyway—downsize, sacrifice, change. All because of . . . what? Who? My father, who'd given me my first pair of ice skates when I was just four years old? My father, who'd worked hard to pay for the lessons, the equipment, the private coach, the entry fees? My father, who'd never missed a practice or competition, always cheering from the sidelines, encouraging but never overbearing, loving but never smothering?

Something kicked me then, right in the chest. I fought to breathe, to keep the sting from my eyes, the shake from my limbs. I looked at my parents sitting in the stands, my father like he'd rather be anywhere but next to the woman he married. I looked at him not looking at me, not looking at her, and for the first time in the history of my competitions, I didn't want to win. I didn't want the money or the Icehouse gear for the club or the TV interviews they'd lined up for me. I didn't want to go to regionals in Lake Placid or sectionals after that. I didn't want any more lessons or competitions or all the big, impossible dreams that came with them. If the ice beneath my feet was the reason for the cracks in my parents' marriage, I didn't want any of it.

I watched them, wanting against the odds the simple gestures that meant things were okay—Dad's arm around my mother, her hand comfortably on his knee. Instead, Dad was still, alone. Mom had suddenly moved several rows in front of him, the camera glued to her face.

Instead of my impressive triple flip/triple toe loop combo, I did a single axel. Then I skipped my camel spin and just kept skating, curving into figure eights as if it were a beginner's lesson. I sensed the confusion from my home team and the coaches who'd seen me nail this stuff a hundred times in training, but I ignored it, pushed it down my legs, out through my skates, deep beneath the ice. When it was time for my grand finale, I did a halfhearted lutz, barely making a full rotation above the rink. On the other end of my jump, I crossed my skates and landed in a score-killing wobble.

The arena was silent.

As the next girl skated out to start her program, I slipped into the girls' bathroom, waiting for my mother to rush in after me.

She didn't come.

"Hudson Avery." At the end of the event, I sat numb in the kiss-and-cry room and listened for my abysmal scores, thinking about all the things that would end that night. The Empire Games. My parents' marriage. The skating career I no longer wanted. And the only shot my fellow Bisonettes had at those much-needed rink and equipment upgrades. I beat them all out in the first round only to choke when it really counted. Mostly, they were too shocked and disappointed to ask, too confused to assume my on-ice meltdown was anything other than an unforgivably bad case of nerves. I left without speaking to my coach or saying good-bye to the girls. I ignored the pinch in my stomach when I saw Kara's face, her eyes glassy and red, her mouth opened in an unspoken question: *What happened out there?*

In the car on the way home, Dad gave my knee a light squeeze and told me things would work out. That I just needed to look forward, to focus on the upcoming regionals—the stuff that really counted. Tonight was just a little setback, he said; I'd nail it next time for sure.

I met Mom's gaze in the side mirror, tired and sad with nothing to say, and I knew what Dad didn't: There wasn't going to *be* a next time. Not for him and Mom. Not for me and skating. Not for any of us.

Chapter One

Damsels in Distress

*Dark chocolate cupcakes
with red peppermint mascarpone icing,
edged with chocolate and crushed candy canes*

In three years of baking for Hurley's Homestyle Diner in Watonka, New York, I've never met a problem a proper cupcake couldn't fix. And while I haven't *quite* perfected the recipe to fix my father, I'm totally on the verge.

"Taste this." I pass a warm cupcake across the prep counter to Dani and lick a gob of cherry-vanilla icing from my thumb. "I think it's the one."

My best friend sighs. "That's what you said about the blueberry lemon batch. And the white mocha ones. Have you *seen* this thing walkin' around behind me? It's the Great Cupcake Booty of Watonka." She turns and shakes it, a few corkscrew curls springing loose from the pile on her head.

"Last one. I promise."

"Nice breakfast. You're lucky I . . . *mmmph* . . . oh my *God*!" Her copper-brown eyes widen as she wolfs down a big bite.

"I used half the sugar this time and buttercream instead of cream cheese. Doesn't compete with the cherry as much."

"Whatever you did, it's delish." She wipes her hands on an apron and goes back to prepping for our open, topping off small glass pitchers of maple syrup. I love baking at the diner on Saturday mornings, especially when Dani's on first shift. There's something peaceful about it—just the two of us here in the stainless steel kitchen, radio on low, the *hiss-pop-hiss* of the big coffeemakers keeping us company while the winter sky goes from black to lavender to a cool, downy gray.

I rinse the mixing bowls and set them back on the counter, rummaging through my stash for the next batch: eggs, butter, raw cane sugar, cocoa powder, heavy cream, espresso, shaved dark chocolate, a handful of this, a sliver of that, no measuring required. Every cupcake starts out a blank canvas, ingredients unattached to any shared destiny until I turn on the mixer. Now Dani stands on her toes to see into the bowl and together we watch it swirl, streaks of white and pale yellow and black, electric beaters whirring everything into a perfect brown velvet.

"You really are an artist, Cupcake Queen." Dani smiles, hefting the tray of syrups onto her shoulder and pushing through the double doors into the dining room.

Cupcake Queen. I owe the newspaper for that one. "Teen's Talent Turns Struggling Diner into Local Hot Spot: Cupcake

Queen Wows Watonka with Zany Creations," by Jack Marshall, staff reporter. The article's preserved in a crooked glass frame on the wall behind the register, right next to an autographed black-and-white photo of Ani DiFranco and three one-dollar bills from Mom's first sale as the new owner. You can see it clearly if you're sitting at the front counter in the seat on the far left—the one with the torn leatherette that pokes the back of your thighs—if you lean over and squint. I don't need to squint, though. I've read it so many times I can recite it backward. *Creations zany with Watonka wows queen cupcake: spot hot local into diner struggling turns talent teen's.*

I never set out to wow Watonka with zany creations or join the royal court of confectioners. When I first started inventing my cupcakes, it was just something to keep me and Bug— that's what I call Max—from going nuts after Dad moved to Nevada. Whenever we'd start to miss him, I'd lure Bug into the kitchen, and together we'd dig through the pantry for stuff to bake into funny little desserts with made-up names and frosting faces. We'd bring the best ones to the diner for Mom to share with the waitresses and Trick, her cook. Soon the regulars at the counter were sampling them, wanting to know when they'd be on the menu, when they could order a few dozen for their next bridge club party. Somewhere between my first batch of custom Bug-in-the-Mud Cakes and now, somewhere between leaving competitive skating and looking for a place to hide out, somewhere between Dad's departure and Mom finding the strength to get out of bed again, baking cupcakes became a part of me—both a saving grace and a real, moneymaking job.

Staff reporter Jack Marshall didn't ask about any of that stuff, though.

My gaze drifts out the window to the snow falling beneath the lights in the back lot. It's so gray and nondescript outside that I could be anywhere, anytime, and for a second the blankness is so complete that I lose track of the hour and forget where I am. Everything is flip-flopped, like the opposite of déjà vu.

"Hudson?" Dani's voice over the whir of the mixer brings me back. *Saturday morning. Twenty-ninth of November. Cupcake day.*

"Sorry. I kinda spaced."

"Yeah, I kinda noticed." She pulls up a tall metal stool and sits next to me at the prep counter. "So, are we gonna talk about your dad's e-mail, or—"

"Not." I recited parts of his latest missive over the phone last night, but here in the Hurley's kitchen, separated from the rest of the world by the double doors and a blanket of new snow on the roof, I'm not in the mood.

"It *is* pretty jackass of him, if you ask me . . . even though you're not." She picks up a batter-covered spoon and licks off all the chocolate. "Like you *really* want to hear about your father's romantic escapades with—"

"Yeah, exactly, thanks." I lift the bowl and scrape the batter into silicone cups, filling each one three-quarters precisely.

"I'm *so* done with his soul-mate-of-the-month crap."

"Did he call her his soul mate?" she asks.

"Who moves to Vegas and falls in love with a female Elvis impersonator? Hello, walking cliché."

I know I should ask him to squash the oversharing, but honestly? Hearing about his special lady friends is better than the alternative. First few months in Vegas? Total radio silence. Now? Let the e-mails flow. Sometimes I wonder if it's the women in his life pushing him to be a better father. "Your children need to be part of your life. Reach out to them." *Ick.* Like I really want Dad to "reach out" over our respective love lives. And by respective, I mean serial (his) and nonexistent (mine).

"Maybe she's all right," Dani says. "You don't—"

"Anyone who goes by Shelvis is clearly not all right."

"I thought it was Sherylynn or something."

"Sheryl*anne*. Shelvis is her stage name. She's on tour this month," I say, making air quotes around "tour." "So instead of visiting us, Dad's using his vacation time to follow her all over the southwest." That's the part I didn't recite last night. I kept hoping it was a joke.

Dani crinkles her nose. "Gross."

"Seriously gross. It's the fourth Shelvis-related e-mail this week."

"Any pictures?" she asks. He sent pictures of the last one— Honey or Candy or something like that—and Dani and I spent the entire weekend on Photoshop, giving her a handlebar mustache and snakes for hair.

I slide the baking cups into the oven and wipe my hands on a dish towel. "I think we can use our imaginations."

"What about video? Now *that* I'd pay to see." Dani clears her throat and breaks into a frightening version of "Love Me Tender."

See, some people politely encourage their tone-deaf friends to sing. Some people even convince them to go on live television and audition for national competitions. But me? I am not that friend. Especially since Dani's parents are, like, jazz virtuosos—mom sings, dad plays trumpet. You'd think she'd pick up on the fact that her voice lacks that certain something . . . called . . . being in tune.

"I thought we already established that your parents' genes totally skipped you," I say.

"They didn't *skip* me. Mom says I'm just underdeveloped. I'm pretty sure Whitney Houston was the same way before she vocally matured."

"Gotcha. Have another cupcake, Whit." I slide the plate of experiments across the counter and load my spent bowls into the giant dishwasher.

I've got enough cupcakes in the oven, so I stick the remaining experiments in the front bakery case and help Dani with her sidework: wiping the menus, rolling silverware into napkins, and setting out metal trays of cut veggies for Trick. In an effort to feel slightly less guilty about our sugar-sweet breakfast, we take five at the prep counter and dine on some fruit salad. Dani recites saucy passages from a novel with a half-naked pirate on the cover as I watch the snow swirl outside, and the entire restaurant fills with the warm, chocolaty scent of fresh-baked cupcakes.

"The calm before the storm," Dani says, closing her book and glancing up at the clock. "Another hour, this place will be a hot mess."

"Don't act like you don't love it. You're a front-of-the-house whore and you know it."

Dani wiggles her eyebrows. "You should try it. I could teach you *all* the tricks."

"I'll stick to baking. It relaxes me." I pull my cupcakes out of the oven and arrange them on wire cooling racks. "How sad is it that the crack of dawn in the Hurley's kitchen is the only time I can get any peace and—"

"Morning, girls!" Mom rushes in through the back door with my little brother and a blast of cold air. "I just heard the weather report—we're expecting a storm later."

"Snowed in at the diner! *Yes!*" Bug pumps his fist, voice muffled by a thick red scarf. His tortoiseshell glasses are all fogged up, so I can't see his eyes.

I kiss the top of his fuzzy blond head and tug off his backpack and jacket. "Winter in Watonka, Mom. Not a big mystery."

"No, just a busy night ahead, and we're already short-staffed." Mom pulls off her hat, her gray-blond hair crackling with static. "Marianne's out of town till tomorrow, Nat's studying for finals, and I'm not sure Carly's ready for more than two tables at a time." Her trademark sigh is laced through every word, and I sag when it lands on my shoulders. That blue-and-white sign with the picture of the fork and knife on the I-190, just before the Watonka exit? Well, that's us—first fork and knife off the highway. Bad weather hits, and all the just-passing-through folks in the world end up in our dining room. There goes *my* Saturday night.

"Nothing we can't handle," Dani says. "We'll just—"

"Mom, can I inspect the mail?" Bug asks. He fingers the envelopes sticking out of Mom's overstuffed purse. "I brought my lab gear."

"Sure, baby. Use my office." She hands over her purse and hangs their coats in the staff closet as Bug skips into the windowless room at the back of the kitchen. "Where's the omelet setup?"

"Already done." Dani hops up from the counter and shows mom the veggies, right where we always put them.

"Ma, chill. We're fine," I say. "It's not even time to open."

Dani and I follow her to the dining room. In flawless, unbroken succession, she pours herself a coffee, starts a fresh pot, checks all the sugar dispensers, and gives the counter an unnecessary wipe-down with a wet paper towel.

You can take the waitress out of the diner . . . but then she comes back and buys the joint.

"Know what you need?" I ask.

"A winning lotto ticket and a vacation? Preferably some-place tropical, no kids allowed?" She sits on a maroon leatherette stool next to Dani, rests her elbows on the counter, and sips her coffee.

"We're fresh out of lotto tickets." I take one of my experimental cupcakes from the case and put it on a pink-trimmed plate. "New recipe. As the owner, you're obligated to try it."

"They're amazing," Dani says. "She's on a roll lately."

"Don't have to convince me, darlin'." Mom smiles and carves out a piece with a fork. After the first bite, she loses the cutlery and dives in with her fingers, just the way you're supposed to.

"They're called Cherry Bombs," I tell her after she inhales the last of it.

"Baby, you're some kinda genius. Love them. And you." She pecks my cheek and drops her dishes in the bus bin underneath the counter.

"I have a bunch more cooling," I say, untying my apron. "I'll be back later to frost."

"You're going on break? But the snow, and—"

"Ma, I've been in the kitchen all morning. I'm just going for a walk. I'll be back before the rush, then I can help wherever you guys need me. Okay?" I grab the bus bin with her dishes and bump open the kitchen doors with my hip.

"Okay," she calls after me. "Say bye to Bug first. Mrs. Ferris is picking him up in an hour."

"Hudson!" Bug flashes a gap-toothed grin from behind his makeshift crime lab in Mom's office, a pair of sandwich bags zipped over both hands. In one, he's holding a white envelope;

in the other, a half-eaten candy cane with a cotton ball rubber-banded to the end of it.

To my early morning eyes, it *appears* he's dusting our mail for fingerprints, but you can't always tell with Bug.

I set my backpack on the floor and plop down in the chair across from him. "Looking for evidence?"

"Nope." He slides the glasses up his nose with the back of his wrist and rubs the envelope with the candy cane. "Anthrax. I'm at a critical juncture."

Critical juncture? Sure. What eight-year-old isn't?

"Find anything interesting?" I ask.

"No powdery residue. But definitely suspicious. Smell." He slides a makeup catalog from beneath a microscope made out of a plate, a toilet paper roll, and an intricate arrangement of pipe cleaners. "Any ideas?"

I take a scientific whiff. "Gardenia. Looks like those Mary Kay terrorists are at it again."

"Don't laugh. Your stuff is on the 'highly suspicious' list, too." He pulls a bright yellow, junk mail–looking envelope from the stack and busts out his game show face. "Hudson Avery, *You're* Future Is Closer Than You Think."

"My future? Hmm. Working at Hurley's *is* pretty dangerous."

Bug sighs. "Don't be so literal. They spelled 'your' wrong. It's one of the signs."

"Of stupidity?" I've asked Mrs. Ferris—our downstairs neighbor, landlady, and chief Bug-sitter—not to let him watch the news. Ever since they busted that terror cell a few blocks over, it's like CSI Watonka in our house. Last month he told me he was installing metal detectors for the bathroom and that starting this summer, I'd need a government-issued ID just to pee. "Hey, I'm sure Mom appreciates your vigilant counterterrorism efforts, but try not to waste the Ziplocs. They're expensive."

"It's cool. I recycle." He flings the anthrax-detecting candy cane into the trash along with a red envelope from the gas company. Miraculously, my grammatically incorrect letter and Mom's makeup catalog get a pass.

"I need this." I dig the bill from the trash and slit open the envelope, even though I already know what it says: THIS IS YOUR FINAL NOTICE BEFORE SHUTOFF. Mom made a partial payment last month, but technically the gas bill's mine—trade-off for keeping the cupcake profits—and there's still a balance due. I'll have to stop by the service center again this week. They probably have my picture on the wall, like those people in department stores who write bad checks. Beware of Hudson Avery, master groveler and avoider of late fees great and small!

"What are you doing now?" Bug asks as I slip the bill into my backpack. "Wanna play Special Victims Unit? You can be the victim this time." He's out of the chair before I can answer.

"Sorry, bud. I have to run out for a while."

He frowns, tiny glasses slipping back down his nose.

"Don't be sad." I kneel in front of him so we're the same height and squeeze his shoulders. Beneath my hands, his bones feel small and hollow like a bird's; I resist the urge to zip him up in my jacket.

"How about we hang out tonight—just you and me. I'll bring home some extra cupcakes." I push his glasses back up and lower my voice to a conspiratorial whisper. "I'll let you stay up late, too. Sound like a date?"

"Hmm." He considers my bribe. "Four cupcakes, and I stay up until midnight."

"I was thinking two and ten thirty."

He hefts my backpack off the floor and hands it over. "*I* was thinking three and eleven, and I won't tell Mom you're ice-skating again."

"*What?* I'm not—"

"I saw you cleaning the skates in your room last night, Hud. I'm not stupid."

Like I needed the reminder.

I swing the bag over my shoulder, skates kicking me hard in the back. "Three and eleven it is, Detective Avery. Just remember the number one rule of good police work: Never rat out your sources."

His eyes go wide. "Don't say 'rat'! You'll give Mr. Napkins a complex!"

I grab his arms. "*Please* tell me you didn't bring your hamster to the diner."

"He's at home, but that's not the point. Just don't say the *R*-word. It offends me."

"Sorry. Don't *narc* on your sources."

"No narcing. Got it." He pulls a pen and a spiral note-pad from the piles on the desk and makes a note. "Hey, don't forget your letter." He stretches to reach the yellow envelope and gives it a closer look. "What's a foundation, anyway?"

"Oh, like a charity. Some gajillionaire sets them up to help a good cause. Why? Rich old uncle Mom forgot to mention?"

He inspects the return address. "Not unless his name is Uncle Lola."

"Uncle *who*?" My throat goes dry, and I cough to clear the knot from it.

Bug scrunches up his face and checks again. "Lola Cap . . . Cap-something."

"Capri*ani*?" I whisper. *It can't be her.*

"Whoa—you know a gajillionaire?"

"Yes. I mean, no. I used to . . . I knew her before. A long time ago." I take the envelope from my brother, ignoring the tremor in my fingers. My stomach twists when I see her name, all fancy black script on canary-colored paper.

"Who is it?" Bug asks.

I crush the letter in my hand. "Lola Capriani was my skating coach."

Chapter Two

Cupcakes of Destiny

*White chocolate cupcakes
with pale blue vanilla icing formed into peaks
and dusted with silver sprinkles*

Dear *Hudson Avery*:

Lola Capriani knew a thing or two about chasing dreams.

The daughter of poor Italian immigrants who settled right here in Western New York, Lola worked hard her entire life, overcoming obstacle after obstacle until she achieved her dream of becoming a professional figure skater. With four Olympic gold medals and nearly five decades as a top-level international competitor and entertainer, Lola returned home to follow a new dream: nurturing athletic talent in young skaters. Through her private coaching practice, she mentored girls like yourself as they worked toward their own dreams.

Following Lola's death last year, her family established The Lola Capriani Foundation for Winter Athletics to provide financial assistance to emerging athletes for training, equipment, travel, entry fees, and other costs associated with winter athletic competition. In honor of that undertaking, and in memory of Lola's lifelong dedication and spirit, we are pleased to announce the Capriani Cup, an exciting new competition for junior and senior class female figure skaters in Erie County who wish to continue skating at the college level. Registered skaters will compete on Saturday, February 1st, for a $50,000 scholarship for collegiate studies and related skating expenses.

As a former Lola Capriani student, you are encouraged to enter this rewarding competition. Additional information and registration forms are available on the foundation website.

We hope to see you on the ice soon, and we wish you success and happiness in all your endeavors, wherever your future takes you!

Sincerely,

Amy

Amy Hains
Director, Foundation Special Projects

I was Bug's age when I met the legendary Lola Capriani. She'd just nailed a triple-axel/triple-loop combo at the Buffalo Skate Club downtown, and I'd just ducked into the third stall of the ladies' room to reconsider my career path (*cough* *throw up*). When I hobbled back out on my rubber skate guards, hair plastered across my forehead and skin as white as the ice, she was on the sidelines with my father, looking a whole lot meaner than she did in the posters on my bedroom wall.

"I got four gold medals and two titanium joints older than you, greenblades," she said to me then, slapping her gloves against her hip and nodding toward the bathroom where I'd just been. "I don't know what *that* was all about, but you'd betta walk it off. *Capisce?*"

I just about peed my pink leotard when she looked at me, but there's something downright *instinctive* about yes-ma'am-ing a septuagenarian with a scorpion tattooed between her shoulder blades and an accent that says *I don't take crap from nobody*—especially when she could still bang out gold-medaling moves like old Lola could. I nodded like a wooden puppet, head on a string, and followed her out onto the rink.

She worked me for nearly two hours.

I found out later it was an audition.

I found out later I made the cut.

My father seemed as humbled and starstruck as I felt. He didn't say anything to me after the workout until we got into the car, and when he finally spoke, his voice was thick with wonder. "This Capriani woman . . . this is your chance, Hudson. Your ticket to greatness. If I can find a way to give you this shot, promise me you won't let her down."

I smiled, and Dad started to glow from the inside out,

like this was his dream, too. Maybe it was. I wasn't sure what brought a globe-trotting ice princess like Lola Capriani back to a busted-up place like Watonka, but I knew what a big deal it was that she'd agreed to train a new student—especially since there was no way my parents could afford her regular fees.

Six years later, after I quit the ice, I learned that she'd agreed to take me at half the cost because of what she saw when I finally shook off my nerves and auditioned that night: drive and potential. Unlimited, unjaded heart. A spark.

When Dad looked at me from the driver's seat with all the pride and hope in the world, asking me to make that one promise, I nodded, same as before.

Head.

On.

A string.

And I *kept* nodding, right up until the night of the Empire Games.

If I'd known about Lola's funeral in time, I would've gone. I wasn't holding a grudge about what happened—it wasn't her fault. She wasn't paid to be my friend or counselor, on the ice or off. She was there the night I threw the event—a sideline seat to the whole disaster. With that single act of unsportsmanlike defiance, I'd thumbed my nose at the ice and severed our arrangement. Left the competition. Walked away from the medals and roses and the promise of a bright future outside of this broken, rusted-out husk of a town. When I turned in my official resignation, Lola took the letter from my hands, nodded once, and walked away. There was nothing more she could do for me, and we both knew it. We never spoke again. I didn't even know she died until I read about it online, three days after her funeral.

But I didn't come down to the beach in the dead of winter today to wallow. I came here to skate. And judging from the solid curtain of white stretched clear across Canada, I've got about two hours before that storm hits.

I fold the letter into a tiny square, shove it to the bottom of my inside fleece pocket, and lace up.

DANGER:

THIN ICE ON LAKE!

NO SKATING, SLEDDING, OR SNOWMOBILING
—*Watonka Department of Parks and Recreation*

I tap the base of the signpost with my toe pick as the white blanket of Lake Erie shifts and blows its bitter breath through my hair. Technically I'm not skating on the lake, just the runoff—a long, shallow slick that freezes over the beach, right near the abandoned Fillmore Steel Mill. It's as close to perfect as an untended outdoor rink can be: level, mostly smooth, swept clear by the constant wind. The air is thick with industrial leftovers, but out here, invisible cancer-causing particles aside, I get to be alone.

As I push off from the post, silver blades scrape against the ice like knives sharpening on an old stone. The memory of each movement is imprinted; bones and muscles and ligaments know exactly how to bend and twist, push and pull, stretch and snap to propel me across the ice. Back and forth, over and over, I engrave the makeshift rink with lines and figure eights. When I return next weekend, the wind will have erased them as though I was never here.

After a solid warm-up, I stop for a hot chocolate break and unpack my thermos, gazing out over the vast stretch of nothingness that lies between here and Canada. They don't make a warning sign for it, but *that's* the real danger—that downright manic-depressive desolation. No joke—winter on the beaches of Watonka is about the emptiest thing you'll ever see in your life. When you're out here alone, contemplating all the things you didn't do and the person you didn't become . . . if you think about it too long—if you stand here and consider the great bleakness of it all—a hush seeps into the gray space, and the wind will hollow out your bones, and the purest kind of loneliness comes up from the inside to swallow you like an avalanche.

I drop the thermos back into my bag and switch out damp gloves for a dry pair. Behind the smokestacks that stand guard around the old mill, the wind shifts, pushing out an invisible plume of burnt air. I tighten the scarf over my face to mute the rotten-egg smell and press on, one-two-three *glide*, one-two-three *glide*.

Glide . . .

Glide . . .

Glide . . .

I left a lot of things behind the night of my last competition, but not this part. I close my eyes and sail across the ice in the dead end of November, and when the wind rushes up to kiss me, I let it. I lick my lips and welcome it in, because the frigid bite reminds me that inside, I'm warm and alive. That inside, my heart still beats for something, calling me to the windburned shores of Lake Erie when fear and regret leave no other haven.

I pump my legs to amp up my speed, closing in on the far edge of the runoff that meets the lake.

Does Hudson Avery still have what it takes? Will she make the near-impossible turn, or will she hurtle across the outer reaches of the ice, destined for a watery, hypothermic death?

The lake is coming up fast, everything around me a white blur. I push harder, legs tight and strong, and just before I cross onto the lake ice, I suck in a cool breath and hold it. I tilt my blades against the world and bank hard, looping around the bend, shooting up a spray of shaved ice. The sound is like a single wave shushing up the shore, a whisper falling out over a blue-white sea. I still hear it in my dreams.

Phishhhh . . .

I race back to the other end, arms out like a great blue heron about to take flight. I hold another deep breath, whip my leg around, and launch into a scratch spin, twirling like a top as I pull my arms tight against my chest. When I'm ready to stop, it's that simple: I set my toe pick on the ice and the world around me halts, immediate, soundless, a snowflake alighting on the soft shoulders of November.

Hudson Avery, ladies and gentlemen! Straight from the frozen

shores of Lake Erie to the international hall of champions, skating
through a shower of roses to take her well-earned place in the winner's
circle. . . .

Behind me, the imaginary crowd fades as the smokestacks
rise up, wind whipping through the iron belly of the mill,
moaning like a ghost. The chain-link fence around it shudders
as if to laugh, and that great bleakness hovers above my skin,
reminding me as always that three years ago, I walked away
from the roses. The cheering crowds. The winner's circles.

Last weekend, alone on this desolate beach, I was certain
the ice-skating part of me would stay locked in the closet forever. Certain I'd torn up my so-called ticket to greatness and
burned all the bridges on the path there. Certain that while
the rest of the world moved on, I'd be stuck in my mother's
old diner, rusting like the gates of Watonka, bound forever to
these shores as my bones turned to ice.

But now?

I look back over the lake and take a swallow of air, lungs
burning with cold and pollution. Generally speaking, I don't
like to spend my work break standing out in the bleached,
bone-numbing cold of Watonka daydreaming about all the
shoulda-coulda-wouldas.

But I can't stop thinking about the letter. The second
chance. *Fifty thousand dollars* . . .

I lift my face to the bright part of the sky where the sun
should be, and in my mind, I hear a new version of that old
saying about trees falling in the forest: *If a girl spends every*

weekend sneaking off to the lake in the dead of winter and no one is around to see her, is she really skating at all?

Twenty feet offshore, an ice volcano erupts, a spout of water shot high in the sky.

Phishhhhhhhhh . . .

It's been a long time since I've run a competitive program. Even with months of dedicated practice, there's no guarantee I'd be good enough to win—especially without a coach. And what about my mother? How could I tell her?

For Mom, my skating was never a career track or even a once-in-a-lifetime shot at something great. It was a hobby. Something to dry off and put away in the closet with the tap shoes, the clarinet, and the Barbie dolls as soon as I was old enough/smart enough/tired enough/broke enough to move on. Now my skates are just another reminder that I used to have a dad around to encourage me, and she used to have a husband to brush the snow from her car and bring her a cup of hot coffee with two sugars every morning before he left for work, and now we don't.

I tighten my legs and propel backward, feet scissoring over the ice, mind drifting into my parallel life—the one where I didn't throw that event, killing my reputation as a top competitor and losing Kara Shipley and my other skating friends. In my parallel life, I don't live in Watonka anymore. I'm a real competitor, always on the road, sending Mom and Bug postcards from beautiful cities as I win medal after medal, title after title. I'm cool and confident, toughened by the difficulties of my childhood but still optimistic as I perform a perfect program for the World Figure

Skating Championships. One by one, the judges rise in applause. They've never seen anything like it. They shout to be heard over the cheers, and then a voice cuts sharply through the din . . .

"Hey! Look *out*!"

I'm cold and horizontal, helplessly pinned beneath a boy. A cute one. Our skates are all tangled up and our hearts are knocking against each other like they're ready to take this outside. His fingers cradle the back of my head just over the cement-hard ice; with his free hand, he brushes the hair from my eyes and I blink.

Josh Blackthorn, co-captain of the Watonka Wolves varsity hockey team, stares down at me, breath mingling with mine in a thin white soup.

"Are you okay?" he asks. His touch across my forehead makes me shiver. I blink again, trying to piece together the evidence. My head hurts, Josh is holding me, and all I can think is . . .

I didn't wash my hair this morning. I totally smell like last night's bacon burger special.

"Can you hear me?" Josh waves his fingers in front of my eyes, his face twisted with worry. Perfect. First time I'm *this* close to a really cute guy in years—and by years I mean *ever*—and save for my adorable pink leg warmers and the lip balm I slicked on when I got here, I'm ninety-two percent hygienically unprepared. He probably thinks I'm a pig farmer or a pig wrestler or some other person who regularly interacts with pork products . . . and I probably have a concussion.

"I hear you." I pull myself into a sitting position to put

some space between the co-captain's nose and my bacon-infused hair. "I'm okay. Just . . . what happened?"

"We crashed." Josh kneels on the ice in front of me. "I sort of . . . sorry. It's my fault." He manages a weak smile. I've never seen his eyes up close before, and when he looks at me full on, I notice all the color in them. Gray-blue with an outer ring of dark purple, flecks of gold near the center. Beneath the left one, there's a tiny freckle hidden behind a row of soft, dark lashes.

I squeeze my eyes shut, breaking through the fog in my head. "How long have you been out here? How do you even know this place?"

Josh pulls off his knit hat and rubs his head, ears going red in the cold. His hair is short and dark, not quite black, and one side sticks out a little funny from the hat. There's a scar near his temple, a tiny white V where the hair doesn't grow. Probably some puck-diving, two-seconds-left-in-the-big-game, one-chance-to-save-it-all kind of injury from his last school.

"I come here to think sometimes. Skate," he says, looking out over the lake. "Get away, you know? I'm Josh Blackthorn, by the way. Hudson, right?" He turns back to me and smiles, his lips an inch closer than they were a moment ago.

"Yeah," I say as if I'm not totally shocked he knows my name and thinks I don't know his. "Avery. I've never seen you out here, though. I never see *anyone* out here."

"No? I've seen you once or twice. But I'm not, like, stalking you or anything. If you're on the ice when I get here, I usually bail. Today I just thought I'd . . . I don't know. Say hi or something.

Be less . . . um . . . creepy?" He raises his eyebrows and gives me another smile, tentative, like he's waiting for confirmation.

No, dude. You're not creepy. You're, like, the opposite of creepy. In fact, you're kind of . . .

My stomach fills with a swarm of bees. As far as stalkers go, Josh would definitely be a good one to have. But I don't do spectators—not anymore. I don't like to be spectated, inspected, spectacular, or even a spectacle. I just want to be a speck. A tiny, anonymous speck in an indiscernible sea of white.

"You okay?" he asks.

I nod as another breeze unfurls over the ice. His jaw tightens, firm and strong as he braces against the chill. We laugh together when the cold hits again, harder this time, our mutual shivering enough to bond us in shared discomfort. In all this frigid whiteness, his mouth looks red and warm, and my eyes trace the curve of his lips as the laughter fades. He watches me, too. When the air stills, his eyes hold mine a millisecond too long.

And right before it becomes, like, I'm-about-to-kiss-you awkward, he looks away.

"I thought you saw me over there." He nods toward the edge of the ice where he must've been standing earlier. Watching. Spectating. "I skated this way, but then you were just speeding up. I tried to warn you, but . . . *impact*." He slams his hands together to demonstrate, startling a seagull out from behind a nearby snowbank.

"I didn't see you," I say.

"You sure you're okay? No dizziness or anything?" He

gets to his feet and reaches down to help me.

"Don't worry about it." I stand and straighten my fleece, ignoring his outstretched hand. "Seriously. But I need to get back to work." I smile a little, even though the mortification meter is exploding off the charts.

"You do? I mean, okay, that's cool." He looks at me straight on again, his crazy-beautiful blue-gray eyes bright and clear beneath the colorless sky, and Parallel Life Hudson goes off on another fantasy. I imagine her sitting at some cozy little café table with Josh, sipping hot chocolate with those irresistible baby marshmallows on top, laughing about their head-on collision. He smiles and tells her she's got chocolate on the corner of her mouth, and she pretends to be embarrassed as he erases it gently with his thumb. There are sparks and laughs and flirty little jokes with lots of subtext, and later, after he walks her back to work, he pulls her into a passionate kiss in the parking lot. The word "bliss" appears in a cloud over her head, surrounded by red and pink hearts, and from that moment on, the frothy feel of hot chocolate against her lips will bring her back to the day they . . .

"So, yeah, I should head out," I tell him, before my fantasyland mind starts naming our unborn children. "Storm's coming, and I'm . . . I'll be late."

Josh's smile fades. Despite the icy fingers of the lake, my neck is hot and itchy under the wool scarf. I lean forward on my toe pick and take a step toward the edge, but the wind hits me again, throwing me off balance. My feet skid, skates connecting with Josh's in a clash of metal.

For the second time in five minutes, the two of us are laid out like a car wreck, that dumb seagull and his motley friends whooping it up on the ice around us.

Stupid birds. Don't you know it's winter?

"Okay, the first crash was my fault," Josh says, standing and pulling me to my feet. "But this one was *all* you. Think you're okay to work?"

"No choice. Time to frost the cupcakes." *Time to frost the cupcakes?* Concussion confirmed. No way I'd say something like that to the hockey boy without some sort of head injury. I've *got* to get out of here.

"Cupcakes, huh?" Josh nods appreciatively. "Okay. But I'm walking you out."

"You just got here. You should stay and skate." I check out his scuffed black hockey skates. They're not new, but they're definitely good quality. Sturdy. Probably fast. "At least until the storm hits."

"Nah. I've had enough crashing and burning for one day. Besides, someone has to look out for you, Avery. You're dangerous."

My breath catches in my chest and my heart speeds up again, but he doesn't seem to notice. He just smiles and puts his arm around me, one hand on my elbow as he guides me off the ice. He trades his skates for boots and I follow suit, slipping rubber guards onto my blades and wrapping them safely in a plastic Fresh 'n' Fast bag in my backpack.

We walk together over a stomped-down opening in the fence, past Fillmore's infamous Graveyard of Signs, every one scrawled with blue graffiti and bent like a broken cornstalk.

FALLOUT SHELTER—IN CASE OF NUCLEAR EMERGENCY, USE BRYANT STREET ENTRANCE. HARD HAT AREA—AUTHORIZED PERSONNEL ONLY. COMPROMISED STRUCTURE—BEWARE OF FALLING DEBRIS. CONDEMNED PROPERTY—DO NOT ENTER. NO TRESPASSING—VIOLATORS WILL BE PROSECUTED. When we reach the end near the parking lot, there's a lone car parked under another sign: LOT B—OVERNIGHT EMPLOYEES ONLY.

"Need a ride?" Josh digs the keys from his pocket. His breath fogs as he waits for my response, soft and even like the plume of a distant train.

I don't have my finger on the pulse of Watonka High's gossip network, but I try to recall everything I've ever heard about him. Co-captain of the Watonka Wolves. Moved here last year from Ohio or Chicago or some other lake-effect place that ends in an *o*. Hangs out with the other guys on the team and their various rotating "hockey wives," though I don't think he has a girlfriend—at least not from our school.

"It's not far," I say. "I like the walk. Besides, if my mother sees me in a car with a strange boy . . . not that you're strange or anything. And not that there's anything wrong with riding in a car with you. It's just . . ." *Brain to mouth! Must! Stop! Moving!*

"Nah, I hear you." Josh smiles and unlocks the car.

I sling my bag over my shoulder and press my hand against my jacket, the foundation letter crinkling softly inside, reminding me of its presence. "Sorry if I ruined your ice time today."

"You didn't. Actually, it was kind of cool . . . um . . . running into you."

"I'm not usually so clumsy out there," I say quickly. "I mean, I just didn't see—"

"I know." He's still smiling at me, but not in a teasing way. It's almost self-conscious, like he's trying to be calm and collected, but he just can't help that smile. Which, of course, makes it that much more adorable and—

"So, see you around?" he asks.

"Definitely. I mean, yes. Okay. Um, bye." I turn away before any more stupid comes out of me.

Josh warms up his car as I jog up to the main road, skates bouncing lightly against my back. The sound reminds me of Lola on that first night, eyes dark and serious as she whacked her gloves against her hip, again and again and again.

You gotta want it, kiddo. Really want it.

I turn back toward the car. It's close behind me now, tires crunching over the snow. Josh pulls up next to me and lowers the window.

"Watch your step, Avery," he says, easing onto the road. "Slippery out there."

I raise my eyebrows and give him a half smile. "That's good advice, Blackthorn."

"Winter in Watonka, right?" He waves and glides down the slick street, break lights flashing at the stop sign. I walk backward in the opposite direction and watch until his taillights disappear around the corner, my boots slipping in the slush only once, all the way back to Hurley's.

Chapter Three

No One Wants to Kiss a Girl Who Smells Like Bacon, So I Might as Well Get Fat Cupcakes

*Double-chocolate cupcakes served warm
in a sugar-butter reduction;
piped with icing braids of peanut butter,
cream cheese, and fudge; and
sprinkled with chocolate chips*

Saturday breakfast is in full swing when I get back, bacon popping on Trick's grill like cholesterol was just recategorized as an essential nutrient by the food pyramid people. If I don't already smell, T minus ten minutes to maximum porkaliciousness.

"There's my girl," Trick says as I throw my stuff into the staff closet and change into my kitchen sneakers. "Thought you went out lookin' for a new man."

"Nah. You know you're the only man in my life." I laugh, but it's basically true, and not in a dirty-old-man way, either.

Trick smiles from beneath his Buffalo Sabres cap, dark brown skin crinkling around his eyes. "Hey, take that box in the office for your brother tonight. I found a bunch of computer parts for his school thing—he left before I could tell him."

"It's not for school." I wash my hands and dig out my frosting gear. "He's building a robot playmate. Says he—"

"Finally!" Dani pushes through the kitchen doors and sticks an order ticket into the strip over the grill. The top of her retro lavender Hurley Girl dress is splattered with the morning's sludge. "You're *never* that long on break. Where've you been?"

"Nowhere." I tie a semi-clean apron around my waist and look at Trick. His back is turned for the moment, but his ears have multidirectional sonar capability and his mouth is even bigger than his heart.

"All right," she says, taking the hint. "Get started on those cupcakes while I do a flyby on my tables. Smoke break in fifteen?"

I nod. We don't smoke, but we break. It's all very complicated.

Fifteen minutes later we're out in the trash alcove otherwise known as the smoking lounge, warming our hands in the heat leaking through the propped-open back door.

She stamps her feet to chase away the ice-blue air. "Spill it," she says. "Quick. My equatorial ass can't handle this cold."

"I ran into Josh Blackthorn from school. We sort of . . ." *Pow!* I slam my palms together like Josh did earlier, imitating our crash.

"Hold up—you *did it*? With the *hockey* captain? On your *break*? What the—"

"No! We crashed on the ice at Fillmore. I was skating. Fully clothed. Besides, I totally reek." I pull my red-blond ponytail across my face for a whiff. "No one wants to do it with a chick who smells like bacon."

Her brow creases. "Everybody loves bacon."

"Not as a signature scent."

"True, but some people—*wait*. You went skating with Josh Blackthorn?"

I play with the zipper on my jacket, yanking it up and down. *Voop. Voop. Voop-voop-voop.* "Not exactly."

Her eyes narrow. When it comes to my on-again, off-again affair with the ice, Dani knows the highlights, but we don't talk about it much. She and I got close during the *post*-skating part of my life, right after Mom, Bug, and I moved to the apartment near her house.

She taps my foot with hers. "Hud, why are you acting all, like, twitchy? What's going on?"

I let out a long, slow breath, remembering how alive I felt today on the ice. I think about the Capriani Cup and the warmth that rises up inside when I land the perfect jump, make the hard turns, nail my favorite moves, even all these years later.

And then I remember Josh Blackthorn's hand brushing the hair from my face.

"Hudson?" Dani asks again, her big, copper-penny eyes searching mine.

"Danielle!" Trick shouts from the kitchen. "Two steak-and-egg specials up for table three!"

"Get Carly to run it!" Dani shouts back. "Sorry. Talk to me, girl. I'm freezing my—"

"Listen." I grab the front of her jacket, pushing out the words in a half-frozen jumble. "I got an invitation in the mail today . . . this thing . . . and after all that stuff from three years ago, and Dad, and Shelvis, and crashing into Josh, something hit me. I think I've been . . . I don't know. Something's just . . . missing. I might—"

"Oh no. Don't *even* say it. You're totally crushing on the hockey boy, aren't you? Jeez. How hard did you hit your head?"

I swat her hand away from my forehead. "I'm not crushing—"

"Trust me. I know hot and bothered when I see it."

"Bothered, maybe. By *you*. You read too many books, you know that? This isn't *How I Met My Half-Naked Pirate Hottie*." I look down at the pavement. "Not even close."

"First of all, it's called *Treasure of Love*, and there's no such thing as too many books. And anyway, you're totally blushing. What is it with you and hockey captains? First Will Harper, and now his number two? This is bad news, baby. Bad."

"Will doesn't count," I say firmly. Will Harper became my first kiss when a rousing match of Seven Minutes in Heaven forced us into someone's basement closet a million years ago— way before his hockey captain days. Honestly, it's not like the stars aligned or anything. Before my brain could catch up to the breaking news of what was happening on my lips, the closet door opened, the light spilled in, and we broke apart. Some guy high-fived Will and everything smelled like Cheetos and root beer and that was pretty much it. "It was just a stupid eighth-grade party game."

"That's because he never spoke to you again."

"Well, Josh isn't like Will. Josh seems really sweet, and he's—never mind. How did we get on Josh?"

"*Who* got on Josh? *I* certainly didn't. Did you?"

I smack her arm. "I don't want to talk about him."

"Look, just because your father's a grade A jackass—"

"Hey!"

"Sorry." Dani tugs on one of her curls, wrapping it around her finger. "I mean, just because your parents' relationship didn't work out doesn't mean all relationships are doomed."

"Crashing into someone on the ice doesn't make a relationship."

"No?" She smiles, her cheeks glowing like smooth red plums. "Maybe you just need to get—"

"Dani!" Trick again. "These cows are well-done, sweetheart," he calls from over the grill, all sizzle-sizzle, scrape-scrape, metal-on-metal. "Ain't gonna run themselves. Carly's got her hands full."

Dani waves him off. "As I was saying . . . wait, you're bright red! Oh, if Josh could see you now. He'd be all over it." She belts out a not-so-kid-friendly, not-so-in-tune rendition of the sittin'-in-a-tree song.

"Highly unlikely," I say. The impassioned skating speech queued up in my head starts to lose steam, my thoughts getting stuck all over Josh and that sincere, post-crash, blue-eyed apology and hot chocolate fantasy.

"Highly *likely*. You look hot today, sweets."

"No way. My ass is *especially* huge in my winter gear."

"Shut *up*! You have a great ass. I'd *kill* for a piece of that." She tries to grab a handful, but I dodge, zipping my jacket all the way up before I go hypothermic. She tries for another grab, but I slap her hand, and when she looks up at the sky and laughs, her shoulders shake and her breath puffs out in big white clouds. Van Morrison's "Brown Eyed Girl" comes on Trick's radio, and I reach for her hands and spin her around, the two of us singing and dancing by the Dumpster under the bright gray November sky.

Even with her off-key voice and the subzero winter air, when it's like this, I don't notice the cold. I don't hear the wind howling through the empty spaces. I don't feel like a small, broken-winged bird trapped in a rusty cage.

I just feel . . . *home.*

But it never lasts.

"Let's *go*, sweet tarts!" Trick shouts. Something crashes to the floor in the kitchen—sounds like a tray of drinks. "And I mean yesterday. Carly's in the weeds."

"Be right in!" Dani calls back. "Man, these new girls. Might as well be working the floor myself. Hey, seriously . . . you okay? What were you saying about an invitation?"

"Oh . . . junk mail from an old skating thing." I wave away

the words, ignoring the imaginary burn of the foundation letter in my jacket, hot against my ribs. "I'm good."

Dani looks at me a moment longer, squinting as if the truth is as easily read as that Cupcake Queen article behind the register. "You know I didn't mean to trash-talk your dad, right?"

"I know." I slide my sneaker back and forth over a patch of ice on the ground. "Go ahead. I'll be right in."

She sighs, checks the bobby pins in her hair, and straightens the half apron beneath her coat. "Don't freeze that sweet, bacon-lovin' ass out here, 'kay?"

"I won't. Smoke break's almost over."

"Good. And don't forget about the rest of those cupcakes, either. There's more buttercream in my future, and you're not *about* to go messin' that up. Sure you're cool?"

"Totally." I flash her my pearly whites to prove it.

Dani scoots back inside and I blow my breath into the air, exhaling all of life's b.s. in a long white sigh. As Buddy Guy sings out over the grill, I close my eyes and lean sideways against the bricks and pretend I'm in some swanky nightclub, hip jutting forward, elbow on the bar, tapping out the long ash from my cigarette. *Ladies and gentlemen, this next song goes out to Hudson Avery, the lovely lady who breaks my heart every time she walks through that door.*

Guitar.

Horns.

Bass.

Mmm, mmm, mmm. Cue those smoldering vocals.

I been downhearted baby, ever since the day we met . . .

The alto sax blows and the guitar moans and here behind Hurley's, a few miles down the hill and across the highway, that old Erie Atlantic train starts up the track, light floating over the engine like some kind of fairy godmother. Ten-oh-five, right on schedule, far away and sad as the sound stretches and bends its way through the approaching storm. Who knows where it goes, but sometimes, when the wheels screech against the tracks and the red lights flash along the crossways, I think about hitching a ride on a coal car just to find out. Then I wouldn't *need* a parallel universe and a skating scholarship to get out of here.

"Hudson? You out there?" Mom pokes her head out the back door, her static-ridden hair now pulled into an old scrunchie. "Third toilet's clogged again."

"Ma, we really need to have that thing fixed."

She blows a loose strand from her face. "I know. But I'm in the middle of the dairy inventory. We'll call the guy next week, okay?"

"No problem." So now I'm a plumber? *Awesome.* The only thing that could make my life even *more* awesome is if Josh and the whole pack of Watonka Wolves march in for lunch just as I'm emerging from the bathroom in my little baker's apron, shirt collar flipped up, hair tousled, restaurant-grade toilet plunger in hand, all kinds of black-rubber-gloves-to-the-elbows sexy.

The train whistle blows like a snowbird into the dead sky and I lean forward on my tiptoes, heels scraping up on the bricks. *Whoooo. Whoooo.* It's not that far, those few miles. I can make it, I think, if I'm careful and the hill isn't too icy. If not today, tomorrow for sure. I'll pack my wool socks and wear my big snow-stompin' boots and stash my stuff out here behind the Dumpster. When I come out for my nonsmoke break I'll snatch up my backpack and ice skates and go, run, dodge, break, *hit it,* straight for the fairy godmother lamplight on the ten-oh-five, black coal train to nowhere.

Cue those smoldering vocals.

Ever since the day we met . . .

"Hudson, you still out there?" Mom rushes past the door again, a clipboard in her hand and a pen stuck behind her ear.

"Yeah! I mean, no! I . . . um . . . third toilet. Got it, Ma." I stamp out the invisible cig with my standard-issue food service sneaker and hobble back through the doorway, careful not to put too much weight on my left hip, semi-throbbing from this morning's two-part wipeout. If she sees me limping . . . no way. My former skating career was Dad's project, and now that he's gone, there's an unwritten, don't-ask-don't-tell policy in our apartment: Mom doesn't ask me to share his dating narratives, and I don't say anything that implies he was ever around in the first place.

"This joint's about to get *mad* crazy." Dani busts into the ladies' room as I'm scrubbing toilet germs from my hands. "Carly's having a meltdown. Girl can't keep it together for five minutes out there."

"What happened?"

"She dropped the F-bomb when that big party asked for separate checks, and now we're comping their whole meal, so of course they all want more food. Their kids made a giant mess, half of them are screaming and eating crayons, and by the way, we're in the middle of a bacon crisis." Dani presses her fingers to her temples.

"You check the back freezer?" I ask, wondering how fast I can squeeze my so-called sweet ass out the little window over the first stall.

"We're totally out."

I close my eyes and magically transport myself to the rink in my parallel life, cool wind running its fingers through my hair as I pick up speed for a triple salchow. I whip my leg around and launch myself into the air over the ice, the world spinning away beneath me and back up again as I land like a feather on an eggshell.

Look at that landing! Incredible! And that form! Amazing!

Right. I shake off the impossible daydream and come back to reality. "Here's what we do. Change the specials board to stuff with ham and sausage to get people off bacon. I'll frost and box a bunch of Cherry Bombs for your big table—that should keep them from ordering off the menu and you can shoo them out before the lunch rush."

Dani smiles, her shoulders relaxing. "Dude, this place

would seriously self-destruct without you." She reaches up to tuck a stray lock of hair behind my ear. "And it's not just your cupcakes. You have—what's wrong?"

"Cupcakes. I have a big birthday order tomorrow, and I just remembered I have to do two more batches for that stupid careers and hobbies thing in French. What are you doing for it? Photography?"

"Of course."

"You figure out your final photo project yet?"

"Still thinking about it." Dani hops up on the vanity counter, legs dangling over the edge. "The theme is passion, so of course everyone's going for lovey-dovey."

"Sounds right up your alley."

"Nah, too predictable. Maybe I should bring in my nude self-portraits for French. *Ooh la la!* Madame Fromme would die!"

"It would serve her right." I laugh. "I swear she only gave us that assignment so I'd bring her something from Hurley's. I should do a plumbing demo instead."

"That'd go over well." Dani switches to a falsetto. "'*Mademoiselle Avery, où est les cupcakes? J'ai besoin des cupcakes!*'"

"It's *les petit gâteaux*. I looked it up."

"Huh?"

"'Cupcakes' in French. *Les petit*—"

"Girls?" Mom barges into the bathroom, still clutching her clipboard. "I just sat three more tables, and Carly's hyperventilating in the kitchen. Dani, I need you on the floor. Hud, Mrs.

Zelasko called about her cupcakes—she wants to pick them up tonight instead of tomorrow. Can you stay late to finish?"

I reach over my batter-mixing shoulder to tighten my bra strap. I should just move in to this place. Set up a cot in back. Hang my clothes on the rack with the pots and pans. "Why not?"

"Thanks, hon. Oh, there's a boy at table seventeen asking for you." She wipes the back of her hand across her forehead. "John something? No, Josh. Josh Black-something. Make it quick, okay?"

The ladies' room door swishes closed behind her.

Dani smirks as I dig into my apron for some lip gloss and/ or a cloak of invisibility. "Interesting development."

"It's a diner, Dani. People eat in them sometimes. Not that interesting." I smear on the gloss and say all this like the inside parts of me haven't turned into lime Jell-O. The prospect of talking to him was much less intimidating when he was driving away from me. "Maybe he's just . . . craving the meat loaf?"

Dani hops off the counter and gives me the once-over. "Craving the meat loaf? Is that what the kids are calling it now?"

"This is really not funny." I take another look at that window over the first stall, but my ass and I both know we won't fit. "You have to cover for me."

"You can't hide in here all day."

"I'm not hiding. Just go take his order and distract him while I break for the kitchen."

She smiles and shakes her head. "All right. But if you're not out in five, I'll come out you myself."

"Grilled cheese and tomato on rye, chocolate shake, and a side of you." Dani breezes into the kitchen where I'm taking my sweet time boxing up those cupcakes for her big party. "Guess he wasn't craving the meat loaf after all."

"What did he say?"

"He's not here to say stuff to *me*."

"Dani—"

"Listen up, sugar smacks," Trick says. I almost forgot he was here, standing at the other end of the prep counter with a butcher's knife and his big sonar ears. "Better go talk to him before *I* do it for you." He brings the blade down on an unsuspecting carrot with a thwack.

"You two suck, you know that?" I wipe my icing-covered hands on my apron and push through the doors.

"*Heyyyy,*" I say when I get to his table, clutching a notepad and pen as if his order isn't already in. As if I'm a waitress. As if I even remember how to write stuff. *Anyway.*

Josh's gaze slides up from the bottom of my apron, stopping to rest on my face. He smiles, but it's different now—muted a little by the harsh lights of the diner.

I scratch a squiggly line onto the notepad. How many times has he seen me skate before today?

"I thought you were trying to escape back there," he says, and I drop the pen.

"No! I was . . . um . . . on break. In the break room. There's a lounge. Outside. Where we take our breaks. When we're on break. I mean, we don't *have* to go outside, but sometimes we do. Because there's air out there and I didn't . . . um . . . how are you? Everything okay?"

Where's Dani with that milk shake? Why can't that family in the next booth set their table on fire? I crouch down as delicately as I can to retrieve the pen.

"Oh, definitely," he says. "I just . . . I feel bad about before. I wanted to check on you." He rubs his head again, hair still messy and adorable. "No permanent damage, right?"

"Nah." *Just the temporary mental kind, causing my mind to wander dangerously into forbidden crush territory.* "I'm totally okay, so enjoy your dinner. I mean lunch. Or . . . whatever." I slip the notebook back into the pocket of my icing-smudged apron. I must look like a total freak show. "I'll go find your waitress."

"Wait," he says, lowering his voice. "I wanted to talk to you about something before, but . . . can I ask a crazy favor?" He looks into his water glass and pokes the ice with a straw, shifting nervously in the booth.

"What's up?" *Need a kidney? Two of them? Where do I sign?* I grab my pen again, just in case.

"When I saw you on the ice . . . you're *really* good." He looks straight at me this time, and the Jell-O formerly known as my bones wobbles. I wonder if he knows how amazing those eyes are. He must. That's how he casts his magic, bone-wobbling spells on unsuspecting cupcake bakers.

"You used to compete, right?" he asks.

"Yeah, but I haven't . . . it's been a few years." Now it's my turn to shift nervously. I stare at the fresh Band-Aids around his index and middle fingers, knuckles undoubtedly scraped when we skidded across the ice this morning. His hands look strong and sure, clean but a little rough, and I imagine them sliding over the curves of my waist. . . .

"Hud?" Mom calls from the front entrance, nodding toward the crowd that just piled in. "Can you help these folks, please?"

"Be right back," I tell Josh. I seat three tables and cash out another while Dani delivers his lunch.

"How's your sandwich?" I ask when I finally make it back. "Grilled cheese is awesome in the winter, isn't it?"

"It's awesome always." He holds up half. "Want a bite?"

"I'll make one later."

"Cool. Listen, about that favor . . ." He bites his lower lip so lightly that I don't think he knows he's doing it. I stare. I can't help it. I see the white edge of teeth against his lips, the thin shadow of stubble along his jaw, the blue sky in his eyes, and Parallel Hudson takes over.

What do you need, Josh? Just name it. Anything. I'm totally here for you.

I knew I could count on you, Hudson. The thing is . . . I don't know if I'm a good kisser. It's not the sort of thing you can figure out on your own, you know? So I was thinking, if it wouldn't be too much trouble, maybe you could kiss me, every day for a year, and then you can . . .

"Hudson?"

I meet his gaze, trying not to think about what it would be like to kiss him. Every day. For a year.

"Is it cool if we skate together sometime?" he asks. "Meet up at Fillmore, maybe you could show me some stuff?"

"What?" I laugh. "You're the hockey captain. You could probably show *me* stuff."

"Not technical moves. Why do you think the Wolves suck so hard? No technique. And don't even get me started on our lame coach. Please? I'd owe you majorly."

My brain starts to replay that cozy little café fantasy from before, but I shut it off. He's not asking me out, he's asking for skating lessons. Planning a solo program in my head was one thing, but skating with another person on my secret spot? Teaching him technique? Forming a team?

Josh folds and unfolds his napkin, and I click the pen inside my apron pocket. The foundation letter was like a seed that took root deep in my subconscious. *Maybe I really* am *good enough to try again,* I secretly thought. *Maybe, with a little practice, I can get into shape and compete, score that prize.* But Josh is asking for help, asking me to show him my moves, show him how it's done. His favor isn't a letter generated by a faceless machine, signed and sent out to an entire mailing list. It's a real request, waiting for a real, face-to-face answer.

And I'm shrinking in the light of it.

He really could've asked me *anything* else—*Can I have that kidney after all? Wanna give the kissing thing a go? Can you dismantle a bomb out on the thin ice of Lake Erie wearing nothing but a feathered bikini?*—and it would've been easier for me to say yes.

I guess I'm not as ready as I thought.

"You doin' okay over here, hon?" Dani appears like a rabbit pulled from a hat, setting a fresh glass of water on the table. The look she flashes me says it all: She heard our conversation, and now she's waiting for my answer, just like he is.

"I'm good," Josh tells her. He traces lines into the frosted edge of his glass with a fingertip, looking at me hopefully. "So it's a date?"

"Sounds fun, but I can't," I say. Dani sighs behind me. "My schedule is kind of—"

"Hudson?" Mom's voice cuts through the din again, this time from the window over the grill that looks out over the dining room counter. "What's going on with Mrs. Zelasko's order?"

"Coming," I tell her. I turn back to Josh. "Sorry. I have to work. See you at school?"

"Of course," he says. His voice is soft, but he flashes an animated smile. "I'll try not to crash into you next time we meet."

I laugh. "Thanks."

I leave Josh with Dani and head back to cupcake central, the heavy doors swinging closed behind me. After checking Mrs. Z's details in my order book, I set up fresh mixing gear on the prep counter and get to work.

Trick looks at me over his shoulder and winks. "What's good, puddin'?"

I hold out a jar of Dutch cocoa for an answer, and he turns up the radio, letting Miles Davis do the talking as Team Diner spins into its bad-weather frenzy. Josh heads out. Other customers come and go. Mom, Dani, and a mostly useless Carly run back and forth between the kitchen and the dining room as Trick cranks out that home-cooked flavor, hot and fresh.

But me? I take my seat at the prep counter, lost in the solo pursuit of the perfect cupcake. It's my place now, back of the house, out of the spotlight, exactly where I belong—no matter *how* adorable the hockey boy is.

Chapter Four

When Life Hands You Lemons, Stuff 'Em in Your Bra Cakes

*Extra-large lemon cupcakes
with light pink vanilla cream cheese icing,
topped with a maraschino cherry and served two on a plate*

By the time I get home, it's dark outside, my feet and shoulders ache, and Mrs. Ferris is chattering on about how Bug is such an *angel* of a little boy. After the third "Bug is so wonderful" story, I connect the obvious dots: Mom forgot to leave the money. Again. I fish a few tens from the stash in my underwear drawer, hand them over, and lock the front door behind her.

"Hudson, what were the primary factors that led to the Civil War?" the squirt wants to know before I have my coat off. He doesn't even ask about the cupcakes I promised him earlier. Which is good, because I forgot them.

"That's a tough one." I slide off my boots and stretch my

toes against the carpet, careful not to step on the plastic ball encasing Mr. Napkins.

Bug waits patiently, clutching a notebook against his slightly too-small alien pajamas, eyes big and hopeful. "Any ideas?"

"I kinda suck at history." Mom should be here to field these important questions, but she's still at the diner making sure all the vendors are paid and the register drawer balances. I hope he doesn't turn into a serial killer on account of my ineffective parenting. "Did you check your textbook?"

"I only have the second-grader version."

"That's probably because you're *in* second grade."

"Hudson, *please*."

"All right, all right. Let's see what you've got." I follow him back to tactical HQ—a.k.a. the coffee table—and check his notes. *The American Civil War.* There's the title, underlined twice, with a bulleted list and arrows and *X*s and an enhanced sketch of one of the plastic army men from his collection.

"You shouldn't have so much homework for at least another three years." I flip through the notebook to an intricate, hand-drawn map dotted with bright green Post-it tabs.

"It's not homework." He rearranges the plastic front line, glasses slipping down his nose. I keep forgetting to ask Trick for one of those tiny screwdrivers so I can fix them. "I was watching a documentary on PBS and wanted to learn more stuff."

"A documentary?" *This kid.* "Must've missed that one."

"Maybe Dad knows. He's, like, Mr. History."

"He's Mr. History, all right." I sink back into the couch

cushions. Bug was so small when my parents split—so young and bendable. He didn't understand why our father left, or that we should have any reason to resent him. All Bug knew was that our dad was gone. And now the hole in his tiny, eight-year-old heart reminds him not that our father is thousands of miles away entertaining some ever-changing flavor of the month, but only that he misses someone he loves.

I look at my baby brother with his giant, hopeful eyes and wish that things were that simple for me, too. That the feeling of missing Dad wasn't all tangled up with the feeling of hating him for not sticking around. That together, Bug and I could whisper about how much we love him, how we wish he was still here, telling us everything he knows about the Civil War. That we could let Mom carry all the timeworn resentment on her own.

"Can we call him?" Bug pushes out from the table and makes for the phone.

"It's two hours earlier in Nevada. Probably dinnertime over there." Briefly, I wonder if Shelvis can cook.

"Oh yeah." He screws up his face and pushes his glasses up his little Bug-nose, and oh my God it just about *kills* me. Really. I might have a heart attack right here on the coffee table, all over the carefully arranged armies of the North and South.

"But we can try," I say, massaging my chest. "We can always leave a voice mail, right?"

He shrugs, gathering up his books and papers and toys. "I'll check online. It's faster."

He zooms to the computer in the kitchen on superfast, round-and-round cartoon feet, stopping only once to rescue a lone little green man who fell to the linoleum in the rush.

Civil War researched and Dad temporarily forgotten, I shoo Bug into bed and start on those cupcakes for Monday's French presentation. An hour later there's the click-clack-jingle-jangle of keys in the front lock as Mom struggles through the doorway with her giant purse and a few bags of leftovers.

"Put this away for me, baby?" Mom hands over the goods and shakes out her snow-dusted coat in the hall.

I transfer two stacks of aluminum take-out containers into the fridge, shove the plastic bags under the sink, and get back to work. "How'd the rest of the night go?"

"Carly quit."

"Seriously?"

"Yep. Said waitressing wasn't what she expected. It's food service, for the love of pie. What's to expect?" She kicks off her boots and flops onto a chair at the kitchen table. "What are you making over there?"

"Carousel Cupcakes. They're for this careers and hobbies thing for French." I hold up my baking notebook to show her the rough sketch—white cake with sunshine-orange icing, a chocolate straw and animal cracker stuck into the top. I really wanted to do these two-tiered lavender honey cakes I saw on a wedding show at Dani's, but I figured words like "bear" and "tiger" were easier to explain *en français*. Besides, no way the masses of Watonka High would appreciate a work of art like two-tiered lavender honey cakes.

Mom's beaming like a normal parent would if her kid just got accepted to Harvard. "You're so clever with those things."

I stir a bit more yellow into the frosting, a drop at a time until I get the color just right. Mom's always been my number one cupcake fan. The other day a lady asked to see our sample book, and Mom gushed over those photos like they were her grandbabies or something. "Look at this one," she cooed, pointing to a shot of my lamb cupcakes—shaved coconut wool, a mini-cupcake head, and chocolate chips for eyes. "My daughter makes them all by hand. Aren't they cute?" I smile when I think about it now, even though it *is* kind of silly. Lamb cupcakes? Honestly. But Mom goes crazy for stuff like that.

"So," she continues, "speaking of Carly—"

"Yeah, I know we have that nondiscrimination policy, but is it illegal to discriminate against psychos? Because she's the third psycho to quit this year, and—"

"Hudson, there's something we need to talk about, honey."

I toss my wooden spoon into the bowl. "Honey" is total red alert stuff in our house. Was she hovering when I talked to Josh at the diner? Did Bug slip up and tell her about the skates?

"Everything okay?" I ask.

Mom taps her fingers on the table. Shuffles through the papers Bug left. Stares out the window as the plastic wall clock ticks off the seconds. Minutes.

"Hurley's . . . ," she finally says, "we're not doing so hot."

"We were slammed today."

Mom shakes her head. "It's not enough. We got a nice boost after your cupcake article, but . . . I don't know. This was the worst month on the books in years."

"That bad?"

"I'm working on a plan to turn it around." Her so-called reassuring grin looks like it hurts, and it reminds me of that day in her bedroom before the Empire Games. *Big night tonight, baby. Let's get moving!*

"You gonna let me in on this plan?" I fill a pastry bag with the sunshine-colored icing. I know from years of overheard arguments that selling the place is not an option. It was the only thing besides me and Bug that she wanted out of the split, and she got it, free and clear. Lump sum settlement, the lawyers called it. The house got sold, the mortgage on Hurley's got paid off, and Dad got to check out, no strings attached.

"We have to cut back hours," she says. "We'll stay open late after the Sabres and Bills games, but otherwise we'll close a little earlier. And what about your cupcakes? Can we put some more variety out there, something special for the holidays? Might give us another jump."

"Easy enough. I'll have Dani take some new pictures for the sample book, too." Okay, so I misjudged the urgency. Shorter hours, a few extra cupcakes to get us back in the black, no biggie. "Don't worry, Ma. We'll be fine."

"Thanks, baby." She sighs again and looks at the clock, the second hand making everything seem like a final countdown.

"Mom?"

"We're not replacing Carly," she announces, fast and blurry like she just talked herself into it. "Things are too tight right now. These new girls want the same benefits the big chains offer, and I can't do that. I'm sorry, Hudson." She looks at me and waits for it to sink in, and when it does, the pastry bag slips from my hands and hits the counter, squirting out a blob of orange-yellow goo.

"I know you don't have direct waitressing experience," she continues, "but you're a fast learner, and you'll have lots of help. Dani and Marianne are strong. Nat's good, too, and she'll be back full time after her nursing exams. I can't give you much more than minimum for an hourly, but you'll make good tips. . . ." She finally meets my eyes, her reassuring grin utterly failing to convince me. "You might actually like it."

Waitressing? I shake my head. I can't do what Dani does— talk to all those people, be friendly and perky as they order her around and drop food on the floor and demand refills and discounts and more, more, more. I can't deal with lousy tippers and picky eaters and adults who try to order off the kiddie menu. I know she loves waitressing, but she's always been a front-of-the-house kind of girl, all smiles and big eyes, bad stuff rolling off her shoulders like kids sledding down a steep hill.

Mom frowns, still watching me closely, and my throat tightens up. No matter how much time I put in at the ovens of Hurley's, no matter how many cupcakes I ice, I've always held on to one simple fact: Baking is the one thing Mom never did.

She was the waitress who got promoted to manager, the manager who became the owner, the owner who gives a little more of her life to that place every day. She's always joked about leaving me the family business, but I never took it seriously. How could I? All this time, as long as I was just baking, my destiny could be separate from hers. Parallel, never overlapping. Close, but not the same.

"I don't want to waitress." My voice cracks. "I like my cupcakes."

"We'll find a way for you to do both." Mom shuffles the papers on the table again, tapping them against the edge three times. "We have to pull together on this."

I take a deep breath and reassemble the pastry bag. *Pulling together.* If only that strategy applied three years ago.

"You're young, Hudson." Mom flashes the everything's-gonna-be-just-fine smile again. "A little more hard work won't kill you."

"You can't prove that. Look at all those people from the steel mill with black lung."

"You won't get lung disease from waiting tables."

"No, but I might get carpal tunnel from carrying the trays, and back problems, and . . ."

"And if I had another choice, I'd take it."

I squeeze a spiral of bright orange icing onto a waiting cupcake, turning it to cover all the edges. *Squeeze and turn. Squeeze and turn.*

"It's only for a little while," Mom says. "Just until things get back on track. And look at the bright side—it's a chance for you to finally learn some other aspects of the business. I was younger than you when I got my start, remember?"

Squeeze and turn. Squeeze and turn.

"Hudson, please?" she asks, softer than before. "I really need your help with this—at least on Sunday to Wednesday dinners. Right now the diner is the only thing paying Mrs. Ferris for the roof over our heads."

Guilt. Guilt. *Guilt.* Pass the freakin' butter.

"Speaking of paying Mrs. Ferris," I say, "you know you owe me forty bucks, right?"

Mom stands, her shoulders slumped. I can almost feel the ache in her bones, radiating out through her skin. Her eyes are red and puffy, dark-circled as if she hasn't slept in days. I know she just wants to kiss me good night and crawl between the cool sheets of her bed, but quickly, quietly, she digs two tens from her purse and hands them over. "I'll get the rest for you tomorrow, okay?"

"Fine." I stuff the money into my pocket and go back to icing the cupcakes.

"Can I . . . you want some help?" she asks.

Yes. I want some help getting out of this job, out of this apartment, out of this place. I want some help figuring out what to do with my life. I want some help believing that there's more to it than unclogging toilets and inventorying milk and sorting money from a drawer that's always just short of enough.

I hand her the box of animal crackers. "I need all the lions, tigers, and bears in separate piles. Um, please."

She dumps the box into a bowl and picks through the crackers, snacking on the ones with missing limbs. While we work, she hums an old Bob Dylan tune, and the melody reminds me of this time we got stranded in the diner during a blizzard, us and Bug, and Dad couldn't get to us because there was a city-wide driving ban. We were there for two days, and without its usual crowds and smells, the place took on a kind of magic. We had all the food we needed and slept sideways in the big booths with the heat cranked up. On the second morning, the wind settled down and Mom took us outside to make a snowman in the parking lot. It had a carrot nose and cut potatoes for eyes and a Hurley's apron tied around the middle. Later, when our noses froze and our fingers ached, Mom made us hot chocolate with scoops of vanilla ice cream and sang that Dylan song as Bug and I drank out of the pink-and-white diner mugs and took turns twirling around the floor, collapsing when we got too dizzy.

. . . *without your love, I'd be nowhere at all. I'd be lost if not for you . . .*

The plows came that night, digging us out so we could finally drive home. I remember watching them mow into our snowman, his raw potato eyes browning in the open air. I wished we could stay snowed in for one more night, but school was set to reopen the following morning and so would Hurley's, and besides, my father was probably worried.

65

It was the last blizzard he ever saw.

I look up and catch my mother watching me over the counter, animal crackers separated on a plate before her, and my heart cracks right down the middle. The left half knows that look on her face from the months following their divorce—her anxiety and worry. All that desperation. The quiet regret, wishing she could have done better for us, wishing the one who *really* owed us the big fat apology was still around to say it.

But the right side of my heart looks at the lines in her face and sees the map of my future. Today I take the waitress gig. Next I'll be managing the schedule. Then in a few years or a decade or maybe even two, I'll inherit the restaurant. Cement my crowning achievement as Beth Avery's daughter, the proud-but-struggling new owner and sometimes-cupcake-baker of a forgettable old diner off the I-190, a pair of scuffed-up ice skates dangling from a hook in the staff closet, a bittersweet memento of another life.

I used to believe that figure skating was my way out, my first-class, one-way ticket to all the good things in the world. "Mom and I didn't have the talent and opportunities you have, kiddo," Dad told me more than once. "If you stay focused, you can skate your way to the top. You can be the queen of everything. You just have to want it bad enough."

For a long time after he left, I didn't want it. And now that I'm finally ready to want something again, it's too late. I'm afraid to skate in front of people. I'm giving up the last of my free time to work at my mother's diner. Queen of everything?

Please. Every one of my chances is gone, and here I remain, stuck outside of Buffalo, the chicken wing capital of the world, queen of nothing but a few zany cupcakes.

"Okay, Ma." I swipe a lion cracker through the sunshine-colored icing and bite off his head. "I'll do it. But Sunday to Wednesday nights blow. After tomorrow, I want better shifts."

She smiles, and the deep lines in her face vanish, temporarily changing the map of my future to a broad, blank canvas. "You got it, baby."

Chapter Five

Opportunity Knocks You on Your Butt Cakes

*Vanilla cupcakes baked over a blend of
chopped pineapples, butter, and brown sugar
inverted on a warm plate and served
with vanilla bean ice cream*

"Oh, Hudson!" Mom fusses with my collar, making a show of it in front of Dani and the whole entire diner. "Don't you look *adorable!*"

I tug at the bottom of the lavender zip-up dress. If I tried to wear this thing to school, Principal Ramirez would personally escort me home just so she could slap my mother for letting me out in public so scantily clad. But tonight? I'm a Hurley Girl—says so in fancy pink letters over my left boob.

"Big step, baby. I'm so proud of you." She wraps me in a hug, her hair tickling my cheek. I blame myself, really. If only I'd been better about attending those spring flings and winter formals, she wouldn't feel compelled to gush over my first day on the job.

"No pictures," I say before she gets any ideas.

"I think you're beautiful," an old man at the counter—one of our Sunday night fixtures—says. He smiles gently and sets down his empty mug, tapping the counter three times. Mom grabs the coffeepot for a refill.

"You passed the Earl test," she says as she pours him a fresh cup.

"Ma, he says that to anyone who still has their own teeth. No offense, Earl."

"None taken," he says. "But you got your own hair, too, so you're twice as pretty."

"See?" Mom says. "You'll do great tonight. Just great."

Yeah, just great. Just awesome. Just . . . kill me.

"Ready, Hurley Girl?" Dani asks.

I tug once more on the dress and take a deep breath. *Only for a little while. Just until things get back on track.* "Let's do this."

"The basic rule is to smile a lot," she says, leading me into the kitchen. "Even when you feel like choking someone, keep on smilin'. The minute you show them you're pissed, you lose."

"Kill them with kindness. Or cheesiness." I flash her a test grin. "Got it."

"Sometimes the rowdy ones get a little grabby," she says, flipping on the tap water. She fills a plastic pitcher and cups and sets them on the prep counter. "If you smack them straight away, they usually back off. You can also try the tray-in-the-lap maneuver, but that takes some practice, and—"

"We training for food service or self-defense here?" I cross my arms over my chest.

"There's a fine line, Hud."

"This gig gets better by the minute."

Dani shrugs. "You get used to it."

I return her easy smile, but the words drop into my stomach like overcooked biscuits. *You get used to it.* According to the crazy, bug-eating guys on those survival shows, human beings are the most adaptable creatures on earth—we can get used to just about anything. Doesn't mean it's okay. I mean, who wants to get used to eating grubs and collecting maple leaves for toilet paper? No thanks.

"Hold this." She passes me an empty serving tray. "I'll load you up with waters, and you balance it. Ready for a cup?"

"A whole plastic cup of water? Hold me back!"

Trick laughs behind us, dropping a pile of stir-fry veggies onto the grill. "You taking bets on this, Dani?"

"Definitely."

"Put me down for seven," he says, squirting oil onto the veggies with a loud hiss. "I lose, I'll make your favorite tonight. I win, you empty the grease traps."

"You're on," she says.

I sigh and steady the tray with both arms extended beneath it, elbows bent, fingers curled up over the edge. "Just load me up so we can get this over with."

"But you're not holding it right. You have to—"

"It's not brain surgery, Dani. Come on."

She shakes her head and sets down one cup first, then another, followed by the water pitcher. "So far so good?"

"Keep it coming," I say.

Dani gives me two more cups, a half smile creeping across her mouth as she holds another one over the tray.

"Hit me," I say, and she drops it. A millisecond later, the tray, the pitcher, and all five cups crash to the floor.

"*Ooh!* Why'd you play me like that, sweetheart?" Trick stomps his foot and curses over the grill as water streams down my legs into a sad little puddle on the floor. Honestly, if this awful dress were any shorter, I'd have to change my underwear.

My so-called best friend laughs as she kneels to pick up the cups. "Looks like I'm gettin' corned beef hash for dinner tonight," she says. "*That's* what's up."

"Just sat a party of ten." Marianne, the resident Hurley Girl lifer who's been here almost as long as the diner itself, makes the announcement from the kitchen doorway. When she sees my predicament, her heavy bosom bounces with laughter. "Learning the tray, huh? On the shoulder, honey, not the arms. Put your back into it."

"You people are full of helpful advice." I grab a clean dish towel from the shelf and mop up my legs, then the floor. "You set me up!"

"Yep. You just lost your tray-dropping virginity," Dani says. "Congrats." She loads up her tray with fresh waters, in actual glasses this time, and hefts it onto her shoulder, nodding for me to follow her to the dining room. Earl gives me an encouraging double thumbs-up as we pass, and I relax, just a little.

"The good news is there aren't any games tonight," Dani

says. "Sports equals booze, and that's bad news, especially if the home teams lose. Remember that."

"Booze, lose, bad news. What else?"

"Watch and learn, Hurley Girl."

After my near drowning in the kitchen, I put the sarcasm on simmer as she delivers the water to that ten-top. We listen in as Marianne expertly takes their orders, Dani schooling me in the background on side dish substitutions, specials, and upselling with appetizers and desserts. She shows me how to prep the salads and mix Coke and Sprite to make fake ginger ale that satisfies all but the most discerning customers. Marianne walks me through sidework and plate presentation and coupons, and then we revisit the tray thing, practicing until I can finally carry it without causing another tidal wave. The dinner rush slows, and after helping me with a particularly rowdy table—the regular Sunday night gathering of the Watonka Sassy Seniors Knitting Club—Dani and Marianne unleash me on my first solo table.

"I've got a date with a plate of corned beef hash," Dani says. "Scream if you need anything." She vanishes into the kitchen, and I approach the booth, pen poised against the order pad.

The woman doesn't look up from the menu when she requests a Cobb salad and unsweetened tea, but the girls do, sitting across from her and snickering like everything is just the funniest joke *ever*. They're both in blue-and-silver Watonka Middle School hoodies, sitting so close together that I can't tell where one's arm ends and the other's begins.

"Two Cokes, please," one of them says. The other girl giggles, and I almost do, too. But then they order the tuna melt platter to share, and I swallow hard through the tightness in my throat, desperate to shutter the rush of memories.

Kara Shipley. Me. Our skate bags stacked across from us as our moms chatted over coffee at the counter. This was *our* booth. The tuna melt was *our* order.

I run my thumb over the table's broken corner, remembering one of our last meals together. A lifetime ago. It was a celebratory tuna melt—Dad had registered me for regionals, and we'd just heard that we'd be competing at the Empire Games with some of our fellow Bisonettes.

"I think I'm in love with Will Harper," Kara confessed that night, picking at the chipped corner. "As soon as we start high school, I'm totally asking him out."

I smiled and clinked my loganberry glass to hers, wishing her luck. She threw a French fry at me and I caught it in my mouth, and though we'd both already landed our double axels, we cheered and clapped like catching that fry was the most incredible stunt anyone had ever performed.

"How could you do it?" Kara demanded the morning after the Empire event, after the dust had settled and she'd called to talk. She knew I'd screwed up on purpose—we were practically sisters, and there was no other explanation. "If you didn't want to compete, you could've let someone else have the chance."

I wanted to explain, but the words weren't there. Maybe Mom had swept them into the dresser drawer with the proof that my father was having an affair. Maybe they were already packed away in his suitcase, saving him a seat on the plane that would take him out west. Maybe the words to explain why I'd thrown away the one thing I'd loved and worked so hard for just didn't exist.

Her breath was heavy through the phone and I meant to tell her how sorry I was, but even those words got jumbled inside, knotting up in my throat on the way out. I couldn't even give her a simple apology, and after a long, uncomfortable silence, she finally hung up.

Weeks blurred into months, and then it was the end of summer, our last weekend before high school. For the first time in history, I wasn't busy with preseason skate stuff during Joelle Woodard's annual summer bash. It didn't matter that Joelle and I weren't friends. It was the kind of free-for-all where no one needed an invite, so I put on a miniskirt and some body glitter left over from my skater glam stuff. I was ready for a do-over—the kind I never got in competitions. It was supposed to be a fresh start without Kara, but suddenly there she was, dressed in a bright green sundress with eyelet trim on the bottom that floated above her tanned knees as she walked down the basement stairs, a can of root beer in her right hand, her left on the railing. I remember it was root beer and not Coke or orange because she dropped it when she saw *me* stepping out of the make-out closet with Will Harper, and from that moment on, the smell of root beer would always remind me of her face, crumpled and confused, her head hung low above that bright green dress like a flower crushed on its stem.

Soon after, she dismissed the closet scene and asked Will out, just like she told me she would that night at the diner. They got together, and I buried my shame in a bowl of cupcake batter. The Hurley's kitchen was a safe place to be; I was finally good at something else. I could forget about Will and Kara. I could erase Lola Capriani and the private lessons Mom could no longer afford and all of the promises that died when my father left, and I could focus instead on making people fat and happy.

I've been doing it ever since.

While Trick works on my order, I take five at the counter with my *Scarlet Letter* homework, a mug of hot chocolate, and one of our best sellers—caramel apple granola cupcakes, a.k.a. Tree Huggers. Two seats over, Earl counts out a stack of dimes from one of those paper rolls you get at the bank, pulls his cardigan tight over his shoulders, and winks at me, hair and eyes and face as gray as the sky. "See ya next time, Dolly Madison."

I walk him to the front door and watch him leave, his footprints making uneven holes in the snow-covered parking lot. Behind his little blue sedan, the I-190 overpass glitters with red and white orbs in the distance, the lights of a thousand cars zooming along to some other destination, Watonka no more than an exit with FOOD-GAS-HOSPITAL, just like the sign says. A crumbling smokestack horizon wedged between the city of Buffalo and its southern suburbs. Exurban, we're called. *Ex. Former. No longer.*

Dani joins me at the door, nudging my shoulder with hers. "You're a million miles away over here."

I shrug and press my forehead against the glass. Outside, Earl flicks on his wipers and coaxes the car out of the lot. With my fingertip I draw an *X* in the frost on the glass over the spot where he used to be. *Ex. Former. No longer.*

Dani follows my gaze past the highway. "I know you don't love the new arrangement, but you're doing great tonight. Don't fade on me now—even on slow nights, we have to stick together. You remember what happened with Carly, right?"

"She's the reason I'm wearing this lovely dress," I say. "No offense."

"None taken. I rock this thing and you know it." She shakes her hips a little.

"Doesn't count. You could make a Hefty bag look hot."

"True. But enough about me. You've been acting funny all weekend. What are you dodging?" The smile vanishes from her reflection in the glass and something hazy passes over her face, gray and sad like a cloudless snowstorm.

I reach into my apron pocket and pull out the letter, wrinkled from all the times I've read and refolded it, carrying it with me ever since it passed from Bug's anthrax detector to my hands.

"Read this," I whisper, keeping an eye out for Mom.

She looks over the letter. "Capriani . . . she was your coach, right?"

"Yeah. Mom was still paying off my lessons after we moved—we must be on an old mailing list."

"Is this the invitation you unmentioned last night?"

I nod.

"Fifty grand? That's pretty sick, Hud." Dani folds up the letter and hands it back to me, her eyes soft and glassy. "I know you skate at Fillmore sometimes, but I didn't know it was like *that*."

"Honestly? Neither did I. But when I heard about this competition, it was like . . . I don't know. Like I could finally have a chance to *do* something with my life, even if Mom can't afford college and my father . . ." His latest e-mail scrolls through my head, sent this morning from a rest stop near the Grand Canyon. God's country, he called it. The soul of the world. "My father just isn't here."

A gust of wind blows across the near-empty parking lot. Snow clouds funnel and swirl beneath the lampposts, and a string of taillights beads along the overpass.

"The thing is," I continue, "when Josh asked me to skate with him yesterday, I thought about what it would be like to do it again for an audience—even one person—and I freaked. I don't think I'm cut out for it anymore."

"What? Hudson, you have to find a way to make this happen. Your whole face lights up when you talk about skating. Look." She touches my reflection in the glass, and I smile, seeing for just a moment what she sees. Nervousness, yes. But hope. Excitement, too.

"You can't walk away from this opportunity," she says. "You'll regret it forever. I know you."

"You're the only one." I look out the door again, the wind

picking up snow and depositing it across the few remaining cars.

"Maybe I can help you train."

"You don't even like the cold." She takes a breath to speak, but I shake my head. "Even if I had time to work on my routine, and I could lose the anxiety, I don't have the cash for another club membership. And I can't train on Fillmore—I need access to groomed, indoor ice."

"What a coincidence. I think we *both* know someone who can get it for you." Dani smiles, wriggling her eyebrows until I connect all the dots.

"Are you serious? Are you . . . *no*. No! That's straight up *crazy*. There is no way I'm—"

"Suit yourself," she says. "But once you figure out you want it bad enough—and I know you do—you'll talk to him."

"Miss?" One of the blue-haired knitting club ladies steps out of the bathroom and joins us at the door. She's a bit winded, and there's a long piece of toilet paper trailing behind her shoe.

"Just thought you should know," she says, leaning in close and pointing a finger at my chest, "the powder room is out of toilet paper, and one of the toilets is overflowing." With that, she waddles back to her table and smooths a crumpled paper napkin over her lap.

I believe this is what Oprah refers to as an "Aha! Moment."

I look at Dani and sigh, a big one for the ages. "Okay. I'll talk to him tomorrow."

Chapter Six

Kill Me, Kill Me Now Cupcakes

*Any cake, any flavored icing,
served in front of the entire school
while wearing your most unflattering,
back-of-the-drawer underwear*

If I detour down the science hall, cut across the gym, head up one flight of stairs and down another, Josh Blackthorn's locker is conveniently en route to my first class.

He totally catches me staring from across the hall like the gawker that I'm not, and I flip open my econ book to a random page as if my sole purpose in this hallway at this moment is to save the lives of hundreds of innocent children by defining the term "gross domestic product."

Here it is! The sum of all market values of goods and services produced by a nation in a given year. Says so right on page ninety-four. Disaster averted! Lives saved! Awards, um, awarded!

Still, he's smiling right at me, and I can't escape. I wave

and head toward him with my best fancy-meeting-you-here-at-your-own-locker face, front and center.

"Hi, Josh," I say, super-originally.

He leans against his open locker door, shoulders shifting under a faded Addicts in the Attic shirt. "How's it going?"

"Good," I say, once again demonstrating my knack for witty conversation. "So, um, you like the Addicts?" *No, idiot. He hates them. Why else would he be wearing their shirt?*

"You know those guys?"

"I once skated a routine to 'Bittersweet.' My coach thought it was unorthodox, but the crowd loved it. I got a perfect . . . anyway. It's pretty much my favorite song." *God.* When did I become such a danger to myself and others? I take a deep breath and try to turn down the spaz-o-meter before someone gets hurt.

"For real?" he says. "I *love* that song. You know the part right after the guitar solo, when he hits that high note? Man, he went to some dark places for that stuff. Sometimes the lyrics just . . . wow. It's so cool that you dig those guys." He looks at me a moment longer like he wants to say something else, something about the band, maybe, or the way one perfect song can make you feel less alone.

He doesn't, though, so I continue with my original mission. "I was thinking about what you said—the skating stuff?"

Josh shuts his locker, fingers tracing the combo lock. The tips of his ears go red like they did in the cold at Fillmore and that tiny, V-shaped scar jumps out again. Not that I'm making a police sketch or anything.

"Sorry if I freaked you out the other day." He turns to face me, and my stomach flutters. "Guess my nonstalker plan kinda backfired."

I smile. "I'm the one who freaked. I wasn't expecting—"

"You have something on your shirt." He starts to point at my chest, but quickly redirects to a spot on his own shirt instead. "Right here."

Hudson Avery's utter grace and all-around awesomeness? Confirmed. The sweater formerly known as white—and by formerly, I mean this morning, right before I dropped off my presentation cupcakes in the French classroom—now sports a giant orange streak clear across the left nipular region. It takes every ounce of willpower I have—plus a visual of last night's plumbing disaster—to keep me from aborting the mission and bolting down the hall.

I close my eyes, shift my econ book so it covers the obnoxious stain, and soldier on. "Josh, um . . . Iwashopingwecould-skatetogetherattherink."

Josh laughs. "Slow down."

I open my eyes and look at the floor, black-and-gray speckled tiles that probably haven't been cleaned since my parents were students here. I take a deep breath. Concentrate. "I thought about it last night, and if the offer still stands . . ."

"You want to skate with me?"

I nod. "But maybe we could use the rink instead of

Fillmore? I'm trying to get back into a training routine, and Fillmore conditions can be unpredictable. Indoor ice would be better for technical stuff."

"Baylor's Rink?"

I sigh. "Sorry, you probably can't, right? It was a stupid idea."

"No, it's a great idea. I should've thought of it sooner." Josh scratches the back of his neck, his gaze drifting down the hall. "Let me talk to Will. He knows the rink manager better than I do. He'll know when we can get ice time."

I try to keep my smile in check, but my whole body is electrified with possibilities. Of the skating nature, *not* the hockey boy nature. Not that hockey boy possibilities aren't equally electrifying, just that they're—

"Not like anyone else uses the place, anyway," Josh says. "What's your number? I'm seeing Will first period, so I'll . . . hang on." He checks the phone suddenly buzzing in his hand. "I need to get this. Talk to you later?"

"Definitely," I say, but he's already answering the call, disappearing around the corner along with half the muscles that hold up my legs and the ones that make my lungs work. One slow step at a time, I head to economics on the other side of the school and sink into my desk in the back row.

Overly Analytical Mind, engaged.

Talk to you later . . . He smiled when he said that, right? Was he asking me, or telling me? Did he mean that he *wants* to talk to me, or just that he *might* talk to me, even if he doesn't particularly want to?

Why did he leave so fast at the end? Who was on the phone? A girl? That's it. He must have a girlfriend. One from another school. One he was just about to call so he could propose to her, but I interrupted, and then he had to run off to take her call, because weddings don't just plan themselves, you know.

"Miss Avery?"

The sound of my name pulls me back to the classroom. Ms. Horner, a.k.a. Ms. Fanny Pack, drags her wooden pointer through the age-old chalk dust on the blackboard. No fancy-schmancy whiteboards and dry-erase markers for *this* establishment, thank you very much.

"Sorry . . . I didn't . . . could you repeat the question?"

"I'd like you to give us a market scenario depicting how the laws of supply and demand impact pricing."

Everyone's looking at me like I'm the chair of the Federal Reserve being interviewed on CNN when all I can think about is Josh's eyes and his smile and how good he must look in his hockey uniform and a whole bunch of other Josh-related stuff about which I can pretty much *guarantee* neither Ms. Fanny Pack nor the actual Fed chairman cares.

"Anytime you feel like participating," she says, "jump right in."

A few people snicker, and someone hums the first few notes of doom from Beethoven's Fifth. I flip through my textbook as though the answer might suddenly appear there, just like it did earlier at Josh's locker. "Um, when there's a low supply of stuff, but a high demand, that means prices will be, um, they'll—"

"Your family owns a restaurant, do they not?" The woman asks me this as if she isn't in there every Wednesday with Madame Fromme for the all-you-can-eat chicken dinner special.

"Miss Avery?"

"Yeah." My voice gets a little stuck inside and I clear my throat. "I mean, yes. My mom owns Hurley's."

"And you work for her?"

Someone chants "Cupcake Queen," and I think of Hester Prynne in my *Scarlet Letter* book, only instead of being tried for adultery, I stand accused of baking cupcakes at my mom's diner. Just wait till they find out I'm waitressing for her now, too—double whammy.

"Yes," I say, face burning. "Sometimes."

"Think in those terms. What if a competing diner opened across town, with better food at lower prices?" She pulls a box of chalk from her—you guessed it—fanny pack and draws a big yellow square with "Joe's Diner" across the top. "In that scenario, supply would increase . . ." Arrows up, drawn in pink. "And demand would decrease." Arrows down, mint green. "How would that affect your prices?"

"We'd have to lower them, I guess."

She nods for, like, ten minutes, tight white curls wriggling on her head like a bunch of geriatric spiders. "Because if you didn't lower your prices . . ."

"People would go to the other diner and we'd lose business." Come on, lady, is this econ, or rocket science?

"Exactly." Multicolored stick people with dollar signs over their heads appear inside the Joe's Diner square. "And then what would happen?"

Well, Ms. Fanny Pack, if you must know, Mom wouldn't be able to pay the rent, and after a few missed payments, Mrs. Ferris would threaten to evict us. Mom would have to sell the restaurant just to keep the roof over our heads, but the bills would pile up until, one by one, the utilities got shut off. Mom would sit at the kitchen table and cry while my brother and I huddled in our sleeping bags to stay warm, eating dry cereal for dinner and cursing my father and the landlady and even poor old Diner Joe. Bug would likely turn to a life of crime—nothing lowbrow, strictly the high-net white-collar stuff on account of him being a genius—and I'd go door-to-door hocking cupcakes made from whatever random stuff I could scrounge from our dwindling pantry. So the real question here, Ms. Fanny-P, is not what would happen, but whether I could keep up with the demand for my Soy Sauce Cap'n Crunch Tuna Cakes. Think so?

"Miss Avery," she says curtly, "I asked you what would happen if your family's diner lost business."

"Um . . . it would . . . we'd . . . um . . ." My entire body is engulfed in flames thanks to this cruel, spider-haired chalk hoarder masquerading as an educator, and while I personally will never leave the apartment again after this public stoning, she'll probably win an economics award and get promoted to the president's financial team. "I'm not sure."

"Well, Hudson, it wouldn't be a viable model for your family's income, so you'd be forced to seek other employment. And then we'd all suffer, because I doubt Joe can do cupcakes like you guys can." She laughs and, certain we understand the cutthroat world of diner economics, erases all the dollar-headed stick people and reholsters the chalk box against her hip.

It wouldn't be a viable model . . . I think about Mom's face as she discussed the books the other night and I laugh, way down deep inside, where nobody can see how desperately unfunny it really is.

Dani has warned me a thousand times that walking and reading is never a good combo, but do I listen? No. And now, with my nose buried in the last few *Scarlet Letter* chapters, I don't see hockey captain number one, Will Harper, lurking near my French classroom until I'm practically on top of him. He flashes me his trademark smile—the award-winning, toothpaste commercial kind—and I start looking for the video cameras. The sooner I get confirmation that the events of my life have been staged for some elaborate, televised prank, the sooner I can collect my royalties and hire a good therapist.

"Hudson, what's up?" He steps closer as I approach, that grin lighting up the dim, beige hallway. "Oh, you have something on your shirt."

Perfect. Not only is this stain like a scarlet letter *M* for "Mortification" on my chest, but Will Harper is standing all up in my space, ogling me as random passersby look on. By Watonka standards, it's practically a *scene*.

"I know. Thanks." I try to make myself a little smaller against a row of lockers. Why is he here? Josh was supposed to talk to Will directly, get this rink thing figured out. The last thing I need is Kara Shipley catching me fraternizing with her ex. Talk about a hanging in the town square, Hester Prynne!

"Saw Blackthorn earlier," Will says, running a hand through his wavy, dark blond hair. "I didn't know you were training again. I thought you quit after—"

"I'm not training again."

Will raises his eyebrows. "Does that mean my co-captain's full of—"

"No. I mean, sometimes I hit the ice for fun. Exercise. It's nothing."

"Not according to Josh. He said you, uh . . . kick ass. More or less." Will smiles again, leaning in a little closer. *Mmmm.* He smells . . . *expensive*. The delicious kind of expensive that erases your mind right while you're standing there, which is why the cologne ads always show a pack of jar-eyed girls draped all over the chesty, good-smelling guy as if they forgot their own names the second *he* showed up.

"Well, Josh said . . . I . . ."

"He asked me about getting you ice time at Baylor's," Good Will Smelling says. "And I think I can swing it, but on one condition." He grins at me like he did that night in the closet, right before he moved in for the kill.

I swallow hard. "Condition?"

"More like a proposition. For the Wolves." Will lowers his voice. "Hear me out. I know my boys are strong. A little unmotivated at the moment, but talented. Thing is, we're not good with technique, edgework, stuff like that. And our coach is useless—he doesn't even call practices. Spends most of his time with the football team. Unlike us, those guys win championships."

"What are you saying?" I ask.

"You need rink time. I need a special techniques coach. I get you the ice . . . and you teach the boys how to skate."

My legs go all wobbly again. Convincing myself to skate with Josh was hard enough. Training an entire pack of notorious thugs who haven't won a single game for as long as I've been at this school? A bunch of puck-slapping meatheads who'd probably rather skate naked at Fillmore during a lake-effect snowstorm than learn a single lesson from a girl?

Has this boy been sniffing too much of his own cologne?

I lean back against the lockers, arms strategically folded over my stained sweater. "I don't know anything about hockey. And I'm already behind on school stuff, and I'm about to pick up a few more shifts at work, and—"

"Where do you—oh, right. The cupcakes. Man, my mom loves those things. I don't know how you do it. I could never work for my parents—they'd take over my life."

"Yeah, well, it's not my *dream* or anything. I have my own life." I don't elaborate. I don't care how amazing he smells. No way I'm getting all self-disclosey with a guy I've only spent about nine minutes of my life with, and that's *including* the seven in the closet way back when.

"Good," he says, his hand landing uninvited on my shoulder. "Because I'm serious about this. We need each other, Hud. Admit it."

I meet his gaze, ready for a fight, but there's an unexpected softness there—a bit of playful humor behind all the cocky attitude that takes me off guard. No wonder Kara fell so hard for him. I'm beginning to feel a bit drugged by the whole thing myself.

"Just think about it, okay?" he says quietly. "I called a practice after school this Friday. Text me if you want to check it out." He grabs one of my notebooks and the pen from behind my ear—the nerve!—and scribbles down his info. I scan the hall for those video cameras again, but my eyes instead find Dani, already sitting at her desk in the classroom. She raises her eyebrows and points to her wrist.

"So you'll text me?" Will hands over my stuff and leans in close, his breath tickling my neck. "Or do I have to work on you? I can be pretty convincing, you know."

"I have to go, Will." I duck into class just as the bell rings and slide into the spot next to Dani, my skin rippling with goose bumps.

"What. The hell. Was *that*?" she asks.

I shrug, shaking off the eau de Harper. "Josh asked him about the Baylor's thing. Not gonna happen."

"He said that? And what's with all the touching and, like, *smoldering* looks?"

I laugh. "Smoldering? You still reading that pirate romance?"

"No. I mean yeah. But whatever—I'm serious! The boy kisses you once, and that gives him perpetual license to put his hands on you? After basically ignoring you for three years? I don't *think* so."

"It's not like that," I whisper as Madame Fromme shoots us *le mauvais œil*—the evil eye. "He wants me to—"

"*Commencez, s'il vous plaît, Mademoiselle Avery.*" Madame beckons me to the front of the class to set up for my presentation. Of course she wants me to go first—she's probably been eye-fondling those cupcakes ever since I dropped off the box this morning.

"*Commencez* handing out the goodies, Cupcake Queen," someone says as I finish arranging the Carousels on the presentation table. I turn around quickly, but I can't tell who said it, and the room goes quiet again. Outside, a tree branch scrapes the window, craggy fingers tapping the glass as Madame Fromme clears her throat, urging me to begin. *Tap tap tap. Tap tap tap.*

"*Bonjour.* Um . . . *je m'appelle* Hudson Avery. I am—I mean, *Je suis*, um . . ." I lean on the table to steady myself, hands leaving damp prints that fade as I fidget. My fingernails are orange like my shirt. It looks like dried blood.

Frosting stains are usually just another part of the gig. An occupational hazard. A badge. *Yeah, I'm the Cupcake Queen, I hand-tint my icing, and I've got the ruined clothing to prove it.* But now, when I look at the color under my nails and the cupcakes lined up neatly on the table, I see my father's suitcases, stacked by the door. The moving trucks that came later to collect the rest of his things, all of us redeposited into separate lives. My walk of shame from the ice rink and all those months I spent hiding out at Hurley's behind an apron and a mixer. I see my mother, too, rushing from the grill to the dining room and back to the office, where each night she counts the till, twice to be sure.

If I don't buck up and do something different, someday that will be me.

"Je ne suis pas mon travail." I am not my job. I mumble it in perfect French, just loud enough for no one to hear. Madame Fromme removes her glasses and squints, and in my parallel life, I say it again. In my parallel life, I climb on the table and stomp on all those cupcakes, lions and tigers and bears crushed under my boot as I scream for the class, for the school, for the entire town of Watonka and anyone who's ever wondered what lies beyond that old smokestack horizon. *Je ne suis pas mon travail! Je ne suis pas mon travail!* I am not Hurley's Homestyle Diner! I'm not a waitress! I'm not the Cupcake Queen! I'm just *me*, alive and whole and happy when I'm skating. When my eyes are closed and my feet glide across the ice. Out there, I forget about my father road-tripping through the desert. I forget about the lines in my mother's face and her chapped hands, red-raw with burns from the grill and too much time at the sink. I forget about the stains on my clothes and under my nails.

When I'm skating, I'm somewhere else. Somewhere better.

But I don't know how to speak the language of impossible dreams *en français*, so I swallow it back, blinking rapidly as if it's just the Lake Erie wind in my eyes.

Tap tap tap. Out beyond the window, past the branches to the barren soccer field, snow dances across the expanse and I want to bolt, straight back to the lake with my skates. But like the old saying goes: It takes forty-two muscles to frown, and only twelve to jam a cupcake in your mouth and get over it. So I smile and begin again, distributing my sugar-sweet merry-go-round confections to the class.

"*Je m'appelle Hudson Avery. Je travaille chez Hurley's Home-style Diner. Oui, je suis la boulangère des petits gâteaux.*"

My name is Hudson Avery. I work at Hurley's. Yes, I am the baker of the cupcakes.

But not for long.

"Those cupcakes rock," Trina Dawes tells me after today's presentations are done. "Are you doing anything January tenth? I'm having a birthday bash. A hundred people at least."

"Can't make it." Wrong date? Wrong address? No way I'm falling for that joke.

"Make it? Oh, no! That's not what I meant." She giggles, her cheeks turning red. "I was asking about ordering cupcakes . . . I mean . . . you could totally come if you want to, though. Do you?" She looks up at me and tilts her head, freshly glossed mouth turning into an awkward frown.

"Wait, you thought . . . that I thought . . . you were invit- ing me to your party?" I pack up the few remaining Carousels, hoping my face isn't the same color as the frosting.

She swipes another cupcake from the box. "I mean, you *could*—"

"I have a thing that night. An art show. With my brother. He's, um, exhibiting his . . . Civil War sculpture. Thing. So I'm busy."

"Can you still make the cupcakes?"

"Not a problem." Where are those horribly intrusive fire drills when you need them?

Trina smiles again, her face rearranging itself to happy and casual. "Should I, like, give you my order now? Or do I have to call Harley's?"

"It's Hurley's," I say with a sigh. "But you can give it to me now."

"You kicked some serious *derrière* in there, *ami*," Dani says after class. "Don't sweat Trina's party, okay? Those girls are like a living issue of *Cosmo*."

"Easy for you to say. The whole junior class doesn't look down on you."

"Please." She empties her backpack into her locker, pack- ing away the Nikon equipment she used in her presentation. "People just don't know you, okay? It's not the same thing."

"They know me all right. Cupcake Queen of Watonka, remember? A real celeb."

93

Dani drops her books into her backpack and tugs hard on the zipper. "There are what—three thousand people up in this joint?"

"So?"

"So why do you assume everyone around here is so tight? You act like Watonka High is this big bowl of awesome and you're the only one who didn't get a spoon. Guess what, girl? It's high school. *Everyone* hates it."

"Not you. You're always talking to people, smiling, whatever. You have friends here."

"So do you—you just keep forgetting it."

"Dani, I didn't mean—"

"Gotta go. I'll catch you at work tonight." She slams her locker, but not that hard, and I let her leave. We never stay mad at each other for more than a few minutes, anyway. I just wish I could be more like her, letting all the bad stuff roll off. Not caring so much what everyone thinks. Full of those confident, front-of-the-house smiles, all the way.

Maybe Dani's right—maybe they don't look down on me. Not exactly. For the most part, they don't even notice me. I spent those all-important clique-forming years on the ice with Kara. While the normal Watonka kids were having playdates and movie nights and sleepovers, we were practicing our lutzes and spins, learning to balance competitive drive with sportsmanship and ladylike grace. By the time I got to high school, I'd lost my skating friends, Kara got swept up in the current of Will's popularity, and fate had sorted everyone else into groups like change in the till. Other than Dani, I was alone; the rest of the nickels and dimes and quarters had moved on—not against me, just without.

Now when they see me in the halls, they remember only one thing: Cupcake Queen of Watonka. That stupid newspaper picture, me cradling a mixing bowl in my arms like a baby. Well extra, extra! Read all about it, Watonka! I used to be good at something else, too. Something that had nothing to do with taking orders from Trina Dawes or following in my mother's dream-sucking, Hurley Girl footsteps. Something with a real future. Something I finally have another shot at.

All I have to do is reach out and take it. It's that simple.

I stash the extra French cupcakes in my locker, flip open my notebook, and turn on my phone. Orange-stained fingertips quick over the buttons, I punch in Will's number, take a deep breath, and send my answer up to outer space.

Chapter Seven

How to Appear Outwardly Cool While Totally Freaking Out on the Inside Cupcakes

*Chilled vanilla cupcakes cored and filled with
whipped vanilla buttercream and dark chocolate shavings,
topped with vanilla icing and a sugared cucumber slice*

Blue-and-silver jersey number seventy-seven, HARPER, skates back and forth in front of his eighteen teammates. From my spot in the player's box, I check the roster and count the boys three times to be sure, looking them each in the eye as I do. It's a thing I learned from that show where the guy gets dropped in the jungle with nothing but a pillowcase, a pack of gum, and a tampon applicator: Make eye contact with wild animals to claim your territory and avoid a beatdown.

Today's primary goal: avoid beatdown. Check.

"It's no secret the Wolves are struggling," Will says.

"Struggle. To flounder or stumble." Thirty-two, FELZNER, defense, taps away on his cell.

"We're definitely stumbling, yo." NELSON, sixty, also defense. He grabs his crotch and spits, then winks at me in the box. Aside from the spitting and groping, which under normal circumstances I don't find all that attractive, Brad Nelson's kind of a dead ringer for that model Tyson Beckford.

I slip off my gloves and lower the zipper on my fleece.

"We've lost focus," Will continues. "We're not playing like a team. Our morale is low. I get it."

"Eh, we bite." DEVRIES, oh-seven, left wing. The smallest of the line, Rowan DeVries sports the unfortunate combination of braces, freckles, and tangerine-red curls. He seems better suited to racing hockey players in a video game.

I flip past the roster and scan the rest of Will's notes. According to the files, the Watonka Wolves haven't been to a national competition in over twenty years. The last time our varsity hockey team even won a *division* championship, these particular boys were still in diapers.

I've certainly got my work cut out for me this month.

As I make my steady, intentional eye contact, the packmates stare back. Hard. Rowan aside, they're all about the same size, big and broad-shouldered, muscle and attitude. Just as Will promised, everyone showed up, skipping their Guitar Hero matches or raw meat–eating contests or whatever it is boys do in their free time, but most of them don't really *mean* it. They're only half-equipped, some of them in worn jerseys while others are just wearing sweatshirts and track pants. Five didn't bother with helmets. Two keep checking their phones, texting and scrolling, counting down the seconds until some-one calls with a better offer.

Will skates to the center of the pack, his skates stopping in a T. He nods toward me in the box. "We have a guest today."

I wave, forgetting all about the cool man-nod I practiced in front of the mirror. Josh smiles at me from the line. *Oh.* Is the pancreas on the left side? Because I think mine just twitched.

"Some of you guys probably know Hudson Avery," Will says. The statement elicits a few grunts. One discernible "yeah." Two sneezes. A yawn. Wow. Just as I suspected, I've made quite an impression at the Watonka Central School District. Per-haps I should refresh their memories with a few stories from the good ole days, like the one where right wing Parker Gilgallon wets his pants during sixth-grade crab soccer, or where defense Eddie Dune got the nickname "Gettysburg" for flashing the crowd during center Micah Baumler's recital of the Gettysburg Address, right after the four score and seven years part.

"She can skate," Will continues. "*Really* skate. And unless you scare her off by acting like your mouth-breather selves, she *might* be able to help us. Off the record, of course."

Shuffles. Groans. Another sneeze. Perhaps my hot-pink zip-up fleece wasn't such an award-winning idea; much more *Barbie on Ice* than the Icelandic barbarian skatetrix Dani and I envi-sioned earlier this week when we discussed the hockey strategy. Still, I expected and planned for this exact scenario, and no one needs to know that behind my confident fuchsia-and-bubble-gum exterior, just above my hockey-boys-you-*will*-take-this-ass-seriously stretchy jeans, my stomach is trying to run up into my esophagus.

Hudson Avery, you are a professionally trained ice-skater. You can do spirals and axels and lutzes around these guys all day long. You are a beautiful woman with the strength of an ox, . . .

Yes! I step out of the box, blades firm on the ice.

. . . the ferocity of a lioness, . . .

Absolutely! I hold my head high.

. . . the grace of a gazelle. . . .

No doubt! Right foot next, firm on the—firm! *No! I said firm! With the grace of a—*

Gazelle.

I'm flat on my stomach, splayed out in an X, cartoon-falling-off-cliff style. As a competitive figure skater, I spent a good majority of my training perfecting the best way to fall on my ass, and I'm not even doing *that* right anymore. What *is* it with me and hockey boys?

Across the ice, thirty-eight black skates are level with my head. White laces looped through silver eyelets. Toes scuffed. Thick blades. Four of them move toward me. *Slash-slash, slash-slash, slash-slash.*

Will and Josh grab my arms and help me to my feet.

"You okay?" Josh's face tightens the way it did after our collision at Fillmore.

"Yeah. I think so."

"You totally bit it," Will says through that megawatt smile. "Blackthorn didn't even have to train-wreck you this time."

"You gonna teach us how to walk, Princess Pink?" GILGALLON, twenty-nine. Pretty ballsy for a pants-wetter, if you ask me. "I wouldn't want you to break a nail."

If I wasn't so utterly *pink* right now, I might just skate over there and knee him in the—

"Back off, Gilgallon," Josh warns. He and Will may be my only allies on the ice. Which is unfortunate, considering there are seventeen other guys staring me down, all looking for a reason to unilaterally dismiss me.

"So, um, why *are* you here, exactly?" *Grab, spit, grab* goes Brad Nelson.

"Seriously, *mami*." Left wing TORRES, lucky number thirteen, shakes his head. "Hockey rink ain't the place for candy-ass little girls. Maybe you should go home and play with your dollies."

"Dude, shut it." Will smacks Frankie's arm while the other guys laugh. "Seriously, you all right to keep going, Hud?"

I press my hand against my fleece pocket, Lola's letter crinkling inside. *You gotta want it, kiddo. Really want it.* I take a deep breath and feel the rink beneath my blades, the familiar solidity coming up through my legs. All winter I've come to the ice sporadically, a secret affair. Without reason. Without direction. Looping like a tiny snowflake swirling on the wind, no idea how far I'd drift or where I'd end up, hoping only that I wouldn't melt before I got there.

But here, now, my reason skates to the surface.

Will and I made a deal. I'm laced up. I'm on the ice. And

---

for the first time since I ditched the competition track three years ago, I have a purpose.

And like old Lola used to say, "I didn't keep myself alive another lousy day just to watch you half-ass your way across the rink, *bambina. Capisce?*"

"Wolf pack, right?" I ask, newly emboldened by the stone-cold Lola-cool in my voice. "That's what they call you?"

"How-*ooooo*!" JORDAN, ninety-nine, goalie. Amir Jordan is actually howling. Head thrown back, olive-brown skin and shaggy black hair gleaming under the fluorescents like a real wolf in the moonlight. The whole thing is pretty frightening, and I don't mean in the sexy "Team Jacob" kind of way.

I suck in a breath of cold air and channel some more Lola, slapping my gloves against my hip. "All right, wolf pack. When was the last time you won a game?"

Slap.

"Tied a game?"

Slap.

"Lost by less than a point?"

"Speaking of points, Princess Pink . . . you got one?" Brad again. You know, for someone so hot, he shouldn't be so wound up.

"Chill out, Nelson," Josh says.

"But homegirl doesn't know *jack* about hockey! You just want to—"

"Ever hear of James Creighton?" I glide toward them, skating along the blue line.

"Who?" Micah Baumler asks.

"Creighton. Father of ice hockey?"

Skates shuffle. Helmets bow.

"He's in the hockey hall of fame," I continue. "And by the way, wolf pups, the father of your favorite sport was also a figure skating judge. So let's drop all this 'homegirl doesn't know jack' b.s. and focus on the biggest challenge this school has ever seen: breaking your flawlessly pathetic ten-year losing streak."

"Ten years?" Rowan laughs. "It hasn't been that long, Hudson."

"Have you *read* the files?"

He looks up at me, lowering his voice as if we're sharing some big secret. Which, apparently, we are. "What files?"

"From the—"

"If you're done with the history lesson, can we *go* now?" Chuck Felzner whines, still messing with his phone.

"Yeah, I'm starving," Brad says. "You guys wanna hit up Papallo's? Ten-cent wings tonight."

Frankie fist bumps him. "Man, you *know* I want in on that."

Josh holds up his hands. "Come on, guys. Practice isn't over."

Oblivious to his protests, the team shuffles collectively toward the locker room.

"You coming out with us, Princess?" Brad winks at me again before he leaves, but I shake my head and he follows the rest of the pack off the ice.

Will and Josh, the only two wolves on the rink, exchange a frustrated glance.

"I'll try again," Josh says. He skates to the edge and slips the guards over his blades, hobbling into the locker room to find his teammates.

"Sorry about that," Will says. "Not bad for your first try, though." He squeezes my shoulder. I remember Dani's "smoldering" comment in French class the other day and gently shrug him off.

"If that's what you call 'not bad,' no wonder your team sucks."

Will laughs, his eyes crinkling at the corners. "Ouch."

"Sorry." I'm not trying to hurt anyone's feelings out here, but . . . not bad? Seriously? On the scale of things going bad, one being my infamous Black Melons cupcake fail—watermelon cupcakes with black licorice icing that even Bug refused—and ten being, let's say, the Cold War, I'd call today's meet and greet about a seven *thousand*. Hot-pink zip-up? Training Watonka's hockey thugs? My so-called candy-ass moves against ten-cent wings at Papallo's?

"It's okay. It's just the first night."

"Will, this isn't going to work. The guys don't—"

"The guys don't realize how much they need you. But they will."

"I don't belong out here with—"

"Yes, you do. It's hard for them—no one wants to admit we need outside help."

"You mean help from a girl."

"I mean help from anyone not on the team."

I slip my gloves back over my hands and flex my fingers. "Why don't we talk to the coach, then? If he signs me on officially, maybe the guys will—"

"No way." Will shakes his head. "Dodd is still technically our coach, but he doesn't care about helping us win. And if he knew about you, he'd flip. Not to mention we're probably violating some school insurance policy. I'm serious, Hudson. You can't tell people about this—especially Dodd."

I shove my hands in my fleece pockets, gloved fingers scratching against the foundation letter. "You're giving me a lot of reasons to walk away."

"I'm also giving you a big one to stay." He looks out across the empty, unblemished rink and smiles, and we both know he's right. Surly hockey boys or not, I need the ice time.

"You don't have to decide right now," Will says. "You wanted the ice tonight after practice? It's all yours. Just let Marcus know when you're done. He's the manager here. He's in the office down the hall—white ponytail, Sabres hat."

"Thanks."

"Have a good workout." Will gives me one last squeeze and skates off toward the locker room.

Once he's gone, I check the laces on my skates, do some light stretching, and push off the back edge. Methodically I loop into my figures, eyes closed, the cut and swish of the blades bringing me back to the only place besides the predawn

Hurley's kitchen that calms me. I'm still mangled from the Wolves firing squad, but a deal is a deal, and holy snowballs—compared to Fillmore, the ice here at Baylor's is a downright dream.

I pick up speed as my legs get a feel for the place, each muscle rejoicing at the smoothness of the groomed indoor rink. I'm much faster here. Looser. Uninhibited. Just like I remember.

I skate hard to the other end and loop back, twisting into a scratch spin, tight and fast, arms high above my head as my feet twirl against the ice and . . .

Bam!

My ass hits the rink with the thud heard round the world.

"This sucks." I drag myself up for another go.

"Rough night, huh?"

I whip around so fast, I almost lose my footing again. *Almost.* Josh smiles and glides across the rink, still in his skates and practice gear.

"Just you and me," he says. "Will went to Papallo's to talk some sense into them. I didn't have any luck."

"No luck, and no wings, either? Talk about a rough night."

Josh laughs and motions for me to follow him around the perimeter. I fall in next to him, both of us taking long, comfortable strides along the edge.

"Hudson, when I first asked you about this . . . I mean, if I'd known Will would rope you into the team thing, I never would've mentioned it to him."

"No. I really need the ice time. I just don't know why he

thought I could help the Wolves. I might as well be invisible out here."

Josh shakes his head. "Will believed me when I told him about you—about what I saw at Fillmore. That's why he thought you could help."

I keep my eyes on the ice, my cheeks burning. "In that case, sorry I let you down."

"You kidding me? The guys are mostly idiots, Hud. Seriously. Sometimes I think we need sensitivity training more than technical work."

"Perfect! Next time I'll bring journal prompts. We can all write about our feelings, and after that, we'll listen to some Indigo Girls and make friendship bracelets."

Josh's eyebrows go up. "That . . . sounds pretty awesome. Hockey with feelings. I can dig it."

We continue our shoulder-to-shoulder loop, picking up speed until we're practically racing. He's taller than me, and definitely strong, but I keep up with him anyway, matching his increased pace at each turn. On our fourth time around, I stop at the box for my water bottle.

"Man, I'm out of shape." I try not to pant like a straight-up dog, but my lungs burn.

"Come on, you're holding your own out there. I'm impressed."

I take another swig and cap the bottle. "Don't be. I'm good on the short bursts, but I suck at endurance stuff."

"I know a trick for that. Something you probably didn't learn at skate club."

"I'm all ears. Um, skates. Whatever." I clamp shut my cornier-than-thou mouth and follow Josh to the center line.

For the next twenty minutes we practice a hockey drill—some sort of sideways run-hop-slide move. I have no idea what it's called officially, but if my lungs and thighs have their say, we'll be calling it the Crusher. Or the Killer. Or the What-the-Hell-Have-You-Gotten-Us-Into-You-Stupid-Girl-er. By the time we finish a few sets, I'm ready to curl up and zonk out, right here on the rink.

"Strange night," I say when we finally change out of our skates and pack up our gear. "Not sure I can handle a weekly dose of this stuff."

"Whatever you're training for, it has to be important, right?" Josh asks.

"Just my only chance at going to college and getting out of here. NBD, as my little brother says."

Josh zips up his bag and throws it over his shoulder. "Then you *have* to do it, right? Give us another shot? Your future totally depends on it."

"That's a fact, fifty-six?"

"Just looking out for your best interests."

"Aww, how selfless." I laugh as we wave good night to Marcus and head out the front door together, my hips already feeling the burn of tonight's workout. Josh walks me to the Tetanus Taxi, the banged-up Toyota 4Runner I inherited from Trick, and waits in the passenger seat until it's warm and ready to roll.

"What do you say? One more chance?" He looks at me and smiles, his eyes softened by the muted green lights of the dash, and I revise my original estimate on the night's badness scale from seven thousand to three.

"The thugs of Watonka can't scare me off *that* easily," I say, thinking of that smooth Baylor's ice. "I'll be back."

"Sweet!" He pulls his hat over his ears and slides out of the truck, breath fogging as soon as it hits the outside air. "See you in school, Avery."

My muscles ache, my bones are battered, and my feet feel like they ran a shoeless marathon over broken glass, but tonight, after I pay Mrs. Ferris, get Bug to bed, and sink my head into that cool, worn pillow, I pull the comforter tight beneath my chin and sleep better than I have all year.

Chapter Eight

The Good, the Bad, and the Cupcakes

Oatmeal pumpkin cupcakes
shot through with chocolate fudge,
topped with a thin layer of fudge icing
and toasted coconut tumbleweeds

"So, the stretchy jeans. Did they or did they not get the job done?" Dani demands, watching me over a bowl of peaches-and-cream batter on our usual Saturday-morning shift. "Usual" meaning I still had to be here before sunrise to bake, only now, instead of hitting up Fillmore for a late-morning break while my cupcakes cool, I'll be working the floor. After nearly a week of training, I'm still not winning any customer service awards, but it *is* getting easier.

I pour the batter into cups and slide everything into the oven. "Promise you won't laugh."

"Are you kidding me with this right now? I gave up ladies' night so you could hang with the hockey boys, and *you're* making conditions?"

"Promise!"

"Okay, okay. No laughing." She drops a stack of laminated menus on the counter for their weekly wipedown. "Now *tell* me!"

I clear my throat for dramatic effect. "For starters, every time I see hockey boys, I bite it on the ice."

"You fell? *Again?*" Dani's cough-that's-supposed-to-cover-the-laugh-she-promised-not-to-do is only slightly muted by the howl of a passing ambulance out back.

"Hey! I said no laughing! This is *so* not funny."

"It's totally funny. You're the most graceful person I know. I can't believe you're such a klutz around your crush."

"He's not my—"

"Mmm-hmm." Dani tosses an unsavable grease-stained menu into the trash. "You know, hon, it occurred to me that this whole Wolves thing might be a *really* bad idea. What kind of a hockey team has not one, but *three* black dudes? No wonder they can't win."

"You think we live in Norway or something? Amir Jordan is Pakistani. There's also an Asian guy, some Puerto Ricans, and the starting left wing has, like, carrot-hair. He must be Irish. It's the whole UN over there."

"Yeah, but did you ever notice there aren't many black guys in the NHL? There's no hockey in the homeland, Hud. It's unnatural."

"I'm pretty sure there's no corned beef hash in the homeland, either, but you dogged that stuff Trick cooked up like it was your job."

Dani laughs. "You're just a regular, hockey-playing Sherlock Holmes, aren't you?"

I scoop some brown sugar into a bowl of buttercream, add two drops of orange tint, and flip on the mixer. "I'm not playing. Just helping out with a few practices so I can train afterward. Which, by the way, was your idea."

"I know." She lets the air out of her lungs, slow and loud, all the funny stuff suddenly erased. "Hudson, listen. I get that you pretty much skated right out of your mother's uterus, okay? No doubt you can rock the rink from here to Antarctica, and that scholarship is a kick-ass opportunity."

"Okay, one: Don't mention my mother's uterus. And two: That scholarship is the only reason I'm doing this."

"I know, and I'm with you. If you want to get back out there, pull on those skates and lace 'em up, girl. I'll be in the stands, stompin' out my Hudson cheer. Just be realistic, too. You have a lot going on right now, and—"

"Hold up." I flip off the mixer. "You have a Hudson cheer?"

"Maybe."

"There's no singing involved, is there?"

"That's not—"

"Trust me, Dani. I can work this. They just need me once a week. And with the extra money from waitressing, I'll pay Mrs. Ferris to stay longer with Bug. All I have to do is keep up with cupcake orders, put in my Hurley Girl time, and fly under the Mom-radar long enough to train for my competition. Two, three months tops."

"Then what?" Finished with the menus, Dani grabs the clean silverware bin and a stack of paper napkins. "The wolf pack comes back from the dead, you score the Capriani thing, and you and the boys dash off into the sunset on your magical golden ice skates? How ro-*man*-tic."

"And leave all this behind?" I sweep my arms around the steel kitchen, air saturated with bacon and cupcakes and my entire family history. "No *way*."

"You know you can't get extra-hot extra–bleu cheese chicken finger subs in any other city. And if you ditch me right after high school, I'm not FedExing them." She tries to laugh, but it comes out too fast, a soft rush that disappears as soon as it hits the light.

Dani's a Western New York girl, all the way. We've talked about going to college in Buffalo together, sharing a dorm or apartment, staying close to home. Even if I got stuck helping out at the diner on weekends, we could still live together, still see each other every day. But now, with this skating opportunity, I could do something else. I could actually leave here. And we both know it.

I lean on the counter as my best friend methodically rolls forks and spoons into napkins, not meeting my eyes. When I saw her the first morning at my new bus stop freshman year, she was like the one-girl welcoming committee, all dimples and crazy black curls that bounced when she laughed. She'd recently moved to the neighborhood, too—from some place in North Buffalo—and everything about her was different from me and the world I'd just left behind. When she smiled, it was like when the sun unexpectedly comes out in the middle of a harsh winter, and I just turned to the light of her.

Still, things had blown up with Kara and I wasn't ready for a replacement. I kept my distance—polite yet cool, friendly but not too inviting. It was the I-fly-solo vibe that I'd spent the aftermath of my father's disappearing act perfecting, but it didn't faze Dani. She'd wait for me at the bus stop every morning and sit next to me for the ride, sharing her cherry-frosted Pop-Tarts and asking me what kind of music I listened to and how I liked our apartment and whether I had any siblings. Nothing about skating or competitions or coaches. Nothing about Kara and the friends I'd ditched. From that very first day, Dani looked at me like no one else had in years—without expectations, pity, or disappointment.

I fell in love with her then.

"Mom will be here any minute," I say softly. "Let's make sure everything's ready."

"Cowboy at table seven's yours today, babe," Dani says, armed with an empty coffee carafe and a devious grin. "Be warned: He likes to send his food back a lot, and he only tips a dollar, no matter what the bill is. Watch his hands. Oh, and don't bend over in front of him."

I tighten the strings on my apron. "Thanks for the A&E biography. If you know him so well, why don't you take him?"

Dani shrugs. "Consider it your final rite of passage. If you can handle Cowboy, you can handle anyone."

"That's what you said about the Buff State frat boys at table twelve." I tug on the bottom of my dress, square my shoulders, and head out to face the country music.

"Howdy," the man says with a cheesy wink. "I'll do the usual."

"Sounds good. Um, what is it?"

He looks me up and down and sighs loudly through his nose. "Large orange juice, hot coffee, black, two sugars, side-a home fries, and a westerner omelet, with extra cowboys and Indians, if you please."

Folks, we've got a live one here.

"OJ, coffee, home fries, western. Got it." I scoot back toward the kitchen to put in the order, but frat house central snags me before I clear the floor.

"Can we get some more nog, please?" One of them points to his empty glass. Mom really needs to reconsider the bottomless eggnog deal. I've spilled so much of it on my Hurley Girl dress, the bacon grease stains are jealous. Besides, I hate that word. *Nog*. Ugh.

"More *nog*, coming right up." I try to smile, but my cheeks hurt.

"And some ketchup," another says.

"Sure thing." I turn back to the kitchen.

"Oh, miss? Can I get a take-out box for this?"

"Take-out box, you got it."

"More coffee, too."

"Okay." By the time I make it behind the beautiful,

protective doors of the kitchen, I'm just one nod-and-smile away from stripping off the Hurley's dress and running out onto the train tracks.

"Looks like a good crowd," Mom says, zipping around the kitchen. "Maybe I shouldn't take off just yet."

"Ma, you can't ditch Bug." Mom's supposed to leave early today—taking my little bro to the McKinley Mall to see Santa. Bug and I have conversed at length on mythical creatures, particularly after Santa missed our house the first Christmas after the divorce, but he lets Mom go on thinking he's a big believer in all that naughty or nice crap. Probably because it's one of the few occasions Mom takes off an entire afternoon just for him.

"Don't worry about us," I say. "We've got it all under control."

"Okay, you're right." Mom scrapes a dried splotch of frosting from my apron with her thumbnail. "You've really taken to this, Hud. When things calm down after New Year's, I'll show you how to do inventory and food orders. Sound good?"

"Cool, Ma." Mental notes: One, add cowboys and Indians to inventory list. Two, jab icicle into eye.

"Thanks, baby. For everything." She leans in to kiss my cheek, and I inhale the scent of her grapefruit shampoo, mixed with the bacon-and-onions smell of the diner. Then I slip my arms around her waist and return her hug. But just for a second, because I have tables waiting, and those Peachy Keen cupcakes aren't going to frost themselves.

"How's it going at the O.K. Corral?" Dani asks at the prep counter.

"I'd rather be at Baylor's falling on my ass in front of the Wolves." I spread a generous pile of buttercream on a cupcake.

"Still crushing on the hockey boy, then?"

I flick a gob of frosting at her boob. "Shut *up*!"

She scrapes it off with her finger and points it at my chest. "You're into him. I can tell—your vibe is totally different when you're into someone."

"How would you know what my 'into someone' vibe is? I haven't had a boyfriend the whole time I've known you. Not to mention ever."

"What about—"

"If you bring up Will and that party again, I'll kill you with this spatula and make it look like an accident. And before you say another word, making out with a cardboard Johnny Depp at the movie theater on a dare doesn't count, either."

"I've got the Johnny pictures to prove it. Remember that." Dani laughs as her gaze shifts to the window over the grill. "Hold up—isn't that Josh Blackthorn?"

"Where?" I whip my head around as my icing-smudged hands rapidly smooth out my dress. But Josh isn't there—just Cowboy reading the paper at table seven and frat guys pointing at their empty eggnog glasses again.

"Wow," Dani says. "You walked right into that one."

I pour a fresh round of nogs and arrange them on a serving tray. "I hate you."

"I'm just saying you shouldn't rule out any possibilities. You never know when love might find you."

"Yeah, in between the pages of *The Swashbuckling Adventures of Naked Pirates*. Speaking of Johnny Depp."

"Waffles up, Danicakes," Trick says.

"Laugh it up, go ahead." Dani grabs two plates of blueberry Belgian waffles and a side of bacon and nudges the kitchen doors with her foot.

"See, hon," Trick says, "guys are like . . . well, take this here." He grabs a peeled white onion, pointing at it with his giant knife. "Lots of layers, and—"

"How's my omelet working, Dr. Ruth?"

Trick smiles, chopping up the onion into fine little bits. "Five minutes. Hey, we're out of the ham quiche. Change the specials board to broccoli and cheese—we gotta move these greens before they die."

"You got it." One less pork product in the atmosphere is always a good thing.

After I deliver those nogs, Dani drags me behind the dining room counter. "You're not gonna believe this, but Josh is here for real. I saw him in the parking lot."

"That so?" I grab the whiteboard from the wall at the end of the counter and redo the quiche. "What a fascinating coincidence."

"I'm not kidding. He's already at the front door."

"Danielle Bozeman, you are *high*-larious." I crouch down to shove the dry-erase markers back under the counter. "Like

Josh doesn't have anything better to do than check me out in my bangin' Hurley Girl dress."

"Apparently not, because he's headed right for you," she singsongs.

"Oh yeah?" No one is seated at the counter, so I bend down a little farther and shake-shake-shake it. "How do I look? Think Josh has a good view of the show?"

"Perfect. I didn't even have to buy tickets."

Um . . . why does Dani suddenly sound like a dude?

"He's really here, isn't he?" I whisper out of the corner of my mouth. Dani nods, barely keeping it together as she slips back into the kitchen. Deserter!

I reach for a mug from the coffee station over my head. In a single swoop, I stand, grab the pot, and turn around, offering it to Josh with a bright, wide grin. "Hi, Josh! Coffee?"

He smiles. "Love some."

"How do you take it?"

"Hot. I mean, cream. No sugar." He parks himself at one of the counter stools and strips off his hat and scarf, hair sticking out funny in all the usual places. "So, was that little dance part of the two-two-two breakfast special?"

"Hudson!" Trick shouts through the window over the grill, just in time. "Bug's here. I'm sending him out with your western."

Bug pushes his way through the doors and passes me the hot plate. "Order up!"

"Thanks, kiddo." I smile at Josh. "Josh? Bug. Bug? Josh. Be right back."

Over at table seven, Cowboy's got his fork in the eggs before I've even set the plate down. Through a mouthful of breakfast, he scowls at me and rolls his eyes.

"Darlin'," he says, swallowing after the fact. "I know you're new round here. But I ordered a bacon and cheese omelet, and you brought me a westernized omelet." He hooks his arm around my waist, the food-coated fork still dangling from his fingers.

"But you ordered the western, sir."

"Miss, can we get some coffees?" A woman calls from the next-door booth. "We've been here five minutes already."

"Be right with you, ma'am."

"I certainly hope so."

"What I wanted," Cowboy drawls on, "was the bacon and cheese."

"We'll remake it for you." I reach over to take the western plate, but he grabs it out of my hands, fingers lingering on my skin. Gross.

"No use letting it go to waste," he says. "Just take it off my bill. I'm gonna need a regular coffee, too." He swirls his empty mug. "The one you gave me was decaf."

I look at him dubiously. You know the old saying—never trust a man wearing assless leather chaps in the snowbelt. Still, no point in arguing. "I'll take care of it."

"Thank you much, sweet thing." He winks at me and clicks his tongue. Dani was *so* not kidding about this guy. And for a lousy one-dollar tip? Speaking of tips, here's a hot one, Cowboy:

Don't piss off the girl responsible for serving your food. A lot can happen on that long, lonely stretch of road from the kitchen to your cozy little booth by the window. Just saying.

"My pleasure, sir." I smile and refill his mug with leaded coffee, pour some for the cranky booth lady, then scoot back to the front counter, where Bug is laughing it up with the hockey boy.

"I see you like my friend," I say to Bug.

"Friend?" Bug leans across the counter and squinches up his face. "Or friend with *benefits*?"

"Bug! Where did you—"

"Mrs. Ferris has cable."

"Now you know why we don't." I top off Josh's coffee and snag a cupcake from the bakery case for my brother.

"Because they took away the box when Mom didn't pay the—"

"Look, a Cookies-N-Creamcake," I say. "Yum!"

He jams a bite in. "Anyway," he says through a chocolaty mouthful, "if someone was my friend with benefits, I could get them free fries. And you make the best cupcakes ever, so I definitely see that as a benefit."

"Got a point there, man." Josh gives him a fist-bump. My brother. Josh. Together. Joking around. I think the planet is seriously falling out of orbit.

"Don't encourage him," I say. "It's bad enough he—"

"Waitress? Can we get some more coffee?" Cranky booth lady again.

"Gotta go." I kiss Bug on the forehead and zip over to refill those mugs as Dani seats three more tables. On my way back, Cowboy waves me over.

"Can I get a little more water, toots?" His hand slips out from beneath the table and makes a beeline for my ass. I lean forward instinctively, still rockin' that happy-to-serve-you grin, water pitcher balanced precariously over his lap—the parts those fashionable leather chaps *don't* cover. Tricky thing, this balancing stuff.

"Oops! Oh my gosh, I'm *so* sorry about that! Here's a few extra napkins." Before he can demand help cleaning up his pants, I run back to the kitchen with the empty water pitcher, nearly crashing into Mom.

"Whoa, what's going on?" she asks.

The pitcher hits the counter with a crash. "Cowboy out there is one grab away from a restraining order. And why are people so impatient around here? Can't they see we're busy? Like I was just put on this earth to fetch drinks, you dumb—"

"It's the diner biz, hon. Difficult customers are just part of the deal." Mom sighs. "Better get used to it."

Get used to it. There's that word again—*used*.

"That guy probably wants his whole check comped."

"He's in here all the time. Just give him a coupon. And if he touches you again, send Trick out for a little chat." Mom smooths her hand over my cheek. "Sure you don't want me to stay?"

Through the window over the grill, I see Bug licking

frosting off his fingers, laughing at something Josh said. "I'm fine. You guys have a good time."

Mom smiles. "All right, we're off to the North Pole. Assuming your brother doesn't engage Santa in another hour-long debate about the physics of flying reindeer, we'll see you after dinner. Take some of the turkey and potatoes home so you don't have to fix anything." She zips up her coat and digs the keys from her pocket, scooping up my chocolate-smudged little brother on the way out.

"Do you like it? Working here, I mean?" Josh inspects one of the new flyers Dani and I put together for my cupcakes, all pink and yellow and creamy-looking.

"It has its moments."

"Seems like there's tons of little stuff to keep track of."

"It's the little stuff that makes it *so* special." I laugh, thinking of that perpetual issue with the third toilet. And the joy of clearing away a table and accidentally dipping your boob in a bowl of cold gravy. And the particular inner peace one finds whilst kneeling under a table, scraping at old gum with a butter knife.

"Anyway, enough about my exotic life. Here." I pass him one of the Peachy Keens from the case. "You're the inaugural taster. Tell me what you think."

"Okay, but first, the real reason I'm here today."

"It wasn't for the award-winning coffee?"

"Not even for the show." Josh winks. "Not that it wasn't highly entertaining."

I turn away to rearrange the salt and pepper shakers on the counter, secretly cursing Bug for not being genius enough to invent a time machine. I've seen enough sci-fi movies to know you're not supposed to mess around with the past, but erasing one humiliating event from the last hour of our lives can't hurt, can it?

"Will sent me," Josh says, draining the last of his coffee. "He's nervous about Friday's game and wants to call an extra practice before Thursday. Can you meet Tuesday after school?"

"She's working Tuesday," Dani announces. I love how she just magically apparates at exactly the right moment.

"What?" she says when I shoot her the patented STFU glare. "Your mom posted the schedule."

I grab the big sugar jar from under the counter and unscrew the caps on the dispensers that need refills. "I'll get Nat to switch. Her last test is Monday—she'll be looking to pick up shifts."

"I thought you—"

I cut her off with another warning look. "It's fine, Dani. Josh, it's fine. Tell Will I'll be there."

A wave of frustration passes over Dani's face, but it's gone in a blink, replaced with something closer to mild annoyance.

"Nat needs the money," I say. "It's cool."

"Just once a week, right Hudson?" She reaches behind me for the coffeepot, still grumbling under her breath. Fortunately, I don't think Josh heard.

"You haven't tried your cupcake yet," I say once Dani goes back to her tables.

"Working my way up to it." Josh makes a show of rolling up his sleeves, hefting the cupcake from the plate, and scarfing down the first bite. His eyes close and I sneak a covert glance, refilling the sugar dispensers as the smile rises on his face. I love that part. I mean, the part when people appreciate the cupcakes, not when Josh smiles. Not that I *don't* love his smile, just that I was thinking more about the—

"Waitress?"

I drop the sugar jar, spilling a bunch on the counter. On the other side of the dining room, Cowboy holds up his empty plate.

"I didn't like these eggs after all," he shouts. "Can I get something else?"

"We're all out of something else." I grab a rag and sweep some of the sugar into my hand, making more of a mess.

"Ready for a few more tables?" Dani scoots behind me to restart the coffee. "Big party heading in. I think it's that birthday group from last month."

"The crazy one with all the Karens?"

"You guessed it. Hopefully we won't get any noise complaints this time."

She speeds back to the floor and I look for something to focus on—a stain on the wall, a chipped mug on the rack below the counter. Anything to keep my head from exploding all over my lavender Hurley Girl dress, right in front of Josh.

"Miss, why don't you have the ham quiche today?" An elderly woman taps on the counter at the other end. "I always get quiche on Saturdays, and I bring some back to the senior center for Bess, and now I don't know what to do, because broccoli gives her gas, and I—"

"Take your seat, ma'am. Your waitress will be right with you." I close my eyes and try to disappear, but that trick never works.

"Hudson?" My name is close on the air, caressing my cheek. I open my eyes. Josh is leaning forward on his elbows, his eyes bright and clear, his smile warm. Behind me, something crashes in the kitchen. Trick swears. The birthday group ladies blow through the front door like a blizzard, bearing presents and balloons and big, cackling laughs. Dani rushes to greet them with an armload of menus and they cheer. The other customers raise their voices to compensate. Cowboy rings the silver bell at the register again and again. *Ding ding ding dingdingdingdingding . . .*

"You okay?" Josh asks. "You look like you're about to—"

"I can handle it." I have to. I swore I could. "Did you like the cupcake?"

"Not really." He smiles again. "Love is a better word. But I should go—you're slammed."

He digs into his pocket and drops a five on the counter, then bundles into his winter stuff. "Hang in there, Hud. Text me later about Tuesday."

He disappears out the front door, and reality rushes over

me like an avalanche. I tighten my apron again, stick a fresh order pad in the front pocket, and swipe the just-brewed coffee from the warmer, armed and ready for the birthday group.

Hudson Avery, ladies and gentlemen! Fresh from the frigid shores of Lake Erie in the biggest comeback of the century!

"Whoa!" Dani jumps out of the way right before I sideswipe her. "Watch it!"

"Ow!" I shake a splash of hot coffee from my hand, recoiling from the sudden sting. "Sorry. Didn't see you."

"You're not paying attention."

"I'm busy!" I reach behind her and grab a clean towel from the shelf.

"Hud, listen to yourself." She sets her tray down on the counter, louder than necessary, if you ask me. "You sure you know what you're getting into with all this?"

"I said I can handle it." I toss the towel over my shoulder and scoot around her, marching off to greet the Karens et al with my best birthday grin.

Two, three months tops.

Chapter Nine

Sticks and Stones May Break My Bones, but Falling Down Hurts Real Bad, Too, Cupcakes

*Red velvet cupcakes with warm raspberry center
and cream cheese icing, topped with mashed mixed berries
and served on a chocolate-drizzled plate*

Tuesday afternoon. Four p.m. Four below zero.

I bombed my eighth-period government quiz.

I'm behind on the reading group questions for *The Scarlet Letter*, and Hester Prynne is totally mad at me.

My tray-carrying shoulder is about to go on strike.

And twelve seconds into Will's emergency extra practice, Chuck Felzner's already starting with me.

"Aw, man," he says when I skate forward. "She's here *again*?"

I take in an icy breath and yank my gloves off. Sure, I could definitely do without the whining, but I'm not here to be anyone's bestie. I just need to show up, get them to improve their game. Show them how much they need me, just like Will says. In exchange, I get the ice time. Quid pro whatever.

"Stuff it, Felzner," I say. "We don't have time for your antics today."

"Ooooh!" Brad Nelson whistles from the front of the line. "Looks like Princess Pink got her balls back. Bring it, baby!"

Josh elbows him in the ribs, which I totally would have done myself if Brad would kindly stop looking like Tyson. Refreshingly, Felzner takes the hint, and in the momentary silence, I plow ahead.

"The other day, you guys asked me if I had a point," I say. "Here it is: Somewhere under all that trash talk, you love this game. You've got a crazy losing streak, but there's no reason you can't end it. Josh and Will say you're good. You could be better. You *will* be." The boys are so quiet I can hear the hum of the cooling machines under the ice, ticking and whirring.

"I *know* skating," I continue, "and I know I can help you. But you need to let me. And I need to see what you've got."

I take a chug of water. When no one protests, Will smiles at me and I press on. "We'll start with drills. Who wants to go first?"

Silence. Eye rolls. One sneeze, two spits, and a cup-adjust.

Just when I begin to sense that my ability to "bring it" has been severely overhyped, Will skates forward.

"Since none of you wolf pups wanna man up," he says, "*I'll* go."

I send him up and down the rink twice, goal to goal with

bittersweet

his stick and a puck. It's like there's an entire eighties *Jock Jams* soundtrack pumping through his head—all those songs the cheerleaders play at the basketball games to psych up the crowd, electrifying his stride. He's hard, fast, and more than a little showy, and the prone-to-swooning part of me flashes back to that kiss in the closet all those years ago. I shudder. He's good. *Really* good.

Thankfully, the objective, focused, professional-skater-type part of me tips her head sideways and dumps that dirty little thought right out on the ice, stabbing the life out of it with a toe pick. *Aaaand, movingrightalong.*

"Aggressive," I tell him on his last return. "Looking good, especially on the straightaway. Watch the right foot near the net—it drags a little on the hard turns in the goal crease."

"Goal crease?" Josh asks as Will skates to the back of the line. "Where did you—"

"YouTube. And Google." I don't admit how many hours I logged on the sites last night, totally blowing off my homegirl Hester Prynne and all that government class stuff about how a bill becomes a law, but that's not important. "Oh, the NHL site, too."

Josh laughs. "You probably know more about this sport than most of us put together."

"Probably. But hey, the Internet is a democracy. Check it out."

I call on Micah Baumler next. Issuing only a minor protest growl, he pulls a pair of goggles over his glasses and follows my instructions. Then DeVries. Nelson. Jordan. Torres. Even

129

Felzner. One by one, they do as I ask. Not without a lot more eye-rolling than should be legal for a boys' varsity team, but somehow we get through it, and I wave them back to the sidelines for a water break.

"Nice work, guys. Looks like we can skip the basics and start with—"

"You do *figure* skating, right?" Nelson again.

I think I liked him better when he was just grabbing himself and winking at me in silence. "That's right."

"I'm not trying to be a dick or anything—"

"Not trying? So dickness just comes naturally for you?"

For a second nothing happens. I cross my arms over my chest, bracing for his next comeback, but he doesn't say a word about it. Suddenly he doubles over, a smile splitting his formerly too-cool-for-school face.

"Damn, I like you. For real." He holds up his hand for a high five, and I concede, smacking his palm.

"You're starting to grow on me, too."

"Look," he says, softer this time. "I'm not saying your kind of skating isn't hard work, but twirls and jumps can't help us against a bunch of Sharks or Bulldogs or Hawks. We need speed, strength, balance, raw stuff like that. So unless you know how to dodge a two-hundred-pound center comin' at you like a freight train, you're wasting your time."

I consider his point. Ten percent valid. Ninety percent I-spent-too-much-time-watching-Rambo-as-a-kid macho bull—

"You guys aren't giving this a chance," Will says. "All those other teams got the same basic training, right? The same stuff Dodd used to give us when he was still around. But who else has a secret weapon like this? She can teach us tons of crazy stuff. They won't even see it coming."

I skate to the center again, buoyed by Will's vote of confidence and the fact that no one has called me Princess Pink for at least five minutes. These practices will be a lot more productive for all of us if I can just get them to see what I'm made of—to see that they really *can* trust me on the ice.

"Will one of you guys try something with me?" I ask.

"*I'll* try something with you." Luke Russet, number twenty-two, defense. Dangerously good-looking in that my-motorcycle-will-definitely-piss-off-your-dad kind of way. He rubs the stubble along his jaw and wiggles his eyebrows at me. Will claps him on the shoulder before his hands complete whatever lewd gesture they were about to make, and I continue.

"Give me a helmet," I say.

Will passes his helmet and skates up behind Luke, nudging him forward. "Go on, Russet," he taunts. "Show her what's up, dude."

I tighten Will's helmet under my chin and point to the net at the other end of the rink. "I'll start down there. Luke, pretend you're the two-hundred-pound center and I have the puck for the opposing team. What do you do?"

"I steal it from you or knock you down trying. Not that I'd mind knocking you up. I mean, down." His eyebrows are still propositioning me, but I ignore them. Honestly, my father is clear across the country—way out of pissing-off-with-a-motorcycle range. Luke's particular charms are lost on me.

"Do it," I say. "Knock me down trying."

Josh steps up. "Hudson, come on—"

"It's okay." I smile. "Trust me."

Luke pipes up again. "Baby, you're just gonna get laid out. I can't do that to a girl."

"Don't worry, you won't."

He laughs and licks his lips. "Look at you, Princess Pink, tryin' to be badass. Wanna bet?"

"Fine, bet me. If you knock me down, you get free dinner at Hurley's every night for a week."

"You're on."

"And if you *don't* knock me down, you shut up. All of you." I turn to face them. "Let's get something straight, wolf pack. I have my own reasons for being here, and they have nothing to do with your sparkling personalities."

"Point?" Felzner says.

"I'm not leaving."

Felzner laughs. "If you say so."

"I say so." I tug my gloves on and skate down the line, beatdown-avoiding, territory-claiming eye contact all the way. "When I'm done kicking Russet's ass, that's *it*. No more whining about who's tired and who's hungry and who needs a diaper change. Got it?"

Nelson oohs again, Josh shakes his head, the rest of the boys laugh, and Luke's eyes lock on mine, smirk erased as he skates backward to the net. "You're on, sweetheart. I like my burgers well-done, fries extra crisp. Vanilla shake, hold the whip. And I'll take one of your mint chocolate chip cupcakes, too. Make a note."

"Noted. Now . . . try to keep up, okay?"

I'm sure his response is laced with more ice than the expanse under my feet, but I don't hear it. I glide to the net at the other end, stop, take a deep breath, and push forward on my toe pick. I zoom across the rink, cold air snapping my face, two hundred pounds of motorcycle-riding hockey god heading right for me.

Slash-slash, slash-slash . . .

A train leaves Los Angeles for New York at eight o'clock, traveling at a hundred miles per hour.

Slash-slash . . .

In New York, a train leaves on the same track at nine-oh-five, traveling at seventy-five miles per hour toward Los Angeles.

Slash-slash . . . slash . . .

At what time will they collide inside Baylor's Rink, causing an explosion of silver blades and hot-pink dust where the girl formerly known as Hudson Avery used to be?

As Luke fast approaches my personal space, my brain checks out and my body takes over, shifting weight to my left leg and bending like a ribbon in the wind. He zooms past me and I pick up speed, pumping harder until I reach the other end of the rink, crossing over into a seamless turn and heading back toward him. His blades grind on the ice and I know he's coming at me faster this time, the rest of the team whooping and shouting from the sidelines. Even Marcus, the ponytailed rink manager, has joined the pack, pumping his fist with the others.

On our second high-speed face-off, I lean into a twist, turning just as he stretches forward and hugs the wind between us. We whip around the rink for another go, and though he's fast and determined and rock steady on the blades, he misses me again, and after the fourth miss, the boys still laughing and whistling on the rails, I signal to Luke that it's over.

I skate fast and furious for the edge, skidding in on my blades, spraying the wolf pack with a shower of ice as I come to a graceful halt.

Marcus winks at me and disappears behind the stands.

No one speaks.

That's right. And you boys haven't even seen my triple/triple!

Luke slides up next to me, panting as he unfastens his helmet. He doesn't say anything or meet my eyes—just pats me on the back once, skates to the rail, and punches Will in the shoulder like he means the hell out of it.

"After today, we've got one more practice before Friday's game," I say to my newly captive audience. "Can I assume we're done with the theatrics?"

All of them nod, speechless. A warmth radiates from my stomach, the tension floating out of my limbs. It's like every air molecule in the rink has registered the change, and now that I have their attention—and maybe even their respect—I *want* to be here. Not just for the ice time, but to help them. To really make a difference, just like Will and Josh always believed I could.

"Excellent," I say. "Now strap on your helmets. You've got drills to do."

Will glides over to me. "I guess this means you're in."

I look out over the boys, all muscle and sweat and swagger, momentarily brought together as they harass Luke about his inability to, in the parlance of our times, "grow a pair."

I turn back to Will, his eyes fixed on mine, and mirror his radiant smile. "Princess Pink, at your service."

Once hockey practice ends, it's time for round two: Capriani Cup training. Certain the Wolves have all filed out into the parking lot, I soar back to the center of the rink alone, and with all the confidence of a girl in a hot-pink zip-up who just kicked about two metric tons of hockey-player ass, launch into a double-axel, double-toe-loop combo jump, landing flawlessly.

Ladies and gentlemen, Princess Pink has officially *brung* it.

Chapter Ten

Red-Hot Double Crush Cakes

*Ginger vanilla cupcakes with
chili-infused dark chocolate cream cheese frosting,
dusted with cinnamon*

"Who's *that*?" Dani stomps into my kitchen on Friday night with her sleepover gear and a bucket of wings, the salty tang of Tobasco singeing my nostrils. "Oh my God, is that your father and Shelvis?"

"You got it. Daddy Dearest subscribed me to his new travel blog."

She sits on my lap to get a closer look at the screen, scrolling down the opening post from Yellowstone National Park. There's an obnoxious close-up of my father and his she-Elvis grinning in front of Old Faithful, his arm wrapped around her waist. Old Faithful? Right. Even though Dad went to Watonka High, he obviously missed Mr. Keller's all-important lecture on irony.

Everyone says that the internet is so awesome because you can connect with people from all over the world, but I think it's the opposite. The internet doesn't make it easier to connect with anyone—it just makes it so you don't really have to. And that's exactly the kind of arrangement my father wants: *Just checking in, no no I can't stay, thanks anyway, don't get up, click here for more, seeyalaterbye.*

"For a female Elvis impersonator," Dani says, "I expected someone hairier."

"Tell me about it." I sigh. Long, dark hair. Good skin. Smile as bright as the new-fallen snow around them. She *is* pretty.

"Sorry, Hud." Dani squints at the screen, tapping the woman with her finger. "Send me the image file. I'll broaden her shoulders and add some facial hair, maybe knock out a tooth or something. Sound good?"

"I knew I could count on you."

"Hey, this'll cheer you up even more. Extra-hot wings for our pregame pig-out, and check it out." She hops up to grab her bag and dumps a pile of homemade DVDs on the kitchen table.

I shuffle through the stack. *Wolves v. Bulldogs, Season XX. Wolves v. Quakers, Season XXI. Wolves v. Raptors, Season XXI.* "Do I even want to *know* how you got these?"

"I didn't do anything illegal, if that's what you mean."

"That still leaves a lot of unsavory possibilities."

She shrugs. "I have Mr. Dodd for gym. He loves me. So

I told him I was doing a spirit club project about the history of Watonka's athletics program and wanted to see the DVDs. He gave me the football ones, too, but I'm saving those for my private collection."

I laugh. "You joined spirit club?"

"I would, if Watonka High had one. I'd be the president of that piece. Holla!"

I return her double high five and flip through the rest of the pile. "This is awesome. Thank you."

"Thank me later," she says. "Let's eat so we can bounce."

With a little bribery of the Andrew Jackson nature for Mrs. Ferris and the Mom-radar jammed under the guise of a French study session at Dani's house, my best *ami* and I hit up the Wolves game. The task of finding good seats proves completely unchallenging. Aside from us, the hockey boys, the opposing Raptors, the coaches, two refs, and the AV club freshman who films the games, there aren't many people here—a handful of families and girlfriends—twenty spectators at most. The highest section is closed off with yellow rope, and only one side of the concessions wall is open.

"Welcome to Ghostville," Dani says.

I hush her as the buzzer sounds and the ref drops the puck between the opposing teams. Raptors take it first, the center forward rapidly slicing his way to the Wolves' goal zone. Amir stops him, cradling the puck and knocking it into Raptor territory. Raptors take it back. Then Wolves. And on it goes for several uneventful minutes until the end of first period, when

Josh finally takes a shot at the net—first attempt of the game. The Raptors dude saves it, ending round one.

From the penalty box, Coach Dodd consults his clipboard, calling out an occasional pointer or swapping players with as much enthusiasm as Trick remaking my screwed-up orders. He doesn't seem to notice the obvious, plain as the white of the ice: Despite the scoreless second period, the guys are skating great. For the first time in a decade, they're not losing. They're holding it down in the goal zone, and other than a few recoverable mistakes, they're keeping the puck away from the Raptors' offense, weaving around the other team, unpredictable yet balanced, aggressive yet controlled.

"I think they listened to me," I say. "They're really keeping it together out there."

"You surprised?" Dani asks. "I'm not trying to join the Wolf Pack Fan Club or anything, but you're an amazing skater, Hud. They should watch *your* DVDs."

"Yeah, but I never thought they'd—*wait*." I lean forward to scope out the seats across the rink where a group of girls just piled in. "Is that Kara?"

"Yep. Looks like she's with Amir Jordan's girl," Dani says. "Ellie something, I think? She's in my English class."

"I know who Ellie is, but what's Kara doing here?" Kara jumps from her seat as the Wolves slice their way toward the goal again, beaming as if Will can see her enthusiasm from the ice. "She and Will are as over as Monday's chicken à la king."

"Eww, don't remind me. My hair still smells like cream sauce." Dani shrugs. "Anyway, she's probably still friends with the other hockey wives. The players, too."

"But—"

"For someone who's supposedly not crushing on these boys, you're getting a little worked up about this."

I lean back in my seat and sigh. "I just think it looks desperate, that's all. I feel sorry for her."

"Mmm-hmm. Watch the game. You're missing your hot little protégés take out their anger on the ice. Quite a sexy display, if you ask me." She pulls out her Nikon and zooms in for some action shots. "And *hello*, number thirteen. Who is that?"

"Frankie Torres. He's in our lunch period."

"Guess I never paid much attention. Mental note: Pay much attention."

I laugh and pat her on the back. "You drool over Frankie. I'm going down for hot chocolates."

Concessions is at rink level, a long stretch of orange shutters that slide up like garage doors to reveal a counter and snack bar. Tonight only the far left side is open, the sweet, dreamy scent of powdered chocolate mix floating down the hall.

I order two cocoas with marshmallows, a bag of salt 'n' vinegar chips, and some Reese's Pieces. After about four hours the half-asleep concessions guy gives me change and piles everything into a little cardboard flat, which, now that I've mastered the fine art of tray-carrying, I can one-hand. I slide it onto my palm, shove the change in my pocket, and turn back toward the stairs that lead to our row.

But I'm not alone.

"What are *you* doing here?" Kara asks, hand on her hip. Red-blond hair spills out from under a baby-blue cable-knit hat, and I want to hate her. I really do. It would be a whole lot easier if she was a cheerleader or something. The all-American bubblegum kind with a prom budget that rivals a celebrity wedding and a red VW Bug convertible with a big pink ribbon dangling from the rearview. It would be easier if her name was Brooklyn or Brianna or Britta or Bree and if she wasn't president of the math club. If her parents were on the boards of elite charity golf tournaments rather than in the Southtowns Ramblin' Rollers competitive bowling league. If she didn't have to endure, perhaps even more tragically than the annual tri-state mathalon, their undying love of Buffalo Sabres lawn decorations.

It would be easier to hate my ex–best friend if it wasn't my fault she was my ex in the first place. *Ex. Former. No longer.*

"Sorry," I say, "but I could ask you the same thing. I thought you and Will broke up?"

Hurt ripples across her face, but she recovers quickly, lips twisting into a scowl. "Unlike some people, *I* have friends on the team, and I've been at every game to support them."

"And I'm sure they appreciate it." I stalk past her, envisioning a mean-girl-style shoulder bump, but the only thing I do is brush her arm, so lightly it might as well be an accident.

She doesn't say anything else, but still, after I turn the corner near the stairs, a shiver passes through me and my neck prickles with guilt, eyes aching from the effort of holding back tears.

"What took you so long?" Dani asks when I reach our seats. "Stop for a quickie in the penalty box? Have to admit, five-six is smokin' tonight."

"Ha-*ha*. No, apparently the concessions dude had to take a nap before he could make the hot chocolates. Hard work, you know?" I pass her a cup and the potato chips.

Back on the rink, Josh, Will, and the rest of my hot little protégés are holding off the Raptors with a combination of strength, intimidation, and a few new tricks for which I'll take full credit. In the final seconds of the game I cling to Dani's arm as Josh runs the puck toward the Raptors' goal, totally unhindered. Closer and closer he gets, Raptors scrambling to reach him as the goalie tries desperately to predict the shot.

Josh passes to Will . . .

Will takes the puck and . . .

If Baylor's Rink were a movie set, everything would melt into slow motion. The seats would be filled with classmates and parents and pro-hockey scouts and other adoring fans, all leaning forward to see the action, and as the buzzer signaled the end of the game, everyone would jump up and spill their drinks and scream and howl and hug the total strangers around them.

Because Will, confident and controlled, taps that beautiful black puck right into the net.

Ladies and gentlemen, he shoots. He scores. The buzzer sounds. The Wolves win.

And the crowd goes . . .

To be perfectly honest, the crowd doesn't go much of anything. For the first time in more than a thousand days, the Watonka Wolves have won a game, and that kind of straight-up, balls-out insanity takes a minute to translate. Even Dodd looks stunned, his mouth hanging open while his brain undoubtedly replays the last five seconds. Dani and I climb down to the edge of the ice where the guys are all hugging and high-fiving, deer-in-headlight grins all around.

"Did that just happen?" Brad asks.

"Hell *yeah* that just happened!" I pull him into a hug. "Congrats. You did it."

"Nah, girl. *You* did it. Did you see those turns? I've been working on my crossovers, just like you said."

"See what happens when you listen to, wait, what was it again?"

He covers his face with his hands. "Don't remind me."

"I believe you said something about a homegirl who doesn't know jack about hockey."

"No need to bring up the past, Princess Pink. We're cool." He holds up his hand for a high five, but before we connect, two arms wrap around my waist and a pair of very soft, very warm lips brushes the back of my neck.

"You rock, you know that?"

Will.

Will? Why is Will . . . *What?* My skin is on fire, but before my brain can invent a semi-intelligible explanation, he lets go, leaving me with nothing but that notoriously dangerous smile as he disappears inside the fist-bumping, stick-pumping mob of Wolves.

Dani gives me a gentle elbow to the ribs. "Hey, Josh," she says to the other captain. The one who has suddenly materialized before us. "Nice game."

"Thanks. You're in my government class," he says. "Danielle, right?"

"Yep. But I go by Dani." She smiles, nudging me forward.

"Was this game for real?" he asks me.

"Um, yes." It's all I can manage in my current state of hot-little-protégé-induced shock.

Josh smiles, running a hand over his head in that adorably nervous way he has. "Everyone's going to Luke's tonight. Twenty-eight Washington, across from the Laundromat. See you guys there?"

"I . . . uh . . ."

"Sounds cool." Dani grabs my hand and leads me toward the exit as the boys hit the locker room. Since I obviously can't remember how to speak in complete sentences, I follow her without protest.

The rush of outside air snaps me back to planet Earth, and I turn to her and smile. "What the hell happened in there?"

"Baby, you are in some *serious* trouble with these boys.

That's what happened." She locks her arm in mine, the haze of our laughter turning white under the night sky as we make our way to the Tetanus Taxi.

We stop at Dani's house to change and speculate and generally obsess, so by the time we get to Luke's place, the party's already jumpin', retro Redman tracks spilling from two giant, eighties-style speakers in the living room. We toss our coats in a heap on the stairs and melt into the crush, most of the faces recognizable from the halls of Watonka High rather than the spectator seats at Baylor's.

In a city where pretty much nothing cool *ever* happens, I guess good news flies fast.

"Hudson!" Will shouts from his perch on the kitchen counter and waves me over. I turn back to Dani, but she's already engrossed in an animated discussion with her photo club friends. I grab a can of orange soda from a cooler on the floor and wander over to Will, hoping he might . . . I don't know . . . explain why he half kissed me on the ice?

"Hudson, you know what you are?" He leans in close. Oh boy—here comes that expensive eau de Harper, trailed by a faint whiff of whatever liquor he's working on.

"What am I?" I ask playfully, knocking into his shoulder. He wobbles before sitting up straight again, bracing himself against the cupboard behind his head. Honestly. This boy probably doesn't even remember *what* happened on the ice tonight, let alone *why* it happened.

"You," he whispers, "are truly a secret weapon. A force to be wrecked with."

"Looks like one of us is a little more wrecked than the other." Will laughs as I clink his plastic cup with my soda, and Josh smiles at me from the other side of the kitchen, raising an eyebrow when I meet his eyes. "Be right back."

I cross over to Josh. "Hey."

"Hey yourself."

"Did—"

"I—"

"You go." I nod toward the monstrous speakers in the other room. "I can't think straight with the music, anyway."

"I made something for you." He presses a black USB drive into my hand. I close my fingers around the device and my heartbeat picks up the pace. How is it that such a little thing can hold so much mystery, so much potential? Anything and everything, or nothing at all. Hope or disappointment. Elation or dread.

"There's some Addicts on there," he says, "but I found some other stuff I think you'll like, too."

"Really?" I *so* want to say something crazy, like how I can't wait to go home and listen, memorizing lyrics and dancing with him in my head. But as a general rule, I try to keep my creeper vibe in check, so I slip the drive into my pocket and stay cool. "Awesome. Thanks."

"Ever hear Undead Wedding's 'Freaktown'?" he asks, leaning in closer so we can talk above the noise. "It's on there."

"No way! I thought that song was an urban legend. Where did you find it?"

"My cousin has this deejay friend in LA who hooks us up. That song reminds me of Watonka. You'll see. The part with the paper birds? I always think of those dumb seagulls."

"I like that Undead Wedding one about the girl in the window."

"'Good-bye, Ghost Girl'!" He turns to face me now, inching even closer as the crowd continues to squeeze in behind him. "You know that part near the end, when he's talking about—"

"The building where they used to live?"

"Totally!" His eyes light up in response, but I keep watching his lips, wondering what it would feel like to kiss them. Soft, I think. Incredible.

"Have you ever—"

"Fifty-six." Will appears beside us and gives Josh a sloppy punch in the arm. "Abby let you out alone tonight, huh?"

Abby? My insides feel like the soda in my hand, bubbling up and then going flat. I take another sip to hide the shock that's probably all over my face. There's no Abby in our class. If he has a girlfriend from another school, why doesn't he talk about her? Why wasn't she at the game tonight? And more importantly, why does she exist in the first place?

Josh looks at me a moment longer, then stares into his drink, ears turning red. "Something like that."

"She here?"

"Not this time." Josh's face changes slightly, his jaw muscles tightening for just a second, and then he smiles. "I told you, she doesn't like you, seventy-seven."

Will strikes a pose, eyelashes fluttering in mock innocence. "What's not to like?"

"I can think of at least eight things." Josh catches my eye and we both smile. "And you know Abby. She's . . . particular."

"I know. Just bustin' your balls, man. Nice pass tonight." Will gives Josh a fist-bump and I go at my soda like Dani on corned beef hash. So Will knows Abby? I don't know Abby. I don't *want* to know Abby. Right now I pretty much hate Abby. And I'd love to say as much for the benefit of the group, but that whole anti-creeper code of ethics gets in the way, so I just stand here like a mime and groove to the nineties rap pounding through the house.

"I can't believe we were so tight out there," Will says, still a little wobbly.

"They get it on film?" Josh asks. "Maybe we dreamed the whole thing."

"No dream. We did it. Thanks mostly to this girl right here." Well I guess we're just the Musketeers now, because Will throws his arms around us and squeezes tight, and our little threesome gets a whole lot cozier.

"How come you never came around before, Hudson?" Will asks, slurring the last part so it's more like *Hud-shon.*

"What do you mean?"

"That day at Baylor's was the first time we really hung out."

"Pretty much." Other than those intimate seven minutes

in the closet a few years back, but who's counting?

"Where did you learn how to skate like that?" Josh asks.

"Yeah, why aren't you at the Olympics or something?" Will asks, a baffled expression frozen on his face. Or maybe that's just the alcohol messing with his reflexes. Either way, he and Josh watch me intently, waiting for my final answer. Where's my phone-a-friend? I finger the cell in my pocket, but there's no way I can text Dani without looking like a total clown.

"I'm definitely not Olympics material. Just took some lessons when I was a kid."

"I guess you could teach *them* now, right?" Josh says.

"It's not like that. I just . . ." I shift my soda to the other hand and take another drink, wondering how much Kara told Will about our on-ice history. Wondering if any of the guys know about my once infamous choke-artistry. "I got busy with stuff. Didn't really have time for training."

Will cocks his head skeptically and I rush to add more. "My parents split up, so priorities changed."

"But you're *seriously* good," Josh says. "I don't know much about figure skating, but whenever I see you at Fillmore . . . and everything with the team . . . wow. You're amazing out there."

"Thanks."

"What the hell are you still doing in Watonka?" Will asks.

This makes me laugh, and I take another sip of Orange Crush to hide it. What am I still *doing* here? Like I'm just waiting around for my scheduled departure, itinerary planned, English-to-French phrase book and first-class ticket to Paris stowed securely in my Louis Vuitton carry-on? *S'il vous plaît.*

"Me? What about you guys?"

"I'm leaving for sure," Will says. "Right after grad, I'm out."

Josh shrugs. "Me too. For real."

For sure. For real. Everyone talks about leaving here, for sure and for real. My father used to say it, too—way before the divorce, he was talking about bigger cities, better opportunities. Even the old people who sit at the counter at Hurley's complain about this place, every day dunking bits of bread into black coffee for a thousand years before now and a thousand years after. We're all gonna leave, right? Today, tomorrow, the next day, one day. Sometimes I imagine the great and final exodus, all of us wrapped in scarves and mittens and puffy coats, piling onto the Erie Atlantic with two suitcases apiece, dousing the place in gasoline and tossing a match, hitting the tracks and never looking back.

But there's something about Watonka, they say. Something that pulls us back, the electromagnet that holds all the metal in place. It's the food, they say, or the chicken wings or the sports teams or the people or the way the air over the Skyway smells like Cheerios on account of the old General Mills plant. None of that stuff brought my father back. And what good are all of those bits of nostalgia when your family—the one thing that truly holds you to a place, the one thing that really makes it home over any other dot on the map—crumbles?

"Oh, what up!" It's Luke, our generous host, clomping up from the basement with a full bottle of something the color of honey, pumping it over his head in time with the beats. A few other guys squeeze in closer, and on the table next to us, Luke lines up a row of plastic cups, sloshing some liquid into each.

"To the Wolves!" Will shouts, followed quickly by Amir's signature *how-oooo*.

"And to our secret weapon," Will adds. "Hudson Avery."

"The most ass-kicking princess I ever met." Luke clinks his cup to mine and downs his shot as the other boys whistle and catcall.

"That's my girl!" Dani emerges from a crowd in the front hall, but Frankie Torres grabs her hand and pulls her into the living room for a dance. She giggles and falls in step against his chest, cheering when he spins her around. Amir howls again and calls for Ellie and someone turns up Redman, bass rattling the foundation, all the framed pictures of Luke's childhood threatening to jump off the walls.

Get down with the irrelevant funk to make ya jump . . .

Will kills another shot and slips his arms around me, pulling me into the mix, a tangle of players and fans and hockey wives clapping and moving en masse. I look back to Josh, but his eyes are already on his phone, fingers texting away as if the entire party is happening on that little screen. Before I can get his attention and wave him over, Will drags me deeper into the crowd. He presses closer, throwing his hands up with the beat, and Josh is still texting Abby and what difference does it make because Will's so loose and fun and he smells so amazing and this warm rush comes over me, like we're all in this giant snow globe together, a perfect moment captured under the glass, all histories and futures forgotten. It doesn't matter that Josh has a girlfriend or that Will doesn't remember our kiss in the closet all those summers ago. It doesn't matter that I screwed up at Luby Arena or that I'm working crazy hours at Mom's diner or that this whole town sucks. Because maybe Watonka was only ever supposed to be a temporary stopover, and maybe I *will* chase that train over the hill, and maybe we're *all* destined to leave this place, for sure, for real, together or alone. But for right now, we're here. I'm back on the ice and the boys are back in the game and all of us are laughing and bouncing and rockin' out, and for a little while, everything is just fine.

. . . until Kara walks into the room.

And sees me enveloped by her ex.

And drops her drink.

Again.

Press rewind. Press rewind. Press rewind if I haven't blown your mind . . .

Chapter Eleven

Shoulda-Coulda-Woulda Cakes

*Miniature banana cupcakes
smeared with a thin layer of
honey vanilla icing*

The halls of Watonka High are buzzing with the news of this weekend's win. No one's volunteering to don a giant wolf head as team mascot, but by Monday morning, everyone at least knows we *have* a varsity hockey team. Baby steps, right?

"Bienvenue, étudiants," Madame Fromme trills as we settle into our seats for another excruciating conversation about nothing. *"Mademoiselle Avery, comment s'est passé votre weekend? Avez-vous cuit beaucoup de petits gâteaux?"*

"Non, Madame. Je . . ." and then, because I forget the French words for "hockey" and "party" and "ex–best friend awkwardness," I revise. *"Oui, Madame.* Lots—I mean, *beaucoup de petits gâteaux."*

I try to smile *en français*, but then I remember the stack of cupcake flyers in my locker—another of Mom's brilliant advertising plans—and I'm not sure the smile translates. She moves on to her next victim and, after a bit of forced banter, hands out the test.

Sacrebleu! Verb conjugations and future tense! I totally forgot. I chance a sidelong look at Dani, desperately seeking confirmation that we're in this big yellow failboat together, BFFs unite *hoo*-rah, but she's already got her head down, pen scribbling frantically across the page.

So much for solidarity.

"The only way I'll pass French is if I keep bringing cupcakes," I say to Dani as we head to lunch later. "I totally forgot about the test today."

"Cupcakes?" Dani laughs. "Not to sound all *après l'école spéciale*, but you could . . . I don't know . . . study?"

"I could . . . I don't know . . . punch you right now?"

"Don't hate on me for being prepared. I tried to quiz you at work yesterday, remember?"

"By translating your pirate fantasy? Not helpful." I grab a tray from the stack in the lunch line and slide it along the metal rails. "Sorry. I'm just distracted with skating stuff."

I don't want to fail French or any other class, but with just over six weeks before the Capriani Cup, I have to focus on training, and right now, *parlez-vous-français*-ing can't do *jacques* for my on-ice game.

"Speaking of distractions," she says, "hockey hottie, twelve o'clock."

Will sneaks into line behind me, smiling at a shy freshman girl who gladly lets him cut.

"Hey," I say, trying to appear cool and calm in the wake of Saturday's touchy-feely fest and ensuing Kara weirdness. "Great game this weekend."

"That was, like, off the *hook* crazy, right?" He loads up his tray with a double order of fries and something that looks like cheese sticks and/or human fingers. Desperate to avoid anything French, I skip the fries and go for a turkey sandwich and carrot sticks.

"You guys should sit with us," he says after we pay. Dani and I follow him to a table by the window. A handful of the guys are there, and they shuffle around to accommodate us. Dani ends up between Will and Frankie Torres, with me and Josh side by side across from them. All the boys are still glowing from Friday's win, and when Josh inches his chair closer to mine and smiles, my stomach fizzes again.

Brain to stomach: We talked about this! Knock it off!

"Carrots?" Josh inspects my tray. "You're kidding, right?"

"Don't tell me you're on a diet," Frankie says. "Because that's some messed-up stuff right there."

"I'm not on a diet," I say. "Just boycotting France. Besides, carrots are good for your eyes."

"So get glasses, Pink," Rowan says. "Baumler's a four-eyed freak and we keep him around."

"Look who's talking, carrot top." Will bounces a fry off of Rowan's forehead and the rest of the guys crack up.

"I totally need glasses," Dani says. "I can barely read that crap Mr. Rooney writes on the board. I'm all, cosine *what*?"

"I have Rooney eighth period. I'm failin' that class," Frankie says. "I'll probably be in summer school. Math blows."

"At least you can *see* what you're failing," Dani says.

I point to my food. "Have some carrots. They're good for your eyes."

"Then *you* have some fries." Josh nudges his tray toward me. "They're good for your . . . I don't know. They're just good."

"Do any of you guys have Keller?" Will flips through a black-and-yellow CliffsNotes booklet. "I flunked his *Scarlet Letter* quiz and now he's making me do an essay on themes. Man, I hate that book. Man, I hate themes."

"I have Keller sixth period," I say. "I like the book. Hester's a tough broad."

"You *would* say something like that, Pink," Amir says.

I hold up a carrot and point it at his chest. "Don't make me bust a carrot in your ass, Jordan. Hester's my girl."

Will looks at me as everyone laughs. "Good. Since you're so in love with her, you can help. You around Friday night?"

"I think so. I should totally charge you, though."

"I'll give you whatever you want," Will says. The boys roar, fries flying everywhere.

"I'd read the fine print on that deal if I were you," Josh says.

Dani taps my foot under the table. "We were gonna check out that ballerina movie Friday night."

"We'll see it over break." I pop one of Josh's fries into my mouth. Yum. Boycott of all things French officially over.

"No ladies' night, then?"

"Hold up," Amir says. "You guys have ladies' night?"

Dani shoots me a look. "We *used* to have them. Then you guys came around and started hijacking all the Fridays."

"How do *I* score an invite?"

"I don't know," she teases. "We may have a spot opening up soon."

"I'll see the movie with you," Frankie says. "Ballerinas are hot."

Dani smiles. "You're on."

Something buzzes next to my right leg, and Josh digs the phone from his pocket. The caller ID confirms my suspicions: *Abby's cell.* Josh sighs and pushes out his chair.

"I'll catch up with you guys later. Hud, eat the rest of those fries. Seriously. Oh, and let me know what you thought of the music mix." He wriggles his thumbs in the international sign for "text me later" and ducks out into the windowed hallway that branches off from the cafeteria, taking my fizzy stomach with him.

Who is this Abby girl, and why is she always calling him during school? Doesn't she have her own classes to go to? Or is she in college? Out of college? Or . . . oh no! What if she's some kind of dyed-blond middle-aged cougar ex-stripper nympho with a smoker's cough who wants to teach him a thing or two about—

"See, this is why I never answer my phone." Frankie reaches for Josh's abandoned fries. "It's like she's got the boy LoJacked."

Rowan punches him in the arm. "You don't answer your phone because no one ever calls your broke fugly ass."

"It's better that way, trust me." Amir nods at Dani and me. "No offense, you two, but females are *trouble*. Uh, don't tell Ellie I said that."

"I don't know, ninety-nine. Some of them are worth it." Will stares at me from across the table, Mr. Razzle-Dazzle himself.

"Oh, *barf*." Dani piles her lunch scraps onto a spent tray. "I'll see you guys later. I have to check on some stuff for photo class. Text me about Friday," she says to Frankie. "You *better* not stand me up. I'll LoJack you for real."

She waves bye and joins one of her photography friends at a nearby table, leaving me alone with the partial wolf pack. The boys trade insults and jokes and food for the rest of the period, but Josh doesn't return. He's still on the phone, still pacing the windowed hallway. I can't hear their conversation, but I watch him through the glass; his face is tight, the lines of his jaw set. He runs a hand over his hair and looks up at the ceiling, as if to ask some unnamed god for intervention.

I look across the room at Dani, but she's already got me in her sights, totally busting me for spying on Josh. I shrug and give her a half smile, but she turns away, folding herself back into the conversation at her table as if I'm not even here.

Amir is totally right. High school girls, French girls, dye-job cougars, adulteresses from the Puritan days—the lot of us are nothing but trouble.

With the promise of a free cupcake at Hurley's every Saturday for the rest of the year, I secure permission from Principal Ramirez to hang a few of those cupcake ads around school. After my government class at the end of the day, I stop by my locker for the flyers and the masking tape Mom shoved in my bag this morning.

But before Operation Mortification commences, someone taps my shoulder, and not all that gently, either.

"Hey," Kara says when I turn around. "We really need to talk."

Perfect. Apparently, since she ran out of the party after catching me and Will together, she's miraculously rediscovered her vocal cords. Judging by the crazed look in her eyes, she spent the rest of the weekend prepping for this confrontation.

I loop the roll of tape over my wrist and hug the flyers to my chest. "I'm kind of busy right now, so—"

"I'm serious," she says. "I wanted to call you this weekend, but I don't have your cell number anymore, and . . ." She trails off.

I turn away from her to close my locker, but she beats me to it, hand slamming against the door. Kara's got me locked down, her arms framing my head, our noses almost touching when I face her again. Some dude in the hallway holds up his cell camera and asks if we're gonna kiss.

"We need to straighten out a few things about you and Will," she says, ignoring our audience.

The presumption shakes me out of my stupor. "First of all, there is no 'me and Will,'" I say with more confidence than I feel. "And last I heard, there was no 'you and Will,' either. So remind me why you're all up in my face?"

"Kiss her!" Someone shouts from the steadily gathering crowd.

She drops her arms and sighs, but doesn't put any space between us. "I don't think you realize what you're—"

"Kara, unless you guys got back together in the last hour, this conversation is over."

The muscles in her jaw clench, her face turning red and blotchy. I've never thought of Kara as a bruiser, but other than Friday night at the concessions stand, we haven't spoken in three years. What do I know about her anymore? That her best friend bailed on her and never explained or apologized? That a few months later she caught said best friend making out with her soon-to-be boyfriend in the closet at some stupid party? And that three nights ago a near-identical scenario played itself out in Luke's living room?

Shared history and risk of suspension aside, I know what *I'd* want to do.

"I have to go." I look down, unable to meet her eyes again.

"I can't believe you!" She swipes the flyers from my arms.

A snowbank of white papers slips across the hall, lost in the boot-slush undertow of the crowd. "Whatever you think you're doing with the Wolves, you better forget—"

"I *know* you didn't just threaten my best friend." Dani appears at my side, calm and quiet, steady, her eyebrows raised in defiance as she takes another step toward Kara. "Because I don't think you're that kind of girl, so I probably misunderstood you. Right?"

Kara looks from Dani to me and back again, eyes glazed with the same tears gathering in mine. She shakes her head and slinks away, and when the crowd finally scatters, Dani scoops up the cupcake flyers, takes my hand, and leads me to the exit.

Dani passes me a cinnamon-smelling Mocha Morris from Sharon's Café, the cat-themed coffeehouse near school, and leans against the bench at Bluebird Park. On this cheery, once-a-decade winter anomaly, the sky is the color of sapphires and the entire world is covered in diamond dust, snow sparkling under the rare, white sun. A yellow lab bounds toward us and I lean forward to scratch behind his ears; I have to hold my drink above his head to keep him from slobbering it all up.

"Feel better?" Dani asks.

"A little." I sip the mocha and let the hot liquid coat my insides. "I don't know why Kara still gets to me."

"*I* don't know why she's being such a bitch. No offense, but was she always so . . . you know." Dani swipes the air with a cat-claw motion. "*Rawr!* No wonder you ditched her."

"It wasn't like that. I . . . it was all my fault." I take a deep, icy breath. There's something about Bluebird that forces me to tell the truth. Maybe it's the trees, stripped of their leafy coats, naked and gray as bone. Or the dogs, living only for right now, running when they feel like running, chasing one another when they're in the mood for company, no thought wasted on drama and cover-ups. Maybe it's just this place, made sacred by our regular picnic pilgrimages in the summer, a safe haven whose hills I wouldn't dare pollute with lies and schemes.

I tell Dani the whole story about the Empire Games and the party with me and Will, how Kara liked him first, how I was more excited about finally getting my first kiss than I was about staying behind that unspoken line that best friends—even ex–best friends—are never supposed to cross.

Dani wasn't the one I hurt, but it still feels like a confession. Guilt creeps over my skin as I speak of my past failures as a best friend, and for the first time in the history of our relationship, I can't look her in the eye.

"I deserve it," I say. "I was a total jerk."

"Honestly?" Dani squeezes my knee. "I think you've beat yourself up for too long. I'm not saying it wasn't messed up—if you pulled that stuff with me, I'd kick your ass. The point is, it happened. It's over. You were both younger, and you had a lot of bad stuff going on. She got together with Will and then she dumped him anyway." Dani sips her mocha, kicking at the snow beneath our bench. "Whatever happened to forgive and forget? All that happy holidays, give peace a chance, can't we all just get along stuff?"

"I never told her how sorry I was. Never even tried to explain. I wanted to, but . . . I lost it. I couldn't. And now it's been so long . . ."

"You could try to talk to her, though. I mean, I'm not telling you what to do. Just that if it's really bothering you, and you want to tell her you're sorry—"

"No. Sometimes it's, like, too little too late." I think back to that day with the cheetah bra, the drive home from Luby Arena with Mom and Dad and all that unspoken tension, the endless shouting match that exploded as soon as they thought Bug and I were asleep. I think back to the days that followed, my father's bags piled by the door like some cheesy brokenhearted country song. The phone call that attempted to explain why this was better for everyone. The news of his planned move out west, the fairy-tale promises that we'd see each other for holidays and vacations and all the important stuff in between. The e-mails and blogs, detailing his perfect new life. And never once did I hear an apology. Would "sorry" have made any difference? Does it ever? It's just a word. One word against a thousand actions.

A springer spaniel nudges my knee, cocking his head as if he's waiting to hear my rationalizations, too. I scratch his ears and swirl the hot liquid in my cup until a thin curl of steam rises from the hole in the lid.

"I *have* to nail that scholarship, Dani." My voice breaks

when I say it, but I realize now how crucial it is, here in this place of truth on a bench beneath the trees. "Do you get it now? Why I have to focus on stuff with Will and the team? I have to keep training. I have to win. It's my way out. Everywhere I look in this town, everyone I see, it just reminds me of the biggest screwup of my life."

"The Empire Games?" she asks. "Kara?"

"That stuff, yeah, but even what happened before. I'm the one that showed my mom the bra. She must've already known Dad was cheating, but that's what made it real. *I* knew. And the second I dropped it on her dresser, she couldn't deny it anymore. Why didn't I keep pretending for her? Maybe they'd still be together . . ." I shake my head and look over the path that leads to the silver maples on the western edge of the park. Their pale branches bend toward one another in a delicate archway, narrow and knobby like finger bones encased in ice. A cold breeze rolls through and the trees shift soundlessly, hardly moving at all.

Dani follows my gaze across the bright white park, eyebrows furrowing into jagged, thoughtful lines. "It wasn't the bra, Hud. Come on. Even if your mom never saw it, she had to know what was going on. You said it yourself. Your dad was *cheating* on her. Things were already messed up, maybe for a long time before that. It's not your fault."

"I know it's not my fault that he cheated. Just that he left."

"No, that doesn't—"

"You know what I remember most about that day? It wasn't

the bra, or even how pathetic my parents looked in the stands. It was what my dad said on the drive home. He kept telling me not to worry, that there'd be another chance. But it was the *way* he said it. Like he wasn't really talking about skating. It was like he was trying to convince himself that it wasn't the end of our family, even though he obviously wanted out. And I kept thinking, all the way home while Mom wasn't saying anything, and all night when I crawled into Bug's bed and covered his ears so he wouldn't hear them fighting . . . I kept thinking that if I'd stuck it out, if I'd just done my best and won that event, that maybe it would've given my father something to root for. A reason to stay."

Dani and I sit in silence for a long time, watching a pair of dalmatians romp on the path, their tails flinging snow all around them.

"Hudson, no one can be your reason to stay. You have to want it. Your father wanted to leave, and you guys couldn't be his reason not to. Harsh, but there it is."

I down the last of my mocha. She's right. And despite our friendship, despite my mother and my baby bird of a little brother, despite the town that's all I've known my entire life, I want to leave, too. More than Will and hockey, more than the mistakes of my past, more than canceling ladies' night, if anything can come between me and my best friend, it's that.

I look out at the craggy silhouette of the steel mill that's always visible in the distance—the backdrop of our lives. Behind our bench, the wind shakes the branches of the oaks, and an icicle dives from the top bough, spiking the snow like a dagger.

"We should head back," Dani says, dropping her Sharon's cup into the trash. "School locks up in an hour, and we've got cupcake flyers to hang."

I toss my cup in after hers and we head out, ducking under the ice-coated finger-bone trees, walking arm in arm as the snow crunches like hard candy under our boots.

Chapter Twelve

Dirty Little Secrets

*Vanilla cupcakes with crushed chocolate cookie crumbs,
topped with Baileys cream cheese frosting
and a light dusting of cocoa powder*

Will lives just a few miles behind me on the other side of the railroad
tracks. Not the movie version of "the other side of the tracks,"
though—it's still Watonka. Same dark alleys. Same tiny, plain
houses. Around here, even the snow looks like an afterthought:
a dingy, threadbare blanket thrown on and stretched thin in the
middle, yellow-brown wheatgrass poking through the holes of it
like the fingers of a dirty kid.

The guy who answers the door is dressed in stonewashed jeans
and a Buffalo Sabres jersey with a white turtleneck underneath.
He has the same broad smile and thick, blond hair as Will, but his
smile doesn't reach his eyes. "I assume you're here for William?"

Well, I'm definitely not here for *you*, Mr. Serious Pants.

"Yeah. Yes. I'm Hudson. We're . . . friends from school."

"Friends, huh?" He eyes me suspiciously. Something tells me he's not the it's-cool-to-have-friends-of-the-opposite-sex-over-for-no-reason type of parent.

"We have a group project for Monday," I say. "I mean, the Monday after Christmas break. In English lit. *The Scarlet Letter.*" Too bad I only brought the paperback—a hardcover would be much better for smacking Will in the head, which he totally deserves for subjecting me to this.

"Upstairs. First door on the left." The man closes the front door behind me and I head upstairs. From the top landing, I hear Will's voice, low and muffled through his slightly open bedroom door.

"I'm trying. It's not that easy. They're better this year."

Pause.

"What am I supposed to do?"

Longer pause.

"Don't worry. You know I want to."

Pause. Laugh. Pause.

"See you Sunday. Later, Coach." Will closes the phone and finally notices me in the doorway, his face reddening and quickly recovering.

"Coach?" I ask.

"Yeah." He tosses the cell onto his desk. "What a jackoff."

"A jackoff you're making Sunday plans with?"

"Spaghetti dinner with the family, every weekend. Lucky me, huh?" Will laughs. "What's in the bag?"

"Tropical Breeze Cupcakes." I hand him the brown paper shopping bag I brought, a box of six of my latest creations nestled securely inside. "Don't get too excited—they're for your mom."

"You serious?" Will opens the box to inspect the goods.

"You said she liked them. Is she home?"

"She works late at Mercy Hospital. Trauma nurse."

"Well, these have pineapple and coconut and they're perfect for a midnight snack. Especially after a long night."

Will doesn't say anything for a few seconds—just stares at the cupcakes, totally zoned out. I know my baking skills affect everyone in different ways, but I've never seen them hypnotize anyone before. Maybe I should raise my prices.

"Thanks," Will finally says. "That was really cool of you." He sets the bag on the floor and hangs my backpack on the hook behind his bedroom door. It's the first time I've ever been in a boy's room other than Bug's. It smells like him, that delicious cologne-and-soap smell.

He sits on his half-made bed and offers me the desk chair.

"Seriously, what's the deal with Dodd?" I ask.

"He's . . ." Will leans back on the bed, watching the snow collect in the screen outside his window. "Listen, if I tell you something, you have to swear it doesn't leave this room."

"It won't. I swear."

Will turns to face me, his eyes dark and serious in a way I've never seen them before—not even during his hardest practices.

"Will? What's going on?"

"Dodd's my father's best friend. My godfather. Known him my whole life. I really don't want the guys finding out.

"Why not?"

"When I first joined the team, I didn't want them to think I was getting special treatment. And now everyone just hates him for ditching us, which I totally get, but . . . you know. I'm in the middle. It sucks."

"But if he's your godfather, why did he bail on your team in the first place?"

Will shrugs. "I know it's lame. But he has a job to worry about, and he's under pressure to show results. Until last weekend, the Wolves *had* no results. Now he's committed to the football team, and they still have another six weeks, plus championships."

"How can you be okay with that?"

"No choice. It's just the way things are."

I shake my head. "That's crap. What about your father? Doesn't he—"

"No. He's out of it, too."

I run my thumbnail over a tear in the desk chair. "No one knows about this? Not even Josh?"

"Nope." Will shakes his head. "Hudson, I'm serious. You can't tell the guys about this. Especially not Blackthorn."

"I'm not. I just don't—"

"Come on. The guys are still high from that win. Think I'm gonna bring them down with this pathetic story? No way. Besides, who needs him? We have Princess Pink."

I smile. "For now, anyway."

"Wanna take a look at my essay? See if I'm on the right track?" He sits up and leans over me to wake up his computer, eau de Harper going right to my head. "Check it out."

I slide the chair closer and read out loud. "'The themes of *The Scarlet Letter* are about how people who commit sins like cheating usually get caught, and if you live in a tightwad society like the people in this book, you also get dissed by everyone else, even when it's not their business.'"

"What do you think?" he asks.

"Okay, I kind of see where you're going with this, but—"

"Good, 'cause I don't. I can't get into that book. Why don't they let us read stuff that isn't two hundred years old?"

"Because then the district would have to buy new books for the first time in twenty years. Anyway, you can save this essay. You just have to put yourself in Hester's position."

"No way I'm wearing a dress and hooking up with a minister."

"At least not on the first date, I hope."

Will shakes his head and laughs. "Not on *any* date."

"So let's start with the getting dissed part. How would you feel if you had a fight with Amir, then everyone took his side and totally ignored you? Like, kicked you off the team, stopped eating lunch with you, wouldn't call to hang out, that kind of stuff? Oppressive, right?"

"Yes! Oppression. Good theme word. Here, switch seats so I can type."

I give Will the desk chair and walk him through sin and

forgiveness, society, the nature of evil, even feminism—though that topic gets rejected after about three seconds. An hour later he's got a complete essay, and at least seventy-two percent of it makes sense. That's usually enough to please Mr. Keller, so he prints it out and flips off the computer.

"You like working with us, huh?" Will asks, sticking his essay into a folder on the desk. "I mean, the skating stuff?"

"Yeah. It's funny, right? I like skating, but . . . you know. Hockey? Plus, I didn't think the guys would be down with it, especially after that first meeting."

"They love you, though."

"They love the game. Obviously you do, too." I look around the room, checking out his hockey paraphernalia. There's a wall of Sabres posters, a bookshelf full of trophies and auto-graphed pucks. At the other end of the room, there's an entire section dedicated to the Colorado Avalanche, including a signed jersey mounted in a frame.

"Hockey's in my family." He nods at the Avs shrine. "That stuff is from my uncle Derrick. Colorado recruited him right out of high school, but he screwed around and partied and totally blew it after his first year. My dad doesn't even talk to him anymore."

"That sounds kind of harsh."

Will nods. "My father's older than Derrick. He got injured senior year and couldn't go pro, so when his little brother got the chance two years later and lost it . . . anyway, now it's all on me. That's my big family legacy—get a Harper back into the NHL."

"Which is why I can't believe your dad isn't pissed at Dodd for—"

"He *is* pissed, but he knows Dodd's in a bad spot. Coach isn't ditching us to go party like my uncle. He's worried about his job. It's just . . ." Will runs a hand through his hair and shakes his head. "Sorry. I shouldn't have laid this on you. I don't even want to talk about it. All I can do is focus on the team and my so-called destiny of greatness, you know?"

"In that case, I'll do what I can to help you fulfill your destiny." I smile, trying to lighten the mood. "It's cool how far the Wolves have come, just in a couple of weeks."

"It's awesome. But you don't have to help with any more destiny crap," he says. "The guys already learned a ton of stuff from you."

I narrow my eyes and give him a playful glare. "What happened to all that 'we have Princess Pink' stuff?"

Will laughs. "I'm just saying . . . I know you're working a ton of hours at the diner, plus your own training stuff, and everything with school . . . I don't know. I don't want us to be a distraction. I feel bad for dragging you into this."

Panic shoots through my insides, and not just because Will is being uncharacteristically sincere. If I walk away now, the deal is off. I'm back on Fillmore, trying to train on that ragged, windblown patch of ice. "Please. My schedule is fine. I really want to keep helping the team. I'm not done with you guys yet." I cross my arms and go for the tough-girl look.

"If this is about ice time, don't worry. Baylor's is almost

always empty. Marcus will let you train as long as you want—he's cool."

I unclench my shoulders. That *is* the most important thing, right? The ice time? Still . . . I made a real breakthrough with the guys last week. And now that they've won a game, they've started to accept me. I know it sounds crazy, but for the first time since the Bisonettes, people are counting on me to skate. I know I have to focus on my training, but I made a deal, too. Not just with Will. With Josh. With all of them.

"No," I say. "I'm staying on. I mean it. I'm learning stuff from you guys, too."

"Okay, okay. Princess stays. But you're already an amazing skater, Hud. I'm not kidding." He sits next to me on the bed, so close that I fall into him a little when the mattress sinks. "Probably the best in Watonka since that two-hundred-year-old Olympics chick."

"Lola Capriani." I wonder what Lola would say if she were in the room with us now. *You're speed skating down the toilet with this boy, Avery. Right down the crapper.* "She was my coach."

"That explains a lot." Will smiles. "I still think you're better than her. Definitely got her beat in the hotness department."

I laugh and cross my legs, casually inching away from him. "Don't change the subject. I was talking about the boys. They need me. They don't have the NHL genetics like you do." I'm teasing, but the smile fades from his lips. He looks back out the window as a gust of wind pelts the house with wet snow.

"I don't know about the guys. I'm just looking for a way out of this place." He meets my eyes, and for a second there's something familiar behind them—vulnerability, maybe. Something empty and unfulfilled. But then it's gone, his usual charm and gregariousness back in place, his fingers looping through the end of my ponytail. "Anyway, I'm surprised they can focus on hockey when you're on the ice."

"Give me a break."

Will moves closer. "That's not what I'm gonna give you." And before I can present him with the trophy for the cheesiest one-liners in a single bound, he wraps his arms around me, pulling me toward him. His lips are millimeters from mine, breath warm and silent, all discussion of hockey boy skills and sin in the Puritan age blown out the window into the swirling snow. Will smiles at me, and for a split second I wonder whether this might be a stupid, pointless venture. For weeks my thoughts have been consumed with a single boy, and his name is definitely not Will. But then, not-Will is *not* here, not now, not running his hand down my back, not slipping his fingers behind my neck, not watching me with ever-intensifying eyes and flashing that deviously sexy smile. He's probably home, waiting for another call or text from someone else. And I'm here. Now. With Will.

So what's wrong with a little harmless flirting of the seventy-seven nature?

Will raises an eyebrow and I lean in closer, our lips touching, then melting together, everything else disappearing into a soft, barely there buzz.

Oh. I kind of forgot what a good kisser he was, even back then, even under less than ideal circumstances. And unless I'm remembering it wrong, he's definitely improved his game. . . .

Thankfully, no clothes were harmed or removed in the making of this movie, because a sudden, impatient throat clearing from the hallway lets us know we've got a live studio audience. Will jumps off the bed and lands in his chair in an instant, the chair rolling back into the desk and rattling his computer monitor.

"I have a feeling this isn't part of your English project." Mr. Serious Pants leans against the doorway, arms folded across the Sabres' bison-and-swords logo on his chest.

"Dad, um, we were just . . . Hudson was—"

"I think Hudson was saying good-bye. You've got a game tomorrow, William." He looks at me with that barely tolerant smile, taps the face of his watch, and vanishes back downstairs.

"Hudson, Dad. Dad, Hudson," Will says under his breath. "Sorry about that. He's always on my ass. He seriously talks like I'm bound for the Sabres—like I have a real shot."

"Maybe you do."

"The man knows my schedule but doesn't come to the games. I don't think he believes it—it's just his mantra. 'Don't be Derrick.' That's what he's really saying." Will's face changes, his eyes far away as he stares out the window. For the second time tonight, he drops the used-car salesman vibe, the I'm-too-sexy-for-my-own-good stuff fading into something a little less certain. Scared. Sad, even. But the moment passes quickly, and by the time he turns his green eyes back to me, they're sparkling with mischief again.

"I should walk you out. But first . . ." He leans in for another kiss, but I turn away, mirroring that flirtatious grin.

"Maybe on the second date, Harper."

"Good. New Year's Eve? Amir has a party every year. Come with me?" He reaches for my hand, his eyes never leaving mine as he waits for my response. "We can have dinner first, then hit the party. At midnight, I get to kiss you again. Unless you already have plans."

I shake my head. Dani always goes with her parents to some jazz fest thing in Toronto for New Year's, and I'm always home with Mom and Bug and my never-aging date, Dick Clark.

But not this year. For once, I have a date with a cute boy. And a party with the guys, besides? Done and done.

"I'll go," I say. "As long as I don't have to do your English homework first."

Will smiles. "No homework. I promise."

I grab my stuff and follow him downstairs. A soft blue glow emanates from the living room at the other end of the house. Will's father chuckles in halfhearted intervals with the canned laugh track.

Will opens the front door. "See you at the game tomorrow?"

"No. I work doubles on Saturdays. Waitressing *and* cupcakes, yay."

"Yay for us, anyway. Thanks again for the cupcakes. Can't promise I won't dig in before Mom gets home."

"That's why I brought six. Try to save her at least one."

"I'm not paying to heat the outside, kids!" Mr. Serious Pants calls out from the living room.

"She's leaving, Dad." Will grabs my hand. "Hey, are we cool? I mean, the stuff about Dodd—you'll keep my dirty little secrets?"

"Hmm. The part about your godfather not being allowed to know about me, or the boys not being allowed to know about your godfather?"

"Yes."

"We're cool," I say. "Good luck tomorrow. Text me the score."

Outside, the evening air tastes like tap water, cold and a little overchlorinated as my lungs turn it into hazy white puffs. As I warm up the truck, thoughts of everything flicker through my head like a slideshow: Coach Dodd. All that kissing. All that smoldering. The New Year's party date. The other party guests. More specifically, *one* other party guest.

This is crazy. I just made out with Will Harper, and all I can think about is his co-captain?

W.W.H.D (What Would Hester Do)? I wonder. Then I totally laugh at myself, because Hester didn't have it so hot, either, what with all the public scorn and sneaking around. Not to mention the fact that I'm seeking advice from a four-hundred-year-old fictional character about high school boys—never a good sign.

I back out of the Harpers' driveway and onto the street. As I shift gears and roll forward, a plastic bag swirls in the current overhead, following me until it tangles into the branches of a bare oak, and I make a right turn toward the railroad tracks, toward home.

Chapter Thirteen

Bah Humbug and a Merry Who Cares to You, Too, Cupcakes

Dark chocolate cupcakes
iced with white peppermint buttercream,
piped with red stripes;
to finish, jam a black jelly bean
right in the middle with your thumb

I know I'm dreaming, because I was just swallowed up by an ice-fishing hole in the middle of Lake Erie and I can totally breathe under-water. I can see, too—all of my fingers are turning blue before my eyes. It doesn't hurt, but I'm shivering. Will swims toward me in his Wolves uniform, but each time I'm about to grab his hand, he morphs into Josh and slips away. Through the bright white hole over my head, a polar bear reaches in and pokes me with his giant paw. "Wake up, Hudson," he says evenly, like he's just passing through Watonka on his way to Antarctica and thought I should know. "Wake up."

I open my eyes. Will and Josh are gone. I'm no longer underwater. And the polar bear has turned into my brother, wrapped up in his silver-and-white astronaut-themed snow-suit.

"Why is it so cold in here?" I sit up, stretch, and pull the blankets to my neck. "It's like there's no heat."

"Mom wants you in the kitchen." Bug's got this weird, you're-pretty-much-dead warning in his tone that's rather off-putting, especially since he just yanked me out of a potentially good dream about number seventy-seven and/or fifty-six.

"But it's freezing in—" Oh *no*. No no *no*! My stomach drops as the red warning strip from the gas bill—shoved somewhere in the bottom of my backpack and forgotten—flashes in front of my eyes.

I throw off my blankets, bolt out of bed, and yank a sweat-shirt over my head, almost flattening Bug. In our tiny kitchen down the hall, Mom's on the phone, pacing, one hand wrapped around a mug. The steam from her coffee is so thick it looks like her hand is boiling the liquid on its own.

"How soon before it can be turned on?" she asks. "I realize that, but it's Christmas Eve. No. I've got two children here. I already—yes. I'll hold."

I make for the coat closet and dig out my boots. Strolling down to the service center in my pajamas is not high on my Christmas Eve priority list, but if I don't kick into proactive overdrive before Mom gets off that call, I might not be alive to see another holiday.

"I c-c-c-can't believe you didn't p-p-p-pay the bill." Bug's teeth chatter as he tucks his hands inside his snowsuit.

"You're the one who tried to throw it out," I remind him.

"Anthrax detection is an imperfect science."

"You're *not* helping." I pull on my gloves and avoid Mom's stare. The gas company—and Mom—knows we're always late, but I've never totally missed a last-chance payment before. Not like this. They don't usually shut off service in the winter. If the pipes freeze, they could burst, and dealing with burst pipes is way more expensive for them than chasing down a few late payments.

They must be really mad at us this time.

"I'm still here," Mom says into the phone. "Oh, thank God. No, we'll make the payment today. Okay, Thursday then. Do I need to do anything else? Thanks again—you have no idea—right. Merry—bye." She sets the phone back into the receiver and lets out a gust of breath. "Should be back on in an hour or two. They'll call later to make sure it's working."

"Mom, I'm sorry. I'll go now. I had the bill in my bag and I totally forgot. I was busy with—"

"It's okay." She downs her coffee, shoves a few things from the counter into her purse, and grabs her keys. "Go on Thursday as soon as they open. And please let me know if you don't have the cash. I don't want to find out like this again."

"Sorry. I won't—"

"Since you have your coat on, run and get some milk? We're out, and Trick needs help with the Christmas Eve specials, and—"

"When are you coming home?" Bug's bouncing up and

down like—well, like a kid on Christmas. "Are we gonna do the tree tonight?"

"I'll probably be pretty late," Mom says. "Hudson will help you."

The bouncing stops. I fight off a shiver.

Mom kneels in front of him. "The good news is that Hurley's is closed tomorrow, and we'll have the whole day together. Just the three of us." She looks at me to confirm. I was planning to hit Dani's for brunch with her parents, but no way I'm risking Mom's disappointment now. I nod.

"Great. Trick's coming for dinner tomorrow," she says. "He's cooking up a bunch of stuff for me to bring home tonight. Sound good?"

"What about pumpkin pie?" Bug asks.

"We don't have pie, sweetie. Maybe your sister can do pumpkin cupcakes?" Mom looks at me with the same anguish that flooded her voice with the gas company. It's quickly becoming her signature scent. What's on everyone's holiday wish list this year? *Desperation*, the hot new fragrance line by Beth Avery.

"Whatever you want," I tell Bug. And I mean it, too, because if one lousy batch of cupcakes is all it takes to give my brother a merry merry and atone for practically freezing out the whole family on Christmas, well . . . deck the halls with boughs of frosting, fa la la la la, la *freaking* la.

They're showing a retro Smurfs Christmas special on TV, so I leave Bug in front of the electronic babysitter with Trick's box of robot parts and an extra wool blanket and head out for Operation Find a Store That Isn't Closed. No way I'll get anything nearby—all the local mom-and-pops are locked down for the holiday, except of course for Hurley's. The world could be in the final throes of the apocalypse and Mom would find some way to keep the coffee on in that joint.

"No room at the inn?" I ask the desolate streets as I pull away from our block. "No problem! Come on down to Hurley's Homestyle Diner, where there's always room for wayward travelers, especially on holidays when we *should* be home with our *own* families, but never mind all that."

Stupid.

As I crisscross from one side of town to the other, I scan the radio. All the stations are doing that 24-7 Christmas cheer crap. I don't feel very ho-ho-ho today, but I hum along with Bing Crosby's "White Christmas" anyway, searching in vain for milk. The sky is still for now, and the crisp white sheets left by last night's flurries have gone gray, mottled and muddied by plows and salt trucks. The houses on this side of town are bigger than the one we share with Mrs. Ferris, but they're older, more weather-beaten. They remind me of the old people at the diner, carrying the collective failure of this town in the slump of their shoulders, in the weariness of their steps.

I downshift as I cross a snow mound pushed into the intersection by the plows, tires digging through the slush, and then, without thinking, I turn onto Sibley Court.

The house is easy to find.

In three years, the place from the outside hasn't changed—green-gray with white trim, badly in need of a paint job. A wreath hangs solidly on the front door, tied with a red velvet bow, and through the windows, the warm glow of the living room radiates into the icy cold day. Inside, behind the gauzy curtains, a woman drapes a strand of blinking colored lights over the tree. They put it in the same spot we used to, right in front of the big bay window.

We were pretty Norman Rockwell-y back in the day—at least, *I* thought so. Dad would take the week off, and even Mom skipped a few hours at Hurley's on Christmas tree day. While we waited for Dad to do the lights, Mom made cinnamon hot cocoa with whole milk in a big pot on the stove, spiking two mugs with Baileys Irish Cream for her and Dad. Lights twinkling, mugs steaming, Christmas music filling the room, we'd cover the tree in ornaments, Bug toddling around the lowest boughs as we hung each glass ball, each handmade noodle wreath, each piece of tinsel with care. When the last box was finally empty, Dad would lift me up so I could place the blue-haired angel—the one he'd made in fifth-grade Boy Scouts, which, with each passing season, lost as much hair as he did—on the treetop. Bug and I were sometimes afraid of her because she looked so haunted and mean, but it was all part of the tradition, part of our family. Mom would take pictures and we'd drink from our frothy mugs and Bug and I would sing carols and when I look through that window now, tiny colored tree lights blurred by the curtains and the frosted glass,

I wonder if I could just walk in the front door, stomp the snow from my boots, stick ole Blue Hair on the tree, and reclaim our old life.

The woman inside stretches on her toes to hang another ornament, and I put the truck in gear and drive on through the slush, all the way across town, all the way back to Blake Street without the milk.

"I wish we could get a real tree," Bug says. "Then at least we'd have *one* real tradition, since that whole Santa thing's a bust. I mean, if parents are gonna make up a cool story, at least do it realistically. Like, have the guy use FedEx or something—no way reindeer can fly with all that weight. Not to mention the Earth is about twenty-five thousand miles around, so to hit every house—"

"You're totally right, kiddo. Physically impossible." I click the last fake plastic branch into the base as Bug enlightens me and Mr. Napkins on the remaining holes in the Santa plot. The lights and tinsel are still wound around the boughs from last year, and when we finally plug in the cords and stand back to admire our work, we both sigh. The heat's not on yet, the poor hamster is shivering in his plastic ball, and let's face facts here, people: This is one sad little Charlie Brown Christmas tree.

"Let's do the ornaments." I wrap the hamster ball in an electric blanket and plug him in. "It'll look better when we're done."

"Okay, Hud." Unfazed, Bug smiles, tugging his mittens

off and opening the ornament box. He pulls out the angel first and places her gently on the coffee table, smoothing her wild sapphire hair with his tiny fingers. "Think Dad will remember to call this year?"

"Maybe. He might be on vacation, though." I blink away today's trip down memory lane and my father's latest blog posts, all sun and smiles from Southern California. Sometimes I think the hardest thing about being the so-called grown-up—a real one *or* a stand-in—is having to pretend that everything is A-OK, that things are looking up, that life will work out for the best, when all you really want to do is roll into a ball like Mr. Napkins and cry it out under the blanket.

"He has a cell phone," Bug says. "With a national plan."

"Yeah, but it doesn't always get reception on the road." I brace myself for the next question, the next bit of logic and reason, but it doesn't come. We sit in silence for a few moments, me stuffing ornament wrappings back into the empty box, Bug tracing the grooves of the angel's corrugated cardboard dress.

"Wanna know a secret?" he asks. "I never liked this ugly angel anyway." Bug wraps his hands around the defenseless angel and twists her in half, ravaging her from halo to toe. He yanks off the wings. Pulls out clumps of spiderwebby hair. Rips at her cardboard dress. Crushes the paper towel roll body. In a final act of vengeance, he grabs her Styrofoam ball head, breaks it off at the neck, and tosses it into my lap, scattering her other remains on the floor between us.

The whole raging episode is over in fifteen seconds, and I wonder if this is one of those things that parents of serial killers look back on as a sign. Maybe it is. But when he turns to me and that ear-to-ear gap-toothed grin rises on his face like a sun on some distant planet, my heart melts. My little brother is just fine. Pefect, even.

"Remember when we used to think she was cursed?" I ask.

"She *is* cursed. I mean, look at that hair. It's like she fell in the tub with the hair dryer."

The fragile foam head rests in my hands, clumps of bright blue hair windblown and hacked, eyes wild with some ancient, silent fury. It's like she's still on my father's side. Like after all these years, she's planning to tell him about this.

I toss her head on the floor. *Good luck with that, Blue Hair. He left you, too, remember?*

"Ready to make those cupcakes?" I ask, standing and holding out a hand for my brother. Bug nods and laces his fingers through mine, stomping extra hard on the fallen angel as we head to the kitchen.

The heat's been back on for hours, but by bedtime, the wind is crazy, railing against the walls with all the power of the lake behind it. With Josh's mix on my iPod and earbuds jammed into my ears, I snuggle into the womb of my blankets, but I can't stop shivering, every icy lash echoing through the music and into my bones.

Whoooosh.

Back in the house on Sibley Court, I used to wait for that familiar roar off the lake. Welcome it, even—the safe harbor of my bed made warmer by the furious beat of winter's hooves against the roof. But here on Blake Street, the wind leaks through the walls, Blue Hair's cardboard wings skittering across my dresser with every gust.

I yank out the earbuds and fold the pillow around my head, blotting out the world. A million miles away, the train whistle blows again, straight through the glass of my windows, straight through every fake feather in my pillow, straight into my head.

Whooo. Whooo.

"Hudson?" Bug's there in the doorway, all black and fuzzy lines, his silhouette lit up like a church statue by the dim yellow light of the hall.

I unfold the pillow and sit up. "What happened?"

"I heard a noise."

"Maybe it was Santa."

"Hudson," he says. "Um . . . well, Mr. Napkins wants to know if you can stay in our room tonight. I think he's a little down. Seasonal affective disorder, maybe."

"Of course, sweet pea." I swallow the lump in my throat and slip out from beneath the blankets, following him toward the hall. When I pass my dresser, I run my hand over the top and sweep the broken angel wings into the trash.

"Mr. Napkins says he loves you," Bug whispers when I climb into his bed.

"Tell Mr. Napkins I love him, too."

Bug pulls my arm across his chest and scoots closer, and I bury my face against his soft blond hair, both of us finally drifting off to sleep.

I didn't hear Mom come home last night, but when I hit the kitchen in the morning on a critical caffeine run, there she is, kneeling in her yellow bathrobe, the dusty bottoms of her slippers sticking out as she tucks two presents under the tree. In the light of the window, she looks young and untroubled, hair falling gently around her shoulders as she hums "The Little Drummer Boy." When she sees me, the smile takes up her whole face, and she's beautiful. It's like the last few years haven't happened yet—like I'm stuck in a dream with my own Ghost of Christmas Past, one last chance to see her and remember how things looked before everything changed.

She waves me over and pulls me into a hug, gray-blond hair clean and soft on my cheek. "Look in the tree outside. Do you see it?"

I follow the line of her finger out the window, across the tiny backyard. The snow is thick and unbroken, dazzling white, and from the branches of a sycamore, a red cardinal watches us, silent and majestic.

"Merry Christmas, sweetheart." Mom wraps me in another hug, longer and tighter this time. For a moment I forget everything but what's here, right now. The smell of her just-washed grapefruit hair. The red bird, keeping watch as the snow falls.

The quiet of Christmas morning, our lives clean and crisp in the new dawn.

From the kitchen counter, Mom's purse warbles suddenly, shattering the fragile peace. She practically trips over me to get to her purse, dumps the whole thing on the counter, locates her cell under a pile of makeup and receipts and loose change, and answers breathlessly as if she'd been waiting on that call her entire life.

While Mom chatters on, I sit beside the Charlie Brown tree and sip my coffee, staring out the window until my eyes water from the bright white intensity.

The cardinal is gone.

"Good news!" Mom clicks her phone shut and refills her coffee, joining me again on the living room floor. "That was Nat. Turns out her sister-in-law works for the Watonka Chamber of Commerce now. You know how they do that big New Year's to-do for local business owners?"

I nod, still watching the snow fall.

"Nat scored me an invitation! Isn't that great?"

"Totally." I smile. "Especially if you like eating food on toothpicks and standing around with a bunch of old people in black clothes."

Mom laughs and swats me with the tie from her bathrobe. "You don't go for the food, hon. It's a good opportunity to chat up the business, especially if they get news coverage. Channel Seven was there last year."

I tug on an old Snoopy ornament dangling from one of

the tree's lower branches. Poor dog's missing an ear. "Sounds fancy."

"It is. Ooh, can I borrow that black dress? The one with the spaghetti straps?"

"The dress is no problem. But Bug might be." I head to the kitchen for a coffee refill. "I already have plans for New Year's."

Mom follows me. "I thought Dani was going to Toronto."

"For your information, I have a life outside Dani."

Mom raises an eyebrow.

"I have a date. With a boy."

"What boy?"

"A guy from my school. He asked me to dinner and a party."

Mom sips her coffee, eyes darkening. "Hudson, we can't find a sitter on such short notice. Not without paying a fortune."

"What about Mrs. Ferris?"

"She's got her grandson this week, and I don't want to impose on her any more than we already do."

"But you never go out on New Year's, Ma."

"This is important. Not just for me, but for the diner. For all of us."

I slump into a kitchen chair. "That's your excuse for everything."

She sets her mug on the counter and pours herself a warm-up, draining the pot. "Who is he? That Josh boy from the diner? You didn't even introduce him."

My cheeks burn, but I don't feel like explaining about Will and Josh and Abby, so I just nod. "I'll introduce you next time. But we need to figure out what to do with Bug, because—"

"What to *do* with me?" Bug shuffles into the kitchen in his camouflage footie pajamas, his morning face all scrunched up and disoriented. His hair is completely flat on one side, totally spazzing out on the other, and his forehead is creased with diagonal sheet marks. Equally disheveled, Mr. Napkins rolls alongside him, fur dotted with hay, his plastic hamster ball bumping into the kitchen table at least three times before he disappears under a chair. "What to do with me for what?"

"What to do with you . . . for breakfast!" I grab Bug into a spinning hug, pretending to bite his neck. "Bug omelet special, today only! Nom nom nom!"

Mom joins in on the munching, and Bug squeals and giggles and finally squirms out of my arms.

He ducks behind the kitchen curtain and peeks out the window, the light illuminating his shape under the fabric.

"Holy tortellini, you guys," he whispers. "I just remembered something important."

"What's that, buddy?" I ask.

"It's Christmas!" He bursts out from behind the curtain and holds out his arms for a group hug, and Mom and I move in for the crush. Mom looks at me over the top of Bug's fuzzy head and smiles, her eyes shiny with fresh tears. Behind his back, I lace my fingers through hers and squeeze.

And dear Mr. Napkins, as if he senses the weight of the

moment, rolls out from under the chair and crashes into my leg.

"Merry Christmas," I say. "Now let's find a way to make this breakfast thing happen."

"No Bug omelets," my brother says.

"No. I'm cooking something special for you two." Mom stands and dusts her hands together. "And after we eat, we'll go outside and make a snowman."

Bug cheers, and I dig out the marshmallows for hot chocolate, and even though Mom's smiling and this is pretty much the best Christmas morning we've had since my father left, I can't ignore the burn in my stomach when I think of New Year's, the way my mother always expects me to be there whenever she needs me, whenever Bug needs me, no questions asked.

I set the bag of marshmallows on the counter and rinse out our coffee mugs, my heart sinking as I picture another night on the couch with Dick Clark, everyone else laughing and dancing and ringing in the New Year together at Amir's.

Missing out on dinner with Will is one thing. But I have to find a way to get to that party.

Chapter Fourteen

Cupcakes with Benefits

*Vanilla cupcakes topped with
whipped peanut butter cream cheese icing,
milk chocolate chips, crushed pretzels,
and a drizzle of warm caramel*

"But you *have* to find a way to come to Toronto," Dani says. "My parents finally caved and said I could bring you. We'll have a suite overlooking the city and everything."

"Don't rub it in." I flip the mixer on high and dump in a pile of shaved chocolate, batter churning into a clumpy mess. First time in history I get not one, but *two* invites for New Year's, and Mom decides it's the perfect night to pimp herself out to the local business community. "I'm rockin' the couch with Bug and Dick Clark."

Dani pouts and stamps her foot, kindergarten-style. "What about Mrs. Ferris?"

"Mom doesn't want to *impose*. Besides, I dropped a small

fortune at the gas company this morning. No way I can cover her New Year's rates—she's a total extortionist." I pour another cup of milk into the cupcake bowl and scrape the sides with a rubber spatula, beaters growling against the paste.

"This is so not fair."

"No kidding. What am I supposed to tell Will about our date? I haven't even . . ." Perfect. *So* not how I wanted to tell her about me and Will, especially after canceling Christmas brunch on her yesterday. I flip off the mixer and tip the beaters upright. "Will asked me out for New Year's. But it doesn't matter, because I can't go."

Dani's eyebrows shoot up under her corkscrew bangs. She's gawking at me like I just pulled a cupcake out of . . . well . . . somewhere cupcakes aren't supposed to come out of.

"Smoke break. Let's go." She grabs my arm and stomps across the kitchen, dragging me out through the back door.

"When did this happen?" she demands once we're outside. "How?"

I lean back on the wall and rub my arms so the cold won't stick. "At his house on Friday."

"Ah, you mean the private tutoring session formerly known as ladies' night?"

I shrug. "We were working on his essay and goofing around, and then . . . well . . . he kissed me. Like, for *real* kissed me. And then he asked me to dinner and Amir's party."

"He kissed you, and you didn't tell me? That's totally

withholding information!" Her mouth hangs open, breath freezing white around the gaping hole.

"Relax, Detective Bozeman." I laugh, but it comes out kind of jagged on account of I'm shivering my ass off in my supershort Hurley Girl getup. "This week was crazy with work and Christmas and everything—"

"You couldn't call me?" Dani folds her arms over her chest. "Or tell me about it any of the five million times I saw you at work?"

"It was only six days ago! I didn't want to get into it on the phone. And Trick and Mom are always around here, and we haven't really hung out alone since—"

"Don't remind me. Know who I spent ladies' night with? Frankie Torres. Who is *not* a lady. And the Friday before that, we ditched plans to go to the game. And before that you had practice, so I didn't even see you. Something wrong with this picture?"

Guilt bubbles in my stomach, but I swallow it down. She's more upset that I didn't tell her about Will two seconds after it happened than she is about an estrogen imbalance in her weekend plans. "You know I have a lot going on right now. I've only got five more weeks to train, and the scholarship—"

"Oh, right. How could I forget the all-important scholarship?" Dani throws her arms up, alerting a seagull that's camped out behind the Dumpster. He screeches at her once and darts back into the shadows.

"It *is* important. Super-important. We're talking about my life's dream!"

SARAH OCKLER

She jams her hands in her apron pocket, shoulders clenched tight against the cold. "How come you never talk about it, then? You're always gushing about Will and Josh and hockey, but you hardly ever talk about figure skating. And when you do, it's never about how much you love the ice or how excited you are for the competition. All you care about is getting out of here, and that scholarship is a means to an end. You act like Watonka's a prison sentence."

The blood rushes to my head, chasing away the chill. "*You* act like it's the only place in the world that matters. But it isn't. There's so much more to—"

"Yeah, yeah, I get you." Dani edges backward to the kitchen doorway. "You hate Watonka, and you'll do anything to leave. So now you're hooking up with random hockey boys in exchange for ice time? Classy, girl. Real classy." She kicks a chunk of ice across the pavement and disappears into the kitchen.

Back inside, I finish up that clumpy batch of cupcakes—passable, but definitely not my best work—and hit the floor for my breakfast shift. Thankfully, everyone in this town must be home ogling their Christmas loot, because it's dead today. Dani and I have the space to work around each other, talking only when we absolutely have to. She runs my food when I'm in the bathroom, I deliver her drinks when she's stuck with a chatty customer. She buses one of my tables, I cash out one of hers. We work as a team to get things done, but we don't look at each other. And when Nat and Marianne show up for the next shift, I don't wait around to split a plate of Trick's corned beef hash at the prep counter or offer her a preview of my latest cupcake experiments. I just hang my apron on the hook, pack two non-clumpy cupcakes for the road, flip open my phone, and text the only person I know who doesn't have any expectations of me—past, present, or future.

My blank canvas.

meet me @ fillmore in 1 hr? :-)

Josh leans against the signpost and tightens his laces, head bent beneath the thin ice warnings so that when he looks up at me and smiles, the Department of Parks and Recreation sends me a totally new message.

DANGER:

JOSH BLACKTHORN SMILING!

"Thanks for coming," I say, returning his grin. "You totally saved me."

He stands and blocks out the rest of the warnings. "Bad day at the diner?"

"Put it this way. Another five minutes and they'd be calling it 'going waitress' instead of 'going postal.'"

"Wanna talk about it?"

"It's stupid." I say. "Things have been a little off with me and Dani lately. And now she's pissed because Will asked me to Amir's New Year's thing and I didn't call her five seconds later with all the gory details."

"Um . . ." Josh rubs his head, looking out over the lake. "Wow."

"Holy melodrama, right? Told you it was stupid."

"No, I . . . um . . . so you're going to the party with Will?"

"I'm not going anywhere with anyone. I have to babysit my brother." I stab the ice with my toe pick and sigh. But then I realize I'm not exactly taking a stand against melodrama here, so I plaster on another smile. "Anyway, in exchange for your heroic selflessness in meeting me on such short notice, I have a present for you." I reach into my jacket and fish out his USB drive.

"You're regifting my music? Can you even do that?"

"No way." I shake my head. "That would be a complete gift violation. This is your drive, but my music. Totally reloaded. There's even some old obscure blues stuff on there from Trick."

"Nicely done, Avery." Josh slips the drive into his pocket and tugs his hat over his ears. "But don't be *too* grateful. My motives weren't all that selfless. I need help with the—shoot. Hang on." He checks his ever-buzzing phone. *Great.* I hope Cougar Mama doesn't show up at Fillmore. An ex-stripper against an ex-skater? Ladies and gentlemen, place your bets.

"Sorry, one sec." He sends out a text, turns off the phone, and buries it in his jacket pocket. "Anyway, I totally suck at those backward crossover things you showed us. So, yeah. Help."

I laugh. "Follow me."

The indoor rink is definitely better for technical work,

but I was actually starting to miss the ruggedness of Fillmore, my original secret spot. If I was more clearheaded when I left work, I probably would've just come here alone. But for once, I didn't stop to analyze everything. I just did what I felt like doing.

I felt like being with Josh. No kissing, no coach secrets and weird family politics, no subtext. Just two friends hitting the ice.

Now I lead him through backward speed drills, slowly working him up to the crossovers. After several falls (his) and laughs (mine), he's finally getting it, and I give him a wide space to perfect his moves.

I run through my figures as he works, looping across the runoff, skates rubbing uncomfortably against my toes and ankles. The leather has stretched with my growing feet; it's thinned and scuffed in spots, torn near the eyelets, but the blades are still sharp. Like all my skates, my father got these for me. A brand-new, custom-made pair. I spent months breaking them in, working them on the ice until they were perfect, soft and buttery.

They fit me a whole lot better back then, just like the pair before that and the ones before that, all the way back to the very first time I ever felt the ice beneath my feet. It was during the winter Olympics more than a decade ago. I was a toddler, mesmerized by the twirls and turns on TV and the way the skaters' feet seemed to float as if they were dancing on water. I'd never before wanted to be anything as much as I wanted to be that—a ballerina on ice. So one morning my father drove me to Miller's Pond, this old place out in the country. He parked the car and came around to my side, kneeling in front of me with a big white box. I took it into my lap, legs dangling over the edge of the seat as I tore off the lid and pulled out miles and miles of tissue paper. Inside, two magical silver blades shone under soft leather boots, bright as snow. Dad laced them up and set me on the ice like dust on spun glass, and he pulled me around and around and around until my face was numb from smiling in the cold, the same question spilling from my lips for hours.

Please, can you take me again, Daddy?

Soon he'd be paying for lessons at the community center two towns over, then private instruction when they started throwing around phrases like "unlimited potential" and "incredible natural talent." Not too long after that came Lola Capriani, and that was it. Pro track, all the way. Before he finally split, my father must've spent a boatload on my dreams, his entire future staked on the destiny I was supposed to claim.

Still, through all the winters of lessons and competitions, through all the dizzying spins and hard-earned bruises and medals, it never meant as much as it did on that first day at Miller's Pond when he surprised me with those magical skates. That day, I really was a ballerina and he was my whole world and if I let myself now, I bet I could still feel the warmth of his hand around my tiny pink mitten.

Don't worry, baby girl. I promise I won't let you fall.

But I don't let myself feel that warmth. Even now, as I

prepare for another competition and wade through all the old memories, the ghosts of my father's promises don't take up nearly as much space as they used to.

"That's it," Josh calls out, skating toward me. "I can't take it anymore." He stops close, his face pink from cold and exertion. "Now that I've thoroughly embarrassed myself, how 'bout showing off some of *your* killer moves."

"You've seen my moves."

"Not *really*." He stretches his arms out before the lake. "All this room. No walls. No rails. No Brad Nelson running his mouth. It's just us and the seagulls. And I promise not to crash into you."

I smile. "There you go, being a hero again."

"You're competing in a month, right?"

"One month, six days, and a handful of hours, give or take."

"Then put your money where your skates are." Josh nods toward the ice. "Come on, Avery. Show me what you've got."

"That a dare, Blackthorn?"

He shrugs. "Call it what you like. You down?"

"Down? I'm about to make you wish you never got *up*," I say, strictly for the cameras. What's a high school action rom-com docu-drama without a few corny but well-placed one-liners?

I hand Josh the puffy outer layer of my jacket and push off with my toe pick, gliding backward to the other side of the runoff. I haven't choreographed my full program yet, but with Josh smiling at me across the ice, I set my nerves to steel and silently count to ten.

A cold breeze rolls over my skin, and in the next heart-beat, the music starts in my head. Not "Bittersweet" this time. Maybe "Freaktown," the Undead Wedding song with the paper birds that Josh likes so much. My muscles recall the beat and tense, uncoiling like a spring to launch me forward. I take long strides, tucking in my arms and head as I pick up speed. As I approach the edge, I look for the perfect spot to curve, looping at an angle as I gain momentum for my first jump. My skates cross over . . . one, two, one, two . . . and *up* . . . my feet drift through the air; I rise to the sky for a single axel. Josh whistles from the sidelines, but *hold it*, boy. I'm just getting warmed up.

I move through another set of jumps and spins, forward and backward, fast and slow, making up the sequence as I go. I speed up again, zipping around the perimeter of the runoff, legs burning from the effort, lungs on fire, heart ready to burst out of its cage, but this is *it*. This is the stuff I was made for, the freedom, the speed, the furious jog of my heart, the cold breeze biting my skin. When I look across the ice and see Josh watching me—*really* watching me—I spring into my triple flip.

But I know as soon as I leave the ice that I won't get enough lift for the full rotations.

I manage to turn it into a double and land without wobbling.

Josh cheers, and I launch into another double, land, and twist immediately into a camel spin. The song in my ears starts to slow, and I let the spin fade into a gentle glide, the bright white sky motionless as I sail uninhibited beneath it. I push off one more time, gaining momentum, zooming closer and closer. Then, in my favorite finish, I cut my blades hard and shower him with ice.

Phishhhh . . .

I can almost hear Lola laughing. *Enough showboating, greenblades. I was making moves like that when I was six.* But she'd smile when she said it. And so would I.

"What do you think, fifty-six?"

"I think I'm glad I don't have to skate against you in the competition." Josh hands over my jacket. "You were wrong about one thing, though. You didn't make me wish I never got up."

His comment hangs in the winter air between us, blood rushing back to my cheeks as I catch my breath.

"I messed up that jump," I say. "I've been working on this crazy triple/triple combo at Baylor's. Back in the day, it was my signature move. Lost my edge a little."

"Could've fooled me."

"You're not a skating judge."

"You'll figure it out in time, Pink." Josh nudges me with his hip, but as usual, I don't see it coming. He grabs me just before I fall, catching me against his chest, arms tight around my waist, neither of us moving for a moment.

"Hudson," he whispers, and I look up into his eyes, so bright and blue in all this whiteness . . . my heartbeat quickens as he leans closer. His grip tightens and my legs go wobbly in a way that has nothing to do with slipping on the ice. He could kiss me. He could kiss me right now, and then I'd know for sure.

We're alone out here, just us and the seagulls and the harsh

December wind. I close my eyes and lean forward, ever so slightly, waiting for him to make the move.

Here's your chance, Blackthorn! Now or never!

"Sorry," he says, letting go of my arms as my eyes pop open. "I didn't mean to knock you over. You okay?"

"I'm . . . um . . . I brought snacks!" My announcement is loud and awkward enough to wake all the ghosts of Fillmore, but it works to break the not-so-momentous moment. I skate over to my backpack and dig out the small box of cupcakes and some balled-up Fresh 'n' Fast bags. Side by side, but not too close, we sit on the plastic bags beneath the signpost and chow down.

At least now I know for sure. Friends. Just friends. I can live with that.

"How lame is it that I have to stay home on New Year's every single year?" I ask between bites of chocolaty goodness. "I swear, if I'm ever allowed out for the ball drop, Dick Clark will accuse me of cheating."

Josh taps the blade of my skate with his. "You and Dick, huh? Sorry, I don't see it."

"Aw, you just don't *know* Dick like I know Dick. Dick and I are like *this*." I cross my fingers and hold them in front of Josh's face. "Like *this*!"

Josh snorts, dropping crumbs down the front of his jacket. "The party isn't all that, anyway," he says, brushing them into the snow. "Believe me—your eight-year-old brother probably needs less supervision than those guys."

"If you ask me, Bug needs *no* supervision. He's the smartest, most well-behaved kid on the planet. I can't believe Mom doesn't—wait. That's it! Josh, that's totally it! You're so brilliant I could kiss you! I mean, not kiss you, but . . . you're really, um . . . smart."

Okay, ice? If you're thinking about killing anyone, now would be a *great* time to crack open and suck me under. No hard feelings, pinkie swear.

"Yeah, well." Josh smiles, looking down the shore. "Last year Gettysburg tried to make out with a mounted deer head and Will woke up in Amir's bathtub wearing one of Mrs. Jordan's nightgowns. I'm still recovering from those images. I'm telling you, you won't be missing much."

"Exactly." I lick the last drop of chocolate icing from my thumb and pull my gloves back on. "I won't be missing it at all."

Chapter Fifteen

Desperate Times Call for Desperate Cupcakes

Um . . . cornbread

By the time I convince Bug to accept my best-in-class New Year's bribe—four custom cupcakes, unlimited television, and no set bedtime— and get to Amir's, it's well past eleven, and everyone inside is well past the "I love you, man" stage. I find Will immediately, his showstopper laugh rising above all the yellow plastic horns and sparkly, dollar-store noisemakers.

"You made it!" Will beams as I enter the kitchen and wraps me in a warm hug.

"Princess Pink, in the house!" Brad Nelson gives me a fist bump and pulls a pink-and-white feather boa from a box on the counter. "Saved it for you. It's pink, get it?"

"Um, yeah. *Thanks.*" I smile and drape it over my shoulders, blending right in with the party people. It's funny to think that just three weeks ago I was at Luke's house with the same crowd of hockey boys, unsure if they'd *ever* accept me. They'd just won their first game in years. Josh gave me the music mix. And then Will pulled me into the crush of the living room, bass thumping through the speakers, all of us laughing and dancing, Will's arms strong and steady as we bounced to the beat.

That night was when it all started—when they let me in for real. And now I'm a part of the group, not just for the hockey stuff, but as a friend, in on all the jokes, wearing my Princess Pink nickname like a badge, hanging out like I've always belonged. Not just with Will, but the other guys, too.

I glance over the mob, hoping against the odds I might find Josh. But I already know he isn't here—I can feel it. He may not be the center of attention like Will, but his absence leaves a palpable hole in the vibe. Maybe after all his stories from last year's party, Abby didn't want to come.

"Where's your friend tonight, *mamí*?" Frankie Torres steps in front of me, hands in his pockets.

"Blackthorn?"

"No. Danielle." He says her name the longest way possible: *Dan-y-elle*.

I raise an eyebrow. "Dani has a family thing in Toronto."

"Oh, right." He looks across the kitchen, like maybe I made a mistake and she's just hiding behind the fridge. "Does she ever say anything?" he whispers. "Like, about me?"

Frankie Torres . . . not a lady . . . something wrong with this picture . . .

"Honestly, we haven't talked much lately," I say. "With work and hockey stuff . . . we haven't seen each other."

"Oh, okay. Cool. I was just—"

"One minute, people!" Amir cuts the music and turns up the television, and Frankie and I merge into the living room with the rest of the crowd. The place is packed, and I end up in a chair across from the couch, separated from Will by a dozen warm bodies. Simultaneously, everyone joins in on the countdown, all of us watching the giant silver ball descend over Times Square.

"Five . . . four . . . three . . . two . . . one . . . Happy New Year!"

The horns and cheap noisemakers muffle the "Auld Lang Syne" trumpets blaring from the television, but that's just fine by me, because that song always makes me cry. Paper confetti snows down around us, everyone drunk and swaying, hugging and kissing. Only Frankie Torres is alone, sitting on the couch and staring out the front windows as if he's still hoping Dani might show. Right now she's dancing in some fancy hotel ballroom while her dad's jazz ensemble belts out this very song, and Josh is making out with Abby, and Mom is schmoozing the locals, and Bug's back home, probably watching the same channel as me, swallowed up by the giant pillows on our couch, and I'm just—

"Where's my girl?" Will calls out across the room. He

smiles when he finally sees me, his eyes lighting up like there's no one else here.

I look behind me, half expecting to see Kara there with open arms and a freshly glossed pout, primed for kissing. But there's only me, rising dumbly from the chair as Will edges through the crowd, drink held high above a sea of people.

"Happy New Year, Hudson." He grabs me with one arm and pulls me into a kiss. The feather boa crushes between us, its delicate feathers tickling my chin. His mouth tastes sweet from the red stuff in his cup, but his movements are intentional, not sloppy or drunk. His hand glides up my neck, tangling into my hair, and the kiss intensifies, my heart hammering so loudly in my ears that I no longer hear the celebration around us; I'm not part of it. My whole body reacts to his touch, skin heating up as his fingers trace lines down my neck, across my collarbone, erasing the rest of my thoughts.

Unnoticed, Will and I sneak down the hallway and slip into a room on the other side of the house. The space is small and mostly dark, some kind of office, illuminated only by the white-yellow glow of a streetlamp outside.

Will closes the door with his foot, his lips never breaking from mine. He backs me against the wall, and as my shoulders hit the cold, painted plaster, I give in to the current of him, melting beneath his touch. Slowly, he tugs the boa from my neck, feathers quivering as it falls to the floor. I slip my hands underneath his shirt, trailing my fingers over the smooth, knotted muscles of his back, all the way up to his shoulders.

Beyond the window on the opposite wall, icy snow falls soundlessly from the sky, but in here, Will's skin is warm, the heat of him radiating through my thin camisole, the ragged, uneven tide of his breath hot on my neck.

"You're beautiful," he whispers in my ear, soft and hungry. I pull him tighter against my body and close my eyes, letting his words linger, his hands expertly moving down my back.

This is it, the kiss he promised, the midnight interlude I'd been warned about. But as good as he makes me feel on the outside, on the inside, I can't stop my mind from wandering. Each time I try to catch my thoughts and bring them back to this moment, every cell of my body pressed against Will's in the newborn moments of another year, I lose my way. It's like driving in a blizzard, slowly inching along the road back home only to realize at the end of a long, cold night that you've pulled into someone else's driveway, someone else's life.

"You okay?" Will whispers, slightly breathless. He brushes a lock of hair from my eyes and kisses my face, but my hand is flat against his chest, holding him back. "We don't have to do anything you—"

"It's not that." I slide my hand down his shirt and close my eyes, fingers tracing the ridges of his abdomen. "I'm sorry. I just . . . I feel kind of light-headed."

"Do you want to sit?" He takes my hands in his and squeezes gently, nodding toward a desk chair behind me.

"I think I need some water." I kiss him once more to alleviate his concern and duck into the hall. The bathroom is thankfully unoccupied; inside, I click the door shut and run my wrists under the cold tap, willing the chill into my veins, counting my heartbeats until they slow to a regular rate.

Will Harper. Until recently, he barely acknowledged my existence. Now, after just a few weeks of hanging out, he's calling me his girl? Looking at me like I'm the only person in a crowded room?

His *girl*? Is that what I want? Is that *who* I want?

My thoughts drift again to Josh, that first day we met at Fillmore, his visits to Hurley's, the backward crossovers, the music, all the jokes and practices. I know we're just friends, but sometimes, when our laughter fades and he holds my glance a little too long, I swear he's looking at me as something more. Not *just* a friend. Not *just* a skating bud, showing him those complicated crossovers again and again until he gets them right. But then his phone buzzes or he starts talking about something else and the thin, momentary thread connecting us breaks and I start to think I imagined the whole thing. Why can't I get him out of my head?

I turn off the bathroom faucet. My hands are shaking, and I'm afraid to look at my reflection over the sink. It's one thing to lie to your mother, your baby brother, even to your best friend. But alone in a tiny beige box of a room on the first of the year, there's no hiding from yourself when you meet your eyes in the mirror.

Will Harper. Josh Blackthorn. The Capriani Cup. So much has happened this winter, so much has changed. *I've* changed. And maybe I'm not ready to see it yet. Maybe I don't want to know the evidence, the smudged makeup, lips red from kissing, eyes burning with some new, unnamed intensity. So I focus instead on the old water spots, the fingerprints of everyone who lives here. I reach for the hand towel on the side of the sink and—

BANG! The door rattles against the frame.

"Just a minute," I say. "Be right out—"

"Or . . ." The door swings open. "I'll just come in."

"What—"

"Yeah. Hi, Hudson. Happy New Year to you, too." Kara shuts the door and leans her back against it, red liquid sloshing out over the cup in her hand. Mascara is smudged beneath her eyes and her long, strawberry blond hair is slipping from its headband, the ends tangling in a black boa around her neck. I didn't see her in the crowd before, but of course she's here.

"Don't worry, I'm not planning to stab you with an ice pick. At least, not with all these witnesses around."

My eyes flicker to the sink, but there's nothing but a bar of soap and a cup full of frayed toothbrushes. Sure, a dental instrument to the eye might sting for a minute, but as far as self-defense weaponry goes, the Jordans' bathroom is severely ill-equipped.

Kara downs her drink and tosses the plastic cup into the bathtub. It rattles against the porcelain, leaving a trail of orange-red dots in its wake.

"Kara, if this is about Will, I really don't—"

"Nope. Over it." She helps herself to one of Mrs. Jordan's lotions from a shelf on the wall and flips the cap. She sits on the edge of the tub, props her foot up on the sink, and massages white goop into her bare legs. The whole room reeks of dried roses and spiked fruit punch, and I have to breathe through my mouth to keep from gagging.

"Hear you're training again," she says. "For the Capriani Cup."

"Who told—"

"You did," she says. "Just now. Not like I couldn't figure it out. They announce a competition, and suddenly you're hanging out on the ice again? Not exactly coincidence."

"No, not exactly." A new thought ripples through my mind, its sharp edges catching behind my eyes. Kara wasn't one of Lola's trainees, but that doesn't mean she wasn't invited to compete. They probably sent the letter to everyone who'd ever set foot in the Buffalo Skate Club, Lola students or not. I can handle the other girls from my skating past. Chances are at least one of them continued skating, at least one of them will be there next month. It won't be easy or pleasant, but I know I can hold my head high, ignore the whispers and taunts, and skate my ass off.

But not in front of Kara.

"So . . . you trying out, too?" I cross my arms over my chest and try for the hard stare, but inside, my stomach flip-flops.

"Parade myself in front of the judges, just so they can tell me all the ways I'm not good enough? No thanks. I'll leave the kiss-and-cry drama to you." Kara gives me the once-over, her eyes landing on my shoulder—the exact spot where we used to pin our matching silver good luck rabbits. The exact spot where mine is still pinned to my old skating dress.

"What I can't figure out," she says, "is the Wolves. Why are you helping them?"

I shrug. "It's a good opportunity."

"Opportunity. Right. Let me guess: Will cut you a deal? Traded a little ice time for some help with the team? Maybe a little something on the side?"

My mind flashes to Will, the feel of his body against mine in the dark room down the hall, his breath on my neck. Heat rushes to my cheeks. She doesn't know anything about Will and me. If there even *is* a Will and me.

"Excuse me." I step around her and grab the doorknob, but she's got her foot against the door, and I can't open it. "Kara, I really—"

"How can you go out for another event?" Her voice breaks suddenly, all the edges of her crumpling. "After everything that happened . . . after I left the ice . . . you never said anything. Ever. And you go out there again like it's just . . . nothing!" Her foot slips from the door and she slumps back against the edge of the tub, tears leaking down her face.

"I know I screwed up that night." I reach for the box of tissues on the back of the toilet and pass her one. "But you didn't have to leave. You were amazing, too. You could've gone on to compete and—"

"You don't get it." She shreds the Kleenex in her hands, little white bits falling into her lap like snowflakes. "It wasn't about the competition. I liked skating, yeah. But it wasn't the same without you. We weren't skating together, we weren't even talking. I skipped the club meets, stopped practicing."

"You just needed some time to—"

"It was more than that. It was like I didn't have it in me anymore. And my parents knew it, so they gave me an ultimatum." Kara deepens her voice to imitate her father. "'We don't have the money for you to screw around. So get back out there like you mean it, or start working on your—'"

"Backup plan," I finish without thinking. I lean against the tile wall across from her, staring at a smear of bright blue toothpaste in the sink. I'd heard the same arguments from my mother over the years, every time I wanted to skip an event or sleep in an extra hour instead of going to five a.m. practice. Every time I came home whining about bruised hips and blistered heels. Every time I fell and swore I'd never do it again, never get up for another try. But somehow, my father always found a way to make it happen. To remind me why I loved the ice.

I'd always assumed Kara's parents would do the same for her.

I hand her another tissue.

"Don't." She pushes my hand away and stands up quickly, wobbling on her heels before steadying herself on the edge of the sink. "I don't know what I came in here for, but it wasn't this. I just . . ." Kara wipes her eyes with her fingertips and opens the door, looking at me one last time. "Forget it."

She yanks the door shut behind her, leaving me alone with the mirror again. I remove her plastic cup from the bathtub and wash my hands, but I still can't look at myself. All I want to do is get home, change into my pajamas, and curl up on the couch with my brother, who isn't old enough to remember my past mistakes and wants nothing from me but a hug, an occasional cupcake, and permission to stay up past his bedtime. My heart aches to think of him alone tonight. I never should've left him. I never should've come.

I find Will back in the living room, half listening to an intense debate between Rowan and Luke on the hotness of various Disney princesses. Jasmine is winning. Kara is nowhere in sight. When Will notices me lingering on the edge of the room, he crosses over and pulls me into his arms.

"You okay?" he asks. "I was getting worried."

"I'm fine. I just need to get back to my brother."

I say my good-byes to the boys and Will walks me to the truck, scraping the ice and snow from my windshield as I warm up the engine.

"Happy New Year," he says again, leaning in through the open driver's side window. He kisses me once more, slow and gentle, and when I finally drive away, he stands in the street and watches me go, shrinking in my rearview until he's no more than a wisp.

Left too long without supervision, most kids would probably finger paint the walls, flush their underpants down the toilet, or, I don't know, set the whole place on fire. Our little genius? He turned the entire living room into an airport, complete with a four-foot-high LEGO traffic control tower and a fleet of paper planes, plastic army pilots taped safely into their cockpits. From deep beneath the couch, a large utility flashlight illuminates some sort of . . . landing strip? I crouch down for a better look.

Oh. My. God.

Stuck to the carpet in parallel, unbroken paths from one wall to the other are two lanes of brand-new maxi pads. Plastic dinosaurs stand guard at every fourth pad—triceratops and T rexes on one side, brontosauruses and pterodactyls on the other—protecting the airport from enemy aircraft and/or heavy flow.

Clear across the room, blissfully content, Bug snores on the couch in an inspiring ensemble of safety goggles, pink earmuffs, blue zip-up pajamas, and one of Dad's old hunting vests in bright orange camo.

"Happy New Year, sweet pea." As quietly as I can, I slip out of my coat and boots and carefully remove Bug's goggles and earmuffs. He stirs and mumbles something incoherent, then drifts back to la-la land while I get to work deconstructing the Blake Street Super-Absorbency Airport before Mom gets home. She'd freak if she saw me throwing these things out—pads are even more expensive than the Ziplocs the kid uses for his anthrax operation.

Landing strip destroyed, I'm about to start on the paper

planes when my phone buzzes on the coffee table. Probably Dani. Things between us may be a few degrees below normal, but she always calls me after her dad's New Year's shows, ready with the full report on the food and the dresses and all the cute Canadian college boys roaming the hotel.

I grab the phone and sneak into the kitchen, checking the screen—not Dani. Josh. I stare at his number as it lights up my phone. Josh is calling me on New Year's? Does that mean he's not out with his cougar hottie?

"Happy New Year," he says when I finally answer. His voice is soft and deep, muffled like he's lying in bed and just on the edge of sleep.

"Hey! I missed you at—well, I thought you guys might show up at Amir's."

"You . . . guys?"

"You and . . . whoever." *Brilliant*, Hudson. "What are you up to tonight, anyway?"

"I'm home with your ex-boyfriend, Dick. He says hi, even though you broke his heart tonight."

I laugh. "He never really loved me, anyway."

"Hey, no judgments here, Avery. You still partying it up?"

I peel a renegade maxi pad from my knee and stuff it in the trash with the others. "Oh, it's a party, all right. I was home by one thirty. Does that make me totally old?"

"Not yet. But if you start eating dinner at four and watching *Golden Girls*, time to worry. Anyway, you near a computer? PBS is streaming the Addicts."

"No way!" I sit at the kitchen desk and pull up the site. "Live?"

"It's a replay of their tenth anniversary tour," Josh says. "Some little club in Denver. They're about to do your song— they were talking about it after the last set."

I turn the speakers on low just in time for the opening chords of "Bittersweet." It's kind of a sad song, slow and mellow and haunted, none of that everything's-gonna-be-all-right fairy dust crap they play on the radio these days, and that's exactly what I like about it. It tells the truth. Sometimes life rocks so hard your heart wants to explode just because the sun came up and you got to feel it on your face for one more day. Sometimes you get the bitter end instead. Life is as gray and desolate as winter on the lakeshore, and there's no way around it, no cure, no escape.

It was always my favorite skating song because it reminded me of the competition itself, how nothing comes without a price, and when you make sacrifices to get what you want, sometimes you screw up and pick the wrong thing.

But once in a while, you pick the right thing, the exact best thing. Every day, the moment you open your eyes and pull off your blankets, that's what you hope for. The sunshine on your face, warm enough to make your heart sing.

Right now, quiet on the phone with Josh and the Addicts while the kitchen clock ticks softly and my brother sleeps on the couch behind his tower of plastic blocks, I know that this is one of those moments.

Those exact best things.

And then my e-mail notifier pings me with a new message, and the song fades out, and the sun disappears.

It's an update from my father's blog.

Watch out, Olympics! the subject says. *Here she comes!*

"Thanks for calling," I whisper into the phone, not trusting my voice to come out right. "I should go. Happy New Year, Josh." I hang up without waiting for a reply and, against every screaming warning in my head, click on the link.

Chapter Sixteen

Lights, Camera, Cupcakes!

*Chocolate Coca-Cola cupcakes
with vanilla buttercream icing
topped with buttered popcorn,
peanuts, Raisinettes, and M&M's*

Two days into the new year, I'm back at Hurley's for the pre-open cupcake shift, hands speckled with exploded chocolate goo, frosting clumped in my hair, and a killer stomachache.

"Hudson, what happened?" Dani asks. We haven't spoken since our argument right after Christmas, but now she's staring at me across the flour-covered prep counter with genuine concern. "Say something."

I toss a spoon into a bowl of useless, runny batter, my own personal comfort food. I probably have salmonella now. "My father."

Dani frowns. "Another e-mail?"

"A blog. A special one for New Year's." The words flash

through my head. *You should've seen my beauty out there on the ice!*

Dani sighs and clears a few crusty bowls from the counter. "Wanna tell me about it?"

I close my eyes. At the other end of the kitchen, the big coffeemaker hisses, and I see the words again. *Watch out, Olympics! Here she comes!* Skiing, sledding, snowshoeing, snowman making, snowball fighting . . . of all the *s*-named winter activities my father could've offered his blushing she-Elvis, he picked the one that was supposed to be *ours.* The very last thing we had together. The thing that no one else could touch—not even my mother. Maybe I turned my back on the rink three years ago, but it wasn't to go skate with another father.

"He took Shelvis ice-skating," I say.

A metal bowl hits the sink with a clang. "That *jackass!* Sorry, but it has to be said." She slams the faucet on, waits until the water gets hot, then soaks a clean dishrag. "Listen, I know it sucks, but you can't let him get to you like this. He's not even here, and he hardly ever talks to you, and—"

"Oh, he talks to me. Always has time to remind me how happy he is without us."

"Hudson . . ." Her voice is soft, just a whisper over my shoulder. The light changes; she's standing right next to me now, so close I can smell her coconut lotion. I close my eyes as her hand squeezes my shoulder, the warmth of it comforting and familiar.

Dani attacks the counter with the rag and I take a deep breath and count silently to ten.

Despite the fact that my baking space is a complete wreck, now that Dani's here and we're getting along a little better, the day ahead doesn't seem so bleak. She's right—I can't keep letting him do this to me. I already spent yesterday locked in my bedroom, crying over my father's stupid blog, wasting my whole day off. Why? He has his own life now, a different life, and just because he tells the world whenever his girlfriend learns a new trick, that doesn't mean I need to read about it. In fact, as soon as I get home, I'm unsubscribing from his stupid blog.

But then I might never hear *anything* from him. . . .

"No. You know what? You're right. Screw him." I push out from the counter and march over to the coffeepot, ready for a fresh cup. "If anything, it just makes me want to nail that scholarship even more." I cross back to the counter and sip my coffee, slightly burnt but nice and hot. "Anyway, enough of my lame family drama. How was Canada?"

"But . . ." Dani reaches for my hands across the counter, but she knows me well enough to realize the Dad conversation is over. "Fine. Canada was . . . it was okay. We got to dress up, take lots of pictures. Dad's ensemble brought the house down."

"Not surprised. Your dad blows. A mean trumpet, that is! *Har!*"

Dani laughs, and the tension between us melts a little more. "Never heard that one before, thanks." She dries my big silver bowl and sets it back on the counter. "The city itself is pretty cool, too. They have a really rich history, and lots of culture, and—"

"You applying for citizenship?"

She smiles. "I'd make a kick-ass *Canadienne*."

"As long as you don't show me up in front of Madame Fromme with your new French accent."

"That's Quebec, not Toronto. *N'est-ce pas?*"

"*N'est-ce* whatever. *Ferme ta bouche.*"

"*Ferme* your *bouche*." She laughs again. "So . . . did you get to have your date with Will?"

"Not really." I wipe off the mixer base and change out the beaters for a fresh pair. "I snuck over to the party for a little while, but I couldn't stay long."

Dani sets a stack of napkins and a silverware bin on the counter. "Are you, like, hanging out with him now? Officially?"

"I . . . guess." I shrug. "He kissed me at midnight. That's something, right?" I laugh. "When I left, he totally brushed snow off my truck."

"All that, just for a kiss? Damn." She smirks and rolls a fork and spoon into a napkin without even looking, starting another set so fast that her hands blur. "Do you like him? I mean, like, *like* him?"

"I'm . . . I think . . . yeah. I do. Maybe." I crack two eggs into a bowl and flip on the mixer. Dani narrows her eyes, but she doesn't press the Will thing.

"Well," she says over the mixer, "what about Frankie and those guys? Who all was there?"

"Everyone but Josh. All the usual Watonka people, plus,

like, ten of Amir's cousins and a bunch of people from City Honors."

"Sounds like a good crowd." She stacks the rolled silverware into a pyramid on her serving tray, not a single napkin corner out of place.

"Yeah. Like I said, I bailed early, so I don't know how it ended up. Can you pass me that flour sifter?" I nod toward the rack of utensils over the sink and she grabs the one I need.

"Were there a lot of other girls there?" she asks. "Like any of the—"

"Can we not talk about the party right now?" I drop the sifter on the counter, louder than I mean to, and she flinches. "Sorry. I'm just really beat, and Mom wants me to make a bunch of extra Sabres cupcakes, and the birthday group ladies are coming for lunch, and I'm trying to break early so I can work on my routine. The competition is in a month, and I'm not even close." I turn to grab the heavy cream from the small fridge next to the sink. "My triple/triple looks like a wounded seagull, and that's supposed to be the best move in my program. Not to mention the fact that I just overdosed on cupcake batter."

I turn back to the counter, but Dani and the silverware pyramid have vanished, the double doors swinging softly in their wake.

Two hours later Trick's singing Lou Reed over the half-empty grill, Dani's slicing oranges for plate garnishes, and I'm hand-icing my twenty-third consecutive blue-and-gold Sabres logo when my phone buzzes with a text from Will:

turn on channel 7—I'm on tv in 5 min!

"Your eyes about fell out of your head just then," Dani says, not hiding the snark in her tone. "That your new man?"

"He's *not* my new—forget it. Would you just come *here*?" I drag her into Mom's office and flip on the television. The tail end of an Old Spice commercial fades out and Channel 7 News returns, Will's old yearbook picture plastered up in the corner behind anchorwoman Marietta Swanson.

"Nice," Dani says. "Now he's a TV star, too? That'll do wonders for his ego."

"Shhh!" I reach over and raise the volume.

"Speaking of unprecedented comebacks," Marietta says in her buttery newscaster's voice, "Watonka High's own varsity hockey team seems to be turning more than a few heads on the ice this season. After a ten-year losing streak, the Watonka Wolves are on a roll. Don Donaldson caught up with the team's captain at Bluebird Park this morning to ask about the sudden turn of events. Don?"

The screen cuts to a bench behind the jogging path at the park. Will, sporting the fresh glow of physical exertion, smiles into the camera, Don Donaldson cheesing it up next to him in his bright blue Channel 7 parka.

"Thanks, Marietta," Don says. "I'm here with Will Harper, Watonka High School student and captain of the Wolves varsity hockey team. Will, your team hit the ice this year with a vengeance, shaking off a record-breaking string of bad luck. What can you tell us about this incredible reversal?"

"Some days I can't believe it myself," Will says, amping up that megawatt smile for the viewers back home. "I think the guys have just really come together this year."

"How do you explain the newfound teamwork?"

"Our secret weapon, of course."

Don chuckles in that robotic newsman way. "Does this secret weapon have a name?"

"Now, Don, you know I can't give away all our secrets." Will cocks his head and winks. I don't think Don realizes that Will is totally making fun of the whole "cool news guy" vibe.

"But I'll tell you this much," Will says. "I've been studying new techniques, working out on the ice with the guys, calling extra practices whenever I can. I also try to really motivate everyone, push them harder when they think they can't do it anymore. We haven't won every game, but we're working on it. There's no secret about a little hard work, Don."

"No, there certainly isn't, Will." Don turns back to the camera and smiles. "Well, there it is, folks. Proof that a little hard work can go a long way, especially here in Watonka, New York. Back to you, Marietta."

"Sounds like the Sabres could use a guy like Will Harper on the team, huh, Don?" Marietta laughs, co-anchors bubbling around her on cue. "Speaking of hitting the ice with a vengeance, let's check in with Dusty Martin on traffic and weather. Dusty?"

I click off the television. "Speaking of hitting the ice with a vengeance, I better finish those cupcakes."

Dani follows me back to the prep counter.

"Let me guess," she says, keeping her voice out of Mom and Trick range. "You thought he'd give you a public thank-you on TV? Better yet, how about a bouquet of *roses*!"

"It's not like that," I whisper. "Will knows my mother doesn't know about the Wolves stuff, and neither does the coach. He can't just out me on television. Besides, he *did* mention me. He always calls me their secret weapon—it's, like, our joke . . . thing . . . whatever."

"You know you're not actually *on* the team, right?"

"I like him, okay?"

"No, you don't. You 'well I'm um I don't know um I guess yeah maybe' him." Dani grabs her citrus knife. "And honestly, Hud? I'm tired of getting blown off just so you two *not*-lovebirds can make out."

"That's not fair," I say. "I had to stay home with Bug on New Year's."

"But you *didn't* stay home. You—"

"Yeah, sneaking out to a party in my own neighborhood for two hours is exactly the same thing as sneaking out to Canada."

Dani taps her knife on the cutting board, nostrils flaring.

"Hey, I don't want to fight," I say. "It's a new year, right? And we still have the rest of the weekend before school starts."

"You're right." She sighs and meets my gaze.

"Sorry I snapped at you earlier," I say. "And that I'm so

230

wrapped up in this skating thing. It won't be forever. Do-over?"

She nods and goes back to her fruit, dragging the knife across the rind. Thin orange slices fall into a neat stack on the chopping board in front of her. "You working tomorrow?"

"Yeah, I'm on breakfast with Nat."

"Feel like coming over after? We could order pizza, see what's on cable? My parents keep asking about you."

"I can't. Maybe Sunday?" I set my mixing bowls in the sink and turn on the hot water, shoulders heavy with new guilt. "There's a game tomorrow, and I promised Will—"

"Girls!" Mom twirls into the kitchen from the dining room, smile brighter than I've seen it in a long time. "I have news."

"You found another waitress?" I ask hopefully.

Ignored.

"I ran into an editor from the *Buffalo News* at the Chamber of Commerce party, and I just got off the phone with him!" Mom presses her hand to her chest, cell phone still clutched in her fingers.

"Ohmygod that's so amazing I don't even know what you're talking about! Yay!" I tighten my apron and pick up a half-iced Sabres cupcake. "If you don't mind, I have a few more bison and swords to make here, so—"

"Hudson, he recognized me from your cupcake article. Remember?"

Creations zany with Watonka wows queen cupcake: Hot spot local into diner struggling turns talent teen's. "Couldn't forget if I tried."

"They're doing a feature on regional diners, and I asked him about including Hurley's. He just confirmed—they're sending a food critic in a few weeks. We're in!"

"Well, all right!" Dani gives Mom a high five.

"That's what I'm *talkin'* about!" Trick cheers from his post at the grill.

"Okay, okay. That's pretty freaking cool, Mom." I set down the cupcake and give her a big squeeze. After the last *Buffalo News* article, we got tons of new business—enough to carry us through another year. A good review could totally put us back in the black. "When's he coming?"

"February third," she says. "Plenty of time to whip this place into shape."

"You got it, Ma." I smile, bullet narrowly dodged. My event is the first. Dani gives me a subtle elbow to the ribs, but I ignore it.

"This is our year, guys. I can feel it!" Mom offers another round of hugs and dips back into the dining room, the echo of her enthusiasm radiating throughout the kitchen.

"It's so close to your competition date," Dani says when Mom and Trick are both out of earshot. "What if she wants to put you on more shifts to get everything ready? What if . . . I don't know. Anything could happen. They're too close together. You should tell her."

"No way. Why do you think I sneak around just to go to Fillmore and Baylor's? Skating stuff totally reminds her of my father. She'd freak."

"That was a long time ago, Hud. Maybe she'd be okay with it now. Maybe things have changed for her, and—"

"They haven't." I think back to that night with the bra, the lines in my mother's face, the way she swept the evidence into the drawer like it didn't exist. I think of all the fights leading up to that final straw, the arguments about ice time and private tutors and moving and how would they ever afford to keep me in the competition, anyway? I see my father's suitcases, his empty promises, and my stomach twists, my eyes hot with stored-up, uncried tears. Not just for me and Bug. But for Mom, too.

"Give it a chance." Dani takes a step closer. "Maybe she'd be excited for you. Maybe—"

"*Maybe* you should stay out of it. *Maybe* I don't want to risk hurting her feelings."

Dani slams her hand on the counter. "Since when do you care about anyone else's feelings?"

"Settle down back there, ladies," Trick says. He twists around and shoots us both a warning look, a cloud of meat-steam rising behind him. The whole effect is quite devilish.

Dani sighs. "But Hudson won't—"

"Me? You're the one—"

"*Enough.*" Trick flips something onto a plate and holds it over his head. "Bacon, egg, and cheese croissant up for table twelve, Dani. Run it."

I strip off my apron and toss it onto the counter. "I'm going on break. Catch you guys later."

She snorts as she heads for the grill. "Say hi to the ice for me—your new BFF."

"No problem. You guys have a lot in common—cold hearts." I grab my gear from the staff closet, stomp out the back way, and slam the kitchen door behind me. From the ledge of the Dumpster, the Hurley's mascot squawks into the air.

"You got something to say to me, bird? Take a number." I zip into my jacket and tighten the backpack over my shoulders, but the seagull is still giving me dirty looks.

"What?!"

He shrugs and dives under a loose cardboard box.

"Yeah, that's what I thought." I yank on my mittens and march across the lot, Hurley's disappearing in the snow behind me. *Stupid bird. Can't you see it's still winter?*

Chapter Seventeen

Chocolate Banana Snap Crackle Popcakes

*Cold banana cupcakes topped with
milk chocolate icing, sliced strawberries, and Rice Krispies;
served in a bowl with a spoon
and a splash of spilt milk (to cry over)*

***That sorry excuse for a triple ain't happenin', sweet stuff. Back on the glass** until you nail it.*

After the tenth consecutive wipeout, I pick myself up off the Baylor's ice for another go, Lola's voice scolding me at every turn. I pump my legs and rush toward the center line, but when I try the lift again, I lose my balance, crash, and skid to a halt on my ass.

Again! Lola shouts.

I stand and dust the cold from my hands, thinking about Parallel Life Hudson. She'd probably be doing this exact thing right now—prepping for a chance at Lola's once-in-a-lifetime skating scholarship. If I'd stayed strong at Luby Arena that night, showed up at regionals, continued working with elite private coaches, I might've ended up exactly here anyway. Maybe I didn't get that far off course. Maybe our divergent paths have finally fused. Maybe there's still a chance. *The* chance.

I push across the ice and leap into a double axel/double lutz combo, pulling off a perfect landing. The crowd roars in my head, and when I close my eyes, it almost becomes real. The shouts and whistles from the stands, the crisp white smell of the air over a freshly smoothed rink, the chill rising from its surface.

Hudson Avery, ladies and gentlemen. The Cupcake Queen of Watonka, back for another shot on the ice. Can she impress the judges one last time? The crowd stomps their collective feet in a unified march, their energy a force field propelling me into another double/double combo.

A perfect score! Folks, this is figure skating history in the making. . . .

I coast forward for one more go, taking the hard turns with speed and grace as I lap the rink. My lungs ache and my cheeks are numb, but I can't stop now. I twist into a death spiral, the white of the ice swirling against the stands above until I stop, take a deep breath of chilled oxygen, and pump my legs toward the other end of the rink.

Swish . . .

I can do this.

Swish . . .

I have to do this.

Swish . . .

I push off from the back edge and spring forward, curling into the air for a single . . . a double . . . a triple flip. Ice-air-air-air-ice. Landing. First one I've nailed in weeks. And the crowd goes . . .

"Damn, girl. You still got it."

I whip my ahead around toward the sound. A single spectator leans against the rails, arms crossed over her chest, strawberry blond braids poking out the bottom of her light blue hat.

Only she's not a spectator. She's laced up.

I swallow the lump in my throat to make room for the sarcasm. "You packin' that ice pick today?"

"Not this time." Kara glides toward the center of the rink, hands clasped behind her back. "Will said you'd probably be here, so I thought . . . I don't know." She looks down at her skates, black leg warmers pulled down over the tops. "Figured I'd dust these things off and see if they still work."

"You talked to Will?"

"Texted him after I saw him on the news. That's it."

I shrug. "Free country."

"Did you catch his interview?"

"Yep." I swizzle backward toward the penalty box, putting some distance between us.

"Hudson, wait." She follows me, her strides as graceful and balanced as ever. "I came to apologize for harassing you at your locker. New Year's, too. I'm sorry I cornered you in the bathroom. I wanted to talk, but I had a couple drinks, and by the time you got there . . . I don't know. Can I blame the booze?"

I grab a bottled water from my pack and take a swig. "You know what they say. Don't drink and . . . stalk people in bathrooms. I mean . . . okay. I don't know where I was going with that."

Kara laughs. "Guess things got a little ridiculous between us, huh?"

"A little bit, yeah." I tuck the bottle back into my pack and skate to the center line. "So, what's up? You trying out for the Capriani thing after all?"

"Think I have a chance?" Kara laughs and follows me to the line. "I don't want to compete, Hud. I told you that already. And I don't want this to come out wrong, but I need to say something about Will. One thing, then I'll shut up."

"Again with the Will threats?" I know she liked him first, but that was forever ago. They had their chance, and it didn't work out. She's the one who dumped him, anyway. And it's not like Will and I are *together* together. And even if we were, it's none of her business. "Sorry, Kara. I don't—"

"Just be careful. I know you're helping with the Wolves, and you two are hanging out now, but as charming as Will is . . . look, once he gets what he wants, he moves on. You saw his interview today. Gorgeous smile or not, Will is all about Will."

"Hockey boys, right? Comes with the territory." I laugh to show her how much she's not getting to me, just in case she missed it.

"I know, but Will—"

"We're not having this conversation."

"Point taken." She fingers a loose thread on her jacket, the sleeve fraying at the end as she pulls. "Speaking of hockey boys . . . is Danielle Bozeman trying to talk to Frankie?"

My stomach knots up at the mention of Dani. "Frankie Torres? Doubt it. Why?"

"Ellie said . . . well, she thought they went out or something. And—"

"They hung out once before Christmas, but it was kind of a joke. She's not into hockey boys."

Kara laughs. "Smart girl."

"Yep." I skate away from her and twirl into a camel spin.

"Your moves are tight," she says, skating a backward circle around me. "You ready for the competition?"

"Mostly. I've been working my ass off after every Wolves practice and whenever I can sneak away from work. I just hope it's enough."

"I'm sure it's fine. You have, like, crazy talent."

"Crazy talent that's been hibernating for three years without a coach." I bend down to adjust my leg warmers, pulling them off my laces a bit. Maybe they're too heavy. Maybe that's what's throwing me off. "I'm still perfecting my triple/triple. I keep screwing up the first jump."

"Looked good to me."

"That was a one-in-a-hundred shot. I can't replicate it consistently, which means I don't have it."

"Let me see."

"What, here?"

"Better than Amir's bathroom, right?" She skates back to the box. "Maybe I can give you some pointers. I remember stuff too, you know."

"You sure you're okay with this?"

"Why not? Come on." Kara resumes her spectator position on the sidelines and I skate back to the center line. This was our routine for so long. For weeks leading up to our events, we'd practice together at Buffalo Skate Club every night, swapping critiques until we'd nearly broken every bone, perfected every move.

Now, after years of not speaking, it's so strange to be skating for her like this again, but it's kind of nice, too. I go through a quick version of some of my program moves, launch into my triple flip, and . . . crash and burn.

"See what I mean?" I stand up and check my laces. Everything's tight. The leg warmers are clear of the blades. The skates aren't a perfect fit anymore, and they're definitely not in mint condition, but I don't think that's the problem. I try two more for her and get the same results: Ass, meet ice. Talk amongst yourselves.

"Your left foot's dragging after the jump," she says. She slides out to the center and demonstrates a version of my pre-jump in slow motion. "You're pushing off the ice strong, but your trailing foot lags. You're not pulling in tight enough for the triple."

"You sure that's it?"

She nods. "Try it again, but this time, lift you left foot a half second earlier."

I skate back to the center, close my eyes, and lean into a glide. I speed up, concentrating on that lagging foot, counting my strokes, two . . . three . . . four . . . and launch . . .

"Yeah! That's it!" She claps from the sidelines, and I open my eyes. I really did it. Triple flip, perfect landing. No missteps, no wipeouts.

"Try another, just to be sure."

I skate back into position, glide up the center ice, and bang out another perfect triple.

"And there you have it," she says. "Put it together with your triple toe loop, and you're golden."

I skate back to the box and grab my water. "Thanks. I've been crying over that move for weeks."

"Should've called me sooner."

"Um . . ."

"Kidding. You still have your old DVDs, right? Might help to watch them again. Make some notes from the outside looking in, you know?"

I nod, picturing the dusty box in the basement.

"You look good out there, Hudson. I'm sure you'll kick ass next month." She looks at me with shiny eyes, and my stomach lurches sideways. If I didn't screw up that night in Rochester, maybe she'd still be competing. Maybe we'd be practicing for the Capriani Cup together, sharing tips and tricks, shouting out cheers and encouragement, may the best girl win. Instead,

I'm training alone, lying to basically everyone I know, and she's here apologizing about some stupid half-drunk bathroom exchange at a party when all she really wanted to do was warn me about Will. Protect me from getting hurt by the boy that was once hers.

I think I'm in love with Will Harper. . . .

"I'm so sorry, Kara." The words sting my throat on the way out. I take a deep breath and try again. "I'm sorry about kissing Will at that party when I knew you liked him. And I'm sorry about throwing the Empire Games. I got out there that night and I was pissed at my dad and kind of in shock and I just . . . I gave up. And after that, I disappeared. I couldn't face up to anything. My parents got divorced, and I went into hiding because I thought it was my fault."

Kara knew that my parents officially split up soon after Empire—everyone did—but by then we were no longer speaking. I never told her about everything that came before the divorce: The nights my father slept on the couch. The clipped arguments and silent breakfasts, forks scraping angrily on plates. All the endless pretending. How that night at the event, just hours after discovering the cheetah bra, I let my own dreams melt, right there on the ice in front of my parents, my coach, my skate club, and my best friend.

"He was having an affair," I say. "I'm pretty sure Mom knew it all along, but I found the real proof that day, fifteen minutes before we left for Rochester. I didn't fully realize what it was in the moment, but somehow I knew they'd split up.

That night at the event, I saw it coming, and I freaked." The ice machines tick below our feet and a shiver passes through my bones. "It's not an excuse, but that's what happened."

Kara lets out a long, slow breath. "I'm sorry you had to deal with that by yourself. But you could've told me the truth. Maybe not that night, but after. Yeah, I would've been mad about losing our shot at the Empire sponsorship, but I would've understood. I would've . . . I don't know. Maybe we'd still be friends today, instead of . . . not."

I look out across the rink, tears blurring the ice into a white sea. "I know."

"I thought I'd moved on," she continues. "It was so long ago, I wasn't competing anymore, we weren't friends, why bother, right? But then I heard you were working with the hockey team, training again, hanging out with Will . . . I'm not the psycho jealous ex here, Hudson. Seriously. But every time I see you with him, it's like watching the last three years unravel in reverse. I didn't . . . I never forgave you."

I turn to face her again and whisper over the tightness in my throat. "And now?"

She sighs, scraping a line in the ice with her toe pick, back and forth, back and forth. "So much happened; things are so different now. *We're* different. But the other night at Amir's, I realized something: Friends or not, I don't want to spend the rest of my life hating you."

"Same," I say.

"So let's call this a mutual understanding. It's the best I can do." She smiles and holds out her hand. Despite the heaviness of her final words on my chest, I take it.

"Does this mean no more bathroom brawls?"

She smiles. "Afraid so. But, Hudson, I'm serious about Will. Right now he needs you for the team, but after that . . . just be careful, okay? And that's all I'll say about it."

I drop her hand and nod toward her skates. "Fifteen minutes before I have to get back to work. Feel like giving those things a workout? Letting me kick your ass for old times?"

Kara raises an eyebrow, and for a second I think she might join me. I know we're not friends anymore—not really. But I want her to say yes. I want her to skate with me again—to *want* to skate with me again. Because after everything that happened, if things can be okay with Kara, maybe it means my skating doesn't have to be an either/or, a bittersweet choice that always leaves something else behind, some other dream unfollowed.

But Kara's smile fades fast, her eyes turning serious and regretful. "I should let you get back to your training."

"No, it's cool. We could—"

"Some other time, maybe." She taps her toe pick against the ice. "Good luck at the event, Hudson. I'm sure you'll win the judges' hearts. You always did."

I nod, blinking back tears. Winning the judges' hearts always meant more to me *off* the ice, after the roses and ribbons and camera flashes, when Kara and I sat side by side with a tuna melt platter in the window booth at Hurley's, the

celebration twice as special because we could share it, no matter who took first.

But things are different now. I made my choices, and so
did Kara, and three years later our paths are as divergent as
fire and ice.

Kara Shipley and I were supposed to skate around the
world together. But now?

"Bye, Hud. See you at school." She glides to the edge of
the rink and slips the blade guards over her skates, and I take
a deep breath, skate back to the center line, and without an
audience, give that triple/triple another go.

Chapter Eighteen

Hester's Scarlet Letters

*Raspberry-vanilla cupcakes
topped with chocolate Chambord icing,
a fresh raspberry, and a scarlet monogrammed* A

"I have news," Will says in the hall outside my French classroom the following week. "Pun intended."

It's the first Friday after winter break, and despite Kara's warnings, he's been walking me to my classes every day, warming up my car in the school lot, dazzling me with his smile and unfailing intensity and all-around good-smelling-ness.

"Give it to me," I say.

"You'll never guess who's coming to the game tonight." Will slides his hand across my lower back, fingers curving around my hip. "My good buddy Don Donaldson. *Heyyy.*" He makes a shooting gesture with his free hand and clicks his tongue.

"Cheesy news guy Don? Why?"

"What can I say? I look good on camera." Will flashes me his TV-ready grin. "I totally boost their ratings."

I punch him in the arm.

"Hey! They like the human interest angle. Hometown heroes, underdogs, all that stuff. We *are* doing better than the Buffalo Sabres this season, in case you haven't noticed."

"Yeah, yeah." I smile. "What about Dodd? He's cool with the media attention?"

"Not a chance. I've been dodging him since the interview last week. I figured I'd set this up now and apologize later."

"You're living on the edge, boy."

"You don't know the half of it." Will leans against the lockers and looks down the hall, his eyes suddenly dark. "Dodd doesn't want any attention on us. My dad thinks he's trying to get Watonka High to drop the hockey program altogether and funnel the leftover money into the football program."

"Why?"

"Dodd wants a college football gig, but first he's gotta make a winning high school team. To do that, he needs cash. Right now the Wolves are a money pit for the athletics department. By the way, this is all highly classified, need-to-know-basis type stuff. None of the guys—"

"Dirty secret, got it." I smile just as the one-minute warning bell buzzes. "Hey, you okay? Should I be worried?"

"I'll worry about me. You worry about this." He slips his hand behind my neck and pulls me in, lips melting against mine in a totally sickening PDA special. Thankfully, the only witness is Dani; she sighs as she ducks behind us into the class-room.

"Gross. Get a room."

It's the most she's said to me all week.

"Bonjour, étudiants. C'est une journée excitante!" Madame Fromme's got her laptop open, rockin' the I-can't-wait-to-torture-you-with-a-pictorial-from-my-1980s-French-excursion glow. From her seat near the projector screen she prattles on, but I don't pick out the French words for "vacation," "trip," or "boring as hell," so maybe we're safe.

"Dani," I whisper as the room darkens and the presenta-tion begins—French Impressionism. Much better than watch-ing Madame traipse through the City of Light with her mall bangs and stirrup pants.

"Dani!" I say again, a little louder. Still no response.

I sneak my phone out of my pocket and send her a text, but when her purse buzzes on the floor, she ignores it, twirling her corkscrew curls around a pencil. Desperate, I go low-tech, pen and paper, and quickly sketch a pirate with Dani's name tat-tooed on his chest. I even dot the *i* with a little heart and add a parrot on his shoulder. At the top I write, "A Pirate Sonnet: Roses *arrr* red. Violets *arrr* blue. I know we *arrr* fighting. But I miss talking to you. *Arr.*"

Pretty impressive, considering I'm not exactly a sketch art-ist. Or a poet.

I fold it into a triangle and toss it onto her desk. Casually, she stretches out her arm and nudges my note to the floor, unopened and unacknowledged.

At least . . . unacknowledged by Dani. Madame Fromme, on the other hand, swoops down like a vulture, capturing my note in her talon and tossing it into the trash without missing a beat on the slide show narration.

For the rest of class, I sit with my hands folded on my desk, face forward, soaking up some art *en français*. It's slightly less lame than I predicted. Madame shows a bunch of winter scenes from Alfred Sisley, and they totally remind me of Watonka. Like first thing in the morning, when the sun's just coming up and everything is quiet and undisturbed, snow still fresh and white, the day uncharted—on those mornings, you look out the window and you know anything can happen, because nothing's gone wrong yet. No best friend fights or lying to your mom or kissing boys in the hallway. It's just clean, pure potential. Hope.

I haven't had a Sisley kind of day in a long time.

When the class bell buzzes, Madame Fromme flips on the lights and Dani packs up her stuff, rapid-fire. Before I can say *attende, s'il vous plaît*, she's out the door, and Trina Dawes is perching her tiny little ass on the edge of my desk.

The girl is glammed to the max, eyes coated with thick black liner and hair pinned into a prom-style updo behind a rhinestone tiara. In her left hand she's holding a thin silver wand.

"Hey, Hudson." The queen bee fairy hooker taps me with

the wand and sticks out her chest, letting her tight white
T-shirt do the explaining:

Kiss Me, I'm the Birthday Girl!

"Happy—" Ohmygod. It's January tenth. Friday, January
tenth. *A hundred people at least . . .*

"Birthday," I stammer.

She whirls her magic wand between us and bounces on her
toes. "Are the cupcakes just *so amazing?*"

I nod emphatically. Bubble-Gum Bling, her signature
theme? I had major plans. Heart-shaped dark chocolate and
white chocolate cupcakes, a thick pillow of pink strawberry
whipped cream frosting with a light sugar glaze, edible silver
glitter, hard candy gemstone accents, all arranged on mirrored trays twined with white Christmas lights. Photo-worthy,
cupcake-archive quality all the way.

Too bad they don't exist.

"*So* amazing," I say.

"Yay! Mom will be at Harley's at five to pick them up."
Trina taps me once more with the magic wand and bounces
into the hallway with her girlfriends, giggling about their *so
amazing* Friday-night party plans. Best birthday *ever!*

"Hurley's," I say, but she's already gone.

I look at the clock over Madame's desk and do some quick
calculations. I still have three more hours of classes, which
leaves less than two hours after school to make two hundred
blinged-out cupcakes for the birthday fairy. That's barely
enough time to mix and bake them, let alone cool, frost, and

hand-decorate. I don't even remember where I stashed the mirrored trays.

Attention, ladies and gentlemen, this is not a test. I repeat, this is not a test. This is a bona fide, break-the-glass cupcake emergency.

And there's only one desperately shameful way to fix it.

Operation Bake-and-Switch commences at the Front Street Fresh 'n' Fast immediately after school.

I check my last shred of self-respect at the entrance, snag a rusty shopping cart, and beeline for the bakery. And by bakery, clearly I'm talking about the shelves where they stack all the stuff that was created by machines on an assembly line in Tulsa, injected with preservatives and high-fructose chemicalness, and shipped here on a truck for our postproduction enjoyment.

I'm pretty sure it's one of those moments where everything is supposed to stand still for a few seconds so you can recognize the impending disaster and redirect the course of your life, but I don't have time for any of that nonsense, because there's a two-for-one special on prepackaged confections today, and I'm about to go bulk wild on this bargain.

Shame creeps along my neck and face, but I ignore it and load up the cart with enough flats of white-frosted cupcakes to feed Trina's party people. Two hundred and ten tasty treats later, I zoom through self-checkout, stack the goodies in the backseat of the Tetanus Taxi, and floor it over to Hurley's, eighty bucks less independently wealthy than when I left the apartment this morning.

Inside the diner, Mom's office door is closed; her all-consuming preparations for the food critic should keep her off my apron strings awhile. In three quick trips, I unload the cupcakes and trash all the packaging, just in case Mom pokes her nose out of the office for a report. I ignore Trick's raised eyebrows as I dive into the walk-in cooler for my leftover stash of buttercream, add a few drops of red tint, whip it into a nice, mellow pink, and load the whole mess into a frosting gun. I'm generally more of a pastry bag kind of girl, but hey, this is war. Or it *will* be, if I don't get these babies done in time.

"What are you *doin'*?" Trick finally demands.

"Target shooting, Trick. What does it look like?" I raise my cupcake weaponry and get to work, squirting pink, lop-sided hearts into the center of the white-frosted Fresh 'n' Fast cakes.

Trick stomps over and grabs my arm. "Hudson Avery, you been doin' some *messed* up stuff lately, but I *know* this isn't what it looks like. Right?"

"Um . . . no." I swallow hard. I've never seen him angry—not even when I screw up orders or we run out of bread on French toast day. "I don't know. What does it look like?"

He lowers his voice and leans in close, bacon fumes emanating from his pores. "It *looks* like you're tryin' to pass off those cupcakes as your own, but I must be wrong. The Hudson Avery *I* know would never sink to that level."

I look at the floor and shrug, eyes burning with near tears.

Trick sighs, but he doesn't loosen his grip on my arm. "Let's forget for a minute that there's probably some kinda tax law against reselling those things. But come *on*, girl. Cupcakes are your art. How can you put your name on something like that? That'd be like Dani buying a frame and telling everyone the fake picture that comes with it is hers."

"No, it'd be like Dani forgetting a major order and trying her best to make it right before it's too late."

Trick shakes his head. "That's a load of crap and you know it."

My cheeks go hot. Trick's the closest thing to a dad I've had in years, and the disappointment in his voice stings. But still, I'm out of options on this one, and the clock is ticking. I pull free from his grip.

"You think I'm proud of this? Think it's my shining moment? I'm barely keeping it together over here, okay?" I continue my mission, applying pink hearts with machine-gun speed. They're actually less heart-y and more round-y, but to the untrained eye, which I hope includes the Dawes family, they still look halfway decent. "Mom's breathing down my neck, Dani's not speaking to me, I haven't seen my brother for more than five minutes all month, and—"

"Your brother's in the dining room," Trick says. "You can see him right now. Last time I checked, Fresh 'n' Fast don't sell stand-in brothers, so get him while he's hot."

"Bug's here? Perfect." I poke my head out the dining room doors and wave him back into the kitchen. "Hey, sweet pea.

Want to learn some cupcake tricks and help me with an order?"

His eyes get huge. "You said I'm not allowed to work on customer projects until I'm older."

"Well, now you're older." I steer him over to the sink to wash his hands, then set him up at the prep counter. Some people call it child labor. I call it . . . let's not get technical.

"When I hand you the cupcake, dip it lightly, like this." I roll the top of a cupcake in a flat bowl of edible silver glitter and set it in front of him. "See?"

"Yum."

"Don't eat it." I squirt a pink buttercream heart over a new cupcake and pass it over. "Let me see you try one."

He's a little slow, but he gets the job done.

"Beautiful," I say. "Congratulations, you're my new Vice President of Glitter. Any questions?"

Bug crinkles up his face. "Can I be Glitter Czar instead?"

"Done."

"One last thing." Bug pulls the spiral notebook from his back pocket and tears off a strip of paper. "Can you give me a blood sample?"

I look deep into my brother's pleading brown eyes and raise an eyebrow. "Bug, seriously . . . did Mom drop you on your head? Like, last night?"

"You can't trust anyone these days, Hud. Even relatives. And I don't want to go into business with someone who won't submit to a basic drug test."

"Give me that." I snatch the paper from his hand and smear

on a sample with red frosting tint. "Does this work? Stabbing myself with a fork is probably a health code violation."

"Good point." The Glitter Czar takes the red-smeared paper, shoves it in his pocket, and gets to work.

With Bug's meticulous help, we finish decorating relatively quickly. I add chocolate piping around a few dozen for a little flair and arrange them carefully into bakery boxes. Then I wrap ten metal trays in foil sheets and stack them together with the order. Some assembly required, but I think we pulled it off.

"Very classy, if you ask me." Bug high-fives me with a glittery hand. "We make a good team."

"The best." I pass him the frosting gun, dinner of champions and Glitter Czars alike. "Couldn't have done it without—"

"Trick?" Nat sticks her pink-haired head through the window over the grill. "Some lady's here for a cupcake order. Did Hudson leave anything to—"

"I'm here, Nat. Tell her I'll be right out."

Operation Bake-and-Switch is a raging success. Back in the kitchen, I lean against the counter and untie my baker's apron, Mrs. Dawes satisfied, cupcake crisis averted. Time to *wolf* down—pun intended—dinner and get to the game. Less than an hour till face-off.

Just as I bite into my chicken Caesar wrap, Mom's office door flies open. "Hud, that you?"

I swallow and give her a half wave. "Hey, Ma."

"Marianne's got the flu. Can you stay for the dinner shift?"

"Not really. Did you call Dani?"

"Tried. She's got plans tonight."

"So do I." As if to remind me, my phone buzzes with Josh's number, but I silence it. What does she mean, Dani's got plans? With who?

Mom crosses the kitchen and takes the stool across from me and Bug. "You going out with that Josh boy?"

"Is that the friend with benefits guy?" Bug swipes one of my sweet potato fries. "He's funny. I like that guy."

Under the table, I kick his foot.

"Ow! Hudson—"

"No," I say. "I mean, I don't have a friend with . . . I'm not going out with Josh tonight. I just wanted to go out. For coffee. With . . . um . . . a girl from my French class. Trina. It's her birthday. Besides, I don't have my uniform here."

Mom frowns and shakes her head. "I'm sorry, Hud. It's only till about eight—Nat and I can handle it after that. It's not a school night, so I'll keep Bug here. You can scoot out after first shift. Sound okay?"

I shrug and jam a few fries into my mouth. Like I have a choice.

"What's wrong?" Mom asks.

"Nothing." I shake my head and smile through the food. I can't let her see me crack. Trick, either—not after the cupcake disaster I so narrowly dodged. I have to find a way to handle this. It's just a few more weeks, anyway. Once I nail that competition, no more Hurley's shifts. No more scraping by. Everything will change. "I really wanted to go out early tonight, that's all."

Mom stands and shoves her stool back under the counter. "Excuse me, darlin', but there's a lot going on these next couple of months, and most of the time, you come and go as you please. In return, I expect—"

"No, it's fine, Ma." She's right. I should be grateful that she doesn't bug me about my every move. I am. I know she does a lot to keep us all going. I just wish those expectations of hers had better timing. "I'll stay."

"Thank you." She leans over and kisses me on the cheek, then swoops in for a Bug-hug. "There should be extra uniforms in the closet. I'll be counting milk cartons in the walk-in cooler if you need me."

I relinquish the rest of my fries to Bug, grab a spare uniform, and change in the ladies' room. There's an unidentifiable red streak crusted down the front of the dress like a jagged zipper. Who knows how many decades old it is.

Mad hot, Hudson. As usual.

My phone buzzes on the bathroom counter—Josh again.

"Hud, where are you?" he asks when I pick up. "It's almost time. The crowd's awesome. The news is here tonight—it's crazy."

I lean against the tiled wall, facing the mirror. "Will told me the news would be there."

"Why aren't *you* here?"

"Dude, I'm stuck at work."

"You can't be! That's so lame!"

I scrape my thumbnail over the red streak—no change. "Seriously. You should see what I'm wearing."

"Mmmm," he says, his voice going low and smoky. "What are you wearing?"

I know he's trying to be all cheesy porn star, but the way he's breathing into the phone sends a squiggly shiver down my back. "Um . . . it's . . . I'm . . . the Hurley's dress . . . thing."

"Kidding, Avery."

"I know." I shake my head at my reflection. Thankfully, Josh can't see my bright pink face through the phone. "So, um, yeah. What's going on?"

"Nothing now. I only spent *all* afternoon hooking up this Deaf Buddha mix. All imports. Guess I'll have to find some other girl who digs—"

"Deaf Buddha? That is *so* not fair, fifty-six."

Josh laughs. "You know I'll save it for you. Just get here as soon—wait, hold up."

He mumbles something to the other guys, all of them suddenly cheering in the background.

"Hud, turn on Channel Seven," he says over the noise. "Hurry! They're about to do a live shot!"

"Okay, I'm going. Hang on." I run to Mom's office and flip on the news.

"I'm waving at you right now!" Josh says.

"I know!" I wave back. I can't help it. "I totally see you guys!"

Unlike Will's solo interview last week, this one features all of them, the camera closing in on each face, then panning out to the crowd. For the first time in recent history, the stands at Baylor's are at least half-full. Tons of people are dressed in the Watonka blue-and-silver, waving homemade signs and banners plastered with wolf heads and puff-paint jersey numbers.

"Told you." Josh tugs on Brad Nelson's jersey and points to the camera. Both of them blow kisses, and on the other end of the signal, though they can't see me, I smile.

The camera pans out again, up to the seats above the center line, where a dozen hockey wives and groupies whistle and cheer. Ellie's standing on her seat, howling just like her boyfriend Amir. Next to her, Kara's shaking a big glittery "Hungry Like a Wolf" sign, waving it over her head.

The camera shifts left and zooms in on the next seat, and my phone slips out of my hand and hits Mom's desk with a thud.

Right next to the hockey wives sits a girl in a blue-and-silver Watonka hoodie, one hand holding a Nikon, the other tucking a fuzzy wolf-eared headband into a sleek, unmistakable fountain of corkscrew curls.

Chapter Nineteen

Desolation Angels

*Chilled angel food cupcakes topped with
white cream cheese icing and shaved white chocolate,
dusted with silver and white
granulated sugar*

I smell like bacon. Again. I smell and my face is shiny and my arms feel like Trick's spinach fettuccine when he leaves it in the water too long. I missed all but the last twenty minutes of the game, which they won, and now I'm standing on the sidelines behind all the other Wolves groupies, staring at Kara's glittery poster board and the back of Dani's wolf ears.

She doesn't notice me. I take a step closer and poke her shoulder. "What are you doing here?"

She turns around, completely unruffled. "Celebrating the win. *Hello.*"

"You don't even like hockey. *Hello.*"

"Not true." She raises an index finger. "I don't like getting blown off *for* hockey. I never said I didn't like the sport itself."

"So now you're all BFF with the wives?"

Dani pulls me aside and shakes her head, but not in a no-why-would-I-be-friends-with-them way. More like an I'm-disappointed-and-saddened-by-your-very-existence-I-wish-we-never-met way. My stomach hurts. Fighting with Dani is one thing. But losing my best friend to a new clique? One that includes my *ex*–best friend?

This can't be happening.

"Not that it's any of your business," she says, brushing a crumb of glitter from her shirt, "but they waved me over when they saw me sitting alone. And then we started talking, and they passed me some wolf ears and invited me to sit with them. Which I did. And now we're down here, cheering for the team. Okay?"

"No! Not okay! Why didn't you just . . . I don't know. Ignore them, or something?"

Dani rolls her eyes.

"I don't get why you'd come here alone in the first place," I say, my voice low. "Don't you—"

"Danielle! Pink! Hey, we tore it up out there, *mamacitas!*"

Dani's entire face changes when Frankie says her name, eyes lighting up even more than they do for corned beef hash. She brushes past me, the sweet scent of her coconut lotion lingering in the air as lucky thirteen pulls her into a hug.

It's clearly not the first time.

My best friend is hooking up with—or seriously en route to hooking up with—one of my hockey boys, and I've been totally blind to it.

It's official. I live under a giant iceberg. And now, watching Dani smile and flirt, Ellie and Kara cooing behind her, all I want to do is crawl back beneath it.

"Hudson!" Josh waves from across the crowd, and my heart lifts. He climbs over the ledge that separates the ice from the stands, pushes his way through the tangle of bodies, and wraps me in a full-body hug.

"Sorry if I'm gross right now," he says, "but Will's in the back with Dodd and this might be my only chance to sneak in a decent celebration hug."

A spark runs through me as Josh pulls me closer, starting in my chest and pulsing outward like a bright, warm sun.

"Three more wins," he says, "and we're in the semis. Believe that?"

"I'm . . . um . . . I'm really proud of you." My voice is shaky despite the truth of the words. My knees turn wiggly and I know we should let go, untwist before any more mixed signals zap my brain. This superpublic display is so unlike him, so much more than just a hug. My heart speeds up as if it can feel that invisible line, that one we just crossed, and Josh must sense it, too, because he moans softly into my hair, almost a whisper. As the cheers of the crowd fade into an indiscernible din, I rest my head on his chest, his heart beating against the wolf on his jersey as furiously as mine, and for the briefest second, I think this might be . . .

"Yo!" Brad hip-checks Josh and yanks me into a side hug.

"Um . . . hi," I manage. While I've come to appreciate inappropriate aggressiveness as one of sixty's endearing little charms, in this particular moment, I might kinda cut him with an ice skate. "Nice game."

He smiles, big and bright. "Nice doesn't even come close, Pink. I think we can finally shake you."

"I'd like to shake *you*." I give him my most intimidating stare-down, but that just encourages him.

"Time and place, baby." He turns his head, spits, and then winks at me. Sexy *and* classy. "You name it, I'll be there. On the ice or off."

"Off," Rowan says, skating closer. "Will promised we could ax the princess as soon as we got our winning streak on." He breaks into this spazzy little dance number, arms flailing.

"Why are you trying to get rid of me?" I ask. "You know I'm your good luck charm."

"I can't speak for these thugs, but *I'm* not letting you go." Josh smiles, eyes fixed on mine, unblinking and intense. When he looks at me like that, the heat of his celebration hug radiates through my entire body again, every nerve reaching out for him.

I close my eyes. *Wrong, wrong, wrong.* Focus. Will. What's taking him so long?

"What's the plan?" Gettysburg asks, breaking into our circle. A few more Wolves crowd around me, some with their girlfriends, some without, everyone knocking into each other and laughing. Behind us, Amir is making out with Ellie like they're in a competition, and from the corner of my eye, I spot Dani and Frankie, way too up close and personal for a couple whose first date was actually ladies' night.

"Showers, then Papallo's," Luke says. "You coming with us, Hud?"

"To the showers?"

"Ooh, I want in on that. You can do my back, and I'll do your front." Brad makes a rather complicated gesture with his hands. I'm not even sure how to translate it, but apparently Josh knows what it means, because he smacks him on the back of the head.

I hold up my hands. "That's a no on the shower invite, yes on Papallo's."

"Stick with me," Josh says. "I have that mix in the car. Wait until you hear—"

"Hud's mine tonight, boys. Sorry." Will appears out of nowhere and puts his arm across my shoulders, settling the debate. He's freshly showered and dressed, wet blond hair curling at his ears. I turn toward him and lean in, letting his rich, familiar scent envelop me. Slowly, the warmth of his body mixes with the feeling of Josh still lingering on my skin, still radiating from my insides.

But when Will kisses my lips, soft and quick, the radiating stops, and I relax. Maybe I just read into it, got all worked up over nothing. Josh is just a good friend, caught up in the moment. It really was just a hug. A slightly-longer-than-usual-yet-totally-platonic celebratory hug.

Will pulls away but I grab him for another kiss.

The guys whistle and laugh and Josh shakes his head and looks at the ice while Will leads us away from the group, and it's just like that nature show again, the males of the species showing their prowess with a bunch of grunts and gestures to officially mark their territory.

Boys. At least I didn't get peed on.

"You okay?" I ask when we get to Will's car. "You seem a little tense."

He tries to smile, but I see right through it, and when I open my mouth to say so, his jaw tightens. "Mind if we skip the group thing tonight? Go for a ride somewhere? I just . . . I need to talk to you about some stuff."

I nod and tack on a smile, hoping it's enough to mask my disappointment at leaving the group. "Was Dodd pissed about the news?"

"Yeah, but that's not . . ." Will's eyes flash, a storm flickering out in a blink. "Let's just bounce, okay?" He puts his hand behind my neck and kisses me once more before motoring us out onto the I-190, Kara's words from last week bleeding into Rowan's and echoing through my head.

Once he gets what he wants, he moves on. . . . Will promised we could ax the princess. . . . Right now he needs you for the team, but after that . . .

We end up on the American side of Niagara Falls, ten below zero, hours after closing time, no other cars or pedestrians in sight. Ignoring the CLOSED signs, Will pulls into a spot near a pathway that snakes around the water and kills the engine.

"Hudson?"

I take a deep breath. I mean, it's been less than a month. He hasn't even tried to sleep with me. And now he's ditching me? Axing me from the team? He doesn't say anything for a full minute. Normally, I think the dramatic pause is a great performance technique, but in these situations? No, not a fan.

"Will, I don't—"

"You okay to walk?" He nods toward the water. "Just for a few minutes?"

I follow him out of the car, gingerly stepping along the icy path. He takes my hand in his and leads us closer to the edge, the roar of water almost deafening.

"I've never been here in the winter," he says. "You?"

I shake my head.

"I thought we should see it," he says. "I mean, it's here, right?"

I lean over the rail, staring down into the white abyss. I heard once that Eskimos have, like, a hundred different words for snow. Growing up in Watonka, I've been hit with all kinds of snow—fluffy, wet, slushy, icy needles, tiny flakes, blustery whiteout clouds of it—but it was always just *snow* to me. Just like ice was always the rink—Fillmore or Buffalo Skate Club or Luby or

Miller's Pond or anywhere else—it was all just the smooth surface beneath my feet. But here, the river's eternal mist has encased
the world in glass. Every twig on every branch on every tree, the
railings and the paths, the lampposts—all of it sparkles in the
moonlight. And as I look into the deep, white maw of the earth,
I see a thousand different meanings, a thousand different words.

Even on my father's blog, in all his pictures and stories, I've
never seen anything so beautiful and amazing.

I wish Josh was here to see it.

We walk along the path to a lookout, and I scrape a thin
layer of ice from one of the signs. "Says here that the Falls
erodes about one foot a year. Eventually it'll crumble all the
way back to Lake Erie."

"Crazy," Will says.

"No, *think* about it! All of this . . ." I spin with my arms
wide, scooping up the landscape. "In forty-eight thousand
years, everything we're standing on will be gone."

"Guess we're running out of time, then." Will slides his
gloved fingers over my shoulders and leans into a kiss, hot and
steamy in the frozen mist.

I pull away slowly, lingering in his arms. "Is this what you
wanted to talk about?"

"Maybe." He gives me that grin, and even though I know
he's hiding something, I'm powerless to push. Talk? What
talk? We half kiss, half stumble our way across the ice-slick
path back to the car. Will cranks the heat, and we continue our
mad race against geologic time in the backseat.

Will kisses his way from earlobe to collarbone, his lips brushing the hollow of my throat, his hair tickling my skin. "I could do this all night."

"Stop! Stop!" I mock push him away, but my giggling makes him more eager, his fingers strumming my ribs. "I'm serious, Josh—*Will*. Will, stop!"

He raises his head, mouth turned up in a partial grin. "Did you just call me Josh?"

"Josh? What? No."

"You did. You went 'Josh-Will' and then—"

"I'm cold. My teeth were chattering."

He raises an eyebrow. "Something going on with you and fifty-six?"

"No!"

Will pulls back, watching me close. "You sure? Because sometimes you guys have this *thing*, you know?"

"What *thing*? We don't have a thing."

"Like an unspoken . . . thing. Like there's this inside joke or something. A thing, you know?"

My heart freezes up, then jump-starts, racing double time. "We're just friends. It's not—"

"Forget it."

"It's not like that," I say. "We aren't—"

"I'm not into sharing, just so you know. If you'd rather be with Blackthorn . . ." His eyebrow arches again to match his grin, sure and cocky and half-joking, and my stomach flip-flops. In a perfect world . . . no. We don't live in a perfect world. And here in the rusty old town of my life, there's the boy who's just my friend, who's hugged me and looked at me a little too long and made me music but never made a *move*, and the boy who's *always* kissing me and calling me beautiful and whispering into my ear, on and off the ice. The boy who's here with me now, the roar of eighteen thousand years of water behind us softened by the warmth of the car, his breath hot and moist on my cheeks.

"I'm not," I say. "I mean, I wouldn't." Still, my throat feels raw around the words, and I look away.

Will sighs, the levity we shared only a minute ago leaking out through the drafts in the doors. The car engine hums, the windows fogging up in the heavy silence.

"So . . . what did you want to talk about, anyway?" I ask. "You said—"

"Yeah. Listen, I really appreciate what you did for us this season. We all do. But I can handle the team now." He refuses to meet my eyes. "The Wolfman. That's what Don Donaldson's calling me." Will stares out the window and shakes his head.

"You're . . ." My heart races, eyes water. "You're kicking me off the ice?"

Will laughs, but it's hollow and cold. "Don't worry about your ice time, Pink. I told you that before."

I don't even process his words. "That's it? I helped you guys get this far, and now that you're Don's pet *Wolfman*, it's over? You got what you wanted, so you're dropping me?"

Will finally turns to face me. Under the pale light of the

moon, his eyes shine, stung. He brushes his fingers across my cheek. "Dropping you? This is just team stuff. It has nothing to do with . . . with *us*." He leans forward to kiss me, but I turn away, my mind spinning.

Once he gets what he wants . . . Kara warned me that he'd call it off. But he's *not* calling it off. Not the way Kara meant, anyway.

"If you're not ending things between us," I say, "why do you want me to leave the team?"

"Because you should focus on your—"

"Don't say it's about my training. Or that the guys don't need help. Something else is going on. I'm not stupid. What happened tonight? Something with Dodd?"

He traces lines into the glass with his finger. "Did you see those guys in suits, sitting in the box with Dodd? My father showed up at the end."

I nod.

"The rest of them were recruiters. NHL Central Scouting."

"Will, that's . . . wow. That's amazing. Do you think they're talking to Dodd and your father about you? Trying to set something up?"

"Yep." Will taps his fingers against the window. "You ever been in a position where you have to make a choice between two things, and both of them are either really good or really bad? Like, it doesn't even matter what you do, because either way you'll have to give up something or hurt someone or ruin stuff and . . ." Will sighs and grabs my hand. "Forget it. I'm totally babbling."

"No, I know exactly what you mean." I lean back against the seat and close my eyes, thinking about Dani again. And my mother. The restaurant. Bug. Cupcakes. Skating and training and the Wolves . . . all the things I've been choosing between this winter. All the things that get left in the cold whenever I say yes to something else.

Maybe that's the lesson I'm supposed to learn from my father, the Avery legacy left with the deed to the diner when he jetted across the country without us. Whenever you make a choice, something or someone becomes the *un*chosen, and that path vanishes forever, unexplored.

Will's voice drops to a whisper. "I'm in a bad spot, Hudson."

"Why? What's going on?" I touch my hand to his face and turn him toward me. "Talk to me."

He looks at me for a long time, eyes glassy and red. "I can't."

"Will, I'm—"

"Believe me when I say it's not about you. And it's nothing crazy like drugs or cops or anything. Okay?"

I nod slowly, swallowing back the hurt. Why won't he tell me?

"It's just . . . it's all hockey stuff," he says. "Family stuff. God. I sound like one of those people who drops this big bomb looking for attention and then acts like everything's fine. I'm not trying to . . ." He closes his eyes and shakes his head.

"If you want to talk, I'm here. Okay?"

"I can't tell you the details." He slips his hand into mine again and I lean my head on his shoulder, both of us breathing softly, water pounding furiously outside, all around us. "I don't mean to be such a downer. I just wanted to say you don't have to practice with us anymore. Dodd's on my ass about everything now, and if he finds out you've been helping us . . ." He sniffs in a deep breath, but he doesn't look at me.

I hate the thought of ditching the team. I hate even more that Will is asking me to. But I knew from the first day that we couldn't tell Coach Dodd. Strictly off the record, that was the deal. And now that Dodd's more involved, and the NHL people are nosing around, I get it. I don't like it, but I get it.

I don't know what else to say to make this okay. I just know that right now, here in this beautiful white palace, I don't want either of us to feel bad anymore. My hand circles his wrist and pulls him closer. He hesitates as he turns to face me. Looks at me dead-on, eyes searching mine in the soft glow of the streetlamp over the car. He leans forward and I look at him and I say it, just a whisper. "Let's forget about everything else. Just for tonight. Just for right now."

He nods slowly and I pull him toward me and we send our obsessions away, over the Falls in an invisible barrel. Will leans against me, hair crackling in the winter air as I pull the shirt over his head. There's no more talking, sad or serious or anything else. His hands are strong as they run along my shoulders and arms, his eyes taking in my face, lips brushing the skin of my neck, whispers hot in my ear until I'm afraid my entire body will turn to mist, leaving nothing of me to bury but the long pale silk of my hair laced through his fingers.

His mouth presses against mine, soft like the gentle snow falling outside. The muscles in his back tighten beneath my hands, and then he kisses me harder. Deeper. He's done this before. Maybe a lot, even, and I let him take over—no awkward fumbling or pointless questions. With Will, I don't have to think; my mind is free to roam, just like that night at the Empire Games. Maybe it's like that for him, too, our mouths pressed together in the car, breath on skin, erasing everything else.

Beneath the weight of him, I close my eyes and let go. I run through the doors of my mind faster than I've ever run before, Will's mouth moving over my skin. Door after door after door, I crash through them all as his fingers loosen the buttons on my shirt, his hands gentle on my stomach, and then I'm gone. Out in the middle of nowhere with nothing but white ice ahead, far from my mother and Hurley's and the food critic, far from Dani and Trina's cupcakes and everything I've messed up this winter, far from school and the team and Fillmore Steel, far from my father's blogs, farther even than the old Erie Atlantic train to nowhere, running until there's nothing left behind but a darkness so black and barren that not even a memory can grow there.

But then, in the utterly cold and empty space, a light flickers. An image. A face. A smile. A tiny white scar and deep blue-gray eyes . . .

The moment is broken. I open my eyes and I'm back in the car, all the old doors shut tight and locked again, Will expertly navigating the landscape of my skin.

"Hudson?" he whispers. My gaze goes blank and fuzzy

until there's two of everything. Two lamps outside. Two gajillion years of water rushing over the edge. Two Wills hovering inches above me, waiting for me to decide what happens next.

"Sorry." I lean forward to kiss him again, to erase Josh and Mom and Dani and the competition from my mind. But he pulls away and all the bad things rush back, impossible and immense, water cascading over a frozen gorge and eroding everything in sight.

"I can't do this," he says. "This isn't . . . where *are* you right now?"

He asks me, but I can't give him an answer—not the real one. The one that admits I'm back on the ice at Fillmore, watching Josh perfect those backward crossovers. Back in my kitchen on New Year's, listening to the Addicts with him on the phone. Back at the game tonight, wrapped in that immense and secret hug while Will wasn't looking.

The spark returns, rushing through my veins, electrifying my entire body. Half-naked in the back of a car perched on the edge of Niagara Falls, I remember Kara's warnings again, how they'd secretly filled my insides with prickles of fear and loss.

But tonight, somewhere beneath this bone-white city of glass, my panic over the thought of Will ending things eroded, replaced by something much more lasting and intense:

Disappointment that he didn't.

"I'm sorry," I say. "I should get back. I have to get up early tomorrow and . . . anyway." I turn away so I don't have to see his face. His touch is light, first on my bare shoulder and then

274

my cheek, but still I don't move. He passes me my shirt and jacket. The back door opens, the dome light blinks on, and the roar of the Falls fills my ears, drowning the guilt, muting the confusion. The door clicks closed. He leans against the car while I dress, his back to me in the window.

"Are you mad?" Outside, I tug on his jacket, desperate for him to tell me no. Or yes. I don't know. Maybe that would make things easier. If he's mad at me, if he tries to make me feel guilty or calls me a tease, then I could have something to hate about him. Something to cling to, some reason to tell myself I shouldn't be messing around with a guy like Will. A guy who—no matter how technically perfect his kisses are— can't chase the cold from the inside.

"No." He smiles without showing his teeth and kisses me on the cheek, just below my eye. "I'll take you back. Come on."

Riding along the desolate I-190, I look at Will's profile in the dark, the lines of his face lit only by the moon on the bright snow, the headlights passing by and vanishing in the north-bound lane. My eyes are all over Will, his perfectly angled face, his wavy hair, his hands on the wheel, but I can't stop thinking about Josh. Wishing he was here. Wishing this was us. Wishing I could kiss him under the moonlight as the water rushed past like the hooves of a thousand horses.

"You know you have to tell him," Will says, as if he can read my mind. He looks at me straight on, eyes so dark and sad that I can't find the courage to argue. "Otherwise, what's the point of anything, right?"

I look away, vision blurring as the snow falls in white needles against the windshield and the long list of tonight's revelations finally hits me.

My gig training the Wolves is over.

My best friend has a new crush and a new crew.

And for all the time I've spent making out with hockey captain number seventy-seven Will Harper, I still couldn't outrun the truth.

I'm totally falling for Josh Blackthorn.

And I have no idea what to do about it.

Chapter Twenty

The Perfect Storms

Eggless white vanilla cupcakes
topped with a thin layer of mashed blueberries
and white meringue frosting;
dusted with powdered sugar and served chilled

Fillmore is empty and unblemished, the sky darkening to a dusty gray as I lean against the signpost and lace up my skates. They're calling for a storm, and other than the seasonally confused seagulls, I'm the only one stupid enough to hang out on the lake. Especially since the only other person who knows about this place is the one I've been dodging for two weeks.

In the wake of my championship make-out fail and subsequent realization at Niagara Falls, I've been too mortified to face Will or Josh. The morning after, Will sent out a group text announcing my retirement from special techniques coaching, and that was it. My time with the Watonka Wolves was over. Done. Since then, I've spent every lunch period alone with a PB and J and a cupcake magazine in the library. Beelined for the nearest bathroom whenever I caught either captain at my locker or truck. Ignored calls and texts and hockey party invites. Dove into the Hurley's kitchen when Josh and Frankie showed up at the front counter, wolfing down hot chocolate and cupcakes with Dani while I hid behind the safety of my mixer.

I still go to the games, but only as a spectator, sitting in the stands with the parents and siblings while Dani cheers with her new friends across the rink and rushes into Frankie's waiting embrace after every win. I've tried to talk to her at the concessions stand, but always after the first greeting and awkward smile, the silence seeps in and pushes us apart again. Even at work we hardly speak—just enough to do our jobs and keep Trick, Mom, and the waitresses in the dark.

Here at Fillmore, the wind whips against my fleece, and I lean back and shake out my arms and legs. Across the white expanse of the lake, the cold rushes me and that dead, desperate emptiness blows straight through my bones.

I know what it's like to miss someone. Despite how mad he makes me, I still miss my father. I miss the way things used to be in our family. Sometimes I even miss Kara, the way we'd calm each other before an event, laugh about it at the diner after, blowing endless bubbles into our loganberries. But I've never before missed someone that I'm physically *with* almost every day. Dani and I work side by side, sometimes for hours on end. We sit next to each other in French. We cross paths in the halls and at the hockey games. We're not outwardly fighting anymore—things are quiet. Civil. Friendly *enough*, but not friends. Every day, she looks through me and I look through her and even though it's like I'm watching her disappear right before my eyes, I can't seem to make it right between us.

After three inseparable years, my best friend and I don't know each other anymore.

I don't know if things are serious between her and Frankie—they're always together in the halls and after the games, but she doesn't call me out for a smoke break to dish the romantic details. She has no idea that whenever I see Josh, my heart beats triple time, and that I'm still too scared to tell him.

I'm clueless about Dani's big photo project, and I never saw the pictures from her dad's New Year's Eve show. I didn't get to confess my cupcake fakery, how guilty I felt when Trina raved about her Bubble-Gum Blings the following Monday in French class. She hasn't seen my father's last three blog posts from Utah, the ones I couldn't bring myself to unsubscribe from. She didn't get the in-person demo of RustBob SpareParts, the robot that Bug finally put together from all that old computer stuff.

And Dani doesn't know about the thing that's tearing a hole in my heart, shredding my dreams. I try to ignore it, to let it pass, but it always comes back, standing on my chest, breathing against my throat.

Doubt.

Despite all my so-called natural talent, the unimaginable potential, my months of retraining, and an intense *wanting* like nothing I've ever felt in my life, some part of me believes that I'm really *not* good enough. That in seven days I'll pour my soul out on the ice for those foundation judges, and sit in the kiss-and-cry room as I wait for the scores that will change my life. . . .

And the numbers won't even come close.

The wind shifts over the lake, pelting my eyes with frigid wetness. Storm's coming. Fifteen minutes, tops.

Just as I've done a hundred times this winter, I recheck my laces and slide out to the center of the runoff, but suddenly, it doesn't seem far enough, daring enough, challenging enough to prove I have what it takes. The wind howls in my ears and I swear I can hear old Lola again, pushing me, reminding me how hard it is to stand out, to truly compete.

Ignoring the warning in my head, I rush forward, faster, racing to the edge where the shallow meets the lake. The cold seeps through my clothes and I glide out farther, slipping over the border from safe to unknown. Across the lake, Canada vanishes beneath a white curtain. The forbidden thrill of imminent danger rises hot from my toes to the top of my head, propelling me farther still. I close my eyes and throw my head back, big impossible flakes landing on my face and blotting out the sound, and for a moment, everything is still. I'm trapped in a giant snow globe, bound to the surface of the ice, nothing left to do but wait for someone to upturn and shake the world, set me back on my feet, and watch the sky fall.

Maybe I've always been waiting for that.

"Hudson!" My name floats on the wind, but it's far away,

or maybe just an echo in my head from a time when things were better, and I ignore it, skating closer to the white wall of the storm against every ounce of logic in my mind. *Hudson Avery, do you have what it takes? . . .*

"Hey—back! You're—far and—I can't—the ice . . ." The words are distant and broken; bright red berries dropped in the snow and carried off by the winter gulls. I barely comprehend that it's not a memory, that someone is speaking to me. I close my eyes. My body wants to keep going, the ghosts of Fillmore beckoning me into the abyss like some evil thing.

"Hudson!" It comes once more, then again, loud and distinct. "Hudson Avery! Come back here!"

Josh.

The words reach me deep inside, shake me out of my fog. I open my eyes and turn toward the sound of his voice, so suddenly grateful he's here. Whatever we are now, whatever we aren't, God I missed the sound of his laugh, the swish of our skates as we carved up the ice together.

This is it. Now or never. I have to tell him. I have to skate right up to him, look into his eyes, and confess. *I listen to your music every night. I close my eyes and replay that postgame hug like a movie and feel it even now, weeks later, my insides still buzzing with the memory. I smile when I picture you doing those crossovers, eating my cupcakes, making my brother laugh. I don't care that you're unreadable and I don't care what anyone says about me and Will and you and Abby, because I can't stop thinking about you. . . .*

I take a deep breath and set my toe pick against the ice,

ready to rush back to shore, back to safety and Josh and whatever comes next. But in that simple movement, the minuscule transfer of pressure from one foot to another, the whole world changes.

I feel it before I hear it, ice moaning softly under my feet. Then there's a crack, a quick snap like the breaking of a brittle bone.

My stomach bottoms out and Josh shouts across the distance, his voice cutting through the pulse of blood, the whoosh of my life passing before me. The ice creaks again and I can't move. Legs immobilized, breath a series of small white bursts as Josh skids to a stop on the lake, just out of reach.

"Hudson, listen to me." He's close now, voice gentle. Soothing. The promise of a warm bath and a crackling fire. "You're fine," he says. "You have to trust me. Do you trust me?"

"Yes," I whisper.

"I can't come any closer. You have to come to me. As carefully as possible, lie flat on your stomach." Josh gets to his knees and motions for me to lie down. "Do it now."

I hold my breath, certain that taking in any more air will upset the balance, that the weight of one more snowflake will send me plummeting. I kneel slowly. The lake moans and I stop, hands flat in front of me as the water rushes beneath, humming through solid ice.

"Stretch out a little more. You have to get on your stomach."

"I can't." I mouth the words. Anything louder will shatter the ice.

"Yes, you can. You're okay. Keep your eyes on mine. Look at me. Look—Hudson—no, right here. I'm getting you out of this, okay? I promise."

"But my arms are sh-shaking. I c-c-can't—"

"Do it, Hudson! Stop screwing around! Just shut up and do *exactly* what I say!"

The panic in his voice sets me on high alert. I take a deep breath, hold it, and press myself flat against the ice.

"Use your arms and legs to inch forward. Go slow. Keep your eyes here." He points to his eyes and I follow his instructions, moving a millimeter at a time, gaze locked on his for all eternity.

"Reach, Hudson. Just a little more. Come *on*!"

My resolve fades and I shiver again, inside and out. Cold and fear suffocate me from all sides. The ice cracks against my ribs like fingers reaching up through the cold and I start to cry and I wonder if the deep blue-gray eyes of Watonka Wolves varsity co-captain number fifty-six Josh Blackthorn will be the very last thing I see before . . .

"Gotcha!" Josh wraps his hand around my wrist and pulls, dragging me as he inches backward. His grip is tight, energy seeping into my limbs. I rise to a crawl, slow at first, faster as we shuffle on hands and knees toward the safety of the runoff. When we reach the edge where the ice ends and the ground begins, Josh stands and tugs me so hard that he slips backward into the snow. I collapse on top of him. I know I should get up but my arms and legs won't cooperate and all I can feel is his heart banging against mine like the first time we met, tumbling together on the ice. I'm still crying and he's shaking beneath me as the wind rushes us, full force.

"I just . . . I thought you . . ." He's breathing hard and jagged, holding me firm against his chest. "Jesus, Hudson. What were you . . . why did . . . *God.*" He takes my face into his gloved hands and I close my eyes, cutting off the tears.

The wind roars across the ice and chokes me with another gale, wet and sharp on my skin. Josh grabs my hands and pulls us up and together we fight our way through the swirling white gusts, collecting my backpack and boots, clomping through deep, heavy snow to the rusted outer building of the mill. We don't stop until we're inside, shielded from the bitter bite of the wind, thrown suddenly into blackness.

"We have to wait it out," Josh says, trying to catch his breath. He pulls off his hat and rubs the snow from his hair and we both look around, eyes adjusting to the dark.

The ground floor is mostly empty. Steel bones jut out from walls lined with white veins, ever-widening cracks where the outside light leaks in. When the wind blows, puffs of snow slip through the gaps, piling up on the floor like loose powder.

I sit on an old wooden crate and change out of my skates, grateful for my boots and an extra pair of wool socks stuffed in the bottom of my bag.

The mill feels hollow and haunted, black inside, the faint clangs of old metal ringing like a ghost ship adrift at sea. The sadness of the place snatches at my soul and I shiver.

Ten minutes ago, Josh saved my life.

"Why did you come?" I ask. "I haven't seen you out here lately, and things have been . . . we haven't talked in a while."

Josh pulls off his gloves and blows hot breath into his hands. "Not since you stopped working with the team. Will isn't saying anything about it, so I decided to stalk you today until you tell me what's going on."

"So you *are* a stalker. I knew it." I smile. I missed this—our easy and familiar banter, still there beneath the sparks.

"I stopped by the restaurant but the pink-haired waitress—Nat, I think?—she told me you'd left already."

"Yeah, I asked her to cover my shift."

"I figured I'd find you here," Josh says. "Only *you'd* be crazy enough to skate Fillmore today. Not that I expected to find you on the actual lake, but—hey, what's wrong?" His eyes are soft and warm, two bright lights in all the darkness. My heart fills with a mixture of happiness and dread, the craziness of the last few weeks finally catching up. I open my mouth to speak, but my throat tightens, tears spilling from my eyes as I think about falling through the ice again. He wraps himself around me and presses my head to his chest.

"You see the videos," I say absently, "but you never think it'll happen to you. If you weren't out there today . . ."

He kisses me on the forehead, caressing my cheeks with his thumbs. "But I was. And you're lucky I've seen a lot of those survival shows."

"With the guy who eats bugs?"

"Precisely."

"You're such a boy. No wonder my brother likes you."

"Your brother likes me? Score!"

"Score if you like robots, army men, and hamsters."

Josh laughs. "Who doesn't?"

Grateful for the levity, I pull away from him and heft my backpack over my shoulder. "Just so you know, I have a granola bar, half a thermos of hot—well, cold by now—chocolate, and some slightly mashed cupcakes. I'm not eating any bugs."

"Good to know. Watch where you step." Josh reaches for my hand, gingerly leading me across the building to another large room, where a bunch of desks and file cabinets line the perimeter, covered in junk and cobwebs. On one end, a rusty sign hangs over a doorway, crooked on a single hinge: DANGER—HOT ACIDS!

"This place is so strange." I swipe a finger over an old desk, leaving a clean line in the dust. "It's like they all just got up and left. Nobody packed or took stuff away or knocked it down. It's just . . ."

"Abandoned."

The wind slams into the wall outside, and the entire building moans and shudders against the onslaught. I shiver and retie my scarf, memories slipping through my head like snow through the cracks in the walls. The horrible, slushy sound of the lake beneath the ice. The frozen expanse cracking against my ribs. Everything changing in an instant. How could I be so reckless? Ten more seconds and—

"Hudson?"

"Sorry." I shove my hands in my fleece pockets, momentarily comforted by the familiar crinkle of Lola's foundation letter. "I was just . . . do you think this place is haunted?"

"Nah, it's not like everyone *died* here. They probably thought it would reopen and they'd get their jobs back. There's tons of places like this in Ohio, too. Welcome to the Rust Belt." Josh picks up a weathered jar of something that looks like bright pink cat litter, but is probably one of the aforementioned HOT ACIDS.

"Careful with that," I say. "There's a reason all the fish around here have two heads and no eyes."

"Ah, good point." Delicately, he sets it back on the shelf next to a row of similarly filled containers, some pink like his and others gray or white. "Help me look through the drawers. We need matches or a lighter or something."

I rummage through file drawers and cubbies until I find an old Zippo lighter with a World Trade Center emblem, *9-11-2001* etched on the back. Obviously, we're not the first urban explorers to visit the place since its closure, though I can't think of anyone who'd willingly hang out here other than Dani, who'd probably shoot a thousand pictures in this creep-tastic corner alone.

I wish I could tell her about it.

Josh drags a metal trash can over near an opening in the wall and fills it with paper and dead leaves and any other dry material we can safely identify as not a HOT ACID. He starts the fire easily with the lighter, gray smoke billowing up toward the glassless window frames.

"Nice job, Boy Scout." I rub my hands over the flames. "If we had a can of beans and a harmonica, we'd rock this joint hobo-style."

"Pull another stunt like that on the ice and I'll throw your ass on the next coal train myself. Then you'll know hobo-style." He sits on a large, empty worktable. "What were you doing that far out, anyway?"

I stash my backpack under the table and take a seat next to him. "I . . . don't know. I was skating on the runoff, then I felt like . . . like I wanted to go . . . away. Something was daring me, and I couldn't get far enough. Crazy, right? It's like I was trying to skate to Canada."

The fire reflects in his eyes, and in the soft orange glow of the flames, he looks older. Serious. "Hudson—"

"Thanks for . . . you know. Out there. What you did." I shudder when I think about it again, imagining the rescue squad fishing me out, blue and gone. Josh explaining to my mom what happened. That he tried, but couldn't save me . . .

The tears creep back into my eyes but I force them away. "Hungry?" I hop off the table and grab my bag. "We can have a two-course lunch, assuming you actually *prefer* cupcakes and granola bars to insects."

"It's an emergency," he says. "I'll make do. But can I ask you a question?"

"As long as it's not about eating bugs."

Josh slides off the table and finds some more cardboard for the fire, dusting his hands together over the popping flames. "You doing okay? I mean, are you warm enough?" *Pop pop pop.*

"I'm fine. Still kind of freaked out, but I'm warm." I resume my place on the table and dig out the goodies. "The fire was a good idea."

"Good." He sits next to me and takes a cupcake from the Tupperware balanced on my lap, our legs touching. *Pop.*

"Yeah." *Pop pop . . . pop.*

"I just wanted to make sure you weren't freezing."

"I'm okay." *Pop.* "It's comfortable."

"Good," he says.

"Not too hot, not too—"

"What's going on with you and Harper?"

POP!

"Nothing." I keep my eyes fixed on the flames.

"So you guys are just . . . hanging out?"

W.W.H.D.? Hester? Any ideas? No?

"Not exactly," I say. *Come on, Hud. Now's your chance. Tell him.* "We're not . . . we kind of . . . it's not like he was my boyfriend or anything." I unwrap my cupcake and toss the paper into the fire, wishing I could channel the fearless determination I felt on the ice the moment I heard his voice. The second before the ice cracked and everything changed. "Anyway, what about you? How's, um, Abby? Angie? What's her name?"

Oh, Hudson. Your suavity is an example to all.

"Abby?" Josh's forehead crinkles. "She's . . . she's good."

289

"She doesn't go to Watonka High, right? How did you guys meet?"

"I see you didn't get the memo." Josh laughs, and then his face turns serious. He looks at me a moment longer, like he's trying to decide how to break the girlfriend news, or how much of his secret relationship he wants to reveal.

He takes a deep breath and rubs his head. "Okay, here's the story. Abby and I go *way* back. We basically met in the hospital when we were born."

"You've known this girl your entire life? Like, literally?" That's flat-out no competition right there. Born on the same day, in the same hospital? They're practically soul mates.

"Yep."

"Whoa. So do you . . . does she . . . um . . ."

"Abby's my sister, Hudson. We're twins."

"Oh thank God! I mean, thank God . . . that you . . . have a sister . . . what a special . . . um . . . napkin?" I pass it over and jam half a cupcake in my mouth to prevent the release of any more stupidity. A sister? He has a sister? And all this time, I thought she was his girlfriend? How hard *did* I hit my head that first day on the ice?

I meet his eyes and he smiles, my stomach launching into its own triple/triple combo.

"It's kind of complicated." Josh downs the rest of his cupcake and tosses the paper into the fire. "I don't talk about it much. I guess I figured Will told you or something."

I shake my head.

"Ever seen *Rain Man*?"

"Mmm-hmm." And that's the most intelligent thing I've said all morning.

"It's kind of like that with my sister. She's, like, off the charts brilliant, but she's super-particular about order and rules. My mom homeschools her. Abby likes it, but she gets a little stir-crazy. That's why she calls me all the time. It's never urgent—just stuff like what happened on *General Hospital* or which neighbor she saw taking out the trash in their bathrobe. But if I don't answer right away, she freaks. Half the time I'm just calming her down, reassuring her I'll be home later. It gets intense. My mom had to get permission from the school so I could keep my phone on during class. Thing is, she'd probably be better off in a place with full-time care, where they could work with her one-on-one. But we don't want to do that to her. She's ours, you know?"

I think about Bug, how I dumped him off with Mrs. Ferris this morning, how he hugged me and waved and pushed up his glasses without a word of protest. I can't picture him *not* being Bug, not being okay, not being home with us.

"How do you . . . I mean, do you guys take her out on weekends or whatever? Do other stuff? Or does she have to stay at home?"

"We go out sometimes. She does okay—depends on the situation. Hockey games are too much for her—she doesn't like the goal buzzer. But she's hung out with me at Amir's a few times. She does better when it's just a few people. Oh, and she doesn't like Will. Too much talking freaks her out."

I laugh. "I don't blame her. Sounds like you guys are close, though. That's cool."

"Abby's seriously my best friend." Josh smiles. "I tell her pretty much everything. We talk about hockey and school and . . . well, whatever. Stuff."

"What stuff?"

"Nothing."

"No, what were you gonna say?"

Josh's face reddens, the tips of his ears as bright as the flames. He stands to stoke the fire with a loose hunk of metal, his back to me. "Okay, so I told her about you, right? How you helped the team, how we've been skating a few times, even about the cupcakes. And now she won't leave it alone. 'How's Hudson, where's Hudson, are you skating today, what does she look like, where does she live, how many cupcakes can she bake in one hour, what's her favorite color, when can I meet her—'"

"Blake Street. My record is two forty in an hour, but they weren't very good. Purple." I take a deep, silent breath as the fire sparks. "And I'd be honored to meet her."

Josh drops the makeshift fire poker and crosses the space between us in two steps, hands gripping my arms. I look up to meet his eyes, serious and determined and the rarest, most intense colors I've ever seen. It's like I'm on the lake again, the rest of the world fuzzing out around the edges, the beauty of his eyes the only thing left. I lean closer, our gaze unbroken, fire crackling and warming the air around us. He swallows and then he's there, right before me. My heart slams into my ribs and my neck goes hot and I close my eyes just as our lips brush and my breath catches and . . .

And Josh pulls away.

"I'm sorry," he whispers, hands sliding down my arms. "Sh— I'm so sorry, Hudson. I didn't mean . . . you and Will . . . I was so . . . not . . . thinking." He rubs his head, his eyes everywhere but on my face.

"Josh, it's okay, I'm not—"

"Can we just . . . can we pretend that didn't happen?" He crosses to the other side of the fire and slumps in an old office chair, the swivel kind with wheels and an adjustable back, and presses his fists into his thighs.

Across the room, the fire is strong between us as he stares at the dusty, broken floor, and my heart rages against his words. After weeks of mixed signals and crossed wires, he finally kissed me—tried to, anyway. And now he wants to pretend it didn't happen?

The wind pelts the walls with a blast of wet ice and his foot bounces on the ground, chair twisting back and forth.

I stand and cross the room. "Will isn't . . . can we—"

"No. I better . . ." He's out of the chair before I get to him. "I'm gonna get some air. I'll be back. I promise."

He doesn't go too far—the shape of him blackens the bright spot of the doorway where we first came in. He pulls the hat from his back pocket and yanks it over his head, look-ing out across the great white bleakness, and I curl up on the desk and watch the flames, trying to figure out how to rewind and instant replay the last few minutes. This time, when our lips brush, I'll lean into him and pull him close. This time, I won't let him talk. I won't let him apologize. I won't let him go.

As Josh dips in and out of the doorway, I unzip my bag and dig out my thermos and the smashed granola bar, occupying myself by making cold chocolate oatmeal in my mouth. I pace the perimeter of the room, tracing lines in the dust on all the desks. I peel swaths of paint from the walls, olive green, probably laced with lead. Toss rocks and metal chips into the standing half of a cracked porcelain sink behind the HOT ACIDS sign. Flip through decaying manuals on treating burns and chemical wounds. Throw paper time cards into the fire, one at a time, yellow flames sizzling like Trick's grill as all the old work hours turn into ash.

"It finally stopped snowing."

I drop the remaining cards and turn around.

"Should we chance it?" Josh asks, rubbing the chill from his hands. He looks at me a moment, and it's like I can read his thoughts as they flash behind his eyes. *No. Let's stay. We'll stay up all night talking about the funniest movies and the best place to get hot wings and what happens at the end of the world, and in the morning, everything will be sparkly and bright, and no one will ever know about this place but us, our forever winter secret.*

"Josh, can we—"

"Yeah. I mean no, you're right." He scoops some snow into the trash can, fire hissing into wet dust. "I just thought . . .

nah, we should head out while we can. Car's buried, though. We'll have to walk."

Josh stomps down a path outside. He looks back at me and smiles, cheeks red from the cold, eyes sparkling like the unblemished whiteness behind him as I reluctantly follow. Together, we make our way through snow-covered streets as the good neighbors of Watonka emerge from their homes to help one another clear footpaths and dig cars from the drifts.

Everyone waves and smiles and asks if we're okay, and yeah, maybe we're fine, just like Josh tells them, but I can't shake that moment in the Fillmore building, Josh's lips brushing mine by the fire. The weight of it sits between us like a magnetic force, drawing us close, then pushing us apart. Is he imagining what it would be like to kiss me again? Or does he wish he could take it all back? Is he really, truly *sorry*?

I stop in the middle of the white street and step in front of him, his jaw set, eyes far away. My voice is rough and my mouth dry, but this much, I know: Josh Blackthorn saved my life. And then he tried to kiss me. No matter what happens next, I'm *not* letting this turn into another two weeks of silence, the entire history of us summed up in a series of near misses and almosts just because neither of us had the snowballs to say anything.

"Feel like stopping at Hurley's for hot chocolate?" I ask. "Hang out with me for a while?"

"Hmm." He finally meets my gaze, his shy, playful smile slowly returning. "With or without marshmallows?"

"With. *Duh*."

"You got yourself a deal, Avery."

We settle in at the front counter and Nat brings us two mugs of hot chocolate with double marshmallows. One sip, and that's it—I can't hold it in another second. "Josh, me and Will . . . we're not together. We hung out for a little while, but it's over. *Over* over."

Josh stares into his mug, dunking the marshmallows one at a time with his spoon. "That's cool, Hud. You didn't have to—"

"Hudson! There you are!" Mom bursts out of the kitchen, practically rocket-launching herself onto the counter to reach me. "I was so worried about you with the storm and—"

"I'm fine. I was . . . we hid out at . . . Sharon's Café. Just until it passed." I look at Josh for confirmation and he nods.

"Next time, answer your phone." Mom runs her hand over my head, her gaze slowly shifting to the adjacent seat. As soon as she notices Josh, her face lights up. "You must be Hudson's boyfriend! I'm so glad to finally meet you."

"*Ma!*"

"I'm Beth, her mom."

Josh takes her outstretched hand, not correcting her on the boyfriend thing. "Nice to meet you. I'm Josh. Hudson and I are . . . we know each other from school."

Mom smiles, checking him out. Meanwhile, my head is about to explode like a marshmallow in the microwave, but no one around here seems too concerned.

"I'm sorry to interrupt," she finally says, "but can I see you in the office when you're done, Hud? I'm putting in the meat order and I want you to learn how it's done."

"Meat order. Awesome." That's what I get for dropping by Hurley's when I'm not on the clock. "Be right there."

Mom disappears into the kitchen and I bury my head in my hands, willing myself to apparate to Parallel Hudson's world. Olympic training, product endorsements, Ice Capades . . . wherever she is, it's got to be better than this.

"Hudson." There's a hand on my back, warm and solid. Slowly, I unfold my arms, and Josh leans in close to whisper in my ear. "Come to the game tomorrow night."

Goose bumps roll across my skin, and I shiver.

"Come to the game," he whispers again, "and then have dinner with me after. Just us. I know a cool place."

I look into his eyes, my heart speeding up like it did the moment his lips touched mine. "Not Hurley's?"

"Definitely not Hurley's."

"In that case, you got yourself a deal, Blackthorn."

"So now you're making fun of me, huh?"

"Never. Well, maybe a little. But mostly never."

"Good. See you on the ice tomorrow, then. The *indoor* ice. Better yet, the *sidelines* of the indoor ice. I'm not taking any chances with you. Got it, Avery?" He pulls on his gloves, his eyes never leaving mine.

"Josh, I—"

"Hudson?" Trick yells from the little window over the

grill, examining his slotted spatula as if he wasn't spying on me. "Your mom wants to get that order wrapped up, hon."

"Thanks for keeping such great tabs on her schedule. Tell her I'll be right in." I look at Josh. "You okay to get home?"

"I'll ask one of the neighbors to dig me out." He zips up his jacket and heads outside, bound for the snow-covered path back to Fillmore. I drop our chocolate-coated mugs and spoons in the bus bin, my heart light, my insides buzzing and alive.

Can we pretend that didn't happen?

Not a chance, Blackthorn. Not a chance.

Chapter Twenty-One

Woolly Mammoth Freeze-Outs

*Chilled chocolate cupcakes with chocolate buttercream icing
rolled in dark chocolate, milk chocolate,
and white chocolate shavings*

Half an hour before the face-off against the Fairplay Sharks, Baylor's is humming, air heavy with the smell of buttered popcorn and anticipation. I grab a hot chocolate from the concessions stand and find a seat near the center line, away from the influx of random new spectators, away from Ellie and Kara and the rest of the hockey wives. Dani's next to a few girls I've seen at the parties, but if she notices me, she doesn't acknowledge it.

Down behind the player's box, Will's local news fan club sets up their equipment, panning across the crowd for the folks watching from home. Even Dodd's got more guests tonight—a bunch of stuffy VIP-looking dudes in suits, all shaking hands with Will's father. Probably the recruiting squad.

I swirl the hot liquid in my cup, heat radiating against my palm. Everyone is glowing, all of them clinging to an unfaltering, unified hope, and when the boys skate out across the ice and wave to their newly adoring fans, the murmurs in the stands give way to a thunderous roar. My heart races as Josh brings up the end of the line, and when he spots me in the stands and raises his stick in the air, my head spins.

I know I'm not part of the practices anymore, but now, as they glide around the rink in their blue-and-silver jerseys in perfect formation, the crowd stomping its collective feet, my whole body tingles with pride. Not to get all mama bear, but it seems like only yesterday the pups were stumbling out of the box, lumbering over the ice with all the grace of bricks.

Tonight they're playing in the semis, heading for the finals, breaking records with the unlikeliest, craziest, most insane comeback in the entire history of Watonka High. Even if they lose this game, they've still performed miracles. When everyone else told them they couldn't do it, they marched out to the rink, banged their sticks on the ice, and raised the dead.

Cheers to that, wolf pack.

I raise my cardboard cup to the ice and take another swig, whipped cream tickling my lips. Down on the rink, the opposition slides out to a boo-hiss symphony, and the starters on both sides line up for the face-off.

The whistle blows. The puck drops. And it's on.

Josh takes it first, cutting across the ice and slapping the puck down the rails to Rowan. Two more passes between them, one back to Gettysburg, back to Rowan, sliding into Sharks territory, over to Josh, Josh lays back to take the shot, but Will cuts across and nabs the puck, shoots hard, and scores, right between the goalie's skates.

First goal of the game, less than two minutes in.

Will dominates the ice again, weaving in and out of the Sharks' defensive line, the tightest turns I've ever seen him pull. When the other team steals the puck, Will steals it right back. He's keeping it away from the Sharks, but he's also keeping it away from his own guys. They're total showboat moves, and in the final seconds of the first period, the opposing defensive line swipes the puck, sends it down the ice, and scores.

One to one at the first intermission, and Coach Dodd calls Will over for a private conference. Dodd's hands flail around, his face red and blotchy, and Will's shoulders slump. Dodd hasn't paid much attention to Will's technique all season, but when you're backed by a pack of recruiters, priorities apparently change. Will should know better. Playing the showman card won't score him any points with the suit committee.

At the start of the second, Frankie snags the puck from the Sharks' center and slaps it to Josh. Josh takes it down the line, passes it to Micah, back to Josh at the Sharks' net. Josh shoots and scores, right over the goalie's shoulder, setting off a crushing roar through the stadium. My heart speeds up each time the boys skate back to the center line, and for the entire game, even though I'm sitting alone with no glittery signs or wolf-ear headbands or blue-and-silver flags, I cheer as loud as I can.

The Wolves are on fire, but Dodd lays into Will again at the next intermission. Josh stands behind them on the ice, bracing against the force of Dodd's secondhand rage. By the time they line up for third period, both co-captains are on edge, elbowing each other as the ref drops the puck.

The score is tied three-three, and in the last five minutes of the game, a chant rises in the stands. By the time it reaches me, it morphs into a song, and soon the entire arena is belting out the chorus to Warren Zevon's "Werewolves of London," changing the words to "Wolves of Watonka," which doesn't have the same lyrical ring, but gets the point across.

The boys are completely pumped.

With one minute on the clock, Amir saves a goal and passes the puck to Luke, who brings it up to Brad, who sends it up to Josh, safely out of Wolves territory. I stomp my feet and sing the wolf song with the crowd, and in the final seconds, Will swipes the puck from Josh, charges ahead, crosses the Wolves' blue line, the red line, the Sharks' blue line, pulls his stick back, and slaps the puck straight at the goalie, straight through his gloves, straight into the net.

The buzzer sounds.

The game is over.

The formerly untrainable, apathetic, obnoxious, and most losingest team in history has just won the semifinals, four to three.

The wolf pack is going to the finals.

I push my way down to the ice, the boys smashed together in a free-form mosh pit, sticks high in the air. I dodge between groups of parents and step out onto the rink in my boots, scanning the crowd for Josh.

Both co-captains hang behind the pack, just out of reach of the celebratory crush. I slide closer. Will is surrounded by Dodd and the suit committee, news guy Don Donaldson edging in with a mic and a cameraman.

"Will, is it true that your coach is already fielding interest from NHL Central Scouting?" Don asks.

"We're looking at our options," Dodd answers for him. It's the first time I've heard him speak actual words all season. "No comment at this time."

"What about you, gentlemen?" Don asks the suits. "Like what you saw out there tonight?"

"No comment at this time," Dodd says again, nodding curtly at the camera and ushering his well-dressed buddies off the ice. Without so much as a congratulatory smile, Will's father goes with them, disappearing behind the stands.

Will turns to skate away, too, but Josh grabs his jersey and yanks him close, their helmets almost touching.

"Josh!" I slide over to them in my boots, trying not to stumble on the ice. "Stop! What are you doing?"

Josh sees me and loosens his grip. "Go ahead," he says to Will. "Tell her about your godfather."

"But . . ." I look from captain to captain. "Dodd? That's what you're fighting—"

"You *knew* about him?" Josh's eyes blaze.

"I didn't think it was a big deal," I say, utterly lost. "Will didn't like to talk about it, so . . . what's *up* with you guys tonight? You just won the semis!"

Josh skates close to me, face red, eyes darker than I've ever seen them. "You two have been scheming together this whole season, and you're asking *me* what's up?"

"What are you talking—"

"That's it, Blackthorn," Will says. "I'm benching you next game. Keep it up, you're out for the rest of the playoffs."

"You're the coach now, too?" Josh shoves Will's shoulder. "Was that part of your sweet little deal with Dodd?"

I wedge myself between them and try to grab Will's arm, but he dives around me, slamming Josh against the glass. I wave for Amir, but the rest of the pack is still hugging and fist-bumping on the center line, oblivious.

"Will, what are you doing?" I shout. "Back off!"

Will lets out a sarcastic laugh. "That's not what you *usually* say."

Josh's face changes from red to ice-white to red again, Will's cocky smirk undoing everything I said at Hurley's yesterday. All the promises I made, the moments between us, erased in the heat of some stupid, testosterone-fueled misunderstanding.

"Josh, don't listen to—"

"Was Hudson part of the package, too?" Josh asks. "Bonus for selling us out? Dodd's really got the hookup, huh?"

Will tells a hundred more lies with a single suggestive

look, but his smirk falls when he sees my face. Something like regret flickers behind his eyes, and then the wall goes back up between us, cold and solid.

"Jealous, Blackthorn?" Will spits at the ice, and suddenly, Josh winds up for a swing. Amir is next to me in a millisecond, the other boys close behind. Before Josh can connect, Amir hip-checks him into the glass, and the rest of the team swarms us, Amir holding Josh while Rowan and Brad pull Will across the ice, back to the locker room.

"What the hell is going on?" I ask Josh, voice shaking. "What do you mean, scheming? And why are you letting Will get under your skin?"

Josh shakes his head, panting and red-faced. I reach out for his hand, but he turns on me, speed skating his way to the other side of the rink, melting into the crush behind the stands before I can ask any more questions.

"Hudson?" Dani pushes through the tangle of undisturbed and still-singing fans. "Are you okay?"

"I'm . . . that came out of nowhere." I shake my head, shock coursing through my veins. Everything happened so fast, a flash hailstorm on the ice. "I don't . . . can we sit for a sec?"

She nods, and I follow her back to the seats at floor level, collapsing into the first empty chair I find. She joins Frankie a few feet behind me.

"You okay?" Kara loops her purse over the chair next to me and sits, face lined with genuine concern. "What happened out there?"

"Will and Josh got into it. Something about Dodd." It's all I can manage without breaking down.

Kara sighs. "Hud, I don't mean to sound like—"

"So don't." I close my eyes. "Sorry. I'm just not in the mood for 'I told you so' right now."

"I wasn't. I just . . . I meant what I told you that day. Be careful with Will. He's got a lot going on, and I don't think he's being honest with the guys about what he wants for the team. He's not—"

"This isn't about me and Will. You have no idea, okay?" My voice wavers, and I close my mouth, willing her to go away. Why is she the one trying to protect me while my best friend is cuddling up with Frankie? Why didn't Dani sit next to me? Why didn't I ask her to?

Kara stands and grabs her purse from the back of the chair. "I just don't want you to get hurt over this. That's all." She watches me a moment longer, but when I don't respond, she finally says good-bye, following the crowd toward the exit in search of Ellie and her other friends.

"Heading home?" I ask Dani.

She looks toward the exit, then back to me. "We're . . . um . . . we're supposed to go for wings after the guys get changed. Do you . . . you could come if you want."

"Maybe I'll catch up later."

"You sure?" Dani asks.

No. I'm not sure. I'm not sure if I'll catch up later. I'm not sure if I want to go out for wings with you and Kara and Ellie, everyone laughing and chatting like this didn't just happen, you and the hockey wives inseparable now. I'm not sure if I want to sit here and wait for Josh to come out of the locker room, try to talk to him again. I'm not sure if I want to scream at Will or ignore him. I'm not sure if you even want me around or if you just feel sorry for me. I'm not sure of anything.

"Yes," I tell her. "Definitely sure."

She squeezes my shoulder and for a second I think she might stay, convince me to go out with her or insist on ditching her plans. Look me straight in the eye, fold her arms over her chest, and call me out. *Talk to me, girl,* she'll say. *Spill it.*

But she just sighs and slips behind me, weaving her way to the exit where the other girls wait.

When I turn around again, they're gone.

Fresh snow blankets the parking lot, but my truck is totally clear, ready to go. Far from the crowds of Baylor's, Will leans against my driver's side door, jacket sleeves coated in snow, waiting.

"I'm sorry, okay?" he says when I get close. He's got his boots and coat on, but underneath it all, he's still wearing his hockey gear. His eyes are glassy, cheeks red from the cold. "I totally messed up. I tried to . . ." He motions toward my clean windshield.

"And now you think I want to hear anything out of your mouth? Just because you brushed the snow off my truck? Excuse me." I push him aside and jam my key in the door lock.

"Let me explain. Please, Hudson."

Behind us, a car crunches over a snow-packed section of the lot, speeding up and spinning into a donut on the vacant other end, the tracks making slippery black snakes in the white-gray slush.

"Two minutes," I say.

Will sticks his hands in his pockets. "I didn't tell you the whole story about Coach Dodd."

"I got that much, Will. Clock's ticking."

"Okay." Will shakes his head, eyes closed as he blows out an icy breath. "All year, my father kept laying into Dodd about giving up on hockey, giving up on me, spending all his time with the football guys. So one night after spaghetti dinner, Dodd looks at my dad and says he's got an idea. Best of both worlds for everyone."

"Why does this feel like an episode of *Friday Night Lights*?"

"It kind of is. Remember I told you Dodd wanted Watonka to drop the hockey program? I was supposed to help make it happen. That was my end of the deal. We already sucked, so all I had to do was keep the team losing and demotivated, and by next season, the school would drop us officially. In exchange, Dodd would hook me up with his recruiting connections."

"On about ten different levels, that makes *no* sense." I look beyond the parking lot to the black silhouette of the steel plant, smokestacks pointing their accusatory fingers into the sky. "If your whole team sucked, why would recruiters look at you?"

"Why does anything happen in this world, Hud? These

guys are Dodd's college buddies. I just had to be good enough to show I was a talented player stuck on a losing team. I could still get noticed if the recruiters saw potential, and Dodd would make sure of that. In return, he wanted the Wolves to crash and burn. I didn't want to screw over the team, but I wasn't about to pass up my one chance to get out of here."

For sure, for real, just like everyone says.

"So you took the deal."

Will nods, drawing circles in the frost on the rusty hood. "But then Josh told me about you, and I got this idea. I thought . . . okay, if this girl can help us train, we might win a few games without Dodd. He could stay with the football team. And chances are we'd still get canceled anyway, but at least I could avoid selling out my friends, and instead of being known as the one talented guy on a suck-ass team, I'd be the guy who led a suck-ass team to break a ten-year losing streak with a couple of unexpected wins."

"Ah. Nice to know your ego hasn't suffered any critical blows this season."

"No, that's just it." Will steps right in front of me. "After a few games, my ego checked out. We came together as a team. For the first time in three years, I felt like I was part of something bigger. Like we could really do this. Win—not just a few games, but a lot of games. Dodd kept pressuring me to tone it down, but he couldn't do anything about it in public. I dodged him for weeks, but tonight, he finally lost it. I was so mad after first period, I just took over the game. I wanted to show Dodd what I could do without him, but that made everything worse. I screwed my friends, embarrassed my father, and Dodd completely freaked. It was like he forgot there were people around."

"Josh overheard?"

"Yep."

I stomp my boots on the ground to warm my numb feet. "Did you explain to him about Dodd and your father?"

Will shakes his head. "You saw what happened after the win. Josh laid into me, and I was so upset about Dodd, and when I saw you looking at Josh like . . . like you *always* look at Josh . . . I don't know. I flipped. I lost it. I'm sorry." Will looks into my eyes, his voice soft and sincere. There's no award-winning toothpaste commercial smile, no expensive cologne, no charmingly cheesy one-liners, no soft and distracting kisses. "You did so much for the team. For me. You're actually kind of . . . amazing. Just like Josh always said."

"Josh isn't . . ." *Was Hudson part of the package, too?*

"Hudson?" He pulls me toward him again, but I press my hand against his chest, holding him back.

"I can't do this."

He sighs and leans in to kiss my cheek, close to my lips, sending a familiar zing across my skin. But it doesn't last; it slips out into the night air, disappearing with Will. He gets into his car, reverses out of the spot, and vanishes down the road, brake lights fading into tiny red specks, the deep gray hole in my chest going black around the edges.

I turn my face to the sky. Heavy, wet snowflakes pelt my

cheeks, sticking in my eyelashes until I blink them away. How can I be upset with Will when he was just doing what he had to do to secure his future? To find his own golden ticket out of here?

I don't even know what's important anymore. What's worth fighting for, even if it's not always a clean fight. Skating? Cupcakes? Hockey? My family? The diner? The scholarship? Dani? Will? Josh? My father? The past? The future? Everything I touch slips through my fingers like spilled hot chocolate. All I have left is the competition, the one thing that really *can* alter the course of my life. Fear and doubts aside, that was the deal. The promise I made myself when I signed up for the Capriani Cup.

Win it, and everything changes.

Now, more than ever, no matter how much it hurts to admit, that promise is the very last hope I'm holding, the only thing in my life that I haven't yet spilled.

In six days, I'll skate for those judges.

In six days, nothing else will matter.

Chapter Twenty-Two

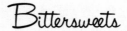

*Bavarian orange chocolate espresso cupcakes
topped with dark chocolate ganache,
chocolate icing, and a flower
of orange buttercream*

A plume of snowflakes swirls through the light of the Mobil sign next door, black lines on a pale blue glow announcing the price of gas and Newport Lights and something else with missing letters. Lake-effect wind lashes my bedroom window and my thin curtains ripple in the early morning draft, swaying at the edges.

I yawn and stretch and reach up to flick the light switch. From Bug's room next door, Mr. Napkins squeaks out a lengthy response on his hamster wheel, which I can't quite translate, because it's too early and I haven't had my hot stuff yet—coffee and shower, priorities one and two.

Twelve minutes later, I set my cup of joe on the bathroom sink as I examine my aching body in the fluorescent light, the parts I crash-landed on in training all week finally standing up for themselves. My triple/triple is solid, but my hip is bruised, a purple rose blooming on my skin. I feel a matching one on my elbow, and when I push up the sleeve of my bathrobe to inspect the damage, the door swings open with a rush of cold air.

"Don't you knock?" I pull my robe tight as Bug looks up with his huge, matter-of-fact eyes, glasses fogging up from the steam of the waiting shower.

He holds up the hamster's water bottle. "Mr. Napkins is thirsty. What happened to your arm?"

"Nothing."

"Can I see it?"

"It's fine."

Bug looks at the shower stall and back to me. "Hudson, if it's bruised, you should ice it. Heat will make it swell."

"Thanks for the tip, Dr. Avery."

"Saw it on *House*." Bug nudges in front of me to get to the sink. He reaches for the faucet. Turns it on. Fills the water bottle. Twists and twists and twists the cap closed. Stretches to shut off the water. Dries the bottle on the hand towel. Turns toward me. And wraps his tiny arms around my waist, pressing his cheek against my robe. "It's from Mr. Napkins," he says, words muffled by the closeness of us.

I run my hand over his head and squeeze him back.

"Almost time for Hurley's," he says. "Mom said I can peel gum off the tables today. Holy cannoli!" He pumps his fist in the air. And then he's gone.

He forgets to close the bathroom door.

I down the rest of my coffee and meet my eyes in the mirror. This is it. The day I've been training for all winter. In ten hours I'll skate in front of a panel of judges for a chance at a fifty-thousand-dollar scholarship. Every one of my nerves stands at attention, my whole body buzzing with equal parts excitement and dread.

In ten hours, I'll finally prove myself.

I'll nail it.

I'll win.

I'll—

"Hurry up, Hudson!" Bug shouts from his bedroom down the hall. "Mom's waiting for us."

"Fifteen minutes!" I call back. I look in the mirror again, one last time before everything changes.

"Hudson, are all the blinds dusted?" Mom asks, zipping around the Hurley's kitchen like some kind of cracked-out, nightmare hummingbird.

"Yep," I say.

"Even the ones in the kitchen?" she asks.

"Did them myself. Twice."

"And the tabletops? Did you check for gum and—"

"Bug's on gum detail." I push open the doors to the dining

room and point to the booths by the window, where my brother diligently scrapes specimens from table underbellies into a small bucket.

"What about the walk-in cooler?" Mom asks. "Did you chuck any expired food and make sure everything on the shelves is alphabetized and—"

"Ma, he's not the health inspector, and he's not coming for two more days. You've been at this all week—calm down."

"Go." Mom points to the walk-in without further explanation, and thirty seconds later I'm knee-deep in dairy, organizing milk products for the third time this week.

"Holy meltdown." Dani ducks into the cooler five minutes later, pulling the door shut behind her. She wraps a sweater around her shoulders and joins me at the shelves. "Girlfriend's on my last nerve out there."

"Tell me about it."

"The dining room is so clean you could eat off the floor." Dani picks through a few bricks of butter, separating the salted from the plain. "The guy's gonna love us."

"I wonder what he's like," I say, eager to keep our non-argument going. "Like, will he show up with a notebook and tape recorder, all official?"

Dani laughs. "Testing, testing, this is Bob Barker, reporting live from Hurley's Homestyle Diner on—"

"Dude, no. Bob Barker is the guy from *The Price Is Right*."

"When did the *Price Is Right* guy become a restaurant reviewer?"

"This year, I guess." I laugh and check the time on my phone. Just under an hour until I make my escape.

"Soooo," she says, stretching it out until it's so long and loaded I already know what's coming next.

"I haven't spoken to either of them."

"That bad, huh?"

I sniff a recently opened carton of heavy cream and set it back on the shelf, face out. "Josh thinks I conspired to get Will in front of hockey scouts and screw the rest of the team. It's this whole mess with the coach—he's Will's godfather."

Dani nods. "Frankie told me that part. But why are they mad at you? You obviously helped the whole team, not just Will."

"There's a lot more to it. I was hanging out with Will, but then Josh and I were supposed to . . . okay, it's a crazy long story."

She reaches for another stack of butter bricks, checking the dates. "You don't have to talk about it if you don't want to. I just thought . . ."

"Are you working brunch tomorrow? Maybe we can go to Sharon's for a late lunch after and talk about stuff?"

"Lunch tomorrow would be awesome," she says. "But I'm working a double tonight, so if you want to start filling me in on the basics . . ."

I check my phone again. "I can't."

"Why are you so antsy?"

"I have the . . . my competition starts in a little while." I pick up a tub of sour cream and inspect the contents. "The scholarship thing."

"That's *tonight*? I totally forgot! Why didn't you remind me?"

"We haven't exactly been on speaking terms."

"Hudson." She leans against the metal shelving that holds all the eggs, hands on her hips. "I know things aren't all lovey-*dovey*, but that doesn't mean I'm ditching out on the biggest event of your life."

"You aren't ditching. It's fine. You don't—"

"What time does it start? I'll call Marianne." She digs the phone out of her apron pocket and flips it open, scrolling through the numbers. "Maybe she'll switch with me so I can—"

"Dani, listen to me." I reach across the small space of the cooler and close her phone. "It's not you, okay? I know I haven't been around much and I don't even deserve your awesomeness, and I totally appreciate that you still want to be there for me. But this event . . . I just . . . I can't really explain it."

"Try," she whispers, eyes shining.

"I need to go it alone."

"Alone. Right." She wipes fresh tears with her fingertips. "Guess you've made that pretty clear, haven't you?"

"Dani, wait." I grab her arm.

"Let go of me." She pulls away and stomps out of the cooler. She tries to slam the door, but I catch it and follow her to the big dishwasher at the back of the kitchen.

"Please listen," I whisper, keeping an eye out for Mom and

Bug. "I've been so stressed about this, and the competition is so hard. That scholarship . . . it's everything to me. You have no idea how—"

"No, *you* have no idea. I've been dealing with your multiple personality disorder for months. I kept telling myself, 'Ease up, she's having a hard time with her family.' Then it was, 'Cut her a break. She's really busy with hockey and skating stuff.' Then, 'Wow, waitressing and baking and school and training—must be tough to balance it all.'" Dani shoves one of my mixing bowls into the dishwasher, followed by a cutting board and a few dinner plates.

"Dani—"

"I tried to convince myself that things would get better once you got the hang of serving, or after the Wolves won a few games, or once Christmas break started, or New Year's, or blah blah blah. But it never happened. Know why? Because there's *always* another reason, Hud, and there always will be. Always something to give you a bad day or put you in a funk. Life is hard—I get it. The thing is, best friends don't use that stuff as an excuse to treat each other like garbage. Best friends don't make you feel like the slush under your boots."

Her eyes are wild and her words hit me like steak knives, but she's right. I can't argue a single point, and hearing the entire soundtrack of my horrible behavior set to the tune of her wounded, angry voice kicks me hard in the chest. I hate that I put that edge in her jaw, the angles in her stance, the stain on our formerly unblemished friendship.

"I totally hear you, Dani. I know I got caught up in my own thing this winter, and I've been a mess of a person, but this is my last chance. I need to be in the zone tonight. No distractions—not even well-meaning ones. If I don't nail this thing, that's *it*. I'm stuck in this hole for the rest of my life."

Dani slams the dish rack into the machine. "Maybe if you weren't so busy trying to bail on this 'hole,' you'd remember that some people call it home, and that you don't have it all that bad. Maybe if you stopped trying so hard to escape, you'd see some of the good stuff, too."

"For you, sure. You still have both of your parents. You know they're going to help you, whatever you decide to do. Look around. Look at this place. *This* is my future. My whole life. Name one good thing—"

"One and two," she says, counting on her fingers. "You have a mom and a little brother who adore you. Three, Trick always has your back. Four, a warm bed. Five, all those friends you made on the hockey team—crushes or breakups or not, those guys *adore* you. Six, a decent job, when you show up. Seven—"

"What about you? Do I still have my best friend, or is that just a regional thing? Because it seems you liked me a whole lot better when you thought I'd be stuck in Watonka, working as a Hurley Girl for the rest of my life."

Dani moves toward me, anger rising from her lungs, coloring her face. But then she changes directions, breaking for the staff closet. She digs through her bag and pulls out a folder, neat handwriting etched across the tab: PHOTO—FINAL PROJ./PASSION.

"Seven," she says, fingers ashen against the plain manila. "Something you love. Something that *used* to make you smile."

"Dani, I—"

"You forgot who you are, Hudson Avery." She flings the folder at the prep counter and a few eight-by-tens slip across the metal surface. I recognize them from the shoot we did months ago for the cupcake flyers. We'd just finished taking some close-ups and I was messing around with a bowl of frosting, licking the spoon mock-seductively. I did it to make her laugh—to make both of us laugh.

It worked. I laughed so hard I didn't even notice she was still clicking away on the camera. And now, staring down at a picture of the former me—the me who only a few months ago could still laugh like that, who still believed a good bowl of icing and a best friend were the keys to happiness—my heart shatters. She's right. She's right and I've risked everything that ever mattered to me, just for one more impossible chance on the ice.

But I've come too far to walk away from it. After all this, I owe it to myself to try. To go after the one thing I *know* will make me happy. Skating. Winning that competition. Getting back out there and proving to the judges that yes, Hudson Avery *does* have what it takes. Knowing that I worked hard for this, no matter who else is standing with me in the kiss-and-cry room when they call out the final scores.

I scoop the photos into the folder and hand the packet to Dani. "If you still want to come with me—"

"It's too late. You made your choice." Dani marches to the other end of the counter and tears the folder in half, dropping the whole thing into the trash. "Good luck tonight, girl. I hope you win that prize. And I hope it's everything you dreamed it would be."

In the third stall of the ladies' room, I shed my Hurley Girl dress and slip into jeans and a sweatshirt, my old, slightly too-small skating dress folded neatly beneath the skates at the bottom of my backpack. My eyes are blurry with tears, but I can't let Dani's words get to me—not now. I have to focus on the competition. Visualize my routine. The applause. The scores. Everything I worked for all winter, all my life, finally happening.

I open the stall door, set my bag and Hurley's uniform on the counter, and splash my face with cold water. I'm okay. I have to be. I have my skates and a passable dress and a date with Parallel Hudson, ready to reclaim the destiny that should've been mine all along.

"Hudson?" Mom sticks her head in the bathroom doorway, face tight and splotchy. "Where's Dani? She's not in the kitchen."

"Did you check out back?" I tear off a paper towel and blot my eyes. "What's wrong?"

"Just got a call from the newspaper. The reviewer has an assignment in New York on Monday."

"He *what*?" I grab my backpack and the crumpled Hurley Girl dress from the counter and follow her out through the dining room, back into the kitchen. "He's not coming? But what about—"

"Tonight, Hudson. He's coming *tonight*." She scans the kitchen, taking inventory. "Nat should be here in fifteen minutes. I called Marianne in, too. See if you can find Dani. Trick? Get those steaks prepped."

"Mom, I can't—"

"What about me?" Bug asks from under the prep counter. His hair is sticking up in every direction, his glasses smudged. "I got all the gum off the tables. And I even found some other stuff, too. Like—"

"You can polish all the ketchup bottles," Mom says. "But first help your sister find Dani."

"Right here." Dani steps in through the smoking lounge door, rubbing her arms. "What's going on?"

"Critic's coming tonight instead of Monday," Mom says. "Can you two change out the specials for the beef tips, put on fresh coffee, and make sure the menus are spotless?"

"Ma!" I step in front of her, finally snagging her attention. "I can't stay tonight. I have plans. It's . . . they're kind of important."

"Important?" She laughs. Like, maniacally. "Hudson, this is the most important night in the life of this diner. If we don't pass this review with flying colors, we're sunk. I don't know how to be any more clear than that. *Sunk*. Do you understand?"

"But—"

"I'm sorry. If I had another option, I'd—"

"You'd take it. Right." I drop my backpack on the floor, still clutching the dress. Grill smoke fills my lungs and makes me cough. I close my eyes to keep the tears in, but soon my heart is racing, blood pounding in my ears. I think back to that night in November when she told me I'd have to waitress, that she wished so badly she had another option, that she'd try to find another server as soon as she could.

"Why don't you and Dani do a quick run-through on the tables," Mom says. "Make sure the condiments are filled, check underneath for any gum Bug missed, and—"

"No."

Mom glares at me, eyes fixed on the Hurley Girl dress in my hand, and it all comes down to this. All the guilt, the money, the extra work, my little brother, the gas bills, the smell of fryer grease, the dropped skating lessons, my father's suitcases by the door, the arguing, the crying, the cheetah bra, and the hours of my life, ticking off against the clock on the wall.

"I can't stay," I say. "I'll come back in a few hours to help, but I have to go now."

She grabs my arm and drags me to the walk-in cooler, fingers digging into my muscle. "Open it."

I do as she says and she pushes us both inside, slamming the door behind us. The skin on my arms prickles, but I'm not cold; adrenaline rushes through my body and warms me all over.

"You're skating on thin ice, Hudson Marissa. *Very* thin ice. This is serious. This is our whole life."

"But it isn't our *whole* life." I shake my head, voice soft but certain. Unwavering. "I don't want to stay here forever, Ma. Not in Hurley's and not in Watonka."

"Since when did home stop being good enough?"

"That's what you want for me? Good *enough*? Whatever happened to aim high? Reach for the stars and all that crap parents are supposed to say to their kids?"

"Do you have any idea what it takes just to keep us fed and housed? To keep this place going?" Mom slams her hand against the metal egg shelf, sending one of the cartons to the floor. "We can't afford the stars."

The yolks soak the cardboard, darkening the edges. The balled-up Hurley Girl dress slips through my fingers and lands on the floor. "It's not fair."

"You're absolutely right." She ignores the eggs, but bends down to retrieve the dress, shaking it out and pulling it against her chest like it's some precious thing. "It's not fair that you have to work so much and take care of your brother. It's not fair that I had to move you guys to a cramped apartment. It's not fair that your father was sleeping with other women during our marriage. So what do you want me to do? Tell me how to make things fair. How to make it work."

Her hand clutches the lavender fabric of the dress, all knobs and angles and bones poking up against the skin, and it reminds me of when she used to dress me for a day out in the snow, tugging my hands into mittens, guiding my feet into boots lined with plastic bread bags to keep out the slush. How much time has passed since my parents took us to Bluebird

Park in the winter? Since they pulled me along the path in a sled, Bug wrapped up in a snowsuit in my arms, all of us laughing as the branches shook and dropped snowflakes on our heads?

I look intently at her face, all the lines deeper in the blue glow of the cooler. "I wish I never showed you that bra."

Mom shakes her head and stands down, turning the handle and pushing open the cooler door. As she steps out into the warm light of the kitchen, her voice goes so low I barely catch her words.

"Some days," she whispers, still clutching the dress, "so do I."

I slip past her through the doorway, everyone waiting silently for the final outcome. Their eyes are on me; Dani shakes her head and Trick's gaze burns my skin from all the way across the room. Bug sits at the prep counter with his head in his hands, face crumpled, glasses sliding down his nose.

My cheeks burn and I can't meet their eyes—the people who've been my family for so long, related or not.

"Hudson?" Bug says softly, tugging the sleeves over his hands. "Can I help you check the tables now?"

"Sorry," I whisper to my brother. To all of them. To none of them. I scoop up my backpack from the floor, grab my jacket from the staff closet, and head out into the ice-cold February air.

Chapter Twenty-Three

Liar, Liar, Cakes on Fire

*Chocolate cayenne cupcakes topped with
cinnamon cream cheese frosting
and heart-shaped cinnamon Red Hots*

One hour—that's it. Three twenties. Twelve fives. Sixty one-minute intervals borrowed from the clock on the scoreboard, all that stands between me and my final, don't-look-back golden ticket out of here. A chance to see the world. A chance to finally live. Because if I don't, it's back to the diner to claim my family legacy, all the unchosen things vanishing, all the lines in my mother's face passed down with the deed to Hurley's Homestyle Diner in Watonka, New York.

We can't afford the stars.

Skaters fill the locker room at the Buffalo Skate Club, each stationed at her own mirror, mothers and sisters and coaches applying a final coat of glitter gel or lip gloss. I recognize two of them from my own club days, former Bisonettes, insepa-rable friends from the west side of Buffalo who were like the brunette versions of me and Kara. I brace myself for the sneers, the *who does she think she is showing her face around here* whis-pers. But the girls remain silent. Focused. They don't remem-ber me, or maybe they don't care enough to cause any drama.

After I slick my hair back into a tight bun and apply the requisite amounts of blush and shadow, I check out the rest of the competition, sparkly and stiff, concentration pulling muscles taught beneath whimsical costumes. I close my eyes and it seems like a dream, so far away and foreign. For three years I haven't watched competitive skating. Haven't seen the girls zipping into their dresses or felt the tension, the pres-sure, the palpable expectations in the locker room before a big, make-it-or-break-it event.

Instead, I've been at the diner, watching Dani, Marianne, and Nat bus one another's tables, run food from the grill to the dining room no matter who placed the order. I've seen Mom tie her hair back and chop vegetables for Trick a hundred times, watched Trick put on a fresh pot of coffee when I was in the weeds with customers, watched Dani pinch-hit when Nat's nursing class ran late, everyone gathering at the end of the long night to count the money and divvy the sidework and trade crazy customer stories. I've been with the Wolves, helping the boys change from a bunch of mouth-breathing hockey thugs to a real team, a real crew.

I look over the girls in the prep area now, so driven and

determined, so willing to put everything and everyone else second, and it hits me: For all my stolen hours on the ice this winter, all those frigid, windblown days at Fillmore and the hard work at Baylor's, the pure competition of it—me against them, them against one another, all of us fighting for a single spotlight—wasn't something I prepared for.

Did I ever prepare for that, really?

"All skaters and coaches, please report to the ice." The announcement crackles through the overhead speakers, setting the locker room ablaze with nervous chatter. "The competition will begin in ten minutes. All skaters and coaches, please report to the ice."

I hobble on my blade guards out to the arena, merging into the line of girls near the edge. One of the west-siders—Paige, I think, or maybe it's Peyton—follows behind me from the locker room, elbowing her way to the front of the pack, catching me in the ribs.

"Nice costume, Sparkles. Shoulda burned that thing after the Empire disaster. Hope it brings you the same bad mojo tonight." She bumps me again as she passes by, a sharp reminder that my single biggest mistake will always follow me, its harsh, black lining lurking just beneath the roses-and-glitter surface of my dreams.

"Skaters, this way, please." A thin man with a walkie-talkie and clipboard waves us over to the box, checking us in one at a time. At his command, we file onto wooden benches and remove our guards. I keep my back to Paige/Peyton and focus on the other surroundings, visualizing my jumps and spins and the cheers that will follow, even from the relatively small crowd—mostly parents and grandparents and a few well-dressed, poker-faced women who are probably part of Lola's foundation, perched unmoving on the center line seats.

I instinctively scan the arena for my parents, row by row, top to bottom. I know it's ridiculous—my father is thousands of miles away and Mom is probably locked in her office, hyperventilating about the foodie. I didn't tell her about the competition, but part of me wishes she'd be here, like she'd somehow found out and dropped everything to watch me, even on the most important night in Hurley's history. Skating was never *her* thing—not like it was with my dad—but maybe now it could be. I could show her how good I am, how swiftly I can win this competition. Earn that scholarship. Remap the course of my life and rediscover the path I lost that night in Rochester. Prove to her, once and for all, that I was born to be on the ice.

But . . . is that why I'm here? To prove something to my mother? To get a do-over on a mistake I made three years ago? Is that the reason I'm zipped too tightly into my old sequined dress, feet anxious to slide and tap and twirl and jump through the right combination of hoops to impress those bored foundation stiffs in the reserved seats? Who are they to decide whose dreams come true and whose die on the ice? Am I here just to win their hearts, to make them fall in love with me?

No. I shake my head, trying to loosen the thought, to jar it free. I'm here because I want to compete. To win. To go to

college and continue training and land on a professional circuit. To . . . what?

The remaining girls pack into the box like glittery sardines,
the seconds ticking off the clock, and my resolve melts away.
This isn't some movie where the dramatic music starts and
Mom bursts through the side doors, teary-eyed as I hit the ice,
all of our problems disappearing in the wake of my flawless
triple/triple combo. This is reality. *My* reality. And though I've
been off the competition ice for a long time, I've done enough
events to know with absolute certainty that something isn't
right—something *else* that has nothing to do with Mom not
being here or all the broken, bittersweet choices I made before
tonight. I can feel it.

More precisely, I *can't*.

That's the problem. I used to get these butterflies before
every event, good ones. They'd swarm my stomach and knock
into each other beneath the surface, a gentle tickle from the
inside out. Kara would massage my hands and shoulders just to
steady them. And then the event manager would say my name
over the announcements, calling me for my turn, and all those
butterflies would stand at attention, calming me, focusing me,
helping to propel me around the ice and ensure I performed my
routine beautifully. They'd stop their flitting just long enough
to see me through, and then, when my scores were announced
and the audience cheered from the stands, they'd reappear,
excited and warm inside, drunk from the victory.

I close my eyes and wait for them to come, will them to fill me up again, but they're not here. And now that I've finally noticed their absence, the hole inside presses on me like a real thing.

Since I've started training again, I've felt that kind of fluttering anticipation *not* when I thought about this competition, but when Dani sampled my new cupcake creations, or when Bug put the final circuit board on his robot. When I finally figured out how to carry a tray full of drinks without spilling a drop. When the Wolves skated toward the net during the semis, feet shushing hard against the ice, arms arched as they prepared to take the winning shots. When Josh's lips brushed against mine in the firelight as we hid from the storm.

"Paige Adamo," the announcer calls. The girl hugs her friend and skates to the ice, music setting her feet on fire, strong and energetic. I want to hate her for everything she said, for everything she is, but I can't. She's beautiful, and her routine is breathtaking.

"Amazing program," I tell her when she slides back into the box. She grabs her water bottle, taking a swig as her coach hands her a towel.

"There's no karma in figure skating," she says, looking right through me. I raise my eyebrows, but she's right. When you're a solo skater, *everyone* is the competition. Even when you're in a local club together, you know that one day, it will come down to the solo, you against your friends. You against the world.

The competition. The grueling schedule. The pressure to

be perfect—a porcelain ballerina, dancing beneath the glass of an unimaginably tiny snow globe. It was all part of the gig.

For so long I wanted to blame my father's affair for my decision to throw the Empire Games and pull out of regionals. I wanted him to be my reason to be mad, my excuse for hanging up the skates and seeking refuge in a bowl of batter. But maybe a small part of me was already there, one skate over the line, ready to leave. I remember it now, all the impossible expectations made bearable only by my pure love for the ice and my friendship with Kara.

I touch the silver rabbit pin on my shoulder, the metal warm and smooth. When I skated with Kara, we protected each other, supported and cheered for each other, our friendship a never-empty well of encouragement. More than the ribbons and trophies and talk of bright futures, our friendship is what made it all worth it. All those five a.m. practices, the blisters and bruises and bone-tiring workouts—as long as we were in it together, we could do anything.

It was never about the competition, just like she said in Amir Jordan's bathroom in the first hours of the brand-new year.

"Hudson Avery," the announcer calls. In my parallel life, the crowd would fall silent; in the stillness before their next collective breath, the butterflies would return. They'd carry me onto the ice and I'd perform my routine as planned, immaculate. Nail a perfect score. Paige Adamo would scowl and pout and stab her toe pick into the ice, but the judges wouldn't waver. It would be unanimous.

The Capriani Cup scholarship would be awarded to . . .

"Hudson Avery," the announcer calls again. I stand and grip the rail in front of the box, steadying myself. This is it. The chance I've been waiting for all winter.

"Hudson Avery, please report to the ice," the announcer echoes. The crowd begins to fidget. Murmur. I close my eyes and wait for those butterflies. If I don't go now, I forfeit. I give up everything I worked so hard for these last few months. Fillmore. Baylor's. Wolves. Cupcakes. Friends. Family. Life.

My heart finally fills, but it's not with butterflies. It's flashes of the Wolves, the new friends I made as I helped coach them into a real team, the joy they shared after each hard-won game. Flashes of everyone at Hurley's pulling together on a busy night to keep the customers fed. Flashes of the pictures Dani took in the kitchen, me with my cupcakes, how they saved me after my father left, gave me something into which I could pour my heart and creativity, something that brought people a few minutes of happiness on an otherwise dark day. Flashes of Mom and Bug and what it means to be part of a family, part of a team—*my* home team.

And then the truth, clear and crisp as the winter sky the morning after a storm: I never really left the ice. I never will. Ever since I blew the Empire Games, I thought I was hiding out in the diner, staying below the radar until the mistakes lost my trail. But I wasn't. Tonight, here, *this* is where I'm hiding. Not from my past. From my present. From my *real* life and everyone I care about.

This competition belongs to Parallel Life Hudson. We're not fused—our paths diverged a long time ago, long before that night in Rochester.

I open my eyes and slide out of the box, but instead of skating to the center of the ice, I give the organizer the cut sign, grab my blade guards, and hobble back to the locker room. Commotion floats through the stands as the announcer receives word of my forfeit and locates the next skater's bio and music, but soon the crowd settles, ready for her to appear.

After I pull on my leg warmers and boots, I peek into the arena one last time. The skater, a tiny blonde in a black-and-silver dress, is in position. She waves to two people in the stands who are out of their seats with pride. The music starts and her face turns serious as she poses for her first step, toe solid on the ice. Maybe she's found my butterflies, or some of her own. Maybe she'll win the scholarship and go on to train and compete and win the Olympic gold, looking back on this night as the one that changed everything—the once-in-a-lifetime golden ticket moment that made all of her impossible dreams come true.

I hope she does.

"Good luck," I whisper, touching the silver rabbit on my shoulder. The skater glides into her first loop, and I slip unnoticed out the back door.

Chapter Twenty-Four

Friend of the Devil Cupcakes

*Red velvet devil's food cupcakes
topped with red, orange, and yellow swirled
buttercream icing peaks and a thin red apple curl*

I pull into a spot close to the Hurley's entrance and kill the engine. It's so quiet I can almost hear the snow fall, big fat flakes plopping on the pavement, the windshield, the roof of the truck. The lights are on inside the diner, but the blinds are drawn, and in the muted hush, I feel it—that edge of wrongness. I shouldn't have come back here. Mom will never forgive me.

I sink back into the driver's seat and slip the keys into the ignition. My heart races and my breath fogs up windows as I reverse out of the spot. I'm leaving tonight. Now. I've got my snow-stomping boots and my backpack and everything I need to escape Watonka, escape New York, escape everywhere. Train or not, this time . . .

It's the old man that stops me.

Earl—the regular from my first day of training. The one with all the dimes. I recognize the blue sedan as it pulls into my just-vacated parking spot. He sees me when he gets out and nods—not a wave or a smile, not a greeting, but something else. Something that in its utter simplicity says only, *I know, Dolly Madison. I know all about it.* We lock eyes for an eternity, conversation floating soundlessly through the winter air, and then the moment vanishes, footprints covered quickly by the snow as he shuffles up the path and disappears inside.

I pull into a different spot and slam the truck into park. No way I'm leaving them again. Not now. Not after everything.

Earl leans on the front counter, tapping his foot to the jazz riff floating from the kitchen. The knitting club is there, along with three other occupied tables, familiar patrons chatting in a low collective hum as silverware scrapes against plates. *Clink clink. Storm's coming back around, believe that? Clink clink clink. We're putting the house on the market this spring. Clink clink. Etta's boy's back from Iraq. Getting married next month. . . .*

Marianne, Dani, Nat, Mom—none of them are in the dining room. Bug's not around, either. I pour a cup of coffee for Earl and push through the double doors into the kitchen. "Looks dead out there. What hap—"

"Close the doors!" A blur of voices snuffs out the rest of my question. Nat, hovering next to the doorway like she's on guard duty, shoves me out of the way and pulls the double doors tight. She's shaking so hard, even her sleek pink bob looks nervous. Some kind of unidentifiable meat is burning on the grill, Marianne and Trick are frantically stacking full plates onto a serving tray, Mom and Dani are crawling around on the floor like someone lost a contact lens, and Bug is tucked into a ball under the prep counter, clutching his backpack and wiping his eyes with a dish towel.

"Nice of you to join us," Mom says. She doesn't get up from the floor.

"What happened? Did the reviewer show up yet?"

"Came and went," Nat says. Her eyes sweep the floor like she's searching for a mouse. "Hardly ate a thing. Lousy tipper, too. And that was after—"

"He didn't like it?" My stomach knots up. "How could he not—"

"Excuse me?" One of the knitting club ladies calls through the window over the grill. "We put our order in a while ago, but I think our waitress went on break."

"Be right out!" Nat's bordering on hysterical. "Hudson, watch the door. Close it right behind me."

"Is everyone in here crazy, or—"

"Close it! I'm not screwing around!"

"Is Nat all right?" I ask when she's out of the kitchen. "Doesn't even look busy out there. What are you guys—"

"May be half-dead in the dining room," Trick says, "but we're kinda scramblin' back here, in case you haven't noticed. So if you could skip the third degree and maybe flip those

Polish sausages, help Marianne run this food, or locate your brother's hamster—"

"Mr. Napkins?" I don't wait for an answer. I duck under the counter and reach for Bug. "Come here, sweet pea. Tell me what happened."

He pulls himself tighter into a ball, shrugging me off. "Mr. *hiccup* Napkins *hiccup* is gone!"

"What do you mean, gone?"

"I had him right here, and now he's"—*hiccup*—"MIA." He opens his backpack to show me the dark space inside, nothing there but a few shreds of hamster hay and an old T-shirt stuffed into the bottom.

"You brought Mr. Napkins here? In your *backpack*?"

Bug blinks behind his tortoiseshell glasses, tears spilling down his cheeks. "I didn't want to leave him home alone again." *Hiccup.* "He gets lonely."

"I know he does, Bug. I'm sorry." My throat is dry and tight, knees aching against the cold tile floor. If I had just stayed here earlier, helped Mom out, maybe things would've gone better with the reviewer. Maybe I could've taken Bug home. Maybe I—

"What if he gets outside?" Bug's crying harder, eyes wild with this new fear. "He'll freeze! What if someone hamsternaps him? What if he gets hit by a snowplow? What if he—"

"Bug, listen to me. Mr. Napkins is the smartest hamster alive. He's not outside. He's somewhere in this diner, and we'll find him. But you have to calm down." I put my hands on his shoulders and inch closer. "I know I haven't given you any reason to trust me tonight. I don't blame you if you're mad, but we have to put that aside so we can find Mr. Napkins. Can you do that for me?"

His big brown saucer-eyes blink twice. One more sniffle. Another hiccup, then a nod, and he follows me out from under the prep counter.

"Do you have your notebook?" I ask. "The one you use to write down clues for important cases?"

He digs out the notebook and a pencil from the front part of his bag and flips to an empty page.

"Good. Now think. What do we know about Mr. Napkins? What kind of environment does he like? What are his favorite hiding places at home?"

Bug's tongue sticks partway out of his mouth as pencil races across paper. "Hates the cold," I read over his shoulder. "Goes near heat vents. Small spaces. Likes food and the dark."

"That's all I can think of." Bug wipes his eyes with the back of his free hand.

"Okay, let's recap." I reread his notes out loud, keeping one eye on the ground in case of a Mr. Napkins flyby. While Mom edges her way around the perimeter, Dani covers the back, searching under the dishwasher with a flashlight.

"Any ideas?" Bug asks.

"Yes." I steer him over to the grill. "He likes food and he likes heat, right? I know where I'd go. Right under there."

Bug and I crouch down and peer under the grill and ovens.

From the dusty dark beneath the warmest place in the kitchen, a tiny pink nose wriggles innocently.

"We have visual contact," I say. With any luck, it's the hamster in question and not some other rodent mascot we've yet to discover. "Bug, keep your eye on him while I find something to get his attention."

"Dani," Trick says, "run this to table eight and tell Nat and Marianne the incident has been . . . located."

"Got it," she says, taking the plates from his hands.

I slip out of my jacket and scarf, drop them on a stool, and scrounge up a tub of peanut butter, an apple, and some sliced cheese. With an elaborately concocted snack and a whole lotta cooing, Bug coaxes his twitchy little friend into the light.

"Mr. Napkins!" He scoops up the hamster and presses him to his chest in a tiny hug. "Don't you ever do that again. I was so worried about you!"

Honestly, I'd be more worried about getting all huggy-snuggy-kissy-face with a rodent that spent half the night trolling around under an oven that's been here since the 1950s, but that's just my personal—

"Hudson? What the . . ." Mom's eyes bulge as she looks me over. In all the excitement of the missing hamster, I forgot about the outfit—my multicolored sequined skating dress just one deep breath away from a wardrobe malfunction, fuzzy pink leg warmers hastily tucked into boots over beige spandex tights. "Where on *earth* have you—"

"Nat's gone." Marianne stands in the doorway, straddling

the dining room and kitchen with her hand against the door. "Guess the ham—" She stops herself when she sees Bug, lowering her voice. "The *incident* really upset her. Between that and the reviewer, she cracked. I don't think she's coming back."

"For someone trying to become a nurse," I say, "she's got a pretty weak stomach."

"Perfect." Mom throws a pot into the sink, metal clanging like an old church bell. "One less person I'll have to ax when that review shuts us down." She looks back to me, head shaking as if she doesn't really want to know. It's all just too much, the lying, our earlier argument, the less-than-enthusiastic food critic, the missing hamster, me in my old skating dress like we just fell back in time.

A month ago—even a day ago—I would've done anything for a chance to burn the Hurley Girl dress, a chance to leave this place free and clear. But now, Mom talking like the diner could actually close, the last of her fragile hope evaporating, my heart sinks. Good or bad, this place was always her dream. Her identity. My mother *is* Hurley's Homestyle Diner.

"Hurley's isn't going to tank, Ma. It's been here forever. One bad review isn't the—"

"A bad review on top of a bad economy, a bad winter, a bad year . . . Hudson, that really was our last shot—we *needed* a stellar mention in the paper. We can't do it anymore. Unless you've got another cupcake miracle up your sleeve that can pack this place every night for the next two months, I can't even afford to keep the grill lit."

"But I thought—"

"Just take your brother home, okay? I need to clean up in here and go over the books. I can't . . ." She rakes her eyes over my dress again, lingering on the silver rabbit still pinned to my shoulder. "I can't deal with you right now." She retreats to her office and gently closes the door, leaving nothing in her wake but the hissing sounds of the grill and the muffled, front-of-the-house scrape of silverware on dishes.

"Doesn't look like anyone heard about the incident," Dani says, sticking an order ticket into the slot over the grill. "I think we're in the clear. Sub mashed for fries on both of those, Trick."

"Dani?" I whisper.

Her eyes flash over me for a minute, then she turns, reaching up into the pantry for condiments. "Well, don't just stand there withholding info again. How'd it go?"

"It didn't."

"You didn't place?" She turns to face me, a ketchup bottle in each hand, her forehead crinkled with concern and confusion.

I shake my head. "I didn't skate. I forfeited."

"So you bailed on us tonight, and you didn't even—"

"Look, I know you probably hate me, and whatever you want to say, say it." I grab the ketchups from her hands and set them on the counter. "But first I need you to do me the biggest favor in history."

Her cheeks go from brown to plum as she takes a step closer. "You've got some kinda nerve coming at me with this. I can't believe—"

"For Hurley's. For my family. I don't have time to explain. Just say you'll help."

"Convince me. Ten seconds."

"Mom says we need a miracle, right?"

"Five seconds."

"I'm changing the specials to half-price apps. Then I'm packing up all of the cupcakes and desserts from the pastry case." I grab my coat from the stool and dig out the keys, dangling them in front of her. "Warm up the Tetanus Taxi and wait for me in the passenger seat. I'll meet you outside in five minutes."

"Hud, what are you—"

"I'll explain on the way. Five minutes!"

"You gonna tell me what's going on?" Dani wipes the fog from the window with her sleeve as we roll out of the parking lot, the entire backseat covered in white bakery boxes and paper plates.

"Mom was really counting on that review tonight," I say.

"Yeah, thanks for caring, like, three hours ago when we could've used the help."

"Just because I'm mad at Mom doesn't mean I don't care. I don't want her to lose the restaurant."

"You should've been there, Hudson."

I smack the steering wheel with my fist. "The guy didn't like the food! He—"

"You still should've been there. It's your *family*."

"I know. And this is the only way I could think of to get Hurley's back on the map."

"What way? Where are we going?"

I downshift, slowing on an unplowed stretch of road. The wheels slip, but I keep us going in a straight line. "Baylor's."

"The Wolves game?"

"Finals. It's a big-deal game."

She shakes her head and lets out a half laugh. "Are you really that selfish, or—"

"The whole school's there tonight, Dani." Snow falls in big, sideways flakes against the windshield. I turn the wipers to a higher speed and downshift again, the engine whining in response. "Half the town, too."

"Yeah, and I'd be there with them if I could, but some things are more important—"

"And they're all probably hungry." I flip on my turn signal and ease into the right lane. "Mom asked for a cupcake miracle? Well, here comes the freaking holy angel of icing, at your service."

Dani looks at the white boxes stacked across the backseat. From the corner of my eye, I catch her smiling.

"Angel of icing?" she says. "That's the craziest, corniest, most whack-ass stuff I ever heard in my *life*." She turns away, looking out the window as the Fillmore smokestacks rush by. "Freaking brilliant," she whispers.

I wasn't supposed to hear that last part, but I did, and I smile, too.

Chapter Twenty-Five

Hudson Avery's Last-Chance Triple/Triple Combo Cupcakes

*Dark chocolate espresso cupcakes
topped with cinnamon café au lait icing,
white chocolate chips,
and chocolate-covered espresso beans*

I bribe Marcus, the Baylor's manager, with two cupcakes in exchange for locating a folding table and setting us up near the rink exit. With only minutes left in the game, Dani and I spread the cupcakes out on plates in a colorful display, chocolate and sugar and mint mascarpone mingling in a wave of sweet air.

"I hope you're right about this." Dani licks a smudge of vanilla frosting from her finger. "And I hope they dig your skatetrix getup."

I drop some plastic forks into a cup at the end of the table and shake my rainbow-sequined ass. "I rock this thing and you know it."

"Oh no, you did *not* just say that." Dani laughs, but we're both startled by the loud, game-ending buzzer. For a split second time stops, and then the cheers grow louder, a roar pushing out from the rink as the arena doors fly open. The crowd is insane, swarming the ice en masse. Above the center line, the school jazz ensemble flashes its brass horns, ready for a victory song.

Trust me—until you've heard Watonka's future jazz stars blow Duran Duran's "Hungry Like the Wolf," you haven't lived.

"They won!" Dani stands on her toes, trying to catch a glimpse inside.

Seconds later the first wave crashes through the doorway, breaking on our table like an avalanche.

"Get your free Wolves victory cakes here!" I cup my hands in front of my mouth and shout over the roar of the crowd as they surround us, mouths open, hands outstretched. "Free cupcakes, courtesy of Hurley's Homestyle Diner! Stop by tonight for half-price appetizers with every meal."

"Free cupcakes!" Dani echoes. "Free Hurley's gourmet cupcakes! Celebrate a sweet season with a sweet treat!"

"Stop by Hurley's on Route Five for more great food and great company!" I say it as often as I can, whenever another hand reaches out from the mob to snag a cupcake. Their rabid, mannerless devouring is the highest compliment, and with every cupcake-muddled thank-you, I make a wish that this crazy plan is enough. Enough to save Hurley's. Enough to mop up the spills. Enough to bring us all back from the abyss.

For the next half an hour we're engulfed in a sea of blue and silver, but the boys aren't in it. No way they would've spotted us from the ice, and by now they're in the locker room recapping their epic win and planning a well-earned night out. Papallo's, maybe, or one of Luke's or Amir's infamous parties.

I hand a Razzle Berry Blast Cupcake to another waiting fan, ignoring the burn in my chest. I miss celebrating with them. I'm sure Dani'll score an invite from Frankie later, but these days, Princess Pink isn't high on anyone's A list.

By the time the crowd blows over, we're completely cleaned out, nothing but cake crumbs and chocolate smudges from table to floor. After we clean up and stash the table with Marcus, I slip into the arena, hoping against logic for a glimpse at Josh. But save for the cleaning crew sweeping up rejected popcorn kernels and other left-behinds, the place is vacant. On the rink the Zamboni machine does its usual circuit, erasing slashes and gouges, the on-ice evidence of tonight's record-breaking victory march wiped clean.

Back on Route Five, in an unprecedented comeback of its own, Hurley's diner is slammed.

Dani and I push our way through a small mob in the front doorway, wading through wall-to-wall bodies to get to Marianne.

"Hudson, you genius little devil!" Marianne calls across the crowd, beaming. "We're on a forty-five minute wait for a table. Get in here!"

Dani throws her coat under the hostess stand and jumps

back onto the floor while I zoom to the back, digging my reserve cupcakes out of the cooler. Dani delivers them as fast as I can thaw and frost, no time for a nonsmoke break, no time to explain this half-baked plan to Mom. Out in the dining room Earl's got the Sassy Seniors Knitting Club taking orders and refilling coffees. Even Bug has a job, writing down names for the wait list in his notebook, Mr. Napkins tucked secretly and securely in the backpack on his shoulders.

From my usual spot at the prep counter, surrounded as always by cupcakes and mixing bowls and white rubber spatulas, I look out through the window over the grill, right into the dining room. The joint's so rowdy, I can't pick out a single conversation. Underneath all that laughter and togetherness, bright circles of red and orange and yellow and white dot every table, some half-eaten, some still untouched. Only a true cupcake connoisseur knows the rules—you wait for when the conversation pauses, the moment you can devote your entire mouth to the all-important task of snarfing down the goods.

Mom catches my eye from across the dining room, and my stomach bubbles. I steady myself and wait for the glare, the portent of oh-honey-red-alert troubles to come. But she just tilts her head and smiles, looking at me over the entire city of Watonka. Most of it, anyway.

Body aching and sequined dress splattered with icing, I smile back at my mother, and her eyes sparkle like they haven't in years.

Me and my bright ideas.

As Trick's radio hums those sad, familiar notes, I lean against the bricks outside, enjoying a long white puff on my noncigarette. I must've been on my feet for two hours straight, running between bowls of cupcake batter, the ovens, and the dining room before we finally got off that wait.

My friend the seagull is still hanging around the Dumpster, scratching at the ground for crumbs. He pretends not to notice me and I close my eyes, loosening the tangle of thoughts and images I haven't had time to sort out this winter. Walking away from the Capriani Cup. My father and his blog. My brief stint with the Wolves. My briefer stint with number seventy-seven. Everything that almost happened with Josh, but didn't. Finally apologizing to Kara. All the arguments with Dani, still unresolved. My mother. The diner. My future, even less certain now. That old Erie Atlantic whistling on the track, still calling me to run as Trick's radio sings into the night.

I been downhearted baby, ever since the day we met . . .

Guitar.

Horns.

Bass.

Cue those smoldering—

"You really are brilliant, you know." Dani bangs her way out the door, startling the seagull into a shadowed corner. "What you did tonight? That was pretty rock star, Hudson. We're still taking tables. And a bunch of people asked about catering and stuff. Your mom is, like, perma-smile. I don't think she even remembers about the food review guy."

Guilt pinches my stomach again, prickling up my spine. If I'd stayed here tonight, maybe we could've been more attentive to him. Maybe I would've recommended a different dish, something he'd like better. Maybe . . .

"Maybe no one else will remember him, either," I say.

"Eh, no one around here reads anything but the sports page, anyway." Dani smiles and looks at me for a long time, silent. Waiting. It's my turn to talk. My turn to undo the knot of our troubles, to save us like the angel of icing stunt saved the night. One chilly winter doesn't seem long enough to kill a friendship, but I guess all it takes is one bad day, leading into another and another and another, excuses endlessly regurgitated. Do it often enough and intention stops mattering, too.

I think again of Kara, all the times I could've said something to explain, to apologize, to try, but didn't. I let our entire friendship die because I was too embarrassed about what I'd done, too eager to go into hiding. I still don't know if Kara and I are on true speaking terms, let alone friend terms. And I have to accept that. It was my choice, after all—three years ago and every day after.

But now, faced with the same opportunity to let it all go? To let another friendship fade into memory while I hide out behind an apron and a mixing bowl?

"Dani, we really need to talk. Not over lunch, not next weekend, but right now."

She lets out her breath, a big white sigh. "I'm so glad you said that. I have so much to tell you."

I flash her a devious grin. "Yeah, you and Frankie Torres, huh?"

She nods and looks at the ground. "We've been hanging out since that night at the movies. It started just as friends, but then he was calling me all the time, inviting me to the games, sitting next to me at lunch. He's a really sweet guy, Hudson."

"I know. You should've seen him on New Year's—when I told him you were in Canada, it was like his puppy died."

"Seriously?"

"Dude, he spent the entire chorus of 'Auld Lang Syne' staring out the windows, pining away. Totally gross."

Dani returns my smile. "I wanted to tell you that I liked him, but every time I tried to bring it up, you either changed the subject or just . . . drifted off." Her smile fades as she meets my eyes, her face crinkled and sad. "It's like you weren't even around anymore, Hud. Like you already left Watonka."

"I've been a crap friend, and I'm really sorry. I screwed up. And I totally miss you."

"I miss you, too." She steps closer, letting the door close behind her as she stomps her feet against the cold.

"I know I made mistakes this winter, but I'm pissed at you, too. I thought you had my back on the skating thing. But the closer I got to the scholarship, the more you clammed up. I felt like you couldn't be happy for me—not because you were jealous, but because you didn't want me to leave Watonka."

"But I *was* jealous," she says. "All of a sudden my best friend had all these new hockey friends and plans that didn't involve me. We didn't even get to hang out at work because you kept giving away your shifts. I knew how much skating meant to you, but after a while, it wasn't about skating. It was all about the guys, then all about getting out of here."

"You *know* I want out. That's how I feel."

Dani frowns, shoulders sagging. "Okay. Watonka isn't the most cosmopolitan place in the world, I get it. But it's still home—at least for me. So not only was I never seeing my best friend, the few times we hung out, she was trash-talking my home. It was crappy, Hudson. And then today, when you said you didn't want me at your skating event . . . It was like I didn't even know you anymore. Like you were already a million miles away from here."

I look out past the lot behind Hurley's, the lights on the highway blurring into two bright ribbons, red and white. For months my single mission was the ice, the competition, winning the scholarship and my one-way ticket out. A hundred, a thousand, a million miles away—nothing seemed far enough. I was so focused on that point in the distance that I didn't bother looking back, didn't consider what I'd be leaving behind.

All the people I love, my family and the friends like Trick and Dani who've become family. All the little quirks that make even the most barren, frigid places beautiful, that make a tiny gray dot on the map the one place you'll always call home, no matter where your glamorous, boring, adventurous, average, ridiculous, impossible, epic, romantic, bacon-infused life leads you.

"I'm sorry, Dani. I *was* a million miles away. But not now. Listen . . . you're my best friend. I can't imagine my life without you in it, no matter how much we fight or who we're with or where we live. None of that stuff matters. We're sisters, you know?"

She nods, wiping her eyes on the edge of her apron. "I'm sorry, too."

"Do-over?" I whisper.

"Do-over." Dani reaches out and squeezes my hand. She leans in for a hug, but I pull back.

"Wait. There's one more issue to discuss. Probably the most important one of all."

"What?" she asks, eyebrows crinkling.

"I'm not sure how to say this." I put my hand on her shoulder and look deep into her eyes. "Dani, does Frankie . . . does he know about your obsession with pirates?"

"Are you *kidding* me? Pirates are *soo* last month. I'm on to ninja spies now. *Bedroom Assassin*, by Ella Drake? *Very* sexy."

"Naked ninja hotties? I dig it." I smile, and Dani finally gets her hug. Inside, the opening chords of Van Morrisson's "Brown Eyed Girl" spill out of the old radio, muffled through the door.

"Listen." I make my voice man-deep. "I think they're playing our song."

"Well?" She tilts her head and holds out her hand, corkscrew curls shining under the silver moon. "What do you think?"

"You asking me to dance?"

"In *that* outfit? Hell yeah, I'm asking you to dance, mama. Shake that fine, sequin-covered ass!" She grabs my hands and we jump and twirl behind the diner, the seagull squawking in vain protest as Dani tries desperately to carry the tune. I keep my hands locked on hers and close my eyes, and my off-key, vocally underdeveloped best friend sings it long and loud into the wintry night, snowflakes falling softly on my tongue.

Chapter Twenty-Six

Not-So-Impossible Orange Dreams

*Vanilla cupcakes iced in swirled vanilla
and orange buttercream,
garnished with an orange slice
and shaved dark chocolate*

When Dani and I get back inside, only a handful of people dot the dining room, families waiting for their to-go boxes, kids licking cupcake crumbs from their plates. As I refill the salt and pepper shakers on the counter, I keep my eyes on the front door, betting against the odds on one final customer. One last chance.

But he doesn't show.

"Hudson?" Mom leans out the kitchen door, hair slipping out of her ponytail, eyes puffy and tired. She nods toward the booth near the counter. On one side, Bug's curled up on the bench with his backpack, a shoeless foot dangling off the seat. "He asleep?"

"Totally zonked."

Mom smiles. "He was quite a trouper tonight."

"No kidding." I replace the big jars of salt and pepper under the counter and line up the shakers against the sugar dispensers. "A few more years and you can give him his own Hurley Girl dress."

"I think he'd prefer a Hurley Man space suit." Mom reties her ponytail and sighs. "Okay, Hudson. Now that we're out of the weeds, we need to have a little chat."

"Start by telling me where you went tonight." Mom closes the office door behind me and takes the seat at her desk. "*Before* the cupcake free-for-all."

I sit in the small swivel chair across from her, smoothing my hands over the silky skirt of my competition dress. All winter I've kept this from her. Now that I have no choice but to tell her, everything I thought I'd be confessing is different. The scholarship, the competition, all those months on the ice at Fillmore—it all means something else now.

I take a steadying breath. Whatever it means, it's time for the truth. And if I'm finally being honest about my dreams, I have to start by yanking them out of the closet.

"I've been skating again, Ma. Training."

Mom doesn't say a word as I tell her the entire story: work breaks at Fillmore, the foundation letter, Baylor's, the Wolves gig, Kara, my guilt about Empire, all the secrets and lies, everything I thought I wanted to achieve this winter. For the first time since my father left, I don't hide behind my apron and a mixing bowl. I don't shy away from honesty just because it's hard and uncomfortable for both of us. I tell her the truth. The real deal about me, about what I want. About who I am. Who I'm not.

My father was the one who bought me my first pair of skates and set me on the ice so long ago. He made sure there was money for private lessons with Lola and all of the equipment I needed. He came to every event, home and away. And he took me skating when I just needed to run around the rink and be silly, no choreography, no moves, no routine. He rented skates and chased me in circles and bought us hot chocolate when we got tired. Skating was ours, mine and his, and in that moment on the ice at the Empire Games, I knew that my mother could no more fill his empty place in the stands than she could fill his empty place in my life. For all the dreams my father and I shared, nothing was strong enough to keep him here with us. And in his absence, I thought I wasn't strong enough to carry those dreams on my own.

But I was wrong. I'm strong enough to carry *any* dream on my own. I was just trying to carry the wrong one.

"Dad's gone," I say, "and I let him take skating with him. For three years I told myself he ruined it. But he didn't. He couldn't. I miss it, Ma. I miss being on the ice. And I'm tired of sneaking around to do it."

Mom leans back in her chair, eyes glazed with tears. "Baby, I had no idea you were skating again. No idea you wanted *any* of this. You could've told me and saved us both a lot of grief. Not to mention money—how much extra cash have you been floating Mrs. Ferris?"

My face goes hot. "Enough to cover a few months of gas bills."

"Oh, Hudson . . ."

"I felt like I couldn't talk about it because you'd get upset, either about the cost of everything, or just remembering stuff with Dad. So when I got that letter, I thought if I could find a way to skate *and* earn a scholarship, I could tell you after. Then you wouldn't have to worry about paying for college, and I could still do something I love."

"Hudson, your father and I have a college savings for you."

"You—*what?*"

Mom reaches for a tissue. "It's not fifty grand—not even close—but it's a start. Enough for in-state tuition, anyway."

"But . . ." I close my eyes, memories resurfacing. "You guys had the lump sum thing. I remember the lawyer explaining it when we sold the old house. Dad didn't have to pay anything else."

"That was for alimony and child support, hon. He's still putting up for part of your education. He makes a deposit every other month. As much as it pains me to say this—and trust me, it does—he's not a *total* heartless jerk."

I fold my arms over my sequins, images of Dad and Shelvis flickering through my head. "I don't want *anything* from him."

"Don't be ridiculous. He's your father, even if he's not

around. Helping with college is the least he can do. *Believe* me."

I stand up and shove my chair back. "No. He bailed on us, Ma. Divorce is one thing, but he totally bailed. He never calls, he barely ever e-mails, and even then it's just to talk about himself."

"I know, and it tears me up that he does that to you kids. But college is expensive, and it's his responsibility as a father to—"

"He's not allowed to feel like a good father just for writing a check. I'd rather have a mountain of student loans than let him buy me a single textbook." I slump back into the chair.

Mom reaches for my hands across the desk. "You don't have to decide about that right now, and I'm not trying to turn this into a conversation about your father's issues. The point is, you could've been honest with me. All this time you've been training for another competition, and I was in the dark. I didn't even know you still had skates. Are you signed up for anything else? More competitions? Scholarships? Lessons?"

I shake my head. "No competitions. But I *do* want to keep skating. Maybe just at a club or coaching little kids or what-ever."

"What about work?" Mom releases my hands and shuffles through the mound of papers on her desk. "You're still on the schedule this month, and you've got a ton of Valentine's orders coming up, and—"

"I know. And I want to do them. All of them. I like baking cupcakes. I like being here with Trick and Dani in the mornings, hanging out in the kitchen, inventing new flavors."

"You do?"

I nod. "I just don't want to work at Hurley's forever. Not as a waitress and not as the future owner. Who knows what'll happen down the line, but right now, I don't want the same things you did. I want my own life."

Mom straightens the papers on her desk, flipping through the stacks with her thumb. I pick at a loose sequin from my dress, pulling it off and rolling it between my fingers. Mom opens her desk drawer and shoves a stack of inventory sheets inside. Closes it. Taps a pencil on the arm of her chair. I roll and unroll my leg warmers, stretch them out, pull them up over my knees.

"So the diner's not your big dream," Mom finally says, dropping her pencil into the abyss on her desk. "I can accept that. It's my dream—always was. The thing is, right now, it's also our family's only source of income. And I really can't make it work without your help."

I lean back in my chair and let out a long sigh, remembering Ms. Fanny Pack and her viable income models. "I know."

"I kept telling you the waitressing gig was only temporary, but I guess it didn't work out that way."

I shrug. "I understand, Ma. I know I didn't make it easy, and I know you do a lot for me and Bug. I want to help. Just, maybe in a different way."

"What way? We got a huge boost tonight, sure. But that review comes out next week, and it could really break us. If that happens, I don't know how much longer I can keep this place open. This isn't a guilt trip. It's a fact."

"Let's just see what he says. Maybe it won't be that bad. Besides, Dani made a good point—people around here only care about the sports page."

Mom laughs. "True."

"Anyway, I'm not ditching again—keep me on the schedule for now. Tonight *was* good. Dani said she got a bunch of catering and party requests, so things might turn out fine. In the meantime, I really just have one request."

"What's that?"

"Eighty-six the uniforms. The Hurley Girl dresses are a little ridiculous, Ma."

She smirks. "Says the girl in skintight rainbow sequins and pink leg warmers?"

There's a knock on the office door, and Dani pokes her head in. "Sorry to interrupt, but there's a table here for Hudson."

"Mind getting their drinks?" I ask.

"Already done. Now they're just getting impatient, banging their silverware on the table and everything. Very middle school, if you ask me."

Bug trails in behind her, rubbing his eyes. "Jeez, your friends are loud. Some of us are trying to sleep!" He crawls into Mom's lap and rests his head on her shoulder.

"Ooh, there they go again. Listen." Dani pushes the door all the way open. From the dining room, all through the kitchen, right straight into the office, a silverware-banging chant floats on the air.

"Pink! Pink! Pink! Pink!"

"Pig?" Mom asks as she arranges Bug on another chair. "No, wait . . . pink? Is that what they're saying? Dani, why are they saying that?"

Dani shakes her head and laughs. "It's . . . a really long story."

"Those are the best kind." Mom tightens her ponytail and ushers us out into the kitchen. "I'll put on a fresh pot of coffee. Hudson, see to your table. You won't have the honor much longer, so make it count." She winks at me, and I turn toward the dining room, still clad in my skating getup and a frosting-spattered half apron, ready to face the music. Er, chanting. Whatever.

I push through the doors. Crammed together around a long row of pushed-together tables, all nineteen of the Watonka Wolves—plus Ellie, Kara, two of Amir's cousins, and a handful of other girls from school—whistle and cheer as I make my dazzling appearance.

After the fight on the ice last week, Will's scandal with Dodd, everything that happened and unhappened between Josh and me, the rise and fall of my big fat skating plans—I didn't expect to see them again. Not like this.

"What are you guys doing here?" I ask.

"Celebrating," Amir says. "Not sure if you heard, but we're kind of a big deal around here. Championship contenders and all. *Howoooo!*"

The other guys join in and pull me into some kind of fumbling group hug, and even Kara gives me a quick squeeze.

"I heard about what you did tonight," she says quietly into my ear. "I'm proud of you, Hudson. I mean it."

After the rousing cheers and generally obnoxious ordering process, the group dogs their postgame dinner, along with twelve large loganberries, seven hot chocolates, three coffees, five fake ginger ales, three dozen cupcakes, and anything else they could cram into their mouths.

The team and their entourage are lighthearted and red-faced from celebrating, but Will and Josh are more subdued than the rest, smiling quietly from opposite ends of the table. Neither looks at me fully, but the tension between them seems to have eased, at least for now. So I refill their drinks and congratulate them again on their win, and in the end, they clap and cheer and pull me into another hug. I'm pretty sure Brad palms my ass and tries to play it off like a too-many-hands-in-the-group-fondle-fest accident, but hey, I can't say I wasn't warned about sporting events and rowdy customers. I let it slide for now, but next time? Adorable championship varsity hockey boy or not, he's totally getting a pitcher of ice water in the lap.

We settle up the check and I watch them leave, the girls huddled together against the cold, the boys fist-bumping and fake fighting in the parking lot as they make their way through the slush.

I trace circles on the glass as they disappear, group by group, couple by couple. Will ducks into his car alone and motors out of the lot, and soon the last remaining Wolf is Josh. He opens his car door, the interior light casting a soft glow on the snow. As if he senses me watching, he turns back to the diner, one hand on the car door, hesitating.

But then he slips into the car and pulls the door shut, the light turning black in the space he left behind. As he rolls across the lot to the exit, his tires carve twin black paths in the slush. The car stops. Break lights flash twice. And then he's gone.

I turn from the window and head to the kitchen for the empty bus bins, ready to tackle the monumental task of clearing their tables.

"I still can't believe they did it," I say to Dani as we scrape food and stack dishes into the bins.

"News dude was right," she says. "Talk about a comeback."

I smile and arrange a row of chocolate-stained mugs in the bin. After a ten-year losing streak, decades out of the finals, the Watonka Wolves are going to the division championships. "I think they might get a felt banner on the gym wall. Finally."

"With your name on it, Princess Pink," she says.

"Hey, stranger things, right?" I heft a full bin onto my hip and lug it into the kitchen, feet aching, shoulders sagging, but heart—at least for now—a little lighter. Even if I can't be part of the team anymore, even if things got weird with Will and didn't work out as I'd hoped with Josh, even if I carry the scars of regret for the rest of my life, I know that this winter, for a little while, I was part of something bigger. Something special.

Cheers to that, wolf pack.

Chapter Twenty-Seven

Have Your Cupcakes and Eat Them, Toos

*Vanilla cupcakes topped with
blueberry vanilla buttercream,
miniature sugared hearts,
gold and silver glitter,
and dark chocolate edging*

They say there's no such thing as bad publicity, and maybe that's true. But I have a feeling if the *Buffalo News* ever learned we put out an APB on a certain missing hamster that night, Hurley's would be in some serious publicity trouble—*not* the good kind.

Fortunately, the restaurant critic never knew that while he feigned indifference over the beef tips two weeks ago, Mr. Napkins launched his own exploratory committee, investigating the leftovers and cobwebs under the grill.

Unlike my "Teen's Talent" piece, our newest claim-to-fame article has only been tacked behind the register for a few days, so I haven't memorized it yet. You can see the headline from across the room, though, even without leaning over and squinting:

"Hurley's Homestyle Diner in Watonka: A Rare Oasis in the Culinary Tundra."

Oasis. Believe that? Thank you, Mr. Poker Face. If the whole food critic thing doesn't work out, you should totally consider figure skating judgery. You've got a gift, friend. A true gift!

The review didn't mention cupcakes specifically, but that didn't stop my zany creations from wowing Watonka again. Between that angel of icing stunt and the Valentine's orders I booked at school—sales really picked up once the hockey wives decided my goodies have more romantic street cred than those cheesy carnations the cheerleaders peddle—the baking biz is booming.

I haven't retired my bangin' Hurley Girl dress yet, but Nat's back after a brief respite, and Mom promised to start interviewing for two new girls. Plus, she promoted Dani to head server and all-around front-of-the-house boss, which was just fine with Marianne, because after working here for, like, a hundred years, she's not looking to move up the exciting Hurley's career ladder anyway. Now, with Dani helping Mom screen potential new girls and keep tabs on everything up front, I can spend more time in the back, training my new recruit.

"You ready?" I ask Bug over the flawless horn work of Charlie Parker.

Bug checks the ties on his apron and pushes up his sleeves, looking at me across the counter. "First, let's get one thing straight. Since I'm no longer just the Glitter Czar, I need a new title."

"Have something in mind?"

Bug nods. "Since you're the Cupcake Queen, I should be the Cupcake King."

I wash my hands and join him at the counter. "How about the Cupcake Prince? You can work your way up."

He considers the compromise. "Okay. One year as the prince, then we reevaluate. I also want stock options."

"Done and done."

"Awesome. Let's do this thing, girlfriend."

As Bug measures out ingredients for his custom-made batter, I make very minor corrections, but otherwise let him experiment. That's how I learned—a blank canvas, trial and error. Sometimes the flavors you think would be perfect together form a disastrous combo, while the ones you'd never imagine hooking up blend to perfection. Sampling and tasting, burning and undercooking, sweetening and mellowing— it rarely comes out great on the first try, but developing the focus and energy and passion for these experiments is what saved me when my father left. What helped me put a smile on my baby brother's face when sadness was all we knew. What kept Hurley's alive at times when our chances didn't look so hot.

Like I always say: I've never met a problem a proper cupcake couldn't fix.

"Dad's never coming back, is he?" Bug asks, showing off

his mind-reading skills. His eyes stay fixed on the mixing bowl as he dumps in a measure of melted chocolate.

"I don't . . . why would you say that?"

"It's okay, Hudson. I'm not a kid anymore."

I smile at my baby brother, his arms stretched across the counter, elbows-deep in ingredients for his first official batch of cupcakes. Maybe he's right; he's not a kid, even though he's only eight. His father left. His mother works a lot. As resident big sister in a single-parent home, it's been my job to look after him. I promised Mom I'd never relinquish the role of chief Bug protector and homework helper, but I think we could all use a little more honesty around here.

"No. He's not coming back."

"Is it that lady? The one who does Elvis stuff?" He licks a smudge of chocolate from his hand and goes back to stirring. "I didn't know he was a fan."

"How do you know about Shelvis?"

"Google. Dad used his real name on the domain registration for his blog."

"Um . . . I don't even know what that means." I lean over his shoulder to check the consistency of the batter and guide his hand into a slower stir. "Dad's gone, sweet pea. I don't think he stopped loving us, he just doesn't really know how to show it right now. Pretty lame, if you ask me."

Bug continues to stir, scraping the sides at regular intervals, just like I taught him. "It makes me sad."

"Me too."

"Then again, if Dad never left, you probably wouldn't be the Cupcake Queen. And if you weren't the Cupcake Queen, I wouldn't be the Cupcake Prince. And then I couldn't do this." He spoons out a huge dollop of chocolate batter and shoves it straight into his goofy, giggling mouth.

"Hey!" I laugh. "Save some for the customers, Prince!"

"It's quality control, Hud. We are a rare oasis in the culinary tundra. We can't feed the good people of Watonka any old garbage."

"Just don't put that spoon back in the bowl, okay? We already dodged one health code violation this month—let's not push it."

"NBD." He flings the spoon into the sink and grabs a fresh one.

I back off and let him work, loading the used bowls into the dishwasher. As I pack up his extra ingredients, I glance at the frame hanging above the pantry—the picture Dani finally submitted for her photo project. She took it last week—me and Mom and Bug, all leaning over a bowl of cupcake batter that Bug accidentally exploded when he set the mixer too high. Mom's laughing with her eyes closed and Bug's got chocolate goo all over his face and glasses. And me, I'm just digging right in there with a spoon.

Passion.

She got an A.

"I think the Chocolate Cherry Fixer-Uppers are ready for the cups," Bug says.

370

"Fixer-Uppers?"

Bug nods, his grin lighting up the whole kitchen. "Once they're cool, we break them apart and then spackle them back together with cherry cream cheese frosting, mini chocolate chips, and chopped Martian cherries or whatever those things are. I was thinking of using a little whipped cream in the frosting so it doesn't get too pasty."

"Um, okay, wow."

He shrugs, pushing his glasses up his nose with a chocolate-smudged finger. "Mr. Napkins thought they had potential when we discussed them last night."

"More than potential." I kiss him on the forehead and set out the silicone baking cups. "I gotta watch my back. These babies are gonna be best sellers, kiddo."

After we pour out the batter and slide the CC Fixer-Uppers into the oven, Bug retreats to the dining room for grilled cheese and gravy fries and I head out back for my non-smoke break. The sky has darkened to a deep purple, flecks of faraway lights flickering on the other side of the hill. Beyond the rise, the train screeches against the tracks, chugging and idling until it decides where it's off to next.

"They never stay long, do they?"

I know that voice.

Josh.

I turn to find him behind me, looking over the hill toward the plume of smoke billowing from the train engine. We haven't spoken since they came into Hurley's after the finals.

A wave at school here, a half smile in the parking lot there, but no real words. Nothing close. Nothing like before.

"Five minutes, give or take," I say.

"Your brother told me you were back here. I hope it's cool. I mean, I know you're on break. I don't want to—"

"It's cool." I force myself to meet his gaze, the icy blue-gray of his eyes, intense as ever. He's got a short, scruffy beard now. They all do—some playoffs superstition thing. I shiver and pull the coat close around my neck.

"Look," he says. "I know things got kind of . . . weird between us. I didn't mean to freak out like that at the semis. I was pissed at Will, and when he said that stuff about you, it just . . . it bugged me. And everything with the coach . . ." Josh shrugs, shoving his hands into his pockets.

"I understand." Until that night at semifinals, I didn't know the extent of Will's plans, but it doesn't matter. I was willing to keep his secrets because I needed mine kept, too. I was doing the same thing—using the team to get what I needed, running away from the truth.

"Will told Dodd about you, by the way," Josh says. "The night after the fight, he told him everything. How you've been helping us, how the whole team came together because of you. He also told Dodd he's not interested in ditching us, and that the coach can either come back and start acting like a real coach, or let us do it on our own. Either way, he's pretty convinced we'll go to nationals, with or without Dodd's stamp of approval."

"Are you serious?"

Josh nods. "You saw what happened this season. And Will's right—it was all because of you."

I shake my head, that train still idling at the station. Catching its breath. Bracing for the long, cold journey ahead, grateful it doesn't have to stay here long. "You guys are really good. You just needed a push."

"And you gave it to us. We made it into the division championships, Hud. We could win this thing." He steps forward, closing the space between us. "I came to say thank you. I mean it."

"You're . . . um . . . you're welcome."

"This is for you. It's from everyone." Josh hands me a package from inside his coat, warm from resting against his chest.

"What did you guys do?"

He grins. "Just open it."

I tear off the paper to reveal a baby-soft pile of blue-and-silver fabric. It can only be one thing.

"A jersey? That's so cool!"

"Not just any jersey. Check it out." He unfolds it and holds it up so I can take a closer look. AVERY, it says, stitched across the back over my very own number: forty-two.

"That's my favorite number!"

"Well, it's yours now, forty-two—no one else can use it. But the best part?" He flips the jersey around. On the front, there's a wolf's head, just like on the boys' jerseys. But mine's a she-wolf. And she's wearing a sparkling pink tiara.

"What do you think, Princess Pink?"

I slip off my jacket and pull the jersey on, right over my Hurley Girl dress. "I don't know what to say."

Josh smiles. "Say that you'll come back and help us train for nationals. We're good, but not undefeated. I think you can still teach us a few tricks."

My heart races, but I force it to slow down. I know in every bone, every muscle, that I belong on the ice. Not as a solo competitor in some glossy-perfect parallel life, but as a team skater. A part of something more than glitter and roses thrown on the rink after everyone else has been eliminated. I think about Amir and Rowan and Gettysburg and even Will, and how much they grew together as a team this season, despite Will's initial solo plans. I helped them get there. And they helped me. And now they want me back.

"Do you remember that day we crashed at Fillmore?" I ask.

"I'll never forget it." His fingers reach for my forehead, but stop just short. "I thought I gave you a concussion."

"Then you came to Hurley's and asked if we could spend some time on the ice together. Just the two of us."

Josh nods. "But you got suckered into training the whole pack. Lucky you."

I pull the jersey sleeves over my hands and sigh. "Josh, listen. I'm not training with the wolf pack again. I promised my mom I'd stick it out at Hurley's until we bring in some new people, and I want to spend more time with Bug. But if the offer's still on the table, I wouldn't mind skating with you sometimes. Just the two of us."

"You sure?" he asks.

"As long as I don't have to give back the jersey? Yes."

"You got yourself a deal, Avery." He pulls me into a hug, but it only lasts a few seconds, the awkwardness of everything creeping back up, fracturing our momentary reunion.

Below us, over the hill, the train starts up again, its breath ragged and loud as it prepares to exit the station. Josh puts his hands back in his pockets, and I know in my heart that this is one of those times, those now-or-never moments that we grow to look back on for the rest of always, asking whether we did the right thing, the best thing, the true thing. Maybe he *doesn't* want me—maybe I misread all the signs and looks and the near kiss. Maybe he really *does* want me, and we'll fall in love and then one day he'll decide he wants a female Elvis impersonator instead. Or maybe there's a real romantic pirate-ninja-assassin love story in there somewhere, just like in Dani's books.

Anything is possible. The only thing I know for sure is that he won't make the first move, and if I let him walk away now, we'll forever be a "just": *Just* hockey player and skating coach. *Just* music swappers. *Just* friends. A *not-quite-almost* whose time passed through as quickly as the train, fading into the distance before it even had a real chance at staying, at becoming something more, because I didn't speak up. Because I waited for someone else to do it for me.

"Josh, wait." I grab the sleeve of his jacket. "That night with Will, when he said that stuff about me—"

"Stop." He holds up his hand. "You don't owe me an

explanation. I overreacted. I'm not . . ." He trails off, shaking his head.

"I need to say this." I grab his hand, holding it tight. "Will and I *were* seeing each other for a while, but it ended a couple weeks before the storm at Fillmore. Because—"

"Hudson, you—"

"Because I realized I was falling for another guy, fifty-six."

He raises his eyebrows and takes a step back, but I force myself to keep going, to follow him, to catalog the intensity in his eyes. All the colors. The tiny scar near his temple. The new, temporary scruff along his jaw. The soft lips that once brushed across mine during a storm.

Josh takes a deep breath. "I don't—"

"Blackthorn? Please. Shut. Up." I grab the collar of his jacket and pull him into me, answering every last protest with a kiss—a real one, deep and intentional.

After months of imagining this moment, his lips on mine fully, unbroken, uninterrupted, nothing could have prepared me for the real thing. Maybe Will was well versed on the technical points of a good kiss, but this?

Josh pulls me tighter, looping his arms around me. Our hearts find their familiar opposite beat, banging against each other through our clothes as Josh slides his hands into my hair, his beard tickling my lips, thumbs caressing my ear, my face, my neck. Being with Josh is like being touched from the inside out. An unexpected blaze of sunshine on an otherwise bleak winter day. Wrapping your fingers around a mug of hot chocolate after walking home in that frigid lake-effect wind. A fire crackling softly beneath your outstretched hands. The perfect combination of cupcake and icing, the kind where you can't quite identify all the secret ingredients, but you feel them melting together on your tongue, and you know that for as long you live, this will be the best thing you've ever tasted.

Not *almost*.

Perfection.

Josh pulls away slowly, shell-shocked and smiling. "Um, okay. Now that we've got that straightened out," he says, a little breathless, "explain to me again how this whole 'friends with benefits' thing works?"

"*Excuse* me?"

"It's just . . . all right. Those cupcakes smell really good, and I was thinking maybe I could score one. Or four." He tucks a lock of hair behind my ear and steps closer, kissing the sensitive skin beneath my jaw. The spark from his kiss travels straight to my toes and I shudder, nearly slipping on the icy pavement.

"Chocolate Cherry Fixer-Uppers," I say, leaning into his arms. "Bug's the one you'll have to bribe, so if you're just doing this for free cupcakes, you're—"

"Doing what—this?" He brushes his lips against my ear again and my bones wobble.

"Don't push your luck, Blackthorn," I whisper.

"Wouldn't dream of it, Avery." Josh's smile disappears. He looks at me again like that first time on the makeshift rink at

Fillmore, playful and serious and a little nervous all at once. He pulls me into another kiss, deeper than the first, initial surprise replaced with utter certainty.

The snow falls on us in soft, white feathers, but I'm not cold. On the other side of the door, the familiar sounds of Hurley's echo through the kitchen—the sizzle and pop of the grill. Trick's radio on low, humming those bluesy old tunes. The whir of the mixer as my little brother blends the frosting for his new confections. Somewhere in the distance, the Erie Atlantic whistles again, fairy godmother lamplight glowing on the tracks, the fleeting call of that old night bird echoing through the icy air as it finally exits the station. For as long as I live in this crazy, lake-effect, chicken-wing-capital-of-the-world town, that old train howling up at the moon will *always* be the sound of someone leaving, the promise of another place.

But tonight, it's not talking to me.

Tonight, out behind Hurley's under the blue-black winter sky, the Cupcake Queen of Watonka is *exactly* where she's supposed to be.

Acknowledgments

Without the love and encouragement of my husband, Alex, my books wouldn't exist. For sitting next to me in the front row on the emocoaster, for dragging me away from the computer to take an occasional hike and/or shower, for inspiring me to turn all of our crazy adventures into stories, and most importantly, for always being my bestie, thank you, Pet Monster.

When I said that cupcakes, figure skating, cute hockey boys, and lake-effect snowstorms sounded like a good combination, Jennifer Klonsky was all, hell *yeah*! Thanks, Jen, for your editorial awesomeness, for your contagious enthusiasm, and for laughing at my inappropriate jokes along the way. It takes a special person, on all counts! Thanks also to Craig Adams, Mara Anastas, Bethany Buck, Jim Conlin, Paul Crichton, Katherine Devendorf, Dayna Evans, Lydia Frost, Jessica Handelman, Victor Iannone, Mary Marotta, Christina Pecorale, Lucille Rettino, Dawn Ryan, Michael Strother, Sara Saidlower, Carolyn Swerdloff, and everyone in the Simon Pulse family who worked so hard to make this book shine.

Ted Malawer, if they made cupcake-flavored Life Savers, I'd send you a whole case. Until then, we'll celebrate with the real thing, extra chocolate icing on top. Thanks for everything you do to keep me writing happily!

Danielle Benedetti, Zoe Strickland, Jordyn Turney, and Sarah Woodard, readers and book bloggers and all-around amazing girls, beneath this bright purple ribbon is a big box of Josh, just for you.

Since my childhood attempt at figure skating lessons ended with me asking to play hockey with the boys instead, I'm grateful that Amanda Crowley so generously shared her insight into the world of competitive figure skating. Any technical skating mistakes are . . . well, they're definitely mine, but let's not call them mistakes. Let's . . . have a cupcake instead! Thanks also to Kate Messner and Mandy Hubbard for early advice on plotting, writing, skating, and everything in between.

Amy Hains, Rachel Miller, Meredith Sale, and Lisa Kenney, I straight up love you girls. I can always count on you to shine the light in my face when I've spent too long in the deep, dark writing cave, and for that, I'm eternally lucky.

Speaking of the writing cave, it may be *crazy* dark, but it's no longer lonely. To my wonderfully talented friends from the 2009 Debutantes, the Contemps, and Lighthouse Writers Workshop, you inspire and amaze me (and prevent me from drinking all this Bombay Sapphire by myself. . . . Cheers!).

My family, my friends, and my family friends (especially Birthday Group), your love, support, and inadvertently inspired character ideas keep me in the storytelling business, in more ways than one. ;-) Group hug!

Finally, I'm forever indebted to you, my fabulous YA readers, bloggers, librarians, booksellers, and teachers (an especially ginormous hug to Paul W. Hankins, a true friend and inspiration to students and writers alike). For as long as you keep reading and sharing these stories, I'll keep writing them. Promise. <3